Bright Day Dawning

ANNA JACOBS

Bright Day Dawning

HODDER &
STOUGHTON

First published in Great Britain in 2006 by Hodder & Stoughton
A division of Hodder Headline

A Hodder & Stoughton Book

I

A CIP catalogue record for this title is
available from the British Library

ISBN 0 340 84075 7

Typeset in Plantin Light by Palimpsest Book Production Limited,
Polmont, Stirlingshire

Printed and bound by Mackays of Chatham plc, Chatham, Kent

Hodder Headline's policy is to use papers that are natural, renewable and
recyclable products and made from wood grown in sustainable forests.
The logging and manufacturing processes are expected to conform
to the environmental regulations of the country of origin.

Hodder & Stoughton Ltd
A division of Hodder Headline
338 Euston Road
London NW1 3BH

My grateful thanks to Doug Hay, architect and friend, who helped me (with many shudders) figure out the poor architectural practices in this book. Any faults in turning his explanations into story events are solely mine.

I

November 1847

Gwynna Jones stared at herself in the mirror. Brand new, the clothes were, the first she'd ever owned that hadn't belonged to someone else first. But the solemn lass she saw there looked like a stranger. Even her hair looked different today, with every single wavy strand pulled back tightly into a bun.

'That navy blue suits you.' Essie walked round her, nodding approvingly. 'It looks neat and trim.'

'I look like what *they* will want,' Gwynna said slowly, still trying to get used to her new self, 'but if they knew . . . they wouldn't want to employ a girl like me . . .'

'None of that talk, lass. You're as good as anyone else. My friend Flora has trusted my recommendation enough to see you. She hasn't promised you the position, but it gives you a chance, at least. You're good with babies and you'll make a fine nursery maid.'

Gwynna nodded. She kept telling herself that, but she still felt terrified of the step she was about to take: getting a job in a big country house.

'Flora and I have known one another for a long time,' Essie went on, 'since we were both young maids together, and she might have risen in the world to be housekeeper to a rich family but she has a kind heart and that won't have changed. She'll make sure you learn your job properly, so that later you can go on to even better things.'

'*If* she takes me on.'

The two women stared at one another solemnly.

'It's all in the past now, love,' Essie said softly. 'If Flora doesn't give you a position, someone else will.'

Gwynna didn't answer, could only manage a tiny nod and swallow hard to keep her emotions under control. She'd been so happy living with Nev and Essie Linney, who'd treated her more like one of the family than a servant, providing her with good food three times a day, her very own bed and clean, warm clothes to wear. She was a different person now from the unhappy waif they'd taken in. There were plenty of mirrors to show her that. But was she different enough?

Once she'd seen how decent families lived, she'd craved the same sort of life for herself, wanting others to respect her, as they did Nev's family. And at least if she got away from Hedderby she wouldn't be embarrassed by the sight of her parents reeling about the streets drunk, wouldn't have to hide till they'd passed because they always pestered her for money. Once, a few weeks ago, her father had taken the shopping money from her forcibly. Nev had had to go round and warn him that it was *his* money and if Mr Jones did that again, Nev would call in the town's new police and have him arrested for theft.

Gwynna never took her own money with her when she went out – well, she was saving her wages, not spending them. In the privacy of her bedroom she sometimes made piles of the coins, counting and recounting them, marvelling that they were all hers.

But the Linneys didn't need her help any more and she was determined not to be a burden on them, so she'd asked Essie to help her find a new job. Today she was going to be considered for a position as nursery maid to the Hungerton family. *Position*, they called it, not a job. The family lived on a big country estate fifteen miles away from the little town of Hedderby, with twelve indoor servants and men working for them outdoors as well. Gwynna found it hard to imagine needing so many people to run one house, let alone having a governess, a Head Nurse and two nursemaids to look after three small children.

Taking a deep breath, she checked that her bonnet was straight and reached for her cloak. 'We'll miss the train if we don't get a move on.'

At the entrance to the railway station she hesitated, glancing at Essie for reassurance. She'd never ridden on a train before and was both excited and anxious about boarding one of the noisy monsters. She'd seen them thundering through the countryside near Hedderby, travelling so quickly it fair made you blink as they thundered past.

Not seeming to notice her young friend's nervousness, Essie went to buy two tickets then led the way on to the platform. 'We're going second-class. I'm too old to stand up in one of those open, third-class carriages, and anyway, we want to arrive looking neatly turned out.'

Within a few minutes the ground began trembling beneath their feet and they heard a clackety-clack in the distance, which got louder as the train chugged into the station. White steam swirled around them as it came to a halt. A few people got out and Essie led the way forward confidently towards a second-class carriage, grumbling about the hardness of the wooden benches as she took a corner seat and gestured to her companion to sit opposite her.

As the train began to move, slowly at first then faster and faster, Gwynna stared entranced out of the window. She'd expected travelling like this to be frightening but it wasn't. A young horse ran alongside them in a field for a few seconds but was soon left behind. It was as if they were flying.

Four stations down the line in the direction of Manchester, the train stopped in the village of Sutherclough. Gwynna could now recognise the S that began the word and the U that followed, though she couldn't fit the rest of the letters together easily. It was such a long word and she'd only mastered short ones so far. One day she'd be able to read properly though, she was determined about that. She hated being so ignorant.

Essie fumbled with the carriage door. Heaving herself ponderously down on to the platform, she waited for Gwynna to follow, then they made their way out of the station arm in arm.

A burly young man wearing a heavy overcoat with two shoulder capes came forward and tipped his hat to them. 'Mrs Linney?'

Essie nodded.

'We've a carriage here to take you to Hungerton House. This way, if you please.' An older man with a weather-beaten face was sitting on the driving bench holding the reins. He nodded politely to them as they were helped inside.

The vehicle began moving and Gwynna stared round, awed by this elegant means of transport. 'I've never rid in a carriage afore – I mean *before*.'

'It's an old one, this.' Essie flicked her gloved fingers scornfully at the worn upholstery. 'Likely they keep it for the servants. Gentry as rich as these wouldn't ride in such a shabby thing.'

The vehicle seemed very grand to Gwynna, who had never before gone anywhere except on her own two feet, and had now ridden in both a train and a private carriage in the same day.

They drove up and down some gentle hills, taking so many turns at unmarked crossroads that Gwynna quite lost her sense of direction. It seemed strange not to have the moors looming to the east and the countryside here was much gentler than round Hedderby.

Eventually the carriage slowed down to turn left between

two wrought-iron gates. The well-raked gravel drive was bordered by trees and a building stood at the end of it. Gwynna gasped. She had never seen such a huge house before. Why, it was as big as the mill in Hedderby! How could any family, even a rich one, possibly need so many rooms?

They turned right halfway along the drive, going slowly round the side and coming to a halt at the rear. When Gwynna would have opened the door, Essie reached out to stop her. 'It's the groom's job to do that.'

Sure enough, the door opened and the young man stood there, one arm outstretched to help them down. 'This way, please.' But once he'd helped Essie down, his polite smile vanished and he scowled at Gwynna. Then his face quickly became expressionless again and as the carriage moved slowly away, he led them to a door at the rear of the house, handing them over to a maid.

Why had he scowled at her? Gwynna wondered. He'd never even met her before.

The young woman took them along a corridor and pointed to a bench. 'Mrs Finch wants to see Mrs Linney first, if you please, so you're to sit here, miss.'

She sat down, feeling even more nervous at being left alone, and watched the maid lead the way down the corridor and knock on a door.

After Essie had disappeared through it, the maid came back, slowing down to stare openly at the newcomer as she passed, but saying nothing.

Everyone else who passed by during the next few minutes – and there seemed to be a lot of them – stared hard at Gwynna. And none of them spoke to her, not even a nod, let alone a 'Good afternoon'. But at least they didn't scowl at her. She hadn't liked that young man. He had mean, piggy eyes and thick lips.

★

Inside the comfortable sitting room Flora Finch came forward to clasp Essie's hands and hold them for a minute. 'You look well, love. Marriage must agree with you.'

'It does. My goodness, you're looking very grand these days, Flora!'

The housekeeper smiled and smoothed her full skirt. 'In my position I need to dress well. Real silk, this is. It doesn't seem all that long ago since we were young maids, does it, and thankful for a cotton print dress in those days?'

Both women sighed and stared into the distance for a moment or two.

'What am I thinking of? Sit down, Essie, and tell me about your protégée. It's the first time you've ever asked such a favour of me. You must think a rare lot of this Gwynna.'

'I do.'

'Tell me more about her – and her family.'

Essie hesitated, then said, 'She's from a poor family, her parents are both drunkards and she wants to get away from them.'

'Brothers and sisters?'

'Two older brothers, three younger sisters. The brothers ran away to be navvies. The sisters are just children. They're not the problem, it's the parents. But our Gwynna's not like them. She's a hard worker and was a great help to my Nev when his first wife died. She looked after his daughter beautifully. She's really good with babies and little children.'

'I wonder you don't keep her on yourself, then, with a stepdaughter to raise.'

'We don't need her help now that Sylvie is eighteen months old. We have a scrubbing woman and there are several grown girls in the house who are my husband's stepchildren by his first wife. Anyway, Nev and I both think it'll do Gwynna good to get out into the world. She'd never even left Hedderby before today.'

'I presume she's able to read and write?'

'A little. She's started learning her letters and knows some of the simpler words. She's got a good brain on her.'

'Hmm. What about young men?'

'She had a fellow, nice lad too, but he was killed in an accident at the mill.'

Flora pursed her lips. 'Well, I'll tell you frankly, I wouldn't normally employ someone with her background, let alone she can't read and write. But the last girl came highly recommended and turned out to be a lazy young madam who ran off with one of the local farm hands.' She patted her stomach suggestively. 'If she hadn't left when she did, we'd have had to dismiss her. So when I got your letter, I decided that since I trust your judgement, I'd meet your girl and if she looked at all capable, give her a trial.'

Essie hesitated, then said quietly, 'There's something else you should know first.' She explained about the trouble Gwynna had been in when they first employed her, knowing that she was risking everything by revealing this. 'I wanted to tell you this face to face. I don't want there to be any secrets that could upset things for her later.'

Flora shook her head disapprovingly. 'I must confess I'd not even have sent for her if I'd known.'

'Which is why I didn't tell you till now. Just meet her and if you like what you see, *please*, for old times' sake, give her a chance to show her worth. Everyone needs a helping hand sometime.' Essie held her breath, praying that she hadn't ruined everything by being so open, only she wasn't one to deceive people, even in a good cause.

Flora sighed. 'Well, it would be foolish not to see her now that she's here.' She rang the bell and the same young maid came hurrying in. 'Fetch Nurse Parker down, then show the girl in.'

Nurse Parker was a stout, grey-haired lady, in charge of

the two nurseries, one for the children of Mr Selwyn Hungerton, the heir, and the other for those of his younger brother Mr Robert, whose family also lived here. After she'd been introduced, she took a seat, studying Essie openly.

As Gwynna was ushered in, Essie's heart went out to the girl, she was looking so white and nervous. And from the way Flora was frowning at her, it seemed fairly likely this had been a wasted journey. No, never wasted. It had given Gwynna some new experiences, she reminded herself as she smiled across at the girl.

'Stand there, please.' Mrs Finch asked a series of sharp questions, before turning to Nurse, who asked more specific questions about the care of babies.

Essie was proud of the sensible way the girl answered, but her old friend's expression still did not lighten.

When they'd finished questioning Gwynna, Flora asked her to go outside again, then looked at Nurse. 'Well?'

'The girl certainly sounds as if she knows what she's doing with young children, but we've never had a nursery maid who couldn't read properly before. I don't like that, I must admit.'

'She's started learning and will soon read as well as anyone else, given the chance,' Essie said quickly, sensing that Nurse was somewhat inclined in Gwynna's favour.

'Well, it's looking after Master Peter that matters most,' the other admitted. 'We don't want someone who'll let us down like the last one did. It upsets young children to lose someone they know. He's been very fretful this week, poor lamb.'

Flora opened her mouth, caught her friend's pleading glance and shut it again, keeping the other information to herself.

'I'd like to see her with him before we decide anything,' Nurse added thoughtfully.

So they went outside and told Gwynna they were taking her to meet the baby.

As they drew near the nursery they heard someone screaming for help. All the women began to run forward but Gwynna got there first. When she burst into the room she saw a baby choking, while the maid holding him didn't seem to know what to do except scream. His face was already a bluish purple shade, so Gwynna snatched him from the other girl, put her foot up on the chair and laid him face down across her knee, pounding his back. Within seconds he had coughed up a mouthful of biscuit.

By that time Nurse was reaching out for him, but she stilled and drew her hands back as his colour returned to normal, watching the younger woman soothe him, pat his back and murmur softly to him.

It was a while before Gwynna noticed how closely she was being observed. 'Did I do something wrong? I'm sorry. I just couldn't bear to see the poor little thing choking like that.'

Nurse Parker smiled warmly at her. 'He chokes easily, does Master Peter.' She turned to the other maid. 'I thought I told you not to give him anything to eat, Mary.'

The maid was still sobbing. 'It was Miss Jane. She came in – and before I knew it, she'd stuffed some biscuit into his mouth. She poked it right down his throat on purpose. You know what she's like.'

'I do.' Nurse's expression was grim as she gestured to the chair. 'Sit down, Gwynna. You can hold him for a minute or two. If you come to work here, he'll be your special charge.'

Flora gestured to Essie to come closer and murmured, 'I'll have to let Mrs Robert know what you told me, but when she hears how the girl dealt with this incident, I think she may be prepared to overlook the past. I like a girl who can think quickly in an emergency, I must admit.' She looked at the clock and raised her voice again. 'I promised to introduce the new girl to Mrs Robert before hiring anyone. Wait here and I'll see if she's free.'

Gwynna sat talking cheerfully to the little boy, who was a bit younger than Sylvie, maybe eleven months old. He gurgled happily back at her, waving his hands and acting as if he understood every word she was saying. When the door opened, she looked up to see a lady wearing a beautiful dress come in with Mrs Finch and stood up instinctively, cradling the baby against her shoulder.

'I'll take him now.' Nurse moved forward.

The lady raised one forefinger imperatively. 'No, leave him with the girl. I want to see them together.' She watched the newcomer try to settle the baby, who was getting a bit restless.

'I think he's hungry,' Gwynna said at last. 'Is there something for him to eat?'

'You take him now, Nurse.' Margaret Hungerton turned to Essie and studied her just as shrewdly as she had been studying Gwynna a moment before. 'We'll give your young friend a trial, Mrs Linney. Three months.'

Essie let out a long sigh of relief. 'I'm sure you'll not be disappointed, ma'am.'

Margaret nodded, then caught sight of the clock. 'I must go. My sister-in-law is expecting callers. Bring Peter to me at the usual time, Nurse.'

'Yes, ma'am.'

Nurse Parker turned to Gwynna. 'Well, young woman, it looks like you've got yourself hired. You'd better go back and fetch your things. We need you to start straight away. Can you come to us tomorrow?'

'Her outfit isn't finished,' Essie said. 'It'll take us at least a week to do the rest of the sewing, I'm afraid. This has all happened so quickly.'

'We can send the things out to be finished by the sewing

woman in the village. I need help with Master Peter as soon as possible. You'll be working for Mrs Robert, the lady you just met, not for Mrs Selwyn.' She could see that this information meant nothing to Gwynna, so explained. 'The lady you just met is the wife of the second son, not the son who'll inherit this house one day. There are three families living here. Old Mr Hungerton and his wife, but she's an invalid, poor lady, Mr Selwyn, the oldest son, and Mr Robert, the middle son. The third son is serving in the Army in India.'

As they walked back down to the housekeeper's room, Mrs Finch didn't speak but when they were inside, she said very firmly to Gwynna. 'You'll behave yourself here or you'll be out on your ear. No flirting with young men, let alone walking out with anyone.'

'No, Mrs Finch.' Gwynna guessed then that Essie had said something about her past and straightened her spine, stung by the housekeeper's tone.

When she and Essie were alone on the train going back to Hedderby, she said in a flat voice, 'You told them.'

'Just Mrs Finch and she told Mrs Robert. Such things have a way of coming out, so it's better to start honestly, don't you think?'

'They didn't tell Nurse?'

'No. The fewer people know the better. It's in the past now, love. You have to carry on.'

'So they won't tell the rest of the servants?'

'No. Definitely not.'

Gwynna stared out of the window, not seeing the scenery this time, but reliving her visit to a grand person's house, trying to make sense of all she had seen there. 'They must be very rich.'

'They are. Old money too, not gained from trade.'

'Is that better?'

'*They* think it is. Consider themselves a cut above mill owners and lawyers and such.'

'It doesn't seem fair to have so much money when some people are clemming for lack of food.' Gwynna could remember being hungry many a time.

'That's what the world's like – unfair.'

She nodded, accepting this because it was her own experience too. But she'd been lucky. Essie and Nev had helped her. Determination filled her to do well so that the Hungertons would want to keep her on. She owed it to Essie and Nev not to waste the chance they'd given her, but most of all she owed it to herself.

Then her face softened into a smile. Eh, but he was a bonny little lad, Master Peter was. It'd be a pleasure to look after him.

Lucas Kemp waited behind after work because Mr Hungerton's land agent had sent a message that he wanted to see him. He put away the tools which belonged to the estate, setting them carefully in the big racks, and slid his own tools into the canvas pouch his mother had made for him when he first started his apprenticeship, rolling it up carefully and tying the strings. He never left his tools here, not even when he knew he'd be coming in early the next day. Some of them had been his grandfather's and he was proud of them, didn't want to risk losing them.

The foreman nodded to him. 'Better go and see Mr Lester now.'

So Lucas picked up his pouch and walked across the yard, whistling under his breath, hardly feeling the cold that had other men wrapping sacks round their shoulders. He had to duck his head to enter the outer room where you waited to see the land agent.

'Is that you, Kemp?' Mr Lester called from the office

before Lucas had time to sit on the hard wooden bench. 'Come straight in.'

He did as bidden, wondering why he'd been summoned.

'Put your tools over there, then pull up a chair.'

Lucas studied the older man's face as he sat down on the hard wooden chair. The land agent's mouth was screwed up in that tight way he had when about to discuss something unpleasant, which was puzzling because Lucas knew he hadn't done anything wrong. On the contrary, his work had recently drawn praise from old Mr Hungerton, because he could not only do the carpentry but the carving that was sometimes needed when they replaced rotten woodwork in the huge old house.

'I've – um – been speaking to Mr Hungerton. We're all very pleased with your recent work, Kemp. Very pleased. You have a real feel for wood.' Mr Lester paused, seeming to have trouble finding words, then went on, 'You're twenty-four now, I believe?'

Lucas nodded, beginning to guess what this was about.

'Not married yet?'

'You know I'm not. I live with my parents.'

'Not walking out with a young woman, either, or I'd have heard about it.'

Silence. Lucas could feel the anger starting to build. They weren't going to go on about that again, surely? He'd marry when he saw fit and not until.

'Mr Hungerton prefers the estate workers to be settled. He thinks family men are more reliable. We've spoken about this before.'

'And with respect, I'll say again what I said then: I'll get wed when I find someone I want to live with, not to suit my employer's convenience.'

'It's – um – not as easy as that. Mr Hungerton has strong views about this matter of young men marrying, very strong indeed. He's given you extra time to settle down because you're a good workman, but he feels you're not playing fair by him. After all, there are several unmarried lasses on the estate and . . .'

'None of whom I fancy marrying, any more than I did when we last spoke.' What his employer really wanted, Lucas knew, was to bind him to the estate for ever. And he wasn't having that.

Another silence, then Mr Lester said curtly, 'In that case, you'd better find someone else to wed because I've been instructed to tell you that you must marry by the end of the second quarter if you wish to keep your job. There's a cottage coming free at that time, which you can have. It's a good one, three bedrooms, so you'll be well set up.'

'Thank Mr Hungerton for his kind offer –' you had to say that sort of thing, Lucas thought, even though you'd like to toss the offer back in his face – 'but I'm not marrying just for the sake of it.'

'I'm afraid he insists.'

'I'd better give my notice then, so that he won't be upset by the sight or thought of me. Four weeks' notice, isn't it?' Lucas had the satisfaction then of seeing Mr Lester lost for words.

'But what will you do, where will you go? You won't be able to stay on with your parents if you've upset Mr Hungerton, you surely realise that, Kemp.'

'I'll have no trouble finding a job elsewhere. There's always work for a good carpenter.' He saw the land agent look at him unhappily, open his mouth then shut it again. The silence seemed to go on for a long time, but Lucas didn't give in, just waited him out.

'Not without references,' Mr Lester said at last, 'and I'm afraid I've been instructed not to give you any if you refuse to do as he wishes.'

'I see.' Rage filled Lucas at this petty behaviour. 'Then I shall have to manage without them, shan't I?' He had his papers, showing he'd completed his apprenticeship. No one could take those away from him. And if it took some time for him to find another job, then so be it. He'd always been careful with his money so he wouldn't starve.

'You won't find another job round here. You can be sure of that.'

Because Mr Hungerton would spread the word not to hire him. Lucas shrugged, still managing to hold back his anger. 'I'll go somewhere else then. I've always had a fancy to see a bit more of the world.' He couldn't resist adding, 'Even *he* can't blacken my name across the whole country.'

'Kemp, *please* reconsider! Mr Hungerton is a very powerful man and he won't tolerate being defied.'

Lucas knew then that he'd have trouble getting away. His master was indeed a generous employer, but only as long as you did exactly what he said and devoted your whole life to his service. If you defied him, he would use any trick in the book to get back at you, lawful or unlawful. Lucas had heard of another man accused of stealing, even when the goods he'd been arrested for taking were known to be his own. The man had received a light sentence from the local magistrate, who always did as Mr Hungerton wanted, and that had been enough to make the poor fellow toe the line from then on, grateful for his job and cottage.

Well, Lucas wouldn't bend on this matter, whatever they said or did to him. He'd no one depending on him and anyway, his mother always said he'd been born stubborn. They'd find out just how stubborn if they tried any of those tricks on him. He knew how unhappy his older brother was in his marriage – a marriage which had been strongly en-couraged by the land agent. Every time he went round he heard his sister-in-law nagging and that had made him vow not to put his own head into parson's noose until he was good and ready.

'I shan't change my mind, sir,' he said quietly but firmly, picked up his tool kit and left. As he looked down at it, he realised suddenly that even this could be used against him. The tools were of excellent quality, though old. They might have been his grandfather's, but if Mr Hungerton said they belonged to the estate, who would contradict him?

He'd have to plan his escape very carefully, and escape wasn't too strong a word to use. They would *not* make him stay here, let alone take a wife he didn't want. But he hated the thought of having to sneak away like a thief in the night when he'd done nothing wrong.

2

Gwynna slept only fitfully that night, her last at Linney's. She hadn't expected to have to leave Hedderby within the day, didn't feel as if she was ready for that. But Essie said she could come back here every year for her two weeks' holiday, so at least she would have something to look forward to. And she was also to come back if she was ever in trouble. She would make sure she didn't do anything wrong, of course, but still, it was a relief to know she wasn't alone in the world.

Nothing would ever make her ask help of her parents again. Nothing! She'd rather starve in a ditch.

When she heard the hall clock strike five, she could stay still no longer so pushed back the bedcovers and got up. She was able to see well enough to dress by the moonlight that filtered round the edges of the curtains. She would miss this small bedroom, the only room she'd had to herself in her whole life, and wondered suddenly where she'd sleep at Hungerton House.

Tiptoeing downstairs, she went into the big kitchen she loved so much, the place where the family gathered to talk and chat or simply be together. Opening the damper, she saw a spark of red in the heart of the big black stove and thrust a spill into it, using the burning splinter of wood to light first a candle then the big oil lamp they always left ready on the table at night. As the fire started to blaze up, she held out her hands to its warmth.

'You're up early, lass.'

She jumped in shock because she'd been so lost in her thoughts she hadn't heard anyone come in.

Raife smiled at her from across the room. He hesitated, head on one side, eyes kindly beneath his sparse silver hair, then walked forward and laid one hand on her shoulder in that comforting way he had.

'I don't want to go,' she blurted out, raising her hand to touch his. He was like a grandfather to her, to all the young people in the family, though he had no blood relationship to anyone except his son Nev and his baby granddaughter.

'I think you *need* to go away, Gwynna love. You took shelter here for a while, but you're too young to hide away from the world for ever. You don't see your old friends, don't even go out on your afternoons off. It's no way for a young lass to live.'

She could only shrug and sit on a stool, holding her hands out to the blaze.

'You're stronger than you think,' Raife said encouragingly. 'You'll do well, I'm sure – learn a lot, meet people, make a good life for yourself. Find another fellow one day.'

'The only people I'll meet apart from Nurse and the other maids will be babies and children.'

'It's a big house, lass. There'll be plenty of other servants to talk to.'

She summoned up a smile, though how she managed that when she felt shivery with nerves, she'd never know. 'You may be right, but I'm – a bit afraid of going to live with strangers. I'm so *ignorant*, Raife! I'm bound to make silly mistakes in such a grand house and then people will laugh at me.'

'If you want a bit of advice . . .'

She nodded several times.

'Laugh at yourself first if you do something silly, then

they'll laugh *with* you. And don't pretend to know every-thing. They won't expect it of any newcomer.'

Footsteps sounded on the stairs and she jumped up. 'I'll get the kettle boiling. They'll be wanting their breakfast.'

Soon the kitchen was full of people – talking, laughing, eating quickly. As usual Nev sat smiling at his stepchildren and second wife from the head of the table, talking less than anyone, but listening far more carefully.

When the younger ones had all gone off to work or school, hugging her and wishing her well in her new life, Gwynna looked at the clock, which had gone on ticking while she'd been helping Essie. 'Would you mind if I went for a quick walk round the town, just to – remember it?'

'Of course not, love. A bit of fresh air will do you good. Wrap up warmly, though. It's a cold day.'

Gwynna went down to Market Street, the main thorough-fare in this long, narrow Pennine town, dawdling and staring round as if she'd never seen it before.

Of course she went to stand outside the Pride, the music saloon that belonged to Nev's stepdaughter and her husband. It wasn't lit up at this time of day, but at night there were bright gas lights flaring outside and lots of people going in, laughing and talking. The Pride was very popular. She'd been to shows a few times herself, because Carrie and Eli were generous about letting family and friends go in free. It was like another world in there, talented people singing, dancing, doing acrobatic tricks – even animals clever enough to perform on the stage. She looked down at her clothes and pulled a face. She didn't like dark colours. They made her feel sad. It must be lovely to wear bright colours and meet so many people, like the performers did.

She turned round, catching sight of the clock just inside the grocery emporium. She had a little time yet, could stroll back.

But before she'd gone a hundred yards she wished she hadn't lingered because her mother came out of a side street. She tried to turn away, but of course her mother saw her and changed course to cut her off.

'Hold on, Gwynna! I was just coming to see you.'

That was a lie. Nev wouldn't let her parents come to Linney's because they were nearly always drunk. Even now, so early in the day, her mother was swaying on her feet.

'I'm in a hurry, Mam.'

Mrs Jones grabbed her daughter's arm. 'Too fine to stop and talk to your old mother now, are you? Well, you're still my daughter and you *owe* me for bringing you up.'

Gwynna knew better than to argue, just held her tongue and waited for her opportunity to get away.

Her mother's tone changed to wheedling. 'I've got such a bad head. Surely you've got sixpence you could lend me, just to buy something to soothe it?'

'No, I haven't. I've told you before, I'm not giving you money for booze.'

'It's not much to ask of a daughter, to help a mother whose head aches so.'

'No!' Gwynna shook off her mother's hand and ran off quickly, not turning round. To her embarrassment, curses and yells pursued her. This was what happened if she didn't keep her eyes open when she went out. She'd given her mother sixpence a couple of times in the early days after she went to work at Linney's, but it had been a mistake. Now, every time her mother saw her, she asked for more money.

Well, no one was wasting Gwynna's hard-earned pennies on booze. One of the best things about the new job was that she wouldn't have to see her parents again. She hadn't even told them she was leaving.

Back at Linney's she banished the incident from her mind,

picked up little Sylvie for a last cuddle, then reluctantly handed the baby back. 'I'm going to miss her.'

'You'll have the new one to look after. But Gwynna – always remember that these aren't your own babies. Don't grow too attached to them.'

She nodded, though she didn't know how you could stop yourself from loving them. The clock struck the quarter hour so she moved across to the stairs. 'I don't want to be late. I'll get my things.'

They came to the front door to wave her goodbye, Nev repeating the promise he'd made the previous evening. 'You know you've always got a home here, love.'

Gwynna nodded and started walking down the street. Her throat was too choked with unshed tears to speak.

Beside her Raife pushed her tin trunk and carpet bag on the family handcart, greeting his many friends and acquaintances as they went but not stopping to chat with anyone, thank goodness, or expecting her to speak to him. He simply gave her a hug when they got to the station and that spoke far louder than words to someone who'd had more blows than hugs from her own parents.

The train came in and soon Gwynna found herself sitting alone in a compartment on a hard wooden bench, her small carpet bag on the seat beside her, her hands tightly clasped on her lap to stop them trembling. Her trunk had been heaved into the luggage compartment at the rear and she was worried about having to let it out of her sight, was worried about everything today.

When the guard blew his whistle, more steam hissed along the platform, making Raife seem a ghostly figure as he stood waving goodbye.

Then he was left behind and she was alone in the world.

She stared out of the train window at the fields and farmhouses they passed, vowing yet again to work hard and make a success of her new life. She counted the stops and at Sutherclough got out of the train, trying to seem confident. 'I've a trunk in the luggage compartment,' she told the elderly porter.

With much puffing he helped the guard unload the battered tin box that had once belonged to Essie. Then, as the whistle shrilled and the train pulled away, Gwynna turned to look for the coachman who was to meet her like last time.

But no one was waiting on the platform of the small station – or in the turning circle for carriages outside it. The porter said he hadn't seen or heard anything, helped her drag the trunk that held nearly all her worldly possessions under the sheltered part of the tiny station, then disappeared through a door. She began to pace up and down to keep warm because there was no waiting room at such a tiny station. The coachman was just a bit late coming to get her, she told herself, and would be here soon.

But the minutes passed and no one came.

She checked the clock on the wall regularly because Essie had taught her to tell the time. Its hands didn't seem to be moving very quickly, but when half an hour had passed she went outside for the third time to look for the carriage.

Why had no one come for her? Had they changed their minds about employing her? But if so, surely they'd have sent someone to tell her?

She felt very alone and afraid.

The Saturday night following his interview with the land agent Lucas waited till his family were in bed, took his savings out of the box under the bed, picked up his tools and papers, and let himself out of the house. Grateful for a moon and a fine night, he walked briskly along the empty roads, hearing frost crunching in the ruts beneath his feet. It took him three hours to walk to Hedderby and then he had to knock up his relatives.

His uncle's first words were, 'What's wrong? Is my brother—?'

'Father's all right, Uncle Fred, except for the way he still kowtows to Mr Hungerton.'

'Well, that's a relief. Come on in, lad, and tell us what brings you here at this time of night.' He looked up the stairs to where his two daughters were standing in their nightdresses, watching what was happening. 'Get back to bed, you two!'

His aunt got the fire going and made Lucas a cup of tea, which sent welcome warmth through his body as he explained what had happened. 'I want you to look after my savings and tools till I've worked out my notice. Someone might say the money isn't mine or that I stole the tools from where I work.'

His uncle stared at him. 'Surely it's not that bad?'

'Oh, it is. You were lucky to get away from the estate, Uncle Fred. Mr Hungerton treats us like he owns us body and soul. I stayed on mainly because of Mum and Dad and because I could gain some useful experience. There's a lot of delicate work to be done on an old house.'

He didn't have to explain to someone who had grown up on the Hungerton estate how easy it would be for its owner to claim that a workman with nearly a hundred pounds in his pocket had stolen it, especially with a compliant magistrate to hand. Most working men never saved even a quarter of that sum, but Lucas had not only saved from his wages but had carved little household objects for his mother to sell at market with her eggs and vegetables, and had added the money he got for them to his savings as well.

'How will you get away, then, lad? If they're that determined to keep you, they'll find other ways to trick you.'

'I haven't worked it all out yet. Oh!' He fumbled in his

pocket. 'I brought my apprenticeship papers too, just to keep them safe. I'll need them to find another job.' He fished in his other pocket. 'And here's Grandad's will. Dad won't miss it, but it says the tools are for me.'

His uncle was silent, frowning, lips pressed together as if to hold his thoughts in. At length he took a deep breath and said, 'I think you need to get yourself a lawyer.'

Lucas stared at him in surprise.

'Do everything legally, even if it costs you.'

'I don't know any lawyers and if I did, they'd only do what Mr Hungerton says, like the magistrate does.'

'Not here in Hedderby. It's a different world here. There's a new lawyer set up a year or two ago, Jack Burtell he's called. He's a bit different from most. I can go and see him for you, tell him what's happened, show him the will. Then he can advise you how best to go about leaving.'

Lucas nodded. 'All right.' He ate the last bit of cake, drained his cup of tea and stood up. 'I'd better get going.'

'You're never walking back at this hour?' his aunt protested. 'I can make you up a bed on the sofa.'

'I have to be back before breakfast. Even my parents don't know I'm here because they'd let it out where I'd gone if Mr Lester questioned them. Write to tell me what the lawyer says and send it care of the Bird in Hand in Lower Sutherclough, Uncle. The landlord's a friend of mine and he owns the place so he isn't dependent on the Hungertons.'

Lucas strode off into the darkness without another word, saving his breath for the long walk home. There was no moon to light his way after the first hour's walking, so he measured his length on the icy ground a couple of times. But he cared nothing for that. He was fighting for his freedom, his lifelong freedom. Eh, it wasn't right that some men had such power over others!

As for marrying, he didn't intend to do that for years.

Once you were wed, you were trapped and could never go your own way in life. He wanted children one day, though, of course he did, but not for a while because he wasn't quite sure yet where life would lead him. He enjoyed working with wood but he wanted more than to be an estate carpenter. Much more.

Nearly an hour after the train had deposited her in Sutherclough, Gwynna heard the sound of a horse and vehicle in the distance but to her disappointment it was only a cart. Then, as it got closer, she saw that it was being driven by the same young groom who had come to the station last time. She shuddered, feeling sick with relief.

He put the reins in the holder and jumped down. 'Sorry to keep you waiting.'

He was only her height, short for a man, and a bit on the plump side. Yesterday he'd been smartly turned out, but today he was filthy, covered in dust and mud.

'What's happened? Did you have an accident?' She indicated a deep graze on his hand.

He jerked it away from her pointing finger. 'Part of the new stable block fell down and everyone had to help get the horses out. It wasn't till they were safe that anyone remembered you. That's why I had to bring the old cart. Half the carriages have been damaged. Eh, it's a right old mess. Now, where's your luggage?'

'I have a trunk and carpet bag back there.' She gestured back towards the station.

She waited until he and the elderly porter had struggled out with the heavy trunk and heaved it on to the back of the cart. Only then did she follow with her carpet bag.

'Get up.' He didn't offer to help her with the bag, so she put it in the back of the cart and climbed nimbly up on to the driving bench beside him, smoothing her skirts so that she was sitting decently. There was still an air of faint hostility about him and he didn't speak to her, just told the horse to walk on.

She didn't want to start at her new place by offending someone. 'Is something wrong? You seem angry at me.'

He turned to scowl at her. 'My sister was going to ask for the nursery maid's job. She'd have got it too, but for you. Our family has served the Hungertons for three generations, and proud of it. We don't want outsiders like *you* coming in to take our jobs.'

He thrust his face even closer and she had to lean back to get away from him.

'You won't last, though. I can tell that just by looking at you. You're not *our* sort. You're rubbish, you are.'

'I wouldn't want to be your sort if that's the kind of manners you have,' she flashed back at him.

He scowled at her even more darkly and shook the reins, so that the horse started moving faster.

She stared straight ahead, holding on tightly as she was jolted about. His words had hurt her deeply. How could a stranger, who didn't know about her family, judge her like that? Was there something wrong with her appearance?

Were all the other servants going to be hostile to her as well?

The rear of Hungerton House was still in turmoil when they arrived and they had to leave the cart some distance away from the back door. One end of the long, low building had completely collapsed but the other end seemed almost untouched. There were several horses in a field nearby and a man was just leading one out of the debris. Its coat was dusty and it had a cut on one shoulder.

'Jabez! Here a minute,' a voice yelled. 'You're good with Misty. We're just getting her out.'

The groom jumped down and left Gwynna sitting on the cart. She stayed there for a minute or two, then decided he wasn't coming back and climbed down.

'Someone see to that horse and cart,' the same voice yelled, 'and get that female out of the way.'

A maid darted out of the back door of the house and pulled at Gwynna's arm. 'Better come inside. Mr Hungerton is upset about the stables an' he can be a bit sharp.'

'I can't leave my trunk and bag sitting out there,' Gwynna protested.

The other lass paused for thought then said, 'You bring your bag in and I'll fetch someone to help with the trunk.' She giggled suddenly. 'You chose a right old time to start here. Who'd have thought that a brand-new building would collapse like that. And Mr Hungerton was so proud of it. He'll be in a foul mood for days now and we'll all have to watch our step. My name's Dodie, by the way.'

She fetched another maid and continued to talk as the three of them lugged the trunk into the house and, with much puffing and panting, hauled it up the narrow back stairs to the nursery wing. Then the other one vanished with a nod.

Dodie, who seemed very friendly, in spite of what Jabez had said to Gwynna, stayed to chat. 'You'll be sleeping in here with Mary to be near the babies. She looks after Mr Selwyn's son, who's two months older than your Master Peter and—'

She broke off as Nurse Parker appeared. 'I've brought the new girl up, Nurse. We had to carry her trunk up ourselves because all the men are outside helping with the stables. They'd have forgotten to fetch Gwynna from the station if you hadn't reminded them.'

'Thank you, Dodie. You can get back to work now.' Nurse nodded to her new helper. 'Unpack your things, Gwynna, then show me what clothes you've still to finish sewing and we'll arrange to have that done by the village dressmaker. After that, you can start getting used to looking after Master Peter.'

She turned to leave, stopped, then came back to say in a near whisper, 'I'd better warn you about Miss Jane, Mr Selwyn's eldest. She's barely eight but she's a little devil, always causing trouble. If she tries to do anything that hurts Master Peter you'll have to stop her, but otherwise there's not much we can do about her, because old Mr Hungerton dotes on her – first-born grandchild, you see, and there weren't any others for years. He won't hear a word against her, whatever she does, the master won't.'

Gwynna blinked. 'I'll remember that.'

'And about you learning to read, I can't have you not knowing how so I've asked the governess to teach you. She's not best pleased but I said you'd do her mending to repay her.'

'I'm only just learning to sew,' Gwynna confessed, remembering that Essie had told her not to pretend about anything. 'I'm not very good at it yet, I'm afraid.'

Nurse's face fell. 'You need to be able to sew in a job like this. I should have asked you about that yesterday, but I was that upset to see Master Peter choking . . . Well, there's nothing to be done about it now but for me to teach you. I'm a good needlewoman, if I do say so myself.'

'I'll be very grateful for any help you can give me, Mrs Parker, and I'll learn as fast as I can, I promise you.'

'Everyone calls me Nurse, so you might as well too.'

'Nurse, then.'

'Go and get that unpacking done. I'll be in to see you in a few minutes.'

The nursemaids' bedroom lay between the babies' rooms and had two narrow single beds and two chests of drawers.

Gwynna paused for a moment to think about her arrival here. The other maids didn't seem hostile, whatever Jabez had said. But she hadn't liked the look in that young groom's eyes. Downright nasty to her he'd been. She'd have to watch out for him.

Lucas finished work on his final day and went up to the foreman. 'I need you to sign this.'

'What is it?'

'It says I've handed over all the tools and things I've been using here.'

The foreman took a hasty step backwards. 'I can't do that, you know I can't, Lucas lad. I'm sorry but—'

Mr Lester came into the workshop and stared across the room. 'There's still time to change your mind, Kemp.'

'No, sir. I'm definitely leaving. I want to see a bit of the world.' He walked across with his piece of paper. 'Perhaps *you* would sign this for me?'

The land agent studied it. 'Where did you get that?'

'My lawyer wrote it for me, said I needed to have it signed before I left here.'

'Well, he told you wrongly. *If* you do have a lawyer, which I take leave to doubt.'

Like the foreman, Lucas also glanced over his shoulder to make sure they weren't being overheard, then said fiercely, 'I *do* have a lawyer and you know why. Other men have tried to leave and been falsely accused of stealing.'

'Rubbish!' But the tone was unconvincing and Mr Lester flushed a dull red, then walked back quickly across the yard to his office without a word.

Which told Lucas that his suspicions were correct. They were going to try to keep him here.

When he turned round everyone else had gone, which meant they'd left far more quickly than usual, another bad sign. He thought for a moment and decided to go out by another route. Returning to the workshop, he climbed into the upstairs storage space and edged his way over the low wooden dividing wall into the hay store next door. Letting himself out through the stables he made his way quickly to the Bird in Hand. But before he'd had time even to say goodbye to his friend, the village constable arrived.

'Lucas Kemp, I'm arresting you for stealing from your employer.'

Lucas scowled at him. *Think!* he told himself. *Think, you fool!* Suddenly an idea came to him and he started getting undressed.

'Here, what do you think you're doing?' the constable protested.

Lucas fended him off and removed every stitch of his clothing so that his friend and two customers, as well as the constable could both see that he was carrying nothing. 'What am I supposed to have stolen?' he asked sarcastically.

'Mr Hungerton sent word that you've stolen some tools.'

'Oh, yes? Did I swallow them, do you think?'

'You could have hid them. You've a bag there.'

'His bag's been here all day and he hasn't opened it since he got here tonight,' Lucas's friend John said at once. 'He's not stolen owt and well you know it.'

'If Mr Hungerton says he has, then he has,' the constable said. 'You're to come with me, Kemp, and if you make a fuss, I'll charge you with resisting arrest as well as stealing. Now put some clothes on, man! Have you no shame?'

Lucas looked at his friend, who gave him a nod, then studied the two men and looked at John again. They didn't work on the estate, so perhaps they'd bear witness that he'd been carrying nothing. John would know who they were.

The constable refused to talk as he led his prisoner across the village and locked him up in the former storeroom the village used for a temporary gaol. But Lucas could see that he looked worried. 'I'm innocent, and well you know it,' he repeated as the door was slammed shut in his face and he was left in darkness. He went and sat on the bench and fumbled around for a blanket, but there was nothing to cover himself with. With a grin he went and banged on the door, yelling loudly enough to be heard in the nearby cottages. No one came but he didn't stop shouting till everyone nearby knew he'd not been given even a blanket, let alone a jug of water.

He wondered how soon his father would find out what had happened to him. He'd said goodbye to his parents that morning, intending to leave quickly after he finished work, so that they wouldn't be involved in any trouble with Mr Hungerton. His mother had wept and tried to give him extra food for the road, but he'd refused gently, telling her he'd eat when he got to Hedderby.

Even if they knew what had happened, they'd not be able to do anything to help him. He doubted they'd dare try, they were so afraid of upsetting Mr Hungerton and losing their livelihood and cottage both.

Time passed slowly. He was known for not feeling the cold as badly as others did, but he'd never spent a winter's night without bedcovers before and found it too uncomfortable to do more than doze for a while, then wake up shivering. He ended up jumping around every hour or so to warm himself up, then trying to doze till the cold got to him again.

By the time morning came he was furious as well as chilled through. If Mr Hungerton thought to wear him down with this sort of treatment he'd find out differently.

Gwynna always had half an hour off while Master Peter was with his mother in the afternoon so she decided to go out for a quick breath of fresh air. As she stood near the back door looking round the busy stable yard, something hit her skirt and there was the sound of a man's laughter. She looked down in dismay to see a lump of horse droppings sliding down, leaving a dirty brown mark on her skirt. Before she could move another piece of muck hit her on the arm and with a squeak she darted inside the corridor that led to the kitchen. A thump on the door she'd just closed let her know that a third missile had missed its target.

As she was standing there, still too shocked to know what to do, one of the kitchen maids came out, gaped at her then tittered.

An older woman came out behind her. 'What are you doing standing about when Cook wants those onions straight away?'

The girl pointed to Gwynna. 'Look at her. She's fallen into some horse muck.' She giggled, her expression spiteful.

The other woman gave her a shove and said, 'Get on with you.' She looked at Gwynna. 'You'll have to wash that off before you go back to the nursery. If you come with me, I'll show you where you can get some water to wash the worst off then you'd better change your clothes.'

'It's my only dress. The others aren't finished.' Gwynna couldn't stop her voice from wobbling.

Her companion looked her up and down. 'You didn't fall, someone threw it at you. Do you know who did that?'

Gwynna hesitated then shook her head. She had learned as a child that people who told tales were not popular and she was sure things wouldn't be any different here.

'I'll help you clean yourself up. I'm the senior upstairs maid, by the way. And I know you're the new nursery maid – Gwynna, isn't it?'

She nodded and waited till the other returned.

'Come this way. We'll see what we can do, though you're going to be a bit damp till your dress dries out, I'm afraid.'

Working carefully, she got the mess off Gwynna's clothing and dried the damp patches as well as she could with an old towel. 'There. That's the best I can do. At least we've got rid of the smell.'

'I'm so grateful.'

'You're welcome, love. It's a poor look-out if we can't help one another. Now, you'd better get back to work, hadn't you?'

Gwynna went off with a warm feeling inside her after this kindness. She'd not go outside again and give Jabez the chance to get at her. Apart from this incident, things seemed to be going quite well. She was fond of Master Peter already, he was such a little love, and she was enjoying learning to sew. Nurse said she had an aptitude for it. Nurse used a lot of long words and was teaching her what they meant, because you had to learn to speak properly as well as dressing properly, it seemed.

Essie and Nev had been right about her needing to get some experience of life, Gwynna felt. She was enjoying meeting new people, living differently, learning all sorts of new things from Nurse about caring for a child.

If only Jabez and the kitchen maid weren't so hostile, she'd be truly happy here. But at meal times they kept making nasty remarks about her. It was hard not to snap back at them, but she'd decided to act as if she hadn't heard them.

The next morning the constable came to release Lucas, looking round suspiciously.

'I've not peed on the floor, if that's what you were looking for,' Lucas said sarcastically, 'but I will do if you don't take me out to the privy straight away.'

With a sigh the constable did so, looking round as if he expected something to happen.

Which made Lucas keep a closer eye on his surroundings

too. 'Don't I get anything to eat or drink?' he asked when brought back into the building.

'You've already been fed.'

'You know damned well I've not been given either food or drink since I was brought here, which means I haven't eaten since yesterday noon. Not even a drink of water, Ted Burroughs! Shame on you!'

The man looked at him pleadingly. 'I have to do as they say. I've a wife and children to find food for. I can't afford to lose my job.'

A voice behind them asked, 'Is that true about the food and drink?'

Lucas spun round, eyes narrowing at the sight of a dark-clad gentleman a little older than himself. 'Yes, it is. Who are you?'

'My name's Jack Burtell. I'm your lawyer. Can you prove it about the food and drink?'

'If you look in the cell –' Lucas waved one hand to the tiny room where he'd spent the night – 'you'll see no sign of food and drink, no water, not even a bucket in which to relieve myself.'

'I've took them out again,' the constable said desperately.

'How many other lies are you prepared to tell?' Lucas asked him scornfully. 'I don't know how cowards like you sleep at night.'

Jack laid one hand on Lucas's arm. 'Better to keep calm, Mr Kemp.'

He took a deep breath and nodded, but even with a lawyer to help him, he wasn't feeling optimistic about today's hearing. 'How are we to prove the truth if everyone is going to lie?'

The lawyer looked at the constable. 'I need to speak to my client privately.'

The man shook his head vigorously. 'I daren't.'

Even as he was speaking two burly men walked in, smiling. 'Is this him?' one of them asked. 'He's a big sod, isn't he? We've come to help you take him to the magistrate, in case he struggles.'

Jack stepped forward. 'I'm Mr Kemp's lawyer and if you lay one finger on my client, I'll have you in court for assault.'

One man took a step forward, but though he was quite small in comparison, the lawyer didn't move from his protective position in front of Lucas. The other man tugged at his companion's arm and said in a very audible whisper, 'He's gentry. Better go careful.'

They stopped where they were and Jack took advantage of their uncertainty to say, 'Shall we go, constable? I'll make sure my client comes peacefully.'

The group of five men walked through the village to the magistrate's house, during which time Lucas explained in a low voice exactly what had happened after he finished work the previous night.

Jack laughed aloud at the thought of him stripping naked. 'You did well, though. It'll be hard for them to refute that.'

'They'll say anything,' Lucas said gloomily, hearing his stomach rumble.

'I hope it does that during the hearing,' Jack said.

'What?'

'Your stomach – rumbles.'

The magistrate, Mr Coulthard, was waiting for them in his rooms, together with his clerk. He raised one eyebrow when Jack Burtell came in. 'Who is this?'

'Gentleman says he's Kemp's lawyer, sir.'

Coulthard bristled at Jack. 'The fellow needs no lawyer.'

'If you're going to declare my client innocent, no, he doesn't. If you consider him guilty before we even start, then it's a good thing I am here.' Jack pulled a card out of his pocket and handed it to Mr Coulthard.

'You'd be well advised to mind your own business, Burtell.'

'Justice *is* my business, sir, as my stepfather, Judge Gerald Haines, reminded me when I graduated from Cambridge.'

At the sound of the judge's name, the magistrate grew very still, staring at the lawyer as if he'd suddenly turned into a man-eating tiger. After a few moments he said in a more polite tone, 'Please take a seat. Your client should stand in front of the desk.'

Jack sat down, Lucas stood where indicated and the police constable moved forward to stand by his side. The clerk cleared his throat and announced that the hearing had begun.

'Charges?' the magistrate asked.

'Stealing from his employer,' the constable said in a faint voice, glancing nervously towards Mr Burtell.

'How do you plead?'

Jack stood up. 'Just a moment. Stealing what?'

'Tools.' It was little more than a whisper from the constable, who was looking more unhappy by the minute.

'How do you plead?' repeated the magistrate, tight-lipped.

'My client pleads not guilty,' Jack said, gesturing to Lucas to keep silent.

'I have Mr Hungerton's sworn statement here about the tools.' The constable held out a piece of paper.

'Is that all the evidence?' Jack asked.

Coulthard scowled at him. 'It's all the evidence *I* need. You surely don't intend to take this fellow's word against that of a gentleman?'

'I intend to see justice done, for which we need proof.'

'The tools went missing,' the constable offered.

Lucas opened his mouth to protest and shut it again as the lawyer put one finger on his lips and winked. A small spark of hope flickered inside him. Was it possible that he was going to get away?

'How do you know that the tools went missing?'

'Well – the land agent sent word to me.'

'I'd like to call a witness,' Jack said.

'Witness?' Coulthard goggled at him. 'Witness to what?'

'To the fact that my client had no tools on him. In fact, there were three witnesses.'

After breathing very heavily, the magistrate said, 'Bring in this witness of yours, then.'

'We haven't brought anyone with us, sir,' the constable said.

'This is a farce,' Jack muttered in Lucas's ear. 'Leave it to me.' He raised his voice. 'I ask for the landlord of the Bird in Hand to be brought in – he's just across the road – and he will tell us the names of the other two men who were with him and who saw my client.'

The magistrate sighed loudly and gestured to the constable, who vanished rapidly.

'While he's gone, I'd like to ask what these two men are doing here,' Jack said.

'Eh?'

'His lordship sent us to make sure the prisoner didn't get violent,' the spokesman offered promptly.

'My client has exhibited no signs of violence, though these two fellows have behaved in a very threatening way both to myself and him. I am considering bringing a charge against them for that. And, sir,' he stared pointedly at the magistrate, 'if the truth isn't sought for diligently, I am quite prepared to bring charges against those responsible for misadministration of justice and bringing the Queen's Law into disrepute.'

Lucas saw Coulthard sag and lose his bluster. The spark of hope inside him glowed still more brightly.

The constable returned with the landlord of the Bird in Hand, who swore when questioned that Lucas had had nothing on him except for his clothes, a handkerchief and a few coins the previous evening. He had also brought Lucas's carpet bag with him to prove that Mr Kemp had taken nothing. 'He brought it to me yesterday morning and he hasn't touched it since. And I'm prepared to take an oath that I haven't opened it, either.'

Burtell insisted its contents should be examined and noted down.

After that the magistrate hesitated, cleared his throat and muttered to himself, before declaring that the case was dismissed for lack of evidence. A bewildered Lucas found himself being led outside.

'Was it as easy as that?' he marvelled.

'This time it was. Whoever told you to get yourself a lawyer was right.'

'It was my uncle Fred.'

'I think it'd be wise if you left here with me today, and on the next train, too. You'll be in physical danger from those two if you stay, and in danger of fresh charges being laid as well.' Jack jerked his head to the right and they saw the two men sent by Mr Hungerton leaning against a wall, watching them closely. 'I'm afraid you'll have to go hungry for a little while longer.'

'It doesn't matter.'

As they waited for the train, Jack said, 'I shall be having a word with my stepfather about this farce. Strange as it may seem to you after today, there are men who do care to see justice done. My stepfather and I disagree about many things, but not about this point.'

'I'm grateful.'

'Can you afford to pay me for my services today?'

'Yes, Mr Burtell. I'm a careful sort and I've money saved.'

'Good. Then it's a guinea and the cost of my train fare.'

'I can't pay you till we get to Hedderby. My money's at my uncle's. I didn't dare keep it here or they'd have said I'd stolen it. I'm not staying there long, though, just picking up some of my money. I've a fancy to see a bit of the world first.'

'Where shall you go?'

'London. I'll look for work, of course, but I've no references, even though I'm a good carpenter. Mr Hungerton refused to give me any.'

'I can give you a character reference, if you like.'

Lucas stared at him in surprise. 'Why would you do that? You've only just met me.'

'Blame it on my fondness for justice again. Besides, I pride myself on being able to judge whether a man's honest or not, and I've dealt with your uncle before so I know your family background. I think it's probably a good thing for you to get away, though, and to stay away for a while. Even in Hedderby we've heard of Hungerton's reputation for holding grudges.'

As the train rattled off down the track Lucas looked out of the window and shuddered at the close shave he'd just had. If his uncle hadn't hired the lawyer for him, if his friend hadn't sent for that lawyer, he'd be in gaol now. He reckoned paying the lawyer would have to be the best guinea he'd ever spend in his whole life.

He looked round the compartment and grinned. 'I've never ridden first-class before and probably won't again, but it's nice to try it once.'

Jack laughed. 'I don't always ride first-class. For all my useful connections, I'm a struggling lawyer and I do more work than is financially prudent for people who can't afford to pay me.'

'For the sake of justice?' Lucas asked softly.

'Yes. I really do believe in it.'

'So do I – now.'

*

Lucas stayed with his uncle and family in Hedderby overnight. The following morning he took some of his money and went into Manchester. He'd visited it a couple of times by train just to say he'd been there, but had only walked round the central area for a couple of hours, then gone home again. Now he had a desire to see more of the city that dominated Lancashire so he spent several days walking round it, talking to people. He'd not felt so free since he was a lad.

He was amazed by the buildings. Even the warehouses near the city centre looked like palaces, with elegant windows and lines that had him tracing them in the air, loving the balance and rightness of their shapes. And more were being built everywhere.

He'd seen the music saloon in Hedderby, now he saw bigger music saloons, equally full of life and activity, and visited two of them, enjoying himself hugely.

But after a few days he was ready to move on to what really drew him, the capital of his country, London. You could get there easily by train in less than a day, which still seemed a marvel to ordinary folk like him who'd had a childhood with no trains in it. He accepted the railways' magic but didn't want to understand how the steam engines worked. What he did want to understand was how people designed the splendid buildings he'd seen, how they made them strong enough to stand for hundreds of years, woodwork and stone combined in a strong, satisfying whole.

In London, Lucas fended off a pickpocket and, with the help of a friendly cab driver, found himself respectable lodgings. Once again he set out to explore a city on foot, but this place was far bigger than Manchester and he soon realised he'd have to confine himself to the central districts. By the end of a week, he was beginning to know his way round them, to recognise the patterns of their streets and parks and buildings.

'Patterns' was the word he used to himself about how towns and buildings were set out, because that's how he remembered them in his mind. You had to wonder at some parts of towns, which were all muddled, as if things had gone wrong, while other parts were graceful and – *right* – that was the only way he could describe it.

And then on the last day of the time he'd allowed himself for a holiday, he found himself a job by sheer chance.

A gentleman was walking along at the other end of a short side street when two ruffians attacked him. Lucas couldn't bear to see that, so joined in the fight, knocking one fellow flying and punching the other so hard his nose spurted blood. The first one scrambled to his feet and dragged his companion away. Lucas didn't bother to chase them because he'd already learned how easy it was to get lost in these narrow alleys.

The gentleman began to gather up the papers that had fallen from a leather case under his arm, while Lucas picked up his hat for him and gave it a quick brush down.

'I'm very grateful for your help, young man.'

'That's all right, sir. I can't abide thieves.'

'From the north, aren't you? You wouldn't be looking for work, would you?'

'I am.'

'Well, I could offer you a job. It's only temporary, but it'll tide you over. If you can read easily, that is.'

'Oh, I can read all right, and do ciphering and simple accounts. Could I ask the nature of the work, sir? I'm a carpenter by trade.'

'Even better! I'm an architect, in the middle of building some houses, and I need a general factotum.' He could see that his companion didn't understand the word and explained, 'Someone to do anything and everything, take messages, help on the sites, check deliveries, whatever is needed.'

'I think I'd enjoy that.'

The man stuck his hand out. 'I'm Reginald Laing.'

Lucas hesitated then took it, not used to gentry who shook your hand. 'Lucas Kemp.'

'From?'

Lucas hesitated.

His companion frowned. 'You're not in trouble with the law, are you?'

'No, sir. But I did offend Mr Hungerton, which is why I've left home.'

'Not old Harold Hungerton?' Laing laughed as Lucas nodded. 'I've met him a couple of times, because he's interested in building ventures, but I didn't take to him, I must admit. A pompous old fool, still living in the eighteenth century, that one. What did you do to upset him?'

'Refused to get wed. I hadn't got a lass in trouble or anything, it's just that he likes his workers to be wed. If you've a family you can't just up and off, can you? When I gave notice, he tried to stop me leaving by pretending I'd stolen my own tools. I had to pay a lawyer to help me.'

Laing rolled his eyes. 'I can believe it of him. You should hear his views on how we should treat the poor. It's amazing what some men can do because of their position. He'd not get away with that in London, I can tell you, only in the country, where he's king of his estate. Anyway, what about this job?'

'I'd like to try it, sir. Er – how much does it pay?' Lucas had already found how expensive it was to live in London. The amount Laing named made him blink and was more than he'd ever earned before in his life, so he nodded. 'That'll be fine.'

After that, Lucas found himself leading a varied, interesting life, learning a great deal and being well paid for it too. His new employer was a cheerful fellow, as well as a successful architect, and pronounced himself well satisfied with his general factotum. Sadly, however, his previous assistant, who had broken a leg, was due back soon, so the job couldn't last.

'I can recommend you to others of my acquaintance,' he offered at the beginning of the last week.

Lucas smiled. 'Thank you, sir. I'd appreciate that.' He was learning so much here about the things that he often wondered about, like how buildings were made strong enough to stand for years or why some buildings looked good and others ugly. Mr Laing said he had a natural talent for that sort of thing, and Lucas admitted to himself that his employer was right. Each new piece of knowledge about buildings seemed to fall into place in his mind without any trouble. Ah, but he desperately wanted that learning to go on.

When he was offered another fairly similar position, he began to think of settling here in the capital permanently.

3

Carrie Beckett woke suddenly, gasping for breath, seeing flames and smoke all around her, then realised where she was. A nightmare, she thought, as she snuggled down again in the bed and waited for her heart to stop pounding. Then she realised it wasn't just a nightmare, but memories of the previous evening. What time was it? It was light already, so must be late.

She looked round and realised she was in a strange bedroom, then saw her husband lying beside her staring at her, wide awake but very still. Eli looked different today, grim, as if his eyes had lost their vivid blue and turned into chips of ice. She reached out instinctively, needing the simple comfort of holding him close after the previous day's disaster – and it was a disaster for them, a very major one.

'I can't believe it. Did our music saloon really burn down?' She felt him nod against her shoulder. She blinked away a tear, trying to be brave, but another followed and suddenly she was weeping.

He held her close, not speaking, not weeping with her, the whole of his body feeling as hard as a piece of cast iron. That helped her regain control of herself. 'We'll cope somehow,' she assured him. 'I know we will.'

'Yes.' Silence, then he said in a gritty voice, unlike his usual tones. 'Before I do anything else, I need to go and see it. Will you come with me?'

'Of course.'

They slipped down to the kitchen where only Raife was sitting staring into the fire, looking old and tired. The clock said it was nearly midday.

'We're going to see it,' Eli explained and the old man nodded.

'Abigail?' Carrie asked.

'Essie took her out in the trolley with little Sylvie, said you two needed your rest.'

'Marjorie?'

'Your sister and Hal caught the ten o'clock train. Told me to give you their love. Can't let the audience down, they said.' He frowned. 'They should have stayed till tomorrow, seen if they could help you.'

'They can't. And anyway, they know we've got you, Nev and Essie.' She went across to give him a quick hug, then went back to Eli. She was getting worried by his silence and his wooden look. And like her husband, she needed to see the ruins of the home and business they'd worked so hard to build up before she could even think about the future.

They grabbed someone's coats from the hooks near the door, because they'd lost all their own clothes in the fire, and made their way quickly down to Market Street, arm in arm. People they passed nodded a greeting, looking at them sympathetically, but to Carrie's relief no one stopped them or tried to say anything. Eli didn't say anything, either.

It was only a short walk. Too short, she thought. She'd have preferred more time to prepare herself. They slowed down instinctively as they turned the corner and each step became more reluctant than the one before until they reached the burnt remains of their pub and music saloon. Without speaking they crossed to the other side of Market Street to avoid the rubble and get a proper look.

As they stopped, Eli let go of her arm and stood there

with clenched fists, his face a mask of pain, while she put both hands to her mouth to hold back more sobs.

The roof had caved in everywhere, but part of the Dragon pub was still standing at the right-hand side of the block, its windows now gaping holes with torn metal shutters dangling and the remaining brickwork soot-stained. Of the music saloon that had been built to the left of the pub, only the far wall was still standing. The rest was rubble, pile upon pile of it, covered in dark muddy ashes with the occasional piece of burnt timber protruding.

She stole a quick glance sideways and saw that Eli was rigid. She tried to put her arm round him but he stepped away from her.

People walked past, eyes averted, offering them what privacy they could to mourn the death of their hopes and dreams.

Carrie summoned up her courage, trying to sound positive. 'We can rebuild it, love. We've done it once and we can do it again.'

'I don't think I've the heart to do it again.'

His voice was still hoarse from breathing in the smoke the previous evening when they were trapped in the building, as was hers. She stole another quick glance at him. When Eli had found out that she'd paid the insurance money he'd wanted to let lapse, he'd seemed optimistic, had talked about building a new Pride with the money. Overnight he'd changed and now he seemed to have lost all confidence in the future. Even his eyes were dull. It wasn't like her Eli to give up on anything, but then this place had meant a lot to him, more than to anyone else, because it was his dearest dream come true.

As he turned away from both her and the sight of the burned buildings, she tugged at his arm. 'Don't talk like that! Of course we'll rebuild.' He shook his head, his expression so bleak she wanted to sob aloud for him. 'Eli?'

He looked at her as if she was his enemy. 'What do you expect me to say? That I can't wait to get started on the rebuilding? Well, I'm empty, Carrie, sick to my soul. I lay awake for most of the night, feeling like I'd been gutted. I worked so *hard* to build that music saloon, put everything I had into it. And one wicked man destroyed it. There's nothing left inside me now. Nothing.'

He started walking away and when she didn't follow him, slowed down and stood there for a minute with his back to her before turning round to toss at her, 'I can't even bear to look at it! Stott meant us all to die when he set it on fire and I couldn't even protect my own wife from him, let alone our home and living. What sort of useless fellow does that make me?'

He looked across the road again, his whole face twisted with agony. 'And if *you* had died, it'd have been because of my stupid dreams and they'd not have been worth it. Carrie love—' His voice cracked and he couldn't continue but stood fighting to control himself, fists clenched, his whole body so taut it was a wonder it didn't break into a thousand pieces.

With a suddenness that was all part of this terrible day, it began to rain again, a slashing grey downpour that had them both soaked in seconds. People hurried past them, seeking shelter. Neither of them moved.

The dismay at what he'd said held her paralysed for a few moments then she flung her arms round him, pressing kisses on his cold, wet face. There was a burn on one of his cheeks and soot still in the pores and creases of his skin. She put one hand on either side of his face and said loudly, 'We *will* rebuild the Pride, Eli. You and me together. You must believe that.'

When he said nothing, she shook him hard. 'Eli, it was a *wonderful* dream, and you made it come true. The whole town benefited from it and people will be eager for you to do it again.'

He shrugged and said in that new, tight voice, 'Maybe my uncle was right when he wanted to sell it. We could live off the money we get for that land. No need for us ever to work again.'

'Your uncle wasn't right, you were. And Athol Stott was a madman. I'm glad he was killed in the fire he lit, *glad*! Now that he's gone, there's nothing to stop us rebuilding our music saloon and doing it better this time. I won't *let* you give up, Eli.' She shook him again and to her dismay, he didn't protest. 'We'll get the insurance money and use it to build a new Pride.'

But whatever she said, he only shrugged or gave her a faint, sad smile, so in the end she took his arm and walked him briskly back to Linney's. Perhaps when he'd had time to recover, had a few good nights' sleep, he'd regain his old confidence.

Essie and the babies were back from their walk and Carrie ran into her friend's arms, surprising herself by weeping again. But it did her good, got rid of some of the lump of pain in her chest.

She wished Eli could cry like this. He was so low in spirits today, so remote, she was afraid for him. Even their little daughter couldn't cheer him up, though he usually loved playing with Abigail.

Gwynna opened the letter, the first she'd ever received in her whole life, and spelled out the words carefully, exclaiming in shock at what Essie had to tell her. She showed the letter to Nurse and asked her to read it out to her, to make sure she'd understood what it said properly. Gwynna knew she still wasn't the best of readers, though she was improving all the time, thanks to the governess helping her and lending her books.

'Mercy on us!' Nurse scanned the letter quickly, then read

it aloud, saying afterwards, 'To lose everything like that. The poor souls! How must they feel?' She folded it carefully and handed it back.

'I can't imagine it,' Gwynna confessed. 'It was so pretty, the Pride, with bright gas lights and happy people going in and out, posters on the walls saying who'd be playing next week. I walked past it on the last day before I came here, to say goodbye.' She looked up. 'Nurse, do you think Mrs Robert would let me go over to Hedderby on my afternoon off tomorrow? I need to see everyone, make sure they're all right. Could someone take me to the station – if she agrees, that is?'

'It's a dreadful thing to have happened to your family. I'll speak to Mrs Finch first, and then we'll ask Mrs Robert. And of course someone will take you to the station and pick you up again. They're always picking up parcels and boxes for the master.'

'Thank you.' Gwynna didn't say that Carrie and Eli weren't exactly family, because they felt and acted like they were.

She stuffed the letter into her pocket and went to see if Peter had woken from his nap yet. At fourteen months he was able to totter about, so you had to keep an eye on him at all times. When she went into the bedroom, she found Miss Jane standing silently by the bed, staring down at the sleeping child with an expression of what could only be described as gloating on her face.

There's something wrong with that girl, Gwynna thought, not for the first time. 'What are you doing here, Miss Jane?' She had to repeat her question sharply before she got an answer.

'Watching my cousin. Wouldn't it be lovely if Peter died in his sleep? He'd go straight to heaven then, before he had time to be wicked, and we could have a big funeral with people crying. Afterwards we'd put flowers on his grave every week.'

A shiver ran down Gwynna's spine. 'Don't be silly! It wouldn't be at all lovely if he died. It'd make his mother and father very unhappy – and me too.' Because whatever Essie said about not loving other people's children too much, Gwynna had found it all too easy to love Peter, who was a sunny-natured child.

Without a word Jane turned and walked out of the room. Gwynna decided there and then not to leave her charge alone again, even when he was asleep. She wondered if she could have her bed moved into this room so that he'd be safe at night. She'd ask Nurse if she could and tell her exactly why. Everyone knew Miss Jane walked in her sleep – and all the servants knew the girl was strange, though of course they didn't say so, even to one another, just exchanged glances sometimes.

In the meantime Gwynna got out her sewing and sat quietly near the bed. She enjoyed sewing, even mending like this. Nurse said she'd learned to do it very quickly, just as the governess said she'd learned to read quickly. She was proud of that.

In another three weeks they'd tell her whether she could stay on. She hoped desperately that she could, because she loved working here. She felt there was a good chance of it, knew she'd proved herself a hard worker. Jabez had been wrong about how the other servants would treat her. She got on really well with all the maids except the one in the kitchen who was a friend of his sister's and had taken against Gwynna from the start.

When Peter woke up, she changed his clouts and fed him, then checked with Nurse as to whether she should take him to see his mother at the usual time today. After hesitating, she told Nurse what Miss Jane had said and done.

The older woman looked at her incredulously and shock made her speak frankly for once. 'She's getting worse, that child is.'

'I know. I worry sometimes that she'll hurt him.'

After a moment's silence pregnant with the things they didn't dare say aloud, Nurse added, 'I'd better report this to Mrs Robert. Let *me* take Master Peter to her today and you get on with your sewing. I'll ask her about you going to see your family while I'm there, tell her how upset you are by what's happened. Mrs Finch thinks you should go and see them.'

Maria Stott watched the two men lower the coffin that contained her husband's body into the ground. The relief that ran through her as she nodded to them to start filling in the grave was so overwhelming that she had difficulty keeping her face expressionless. He was dead! At last, after nine interminable years married to a wicked man, she was free to live her life decently and bring up her sons to be happy and honourable – two qualities totally alien to her vicious husband.

Normally, for someone of his class and wealth, there would have been a crowd of mourners come to pay their last respects, but if Athol Stott had been hated in Hedderby before, he was hated even more now that he'd burned down the music saloon which many people had enjoyed visiting. So there were only his wife and his cousin Edmund to farewell him, and they were here solely out of duty. She looked down at her black gown. She wasn't going to wear it again after today or make the slightest pretence of mourning Athol, and if that upset the good ladies of Hedderby, she didn't care.

As a bitterly cold wind whined around her, she saw the top of the coffin that contained her husband's charred remains vanish beneath the earth that was being shovelled in rapidly by a shivering gravedigger.

She hadn't brought her sons here today and intended to do

all she could to wipe out their bad memories of recent years, though she doubted she could do it completely. Eight-year-old Isaac's last memory of his father was of being whipped till his back bled. You never forgot such vicious treatment and the doctor said that the boy would bear the scars of that whipping for the rest of his life.

She fingered the ridge of flesh on her cheek, another legacy of Athol's temper, given to her for trying to protect her son. The doctor said that scar would also remain, though it would fade from its present livid red. But it had been worth it, a stripe of honour across her face as far as she was concerned, since her intervention had stopped the whipping of Isaac that had gone beyond reason.

There was only one thing of which she was quite certain now: that she would never, ever get married again. She wasn't sure what the future would bring her – quiet joys, she hoped, small triumphs. Nothing could be as bad as the past, surely?

She watched the gravedigger step back for a rest, leaning on his shovel. As she looked at the pile of damp, muddy earth she thought, *It's over, it's really over now.* Without a word she turned and led the way out of the churchyard.

'Are you all right?' Edmund asked, keeping his long legs to her slower pace.

'Yes.' She didn't speak as they got into the carriage to be driven the short distance home. Inevitably they passed the ruins of the Pride and she shook her head sadly but there was nothing she could do about that.

At home the housekeeper was waiting to take her mistress's cloak and fuss over her. Maria smiled her thanks. Mrs Ibster was a loyal friend after all they'd been through lately. 'Could you bring us some tea, please?'

'Cook's kept the kettle on the boil, ma'am. Oh, and Mr Hordle is here. I showed him into the library.'

'We'll join him there, then.' It was good of the lawyer to come when he'd refused a few months ago to act for Athol any longer. Greeting the elderly man, Maria took a seat near the fire and held her hands out to it, feeling chilled to her soul. The huge leather armchair Athol had favoured was gone from the room, thank goodness, but she felt as if its shadow – and his – still hovered there. She'd told them yesterday to remove the chair, burn it or do what they liked with it as long as she didn't see it again.

When they'd drunk their tea and made some polite conversation, Maria set down her cup. 'Now, please tell me how things are left, Mr Hordle.'

He hesitated. 'You won't like it, I'm afraid.'

Her heart sank. Surely there would be enough money for them to live off? Even Athol couldn't have left his money to others when he had a wife and two sons. 'Tell me.'

Mr Hordle cleared his throat. 'Everything has been left to your sons and they – together with their inheritance – are to be under the guardianship of his second cousin.'

She was startled. 'Second cousin? I didn't think he had any relatives apart from you, Edmund. He always said there were none.'

'We have a few distant connections, but Athol would never have anything to do with them, so I didn't think it worth contradicting him,' Edmund explained quietly. 'Which cousin has he chosen, Mr Hordle?'

'Jeremiah Channon.'

Maria saw Edmund's face tighten. 'You know him?'

'No, I've never met him. But I know of his father from mine. The man is the sort of holy bigot who makes his family's life miserable. With that upbringing, I doubt the son will be much different.'

She shuddered and closed her eyes, willing herself to stay calm. As if her boys had not had to suffer enough!

The lawyer looked at her sympathetically, waiting until she opened her eyes again to add, 'I'm afraid that's not all.'

She pressed her lips together and waited numbly.

'Jeremiah Channon is to take over the running of this house, for which he will be paid an annual sum, and you . . .' he hesitated, then finished, 'are to submit yourself to his governance or else you are to be cast out with only the clothes you stand up in.'

She couldn't hold back the angry words. 'How *could* you let Athol make such a condition?'

'How could I have stopped him? He'd only have gone else-where to have the will drawn up. That will was one of the things which made me ask him to find another lawyer to handle his affairs, I must admit.'

Anger made her unable to speak for a few moments. Hadn't she had enough to bear? Then she took a deep breath and said as levelly as she could, 'I must pray that Mr Channon will be a reasonable man.'

After another hesitation, Mr Hordle said, 'It would be wrong to keep this from you, though it grieves me to tell you and indeed, it was the thing which upset me most about the will. Your husband insisted on including a statement explaining why he had left things like that. He said you had a weak, unprincipled nature and a limited understanding, which is why you were not to be trusted with the care of his sons, or even the care of any money left to them. I know this to be a lie and so I shall tell Mr Channon, but I can't refuse to give him the written statement.'

She felt Edmund's arm go round her shoulders. 'Has Athol left me anything at all?'

'No, nothing. Everything you possessed was his by law, even the clothes on your back.'

The desire to weep left her abruptly. 'No, it wasn't! There was money set aside for me from my dowry, a legal settlement made before our marriage in case I was widowed. My father made certain of that and explained it to me.'

Mr Hordle frowned at her. 'Your husband said nothing about it.'

'Which was typical of him.' A dreadful thought occurred to her and she looked at him pleadingly. 'Surely he can't have taken my money? It was lodged at the bank for me. Surely there are records of it in your rooms? Your father dealt with it, I think.'

'I'll look through the records straight away. I do apologise if there's been an error, but I'm certain there were no other papers in your box.'

'It isn't a huge amount of money, but there should be enough for me to live on modestly if . . . if things grow too difficult. Though I don't wish to be separated from my sons.' After a moment or two's silence, she added quietly, 'This will is Athol's revenge on me.'

'For what?' Edmund's voice was sharp with anger. 'You've been a model wife, better by far than *he* deserved. A loving mother, too.'

'Revenge for me being whole in body when he was so horrifically injured. After the accident I sometimes thought he hated everyone who was able-bodied. He hated you too, Edmund, as you were no doubt aware. But he needed you to run the engineering works for him, so he did nothing about that hatred.'

Mr Hordle cleared his throat to gain their attention. 'I must now inform Mr Channon of the will and ask what arrangements he wishes to make, but I wanted to tell you exactly how things were left first, Mrs Stott.'

'I'm grateful. Let me know when he is to arrive. I'll have a room prepared for him.'

'I can't believe that even Athol could have done this,' Edmund muttered.

But she could. She could believe anything of her late husband. She looked at the man beside her, as unlike his first cousin as a man could be. Decent, upright, kind and loving towards his wife. It was hard sometimes to believe that the two of them were related. Why had she not married a man like him? Why had she been taken in by Athol's good looks and charm when he came courting her? That charm hadn't even lasted a day beyond their wedding.

'You can come and live with us if things get too bad, Maria,' Edmund said gently. 'I don't even need to ask Faith. I know she'll agree with me about that.'

'Thank you. It'll be good to know there's somewhere I can take refuge if I need it, but I'd have to be very desperate to leave my sons.' She turned to the lawyer. 'Can I contest the will?'

'It would cost a great deal and the outcome would be uncertain.'

'I could sell my jewellery. I have some good pieces, but they mean far less to me than the boys.'

Mr Hordle hesitated.

She stared at him aghast. 'Athol *can't* have left my jewellery to someone else. It was my mother's, part of my dowry, and I know it was listed in the marriage settlements. He never bought me any jewellery apart from the wedding and engagement rings, you know.'

He looked at her in sympathy. 'He gave me a list of your jewellery, said he'd given it all to you and if he died it was to be kept in the bank for your sons' wives. Since I didn't find the papers about your marriage settlement, I couldn't contradict him about that.'

'It's not true.'

Edmund cleared his throat. 'Since the list is a lie, surely you don't need to include it in the information sent to Mr Channon? Can we not regard it as the product of a deranged mind? For you can't deny that Athol was insane towards the end.'

Mr Hordle hesitated. 'Yes, but it's in the will that your jewellery is to be stored in safety.'

She smiled suddenly, a grim smile. 'We won't need to go against that. I shall be happy to give you my wedding and engagement rings. Indeed, I'd appreciate it if you'd take them now.' She pulled them off even as she spoke and went across to drop them on the table next to the lawyer, not caring that he was visibly embarrassed by this gesture.

He picked them up and held them out to her. 'My dear lady, there's no need for this, no need at all. As soon as I find the settlement papers, I'll destroy the list of jewellery. It's not that I don't believe you. I just – can't break the law.'

She made no attempt to take them from him but looked at him questioningly. 'Would you be willing to act as *my* lawyer from now on?'

'I'd like to, but it might be better if you found yourself another lawyer, so that I could keep an eye on things for the boys in case Mr Channon should prove – difficult. I'd suggest my young colleague, Mr Burtell. Indeed, I'd be happy to brief him for you.'

'I like and respect the man,' Edmund said quietly from across the room.

'Then I'll ask his help.'

Mr Hordle looked at the two rings lying on his outstretched hand. 'I'd much rather you took these back, Mrs Stott.'

'I shan't wear them again. You can give them to Mr Channon to dispose of.' She frowned in thought. 'I think I'd like to see Mr Burtell as soon as possible. Could you ask him to call on me, please?'

He nodded, then looked at Edmund. 'I presume you'll continue to run the family engineering works in the mean-time?'

'Yes, for as long as I'm allowed to do it my own way. I was hoping to buy into it now that Athol is dead, because we need some new machinery and my capital would provide that. If Channon tries to interfere, however, or if he's anything like his father, I'll start my own business instead.'

'I'll inform him of that.'

When the lawyer had gone, taking the two rings with him, Maria went to sit down again, saying nothing, only clasping her hands in her lap and staring bleakly into the fire.

Edmund came to stand on the other side of the hearth, resting one forearm on the mantelpiece. 'Are you all right?'

She took a deep breath and straightened her spine. 'I'll have to be, won't I? My boys' future depends on me.'

'What shall you do now?'

'Tell the boys what's going to happen. Get ready for Mr Channon. See what he intends. What else can I do?'

4

Jack Burtell sent word that he would call upon Mrs Stott at ten o'clock the next morning, if that was convenient. She studied her reflection in the mirror as she got ready to see him. Pale still, her eyes dark-rimmed because she wasn't sleeping well and kept waking with a start thinking she heard Athol stumping along the landing towards her room on his artificial leg. *Concentrate!* she told herself. *What are you going to wear?*

After some thought she donned a lilac gown she'd always been fond of. It was old-fashioned, like all her clothes.

She liked Mr Burtell on sight, a bright-eyed man of about her own age, short but with a presence that made you respect him and an expression that was both kindly and yet seemed to challenge the world to do its worst.

He took a seat opposite her. 'Mr Hordle has explained the situation. It must be – difficult for you.'

'Yes. But not as difficult as living with my late husband was.'

'I can imagine.'

And for some reason, she believed he could because he looked intelligent enough to see behind the invisible curtain people often drew in front of their private lives.

'I have one piece of good news, at least. Mr Hordle has found the deeds for your marriage settlement. They'd been mistakenly placed in a nearby box by an old clerk, who has since died. Mr Hordle is very mortified about that and sends his apologies to you. Do you want me to explain the settlements to you?'

'Not unless something has changed. My father explained exactly what was involved before I married. He was a prudent man.' She saw the lawyer looking at her speculatively. 'I believe I've a fair understanding of business matters, Mr Burtell.' To prove it she summarised the settlement details and saw him smile.

'You're an intelligent woman, Mrs Stott.'

'Am I? Let's hope Mr Channon believes that. Now, one of the first things I want to do is place my jewellery in your care.'

'Surely that's not necessary? It's yours from the marriage settlement.'

'I've learned the hard way to leave nothing to chance. If Mr Channon believes me to be of weak intellect, he may try to take the jewellery away from me. The sale of it would buy me a cottage, at least, if I have to leave my sons.'

'Why should you have to do that?'

'He's Athol's cousin.' She shuddered at the mere thought of what that might mean.

'Very well. I'll lodge the jewellery in the bank for you but in an account with your name on it as well as mine.'

'I'll go and fetch it for you now.'

When she got back he was looking out into the garden, where Isaac and Ben were playing, with Renny encouraging them to run and shout. She went to join him. 'Renny came back the day after Athol died and I was happy to employ him again. He's good for the boys, keeps their spirits up. If anyone can heal the scars left by their father, he can. I'm hoping Mr Channon will let him stay on here.' She was hoping a lot of things.

He hesitated then said, 'Forgive my frankness, but don't you think it would be better if you wore black? It's bound to set people's backs up to see you dressed in colours.'

'No, Mr Burtell, I can't mourn my late husband and won't pretend to. It was my happiest day for many years when he was killed. Though I shan't say that to anyone else, I hope I can be truthful with you?'

'You can indeed, Mrs Stott.' He sighed and shook his head. 'I must go now, but if you need me – for anything! – you have only to send a message and I'll come as quickly as I can.'

When he'd gone she went back to the window to watch the boys and the dog that had caused so much trouble with Athol. Migs was a strange-looking creature, tall and leggy, with one ear permanently drooping, but he was a friendly fellow. She was delighted at her sons' pleasure at having their pet returned. Their father had tried to kill it. And it was a relief to have Renny here to look after them as well as the governess. He was a strange man who seemed to have the power to heal people, to see into their souls almost, and she was sure he'd be the best person to help her with the boys now.

All that remained was to meet this Mr Channon. Until he came she was in limbo, waiting for her new life to begin. She prayed he'd be a reasonable man, would not impose a strict and unhappy regime on her poor boys, who had suffered enough.

But it sounded as if he had the power to do what he wished with all their lives. That terrified her.

When the maid had cleared away the breakfast things, the mail was brought in, as usual. Jeremiah Channon suppressed his irritation at the way his father studied each envelope before passing it on to the person for whom it was intended.

'Whom do you know in Hedderby, Jeremiah?'

'No one, Father.'

'And yet this is a substantial communication.' The old man fingered the bulky envelope, frowning. 'One of the new gummed envelopes, too. A ridiculous extravagance when papers can be folded and secured with sealing wax.'

Jeremiah reached out and took the envelope from him, hesitated, then slit it open, not wanting to provoke a tirade about secretive behaviour by taking it away to read in private. He studied the contents and could not hold back a gasp, which drew his father's attention again.

'Bad news?'

'Yes. Surprising too. It seems that Athol Stott has passed away – he was only a year older than me – and he's named me guardian to his two sons.' The thought of the children brought the pain of his own loss flooding back so that Jeremiah could hardly breathe for a moment or two, let alone talk.

His father immediately bowed his head and began to intone a prayer for the soul of their dear departed relative, though he'd not had a good word for the Stott connection previously. His voice came out muffled and spittle trickled from the corner of his mouth because of the seizure which had made one side of his face droop, but that didn't prevent him from launching forth into loud prayer whenever he saw fit.

Jeremiah suppressed a sigh as he bowed his head. Since the death of his wife and little daughter he'd come back to live with his parents and it had been a serious error of judgement. He had remembered how difficult his father was to live with and mentally allowed for that, but hadn't realised that the old man had become even more rabidly religious since his seizure. But at the time Jeremiah had been distraught with grief and had literally had nowhere else to go.

If it wasn't for his mother, he'd have moved out of here before now, but she was so happy to have him living with her again, and he was their only child, so he didn't want to hurt her. She had enough to bear from his father. But it seemed that fate had now given him the opportunity to leave this dreary house without offending anyone and he meant to take full advantage of that. 'I'll have to go over to Hedderby immediately and speak to the lawyer.'

'When exactly is the funeral?'

'It's been held already.'

His father dabbed the drooping corner of his mouth with his table napkin. 'I wonder why such unseemly haste? I shall go with you.'

'Thank you, but no, Father. This is something I wish to do on my own.'

'It's my duty as the last of my generation in the family to pay my final respects!'

'I'm afraid I must nonetheless decline your offer.' Jeremiah got up and left the table before the two of them could get into another argument. His father seemed not to be thinking clearly since the seizure and had begun to treat him like a lad who needed guidance, instead of a man of four and thirty. The old man had even dared to criticise the house designs for which Jeremiah was making a name as an architect in the town – or had been making a name until the tragedy that took his wife and three-year-old daughter from him. It was two years since it had happened. Time enough to be over the sharpest of the grief, more than time for Jeremiah to make a new life for himself instead of this half-life.

But what to do, where to go, that had been the unanswered question that had held him back? The only thing he knew was that he didn't want to stay in this town any longer. It held too many memories. Now, it seemed that fate was offering him the opportunity to move and do something worthwhile.

He went along to the room at the side of the house which had been set aside for his office, wondering what Athol Stott's sons would be like. He paused for a moment or two, frowning as he remembered his second cousin. They had only met a few times but none of his memories was good, for Athol had not only been older and bigger than him but a bully. He hoped the sons weren't cut from the same cloth as their father. If they were, Jeremiah would make sure they were pulled into line, taught how to behave decently.

And the wife . . . what sort of woman would marry a man like that? A fool, undoubtedly. Even by the time he was twenty, Athol had had a bad reputation in the family.

Jeremiah unlocked his desk, rolled up the front and sat down. Pulling a piece of writing paper out of its slot at the back, he unscrewed the inkpot, dipped in his pen and began replying to the lawyer who had contacted him.

Gwynna was able to get a ride from Hungerton House to the station on the cart going to fetch some parcels due to arrive by the morning train. The coachman, who organised all the vehicles in the house, promised to send someone to fetch her on her return, because the house was far out in the country. She hesitated, wondering if she dared ask him not to send Jabez, but as that young man came round the corner just as she was opening her mouth, she couldn't do it, so thanked the coachman and went to get her things.

When she arrived in Hedderby, her first thought was to go and look at the Pride. She could only stand and groan at the sight of the ruin. Men were working to clear the ground, all of them covered in black dust, so that it was hard to tell what colour their hair was. Only their teeth and the whites of their eyes broke the temporary darkness of their skin. There was still one wall of the Dragon standing and that seemed to make the rest of it look worse, somehow. Shuddering, she hurried away, up the hill to Linney's.

At the side door she hesitated then knocked and waited. She didn't live here now. She must remember that.

Essie opened it. 'Gwynna! Why on earth didn't you come straight in? We told you to think of this as your home.'

'I didn't like to presume.'

The older woman gave her a big hug, then held her at arm's length. 'Presume indeed! Don't you dare knock again, lass. This is *your* home too, and you can walk right in at any time of day or night. You're looking well, I must say. Is the food all right? And surely that's a new blouse?'

Gwynna gave her another hug, suddenly close to weeping at the welcome, which was warmer than she'd dared hope. 'Oh, Essie, you never miss a thing, do you? Yes, it is a new blouse. Nurse is teaching me to sew, so I made this myself, and the governess is teaching me to read and . . . well, everything's fine. It's Carrie and Eli I was worried about, the reason I came back today.' She looked round. 'And where's little Sylvie? She must have grown so much in two months.'

'She has. Raife's taken her out for a walk, but they'll be back in a few minutes. She's walking more strongly now and we've had to buy her some new boots to support her ankles, not that she can walk very far yet, so he's taken the trolley for her to ride back on. As for Eli, he's gone down to the site to work out how to pull the dangerous bits down. I'm surprised you didn't see him.' She hesitated as if she was going to say more about him, but didn't. 'Carrie's gone upstairs to fetch Abigail who's been having a nap. There, that's her coming down now.' She raised her voice. 'Look who's here!'

Gwynna wasn't surprised to see how strained Carrie looked, so held her arms out to the baby to hide her feelings. And like all children, Abigail went to her with a smile, so she hugged her close and said quickly, 'I was sorry to hear about the Pride, Carrie. That's why I came home. I wanted to see everyone and well – I was worried about you.'

Carrie gave her a sad smile and went to get a drink of milk for her daughter. 'I'm all right. It's Eli we're all worried about. He's having the site cleared but he isn't making plans to rebuild. He's not himself at all, seems to have lost heart.'

'Oh.' Gwynna didn't know what to say to that. Impossible

to imagine Eli Beckett not taking charge of things vigorously. 'And the others, are they all right? I do wish I could stay to see Dora and Edith when they come back from work, but I only have two hours before I need to catch the train back.'

She spent a happy afternoon catching up with everyone's news and cuddling little Sylvie, who had been her special charge. But after a while she sighed and looked at the clock. 'I suppose I'd better be going. I daren't miss my train.'

'I'll walk you to the station, lass,' said Raife.

They didn't say much, but as always, it was a comfort just to be with him.

It had been so wonderful to see the people she thought of now as her family that when she got on the train, she sat there trying not to cry, relieved that there was no one else in the compartment to see her weakness. She wished she had been able to find a job in Hedderby, so that she could see them all more often.

When she got out at Sutherclough she found Jabez waiting for her with the cart, his expression as hostile as ever. Her heart sank. The last thing she needed at the moment, when she was feeling homesick and upset, was him making nasty remarks.

He didn't offer to help her get up and started the horse moving before she was properly settled, making her heart thump with panic as she desperately clutched the edge of the seat, trying not to fall off. He laughed at that as he drove out of the station.

When they were halfway home, he stopped where the lane widened. 'How about a kiss?'

She gaped at him in shock. This was the last thing she'd have expected from him. 'Certainly not!'

'I've heard you give some fellows more than a kiss. My sister's met a lass from Hedderby who says you've been in trouble, had a baby. What'll you give to stop me telling the mistress about that, eh?'

His smile was more of a leer and he stretched one hand out to paw at her breast. She batted it away desperately, but he laughed and reached for her again, so that she had to fight him off while still trying to stay on the narrow bench seat, perched high above the road.

'Let go of me!' she yelled. 'Ow! Leave me alone, will you!'

Neither of them heard the sound of a horse's hooves but a voice suddenly boomed out from the field at one side. 'Stop that at once!'

Jabez turned to see Mr Robert glaring at him from the other side of the hedge, mounted on his tall grey and in a good position to see everything that was going on.

'Do you always pester the maids like that, you young scoundrel?'

'She was egging me on, sir.'

'I heard her myself telling you to stop, saw her trying to fight you off.'

'She changed her mind,' Jabez said sullenly.

'I don't think she did. And if I ever catch you annoying one of our maids in that way again, you'll be out on your ear, my lad. Now, drive back to the house at once and don't you dare lay a finger on her again.'

Jabez picked up the reins and told the horse to walk on, but as it began to trot towards the house, he muttered, 'I'll get back at you for that, see if I don't.'

'Get back at *me*!' She glared at him. 'It was you who started it all.'

'You were asking for it. I knew you were rubbish the first time I saw you, and I was right.'

When they arrived she jumped down and ran inside, rushing up the stairs to her room to tidy her hair, which had come loose in the struggle. But Nurse saw her and called to her to stop.

'What on earth have you been doing, girl? You're in a right old mess.'

Gwynna burst into tears. 'It was that Jabez. While he was driving me home, he tried to – to paw at me. If Mr Robert hadn't come riding along and seen us, I don't know what Jabez would have done to me.'

Nurse gaped at her. 'Well, who ever heard the like? And his parents are decent folk too. You'd better tidy yourself up quickly. Peter missed you.' When Gwynna didn't move, she added, 'Cheer up. It's not the end of the world and I'm sure Jabez won't lay a finger on you again.'

But Gwynna couldn't even manage a smile. She was worried sick about what Mr Robert's wife would say when he told her what had happened. Even if they believed her side of the story, mud always stuck. And she'd still not been told whether she could stay on here. This couldn't have happened at a worse time.

She spent a restless night and at one stage thought she heard a sound from Master Peter's room, so crept out of bed and tiptoed along to it. There she found Miss Jane standing by the bed, a pillow in her hands.

Gwynna snatched the pillow and hurled it aside, then picked up the baby, who immediately began to cry. Shuddering with relief that he was all right, she turned back to deal with the girl and saw her hurrying out of the room.

That did it! She was sleeping in here every night from now on. She put the little boy into bed, soothing him, and sliding in next to him, taking comfort from the warmth of his body and the little murmuring sounds he made as he sucked his thumb and went back to sleep.

Early the next morning she went to find Nurse, carrying the baby with her, and told her what had happened. The older woman goggled at her, then sagged back in her chair.

'They won't believe us if we tell them – or at least they won't believe she meant to harm him.'

'I'm sure she did, though. And children do die in the night for no reason, so I doubt she'd have been caught out.'

'You're not making this up, Gwynna, not imagining it to be worse than it is?'

'No, Nurse. She was holding the pillow above his head, as if she meant to smother him. And anyway . . . we've both been worried about that girl for a while, haven't we?'

The other nodded. 'I'll have to tell Mrs Robert. I've mentioned things to her before, and I know she'll believe us. She worries about Miss Jane too, but what can she do when the old master is so besotted with the girl? You'd better keep quiet about this, though. The gentry don't like washing their dirty linen in public. I'll speak to Mrs Robert before she goes down to breakfast.'

When Nurse came back she took Gwynna aside. 'She believed me. She'd heard Miss Jane a few times talking about how lovely funerals were, especially funerals of little children. So you're to have your bed moved into his room. Just tell the others he's waking in the night upset and you want to be there to comfort him.'

Later that morning Dodie brought a message that Mrs Finch wished to see Gwynna at eleven o'clock. With a sinking heart she went down the stairs just before the hour.

Mrs Finch greeted her unsmilingly. 'I heard that you had some trouble yesterday.'

'Jabez tried to—'

'I know what that young man is like, but you must have been encouraging him and I'm telling you now that if you ever do such a thing again, you'll not keep your job here. You wouldn't be doing so now, except that Nurse spoke out for you, said she didn't know what she'd do without you.'

'But I *didn't* encourage him, I swear I didn't, Mrs Finch! He's got a down on me because his sister wanted my job.'

'That wouldn't make him attack you like that.'

'He's found out – about the baby I had. Well, it was his sister who found out. He says he's going to tell everyone unless I . . .' She broke off, unable to put it into words.

Mrs Finch breathed in deeply. 'Then you'd better be even more careful how you behave, hadn't you? I'll tell him to keep quiet about what he's heard. But I shall be keeping an even closer eye on you from now on and we'll wait another month or two before we decide about keeping you on here.'

That night Gwynna cried herself to sleep in the new bedroom, muffling her sobs in the pillow so as not to wake Peter. She was going to lose her job, she knew she was. And then who'd watch out for her little darling?

Two days before his employment with Mr Laing ended, Lucas received a letter from his distraught aunt that dashed his hopes and dreams. His uncle had had a seizure and was unable to work. The family had no money coming in and had no one else to turn to except Lucas.

He didn't hesitate. Apart from the fact that they were family, they'd helped him when he was in trouble so how could he not do the same for them?

It was with a heavy heart that he explained the situation to Mr Laing and the man who would have been his new employer, packed his bags and set off for Hedderby.

The world outside seemed as cloudy and grey as his future, and he was glad to be on his own in a compartment, lost in his thoughts.

Jeremiah stepped off the train in Hedderby and looked round with interest. He had directions to Mr Hordle's rooms but had deliberately taken an earlier train, wanting to get a feel for the town because he was seriously considering settling here for a while. Devoting his life to bringing up two fatherless boys made a lot more sense than pretending to design houses when all his old skills and enthusiasm seemed to have vanished. For the past two years he'd been bringing out old designs for clients because he couldn't think of new ones, and people had noticed, he was sure, because commissions to design houses had dwindled. Or maybe he hadn't tried to find and woo new clients.

Nowadays he often idled away the time designing palaces, imaginary places with soaring ceilings and ornate embellishments. How childish could a grown man get? But no one knew about that, at least.

The situation of Hedderby pleased him. It nestled comfortably at the foot of the moors and was built mainly of millstone grit, the newer buildings golden, the others weathered to a grey tone. It had a long main street with the station at one end and at the other the remains of a large, burnt-out building. When he got to it, he stopped to stare, lost in memories of the fire that had destroyed his own home and life. This conflagration had been recent by the looks of it. He pulled himself together and turned to a passer-by, who had also stopped to look at the ruins. 'Excuse me, but could you please tell me what happened here? What was this place?'

'It were two places, really, a pub and a music saloon. The Dragon, the pub were called and the other place were the Pride. Eh, I've spent some happy nights there. Me an' the wife miss it sore. It were the only place a decent woman could go out to of an evening and now that the childer are all grown up, we used to go to the show every Saturday. It were like when we were courting.' He sighed and contemplated the building with great regret, then noticed the clock hanging outside the grocery emporium. 'Is that the time? I'm sorry, but I've to get on now.' With a tip of his hat he strode away.

Jeremiah walked slowly back towards the station, frowning. It was a strange way to talk of such a place. His father called pubs 'dens of iniquity' and their minister had railed at length in a recent Sunday sermon about the new music saloons that were, according to him, springing up everywhere to entice working men from the path of virtue. Yet the passer-by to whom Jeremiah had just been speaking had seemed respectable enough. He'd not only considered the Pride a decent place but had said he used to take his wife there regularly.

Wondering who was right, Jeremiah followed the directions he'd been sent and made his way towards Mr Hordle's rooms. As he walked one or two people stopped dead and stared at him in a way that said they thought they recognised him – and didn't like him. He looked at them in surprise and they shook their heads as if acknowledging a mistake and hurried on.

When he went into Mr Hordle's office, the lawyer also stared at him in shock and this time Jeremiah was able to ask why.

'You – um – resemble your cousin Athol. As he used to be before the accident that left him maimed, not as he was just before he died. You're not totally like him, but there's enough of a resemblance to give people a shock the first time they see you.'

'Oh.' That must account for the unfriendly glances in town, then.

He forgot what the lawyer had said about his appearance as they settled down to discuss the will and Jeremiah's new duties.

'I think it best if I tell you something about the – the background, then leave you to read the will at your leisure.' Mr Hordle hesitated before saying in a rush, 'I don't know how to say this to you, but someone must. Your cousin, Athol Stott, was not a good man. Indeed, there were some doubts as to his sanity during the last year or two of his life. I myself am convinced he had totally lost his reason in the few months before he died. And this will of his – it wasn't well thought out, or kind. He has left his widow without any means of support except for your charity – and she didn't deserve that.'

'How did he die? You gave no details in your letter.'

Another hesitation, then, 'In the fire that recently destroyed our town's music saloon, a fire he set himself, deliberately.'

Jeremiah was so astonished by this that he couldn't speak for a moment or two. 'Are you *sure* he set the fire?'

'The whole town is certain of it. There can be no doubt whatsoever. If he hadn't been killed, Athol Stott would have been brought to justice and hanged, so perhaps it was better this way. Did you – know your cousin well?'

'No. I'd not met him since we were boys, and not often then. I must confess I was surprised to be named guardian to his sons.'

'I hope you'll take my word for his character. I don't want to go into too much detail. I detest gossip. But you need to be aware of the – the background. There's one more thing I must tell you.' He flicked his fingers towards the pile of documents, an expression of deep distaste on his face, 'Among those papers is a statement I am duty-bound to pass on to you, a statement which questions Mrs Stott's intelligence and moral integrity. I have to tell you, sir, that it is a lie. She is one of the finest ladies I've ever had the honour to meet and there is nothing wrong with either her wits or her morals. She is a devoted mother and was sorely tried by her marriage to *that man*. She and the boys are well rid of him.'

Jeremiah sat very still, astounded by these revelations.

'If you have no further questions at this point, Mr Channon, I'll leave you to peruse the documents. Please let my clerk know when you've finished and he'll fetch me. Ah, here he is with the tea. Very timely.'

Jeremiah read the will carefully, then the statement left by his cousin. It wasn't his habit to make hasty decisions. The only time he had done so in recent years had been when he moved in with his parents again, and that had proved to be a serious error of judgement. The lawyer had spoken very strongly on Mrs Stott's behalf. However, Athol's statement said she was of unsteady character. Who was right?

Could the lawyer be over-fond of her, perhaps? He didn't look the sort and was rather old for that sort of thing, but then men's characters didn't always show in their faces and older men could make fools of themselves as easily as younger ones. Look at his own father! A laughing stock in the town lately for his religious ranting.

Still wondering where the truth lay, Jeremiah went to the door and told the clerk he was ready to speak to Mr Hordle again.

'Is it possible for me to visit the family, so that I can meet my charges and their mother? I have some time yet before I need to catch a train back.'

'Yes. I warned her you were coming today and suggested the same thing. She said it would be quite convenient for you to call. Indeed, she's anxious to find out what you intend to do so that she can get the boys settled into a new way of life, poor things.'

The two men walked across town, Jeremiah adjusting his pace to that of his rather portly companion, still keeping his thoughts to himself.

The house was an elegant villa set in walled grounds not far from the city centre, just up the hill from a large building that seemed to be used as a manufactory of some sort.

'That's the family engineering works,' Mr Hordle said, stopping just before the gate and pointing down the hill.

'It's quite large.'

'Yes. It used to be a thriving concern.'

Jeremiah was puzzled by that remark, but decided to find out more about the works later.

As they paused at the gate, two little boys came running round the side of the building chasing a dog which had a stick in its mouth. A man who looked like a servant followed them and stood at the corner watching with a fond smile as they caught the animal and took it back round the side. None of them noticed the two men standing in the street near the gate.

'Surely it isn't fitting that they play out like that with their father so recently dead?' Jeremiah murmured.

Mr Hordle scowled at him as he opened the gate and began walking towards the front door. 'It's very fitting. Those boys have a lot of bad memories which need replacing with good ones.'

The door opened and a woman stood there, an upper servant by the looks of her. She stared at the stranger with the same shock everyone else had shown, and it was a moment before she spoke.

'I was just dusting the front parlour, Mr Hordle, and saw you coming up the path.'

'How is she, Mrs Ibster?'

'Bearing up. She's not eating though. Fretting about what's going to happen to those poor boys.' She cast a worried glance at the stranger. 'Perhaps I should warn her you're here.'

Jeremiah was puzzled by her choice of words as the 'poor boys' had had every appearance of health and energy. He hoped she would warn Mrs Stott about his resemblance to his dead cousin.

Mrs Ibster lowered her voice. 'Isaac is still having nightmares about it all. She was up with him twice last night, Mr Hordle, that I heard.'

The lawyer tutted sympathetically as the housekeeper walked away.

Shortly afterwards a door opened at the rear of the hall

and a lady came towards them. She was dressed in lilac, so she couldn't be the widow, Jeremiah decided. Perhaps a friend of hers.

Mr Hordle moved forward a couple of steps. 'My dear Mrs Stott, how are you?'

'I'm well, thank you.'

As her gaze turned to the stranger she gasped and lost every vestige of colour, swaying so that Jeremiah instinctively stepped forward to support her for a moment. But she flinched away from him so he moved quickly back, waiting for her to recover.

'I'm sorry. I wasn't prepared for the resemblance. It shocked me, even though Mrs Ibster warned me.'

She searched his face with something of desperation in her eyes. Fear too, Jeremiah thought.

'As you have surmised, my dear Mrs Stott, this is Mr Jeremiah Channon.'

He shook her hand, surprised by how thin and fragile it felt. As she moved into the light he saw that one of her cheeks was crossed by a livid scar, a recent injury by the appearance of it. He forced himself to look away from it out of courtesy but couldn't help wondering how she had received such a deep weal. It looked like, but of course it couldn't be, the mark of a whip.

Her voice, now that she had recovered her composure, was low and pleasant on the ear. 'Would you like to leave your hats and coats here, gentlemen, and join me in the front parlour?' She turned and led the way, waiting till they'd come into the room then indicating places for them to sit. She took a seat near the fire, sitting very upright on the edge of it, her full skirts falling gracefully around her.

Jeremiah could see that her eyes kept going back to his face, such dark eyes and full of pain. 'I'm sorry about your loss.'

She looked at him in surprise, then at the lawyer. 'Didn't you explain how things were, Mr Hordle?'

He spread his hands helplessly. 'I did – um – outline the situation, but it isn't easy, I'm not in the habit of speaking ill of the dead.'

Maria pressed her lips together and stared at the floor for a minute, then took a deep breath and looked across at Jeremiah, 'What did Mr Hordle tell you about my husband?'

'Just that he wasn't himself for the last year or two and that he set fire to the music saloon, a fire in which he lost his own life.'

She knew that the two of them could not hope to deal together unless the boys' new guardian understood what she and her sons had been through. In cold, controlled phrases Maria explained that her husband had been a cruel madman, who had tried to murder several people by locking them in a burning building.

She couldn't bring herself to go into details about her personal life and marriage to a man who was a complete stranger, so ended, 'He was neither a good father nor a good husband, and our home life was – extremely difficult. I hope you will make allowances for that when dealing with the boys, who are very nervous now of strangers. Your resemblance to their father will upset them.' She gestured towards herself. 'Athol's death was a relief, not a loss, to all in this house and I refuse to wear mourning for him.'

Her visitor didn't say a word or interrupt her, and his expression didn't betray any reaction to what she had said, apart from the slight frown that creased his forehead, so she didn't go into further detail but waited for him to speak.

'I can assure you that Mrs Stott has spoken nothing but the truth,' Mr Hordle said, as the uncomfortable silence dragged on. 'I know that from my own experience of the man. And your cousin Edmund will also be able to confirm what she has told you. He is at present running the engineering works. We could go there later if you wish.'

Jeremiah took out his pocket watch and consulted it. 'Perhaps next time I visit. It's more important that I meet the boys today.' He was shocked to the core by the widow's revelations, which had been made in short, terse phrases and a toneless voice, as if she were reciting a lesson. But he had noticed how tightly she clasped her hands in her lap and how white her knuckles were – as white as her face, except for that single red weal. 'I find it hard to comprehend,' he said at last, 'that a man could . . .' Words failed him and he could only shake his head in bafflement. Surely she must be exaggerating? 'I'd like to meet my wards now, if I may?'

'Certainly.' She rang for the maid then crossed her hands in her lap and waited.

It was the same man who shepherded the boys into the room. He'd obviously tried to smooth their hair and straighten their clothes but there were grass stains on their breeches and their faces were ruddy from playing out. They both stopped in the doorway and stared in horror at Jeremiah.

Isaac backed away and Renny had to catch hold of his arm to stop him bolting. 'It's not your father, just his cousin. And he doesn't really look like him. His eyes are quite different and his mouth too.'

Jeremiah was astonished to hear a servant speaking so familiarly.

'Thank you, Renny.' Maria got up and went to draw her sons forward, keeping one arm round each of them. 'This is Isaac, who is nearly nine now, and Benjamin, who is six. Boys, this is your Cousin Jeremiah, who is your guardian now.'

Both boys pressed closer to her as they muttered how do you do.

'Come over here and let me look at you properly,' Jeremiah said.

They took a couple of steps forward, but when he moved towards them, they both flinched backwards, clutching their mother again. He stopped where he was. Why were they so afraid of him when they'd never even met him before? He sought for something to say that wasn't threatening. 'Was that your dog I saw you playing with earlier? What's his name?'

The elder lad looked at him dubiously and then, at a nudge from his mother, said pleadingly, 'His name's Migs and he's a good dog. We look after him properly and we won't let him disturb you, I promise.'

'I like dogs. I've never had one of my own but I've always wanted one.'

'You won't – send him away?'

'No, of course not.'

Relief made them sag against their mother but they were still suspicious and his other questions drew only monosyllabic answers from them. In the end he gave up trying to get acquainted with them. Suffice it for the moment that they were clearly well cared for physically and that their mother loved them. That shone in her face, echoed in her voice, showed in the way her arms went round them protectively when they were afraid.

'Why don't you go outside and play again?' he suggested, waited till they'd left and turned to the mother. 'We must hope they'll get used to me. I can assure you that I intend to carry out my duties towards them to the best of my ability. If it's all right with you, I'll take up residence here next week.' For this meeting had only reinforced the need for him to be here. These were two very unhappy children and something needed to be done about that. He would reserve judgement on the mother's ability to manage their lives. She didn't seem a foolish woman, but she was very nervous and indeed, she was looking at him almost as apprehensively as her children had.

'I think,' he went on, 'we should call one another "Cousin". If I'm the boys' guardian, Mr Channon is too formal. Would that be agreeable to you?'

'Yes. Yes, of course. Whatever you wish.'

'Good. Then I'll be back next week to stay if you could have a bedroom prepared for me. I'll write and let you know exactly when I shall arrive.'

He was irked by her wariness, her nervousness, her obvious fear for her sons, so before he left he stopped by the door to say bluntly, 'I am not in the habit of ill-treating children, Cousin Maria. You have nothing to fear from me in that respect.'

'They've – had to endure difficult times. My husband didn't even like to hear them playing.'

'I'm not your husband and I do like to see and hear children playing. I intend to make sure their lives are peaceful and orderly from now on.'

She nodded, but he could still see mistrust in every line of her too-thin body.

As they were walking back into town, Mr Hordle sighed and said, 'You see how it is.'

'I don't. Not really. But I shall.' To his surprise the lawyer looked at him just as warily as Cousin Maria had.

'Please treat them all kindly, Mr Channon.'

This un-lawyerly remark startled Jeremiah. He had a lot to think about as he sat in the train going home. Most of all, how much to believe about his cousin Athol. Surely the man could not have been that wicked?

5

Carrie waited till they'd finished their evening meal, then said, 'We need to talk, Eli. Let's go out for a walk.'

He looked at her in puzzlement. 'A walk? It's freezing cold outside.'

'We can wrap up warmly. It's not raining. Eli, *please!*'

With a sigh he let her arrange for Essie to keep an eye on their baby daughter and put on his hat and overcoat.

Carrie led him down to the bare site where the Pride and the Dragon had once stood, let go of his arm and set her hands on her hips, the moonlight bright enough to show her determination. 'You've cleared the site, but you haven't done anything about finding an architect.'

'I'm still not sure what to do.'

'Rebuild the Pride of course. People keep asking me how soon it'll be running again and I can't tell them. They miss it, especially the women. Where else can they go that's respectable?'

He sighed and stirred the soil with one toe. 'I can't seem to get a feel for what to do. I think I used up all my energy the first time we built it.'

'But the night it burnt down you said you were going to build a new one, a real theatre this time, using the whole site.'

'I can't seem to see my way forward at the moment. It's as if I lost my old enthusiasm for making things happen in the fire. And I keep thinking . . . maybe I was too proud of what I was doing, maybe I was *meant* to fail.'

She was tired of treading on eggshells when she talked to him. 'I think you had such a shock that it's taking you a while to recover. But it's time to pull yourself together now because if *you* won't find us an architect, then I shall. Oh, Eli, *please* make an effort! We can't just leave the place like this.' She waved one hand to the empty space around them. 'Remember what it was like? Bright lights, happy people. You were a wonderful Chairman. Let's find an architect and get started.'

He shoved his hands deep into his overcoat pockets. 'Actually, an architect has written to me. He said he'd heard about our troubles and offered to build us a new theatre. He's built one or two others already, it seems, specialises in them.'

'Why didn't you tell me?'

'I don't know. I couldn't seem to think my way round to doing anything about it.'

Her tone was softly chiding, but full of love. 'You wouldn't have been alone, Eli.'

Slowly he raised his head and stared at her, and it seemed as if his eyes had lost some of their icy look. 'What fortunate fate brought me you, Carrie lass?'

He took a step across the gap between them, pulled her into his arms and held her close, so close she could hardly breathe. For a few minutes they stood there pressed against one another, heedless of everything around them.

As he held tight to his wife, Eli took a deep breath and forced himself to speak more positively because she was right. He had to pull himself together. 'I'll write to this Mr Trevin and ask him if he's free to come and see the site, discuss things.'

She looked at him searchingly in the moonlight. 'You still don't sound like your old self.'

His smile was tender. 'Maybe I'll never be as brash and

confident as the old Eli. But with you beside me, I'm sure I can make a go of this again.' For a moment, he almost believed that – almost.

It seemed to her that something was still amiss, but she couldn't put a finger on it and decided to push her doubts aside for the moment. 'So, we'll make a start on the new Pride.'

'No. Not the new Pride, love.' He waved one hand towards the ruins. 'We'll call the new one something different . . . I've been thinking about the Phoenix as a name for it!'

She didn't see the need to change the name, but was happy to humour him as long as he started rebuilding. 'What's a phoenix?'

'A legendary bird that burns itself every year and rises out of its own ashes as a bright new creature. Could anything be more appropriate as a name for our music hall?'

'Music hall, is it now, not music saloon or theatre of varieties?'

'Yes, that's what they're calling them in London. I've seen the name used a few times in the *Era* newspaper. And if we don't rebuild the pub we'll have enough space to make it a proper theatre, not a long, narrow room like the old place.' He pulled her back towards him for another hug. 'Eh, lass, you give me heart, you're like a phoenix yourself, a bright, shining, splendid creature that I love more than life itself.'

She chuckled against him, feeling almost light-headed with relief at the thought that he was coming out of the bleak mood. 'Get away with you, Eli Beckett! You and your fancies. Though I'd still like to keep the old name, I must admit. I can't think of it as anything but the Pride.'

He pulled her to his side so that they could start walking back, arms round each other's waists like young lovers.

'You can do it, Eli,' she said softly. 'You can do anything you set your mind to.'

'*We* can do it. We're more than husband and wife, you and me, we're friends and helpmeets. And anyway, you're the one who can always see how spaces fit together so I'm going to need you to be part of the planning. I'll write to that architect this very night and if he seems all right, we'll let him design us a proper theatre, then we'll call it the Phoenix Music Hall. Or the New Pride. Or anything else that takes our fancy. And it'll be better, far better than the old Pride ever was.'

She felt much happier as they made their way quickly back to Linney's, where they were still staying. Nev had changed it from the old days when the rear had been a common lodging house. He'd made proper bedrooms for lodgers there now and put in the modern novelty of a bathing room, a place just for washing yourself in. There was another bathroom for the family as well. The place was perfect for visiting performers – only there wouldn't be any for a long time to come. And Nev had lost his main source of income until the new music saloon was built, which was another reason she'd confronted her husband tonight.

When Eli was asleep beside her in the comfortable bed, however, the faint uneasiness returned and Carrie lay staring into the darkness. It was too much to hope that Eli would stay optimistic, because he'd been hard hit by the loss of his dream, but perhaps he'd taken the first step back to recovery today. He turned over and muttered something and she held her breath. He was sleeping so badly lately. But he settled again.

She could only hope and pray that he'd continue to move forward now that she'd given him a push. Well, you had to keep going when something bad happened, didn't you? Who knew that better than she did? Terrible things had happened to her at various times in her life and no doubt would again. That was one lesson she'd learned very early on. Eli had had an easier life in many ways, always enough to eat, warm clothes, unlike her and her nine brothers and sisters.

He groaned and flailed one hand. What was it that was haunting him? He not only slept uneasily, but got up during the night and hadn't made love to her since the fire. She tried to be patient with him about that, but she had her needs too, and one of them was for his love.

'Phoenix,' she murmured to herself and pulled a face in the darkness. She preferred the old name, the Pride, so called because Eli had wanted to make his music saloon the Pride of Lancashire. She wondered what people in Hedderby would think if they changed the name. She'd have to persuade him to keep the old name. But she wouldn't even try to do that just yet. One step at a time. It would be enough for now to make a start on rebuilding.

When she woke in the morning the place beside her was empty and Eli wasn't even in the house.

Nurse kept a close eye on Gwynna, who seemed her old self only when playing with Peter. Something had been upsetting that girl ever since the trip to Hedderby, and it wasn't just the worries about Miss Jane. Surely a young fellow pawing at her wouldn't cause anxiety this deep? From the looks of her Gwynna was crying at night. Nurse didn't like to see that in a young lass.

She decided that this couldn't go on, waited until Peter was asleep, then called Gwynna into the next room. 'Sit down, dear. Now . . . tell me what's upsetting you.'

No answer and the girl was avoiding her eyes, so she repeated her command, reinforcing it by, 'You're not leaving this room till you do tell me.'

'I'm worried about my job.'

'And what else?' Nurse waited patiently, watching Gwynna

twist the edge of her starched white pinafore. 'I shan't let you go until you tell me.'

She burst into tears.

Nurse went to sit next to her, putting her arm round the sobbing girl. 'Did Jabez do more than just touch you that day? Is that what this is about?'

Gwynna shook her head, then could bear the burden of her worries no longer and blurted out her story, letting herself be comforted by the thought that the mistress knew about this already.

Nurse was silent for a while, then shook her head. 'I'd never have thought she'd have taken you on. You're a lucky lass.'

'I know.'

She sounded so desolate that Nurse gave her a hug then sent her back to sit with her charge.

Neither of them noticed the shadow that had moved across the doorway as Jane walked back towards the nearby schoolroom, hugging her new knowledge close.

The next day Jane went to find her grandfather, confiding her worries to him that a nursemaid of low morals was looking after her little cousin. He erupted into fury – not with her, never with her, he assured her – but with the maid-servant who had tricked them all. When he'd comforted the sobbing child, he set the bell jangling and roared at the maid who answered it to fetch his daughter-in-law *this minute!*

Jane sat smiling into her handkerchief as she mopped her eyes. It was useful being able to cry whenever she wanted to; it had got her her own way many a time, or saved her from trouble.

Servants went running and word spread through the household that old Mr Hungerton was in one of his furies.

Margaret was startled to be interrupted in her cosy chat with a friend who had called to see her.

'I'm sorry, ma'am, but it's the master. He wants to see you straight away.'

'Tell him I have a visitor and I'll come to him later.'

The maid stood there wringing her hands. 'I daren't do that, ma'am. He said straight away – and he was shouting ever so loud.'

Margaret understood at once that her father-in-law was in one of his tempers and stood up. 'Stay there, Barbara. I'll be back shortly.'

'I think I'd better leave, my dear. Everyone knows how – difficult things can be for you sometimes and there's no telling when you'll be free. You'll come to tea with me tomorrow?'

'I shall look forward to it.' And she would, as she always looked forward to getting out of this house. If certain plans her husband was making came to pass, maybe they could soon leave for good. If not, she didn't know what she would do, especially with the new worry about her niece Jane's threatening behaviour towards Peter. She didn't take Gwynna's concerns about that lightly, because she too found her niece strange.

Margaret went to the library, which was her father-in-law's domain, and found him pacing up and down, with Jane sitting to one side, looking smug. Her niece only got that look on her face when she was causing mischief. What could it be this time? 'You wished to see me, Father?'

'Yes. Did you check up properly on the new girl who's looking after Peter?'

'What do you mean?'

'Did you know that she'd had a baby *out of wedlock* before she came here?'

'Yes, I did. However, I don't think this discussion is a proper one to hold in front of a child.'

'It was *this child* who found out and informed me, though

she was too innocent to fully understand what she was telling me. But I understood! How dare you bring such a slut into my household?'

His face was so dark red that Margaret was worried he'd have an apoplexy. 'This is not something to be discussed in front of Jane,' she repeated.

He stared at her for a moment, then said curtly. 'There's no need for any discussion. You will dismiss the girl immediately.'

'But she's wonderful with Peter. And she's not a slut, she—'

'Are you defying me, Margaret?'

She braced herself, trying to stand up to him for once. 'The care of my son is *my* province, Father. What's more, if you'll let me tell you the girl's story, you'll see that it's not as bad as you think.'

Instead he went and pulled the bell pull, jerking it several times so that it broke off in his hand. Someone approached the room at a run. 'Fetch Mr Robert!' he roared, throwing the bell pull at the man who came in. 'At once!'

'Certainly, sir.' The butler picked up the piece of plaited cord and backed out, warning the maid he sent running for Mr Robert to spread the word that the master was in a right old state, as bad as he'd ever been, and everyone was to watch their step.

In the meantime, though she was shuddering inside, Margaret once again refused to discuss the matter in front of Jane or promise to do as her father-in-law wished. When her husband came into the room, she turned to him in mingled relief and anger and tried to explain what was happening, only to be shouted down by his father.

Robert closed his eyes for a moment, then put his arm round her. 'I'm sorry, Father, but I agree with my wife. This is not a suitable discussion to hold in front of a child.'

The tirade that was let loose made it impossible for anyone

else to speak until the old man had finished shouting
and threatening them. While that was happening, Robert
glanced at his niece and saw her smiling as if enjoying the
fuss she'd caused. He waited until the noise had died down
and said coldly, 'Margaret and I are not children to be
chastised, sir, and certainly not in front of our niece.'

'While you're living in my house, you'll do as I tell you,
as will everyone else.'

And suddenly Robert had had enough. He looked at his
wife questioningly and she nodded, taking his meaning at
once. 'Then the remedy is quite easy. We'll leave your house.'

'If you do, you'll not inherit a penny from me.'

'I have some money from my godmother. I've been
considering investing it in various business ventures and I
think I shall manage well enough.'

'You'll leave this very day, then.'

Jane smiled at them from behind her grandfather's back.
Robert put an arm round his wife's shoulders. 'Perhaps you
should go and start packing, my dear?'

'I'll do so at once.'

Mr Hungerton glared at her, turned to his son and opened
his mouth—

There was a knock on the door and Selwyn came in. 'I
heard there was trouble.'

Margaret walked out past him, head held high. Her
brother-in-law never supported them against his father,
would do anything to maintain the peace, and she couldn't
bring herself to tell him how worried they were about his
daughter.

Mr Hungerton summed up the situation as he saw it to
his oldest son. Selwyn, who had acted as peacemaker more
than once, sent his daughter out of the room.

She hesitated, caught his eye and went meekly.

He managed to calm his father down by agreeing with

everything he said, while muttering asides to his brother in a voice too low for his father to catch. The old man was rather hard of hearing and his eyesight wasn't sharp enough to make out a mouth moving.

'Just go and visit some friends for a few days and I'll get him to change his mind. This should never have happened and I agree with him: Margaret was foolish to hire the girl, knowing her background. The creature must leave today.'

Robert shuddered at the thought of leaving his son unprotected against Jane. 'I'll have the nursemaid driven to the station. But *not* by that Jabez of yours. I caught him trying to force himself upon her yesterday. You want to watch who *you* hire, too.'

'What are you saying? I won't have you whispering behind my back.'

Selwyn turned and said smoothly, 'I'm persuading Robert to send the girl packing at once, Father. And trying to get him to see sense.'

'He's not staying unless he apologises.'

'I'm not staying.' Robert glared at his brother and left the room.

Upstairs, Margaret went to see the new nursery maid, to tell her why she would have to leave and to pay her what was owing.

Gwynna listened in silence, tears filling her eyes. 'I'll miss Peter so much.'

'I'll give you good references,' Margaret said. 'I know this isn't your fault. We've been more than satisfied with your work.'

'Thank you, ma'am.' She hesitated then asked, 'Who's going to watch out for him at night now?'

'My husband and I are leaving here today ourselves.'

'Leaving?'

'Yes. We'll be staying with my sister and there simply won't be room for you.' Margaret hesitated, then turned back to Gwynna. 'Where shall you go?'

'Back to my family in Hedderby.'

'Give me their address. I'll send you a character reference once we've moved, so that you can get another job.' She looked at the gold fob watch pinned to her bodice. 'And now I must get on. I have a lot to do.'

Gwynna said goodbye to Nurse, who wept and told her she was a good lass. Then Gwynna quickly packed her things and was driven to the station by a groom, who didn't say a word to her on the way. He dumped her and her big trunk outside the station and drove off without a backward glance. She couldn't find the porter so had to drag the heavy tin box into the station by herself.

When the train was due, the porter appeared from wher-ever he'd been hiding and grudgingly helped her load her trunk on board.

She was too lost in thought to see the figure running to catch the train and getting into the end carriage as it moved off. Her future might actually be brighter than it had looked before, she decided. Had she not wished for a job in Hedderby?

But had Mrs Robert meant what she said? Would she remember the references? They were so important when you were seeking a job and Essie had no more friends who could give her a chance.

At the next station, the door to her compartment opened just as the train was pulling out and a man got in.

Gwynna looked up and cried out in shock to see Jabez close the door and sit down in the corner, smiling at her in a way that frightened her. She tried to open the door and jump out but he threw her back. By then the train was now going too fast to throw herself out.

'It's quite a way to the next stop,' he said with a smile. 'Time enough for me to finish what I started the other day.'

'If you hurt me, I'll tell Mrs Finch and you'll lose your job.'

'No, I won't. It was old Mr Hungerton who told me to come after you and make sure you knew what your place was in the world.' Jabez grinned and began to unbutton his trousers as he moved slowly along the seat towards her. 'Come here, Gwynna.'

She stared at him in horror and moved back until she was pressed into the corner. She was terrified. The train was rattling along, no one could get into the compartment until it stopped again and she knew Jabez was much stronger than she was.

As he grabbed her arm and pulled her towards him, she began to scream and try to fight him off. She kept screaming at the top of her voice and struggling, but he just laughed as he pinned her down with the weight of his body and began to lift her skirt.

Lucas, who was journeying back to Hedderby, was jolted out of his worries about his uncle by the sound of a woman screaming nearby. He jumped to his feet instinctively, steadying himself in the swaying train as he listened. The screams for help sounded to be coming from the next compartment. He let down his window and peered out, but the train was travelling so fast he knew there was no way he could reach her.

What was happening? Was someone trying to murder the poor woman?

He thumped on the wall between their compartments and yelled, 'What's going on?' but it seemed to make no difference to the screams.

Then suddenly the train began to slow down, jerking and

jolting so that Lucas was flung down on the seat. His bag fell off the rack, narrowly missing him. Metal screamed on metal as the brakes were applied, and the thin screaming sound seemed to blot out all other noises. He pulled himself across to the window in time to see a man standing beside the track waving his arms and staring anxiously in the direction they were heading. A moment later there was a thump and the train rocked furiously as if it had hit something.

Lucas was thrown about again and tried to brace himself on the floor because he thought the carriage was going to jump the tracks. The noise of the brakes gradually lessened and the wild rocking stopped as they slowed down.

Even before the train came to a halt, he flung open the compartment door and jumped down. Steam blew round him and further ahead he heard men yelling. Voices were calling, women were sobbing and somewhere a baby was wailing.

Running back to the compartment from which he'd heard the woman screaming, he yanked open the door in time to see a man hastily buttoning up his trousers and a young woman lying very still on the floor. As he hauled himself up into the carriage, he recognised the man as one of the grooms at Hungerton House, but he couldn't remember the fellow's name. He kept hold of him as the man tried to push past him and as they struggled, a voice behind him called, 'What's happening here? I heard someone screaming.'

'So did I,' Lucas panted.

The woman groaned just then and his attention was distracted for long enough for his captive to wrench himself out of his hands, shove aside the elderly gentleman who was peering into the compartment and jump down. He took off running swiftly across the field.

Lucas couldn't hold back a growl of anger, but after one quick glance at the fleeing figure he turned back to the

woman, lifting her gently from the floor, noting with a tight-
ening of the lips that her upper clothing was torn. 'Someone
find me a female to help her!' he tossed over his shoulder
at the small group of spectators who had gathered.

Instead someone called the guard, who was going along
the train checking that no one was seriously hurt.

The guard clambered up into the compartment. 'What's
going on here?'

Lucas was sitting on the bench by now, cradling the young
woman against him, worried that she was still unconscious.
He explained briefly what he'd heard just before the train
had stopped so abruptly, and what he'd found when he
opened the carriage door.

The gentleman who'd been peering in was still there in the
doorway and agreed that that was indeed what had happened.
'It's a disgrace. Fellow like that should be whipped and
hanged. I kept an eye on the brute but he vanished into those
woods. You'll never catch him now, more's the pity.'

Lucas waited for the guard to offer to help, but the man
was staring at the young woman, his eyes lingering on her
torn garments. After a moment he whispered, 'Do you think
he had his way with her?'

'I don't think so, but he would have done if the train hadn't
stopped. What happened?'

'Some cows on the line. A lot of them milling around. The
idiot in charge couldn't get them off in time, so someone
ran down the track to warn us and luckily the train driver
saw him in time to slow down. We still hit one of them,
though, and it's a miracle we didn't come off the rails. No
one seems badly hurt, thank goodness.'

'Except for this young woman, who's been knocked
unconscious,' Lucas corrected him.

'Yes. Well, I'll have to go and check the rest of the train.'
Just then she groaned and moved her head to and fro,

whimpering as if it hurt. When she opened her eyes, Lucas said gently, 'The train hit a cow. You were thrown about and bumped your head.'

She looked at him dazedly for a minute or two, then gasped and looked round, a terrified expression on her face.

'The man who attacked you ran away. Did you know him?'

'Yes.'

'I recognised him, know where he works. If you can tell the police his name—'

She looked at him and tears filled her eyes. 'It won't do any good.'

'What do you mean? He must be brought to justice.'

She closed her eyes and shook her head. A tear leaked out from under her closed lids, then another one. 'His employer's rich and *he* sent the man to frighten me.'

'Hungerton did?'

She opened her eyes again. 'Yes. Do you know him?'

'Yes. I used to work for him. And he treated me badly too, had me wrongfully arrested. I was lucky to escape without going to prison.'

'So you understand.'

Lucas sighed. Oh yes, he understood all too well what the old devil was like! He could do nothing but hold her close. 'You've been hurt. You need to see a doctor.'

She nestled against him trustingly. 'I just want to go home.'

'Where is your home?'

She stared up, her eyes searching his face. Something about it seemed to reassure her. 'Hedderby.'

'I'm getting off there too. I'll see you get home safely. What's your name?'

'Gwynna. I live at Linney's. My trunk's in the guard's van. Oh, it hurts.' She lifted one hand towards her forehead, then her eyes rolled up and she fainted again.

'Is she dead?'

Lucas looked at the guard, who had just returned. 'No, she's just fainted again. But she's told me her address. She lives in Hedderby. I'll see her home.'

'I'll go and tell the driver we're ready to leave, then.'

'I need a woman to—' But he was talking to himself. Even the older man had gone back to his compartment.

The guard returned five minutes later, calling out loudly as he walked along the train, 'We can proceed slowly. If you'll all get back into your compartments, please . . . Everyone inside again, *if* you please!'

He stopped to ask Lucas, 'Can you keep an eye on her for now, sir? We've lost a lot of time.'

'If you'll fetch my bag from the next compartment.'

The man was back with it a minute later and Lucas watched as he closed the compartment door. A few minutes later the train began to move slowly forward. They passed the mangled corpse of a cow and continued on their way, gradually gathering speed.

Lucas looked down at the unconscious woman – well, she was hardly more than a girl, really. She was too thin, but from her clothing he'd think her to be respectable. She'd be mortified by the torn bodice. Without hesitation, cold as it was, he took off his overcoat and wrapped it round her. He'd recognise that fellow again if he ever saw him, and if the law couldn't punish him, then Lucas hoped for a chance to give him a lesson he'd not forget in a hurry. What was the world coming to when a young woman couldn't travel in safety on a public vehicle?

Or when rich men treated their poorer fellows so badly? What had old Hungerton got against the girl, for heaven's sake?

When the train stopped at Hedderby the guard reappeared, opening the door. 'Do you need help getting her out?'

'No, I can manage.' There were some advantages to being

tall and strong. 'If you could get the bags out for me? That one must be hers. And she said she had a trunk in the luggage van.'

With the help of the guard and two very interested porters they got all the pieces of luggage out of the train and Lucas was directed to carry Gwynna into the waiting room.

'Station master says could you wait for him here, please. He needs to write a report on the accident.'

'Very well.' Lucas sat down on a chair with her still in his arms since there was nowhere but a rather dirty floor to lay her.

Once the train had left again, the station master came to speak to him. 'The guard said there's been an assault on this young person.'

'Yes. I heard her screaming for help just before the train hit the cow, but I was in the next compartment and couldn't go to her aid.'

'The fellow got away, it seems.'

'Yes, but she knows who he is. She said she was coming to Hedderby and had to go to somewhere called Linney's. Do you know where that is?'

The man's face cleared. 'Oh, yes. It's a boarding house. I'll fetch you a cab and you can take her there. The railway will pay for that. I'll mention the incident in my report, but she'll have to make her complaint to the police.'

So for lack of anyone with the sense or kindness to help him, Lucas continued to hold the stranger in his arms. Actually she felt right there, which was a strange thing for him to think. But he liked the way her light brown hair waved softly round her face where it had escaped from the bun at the nape of her neck, tickling his hand. And her skin had a creamy texture that made him want to run his finger down her cheek. He didn't, of course.

When they got to Linney's the cab driver went to bang

on the front door and this time Lucas got the help he required, because the woman who answered it recognised the unconscious girl in his arms at once.

'Gwynna! Mercy on us, whatever's happened?'

'There was a train accident.' He carried her inside, then helped the cab driver carry in her trunk and their bags, by which time she was again regaining consciousness. He sat quietly watching her, seeing the way she sobbed in relief when she saw where she was and the way the woman hugged her.

Sure that she was in good hands, he stood up. 'I must go. I've urgent business of my own to tend to. I'll call tomorrow, if I may, to see how she's going.'

'Wait. What's your name?' the woman called after him.

He didn't answer, didn't even hear what she said because now that he'd got the girl safely home he was worrying about his family again, especially his uncle, who sounded to be at death's door.

Lucas went from Linney's to his uncle's house. He knocked on the door but no one answered, so he opened it and called out, 'Is anyone home? It's me, Lucas.'

There was an exclamation from upstairs and his ten-year-old cousin Belinda came running down to fling herself into his arms and burst into tears.

He held her close, making soothing noises. 'Nay, Belinda love, calm down. My uncle hasn't . . . ?'

Her sister Peggy stood behind her, hands tightly clasped, a look of great anxiety on her face.

Belinda spoke in a low voice, glancing upstairs as if to indicate she didn't want to be overheard. 'Dad's alive, but it's awful! He's just lying there, Lucas. At first he couldn't move at all, but now he's able to move his right hand a bit, though all that side of his body is stiff and his face is all twisted. He can't go to work, and me and Peggy haven't been to school since it happened. We're all of us that upset and we don't know what to do. Mum sits by his bed and cries most of the time. I've been doing the cooking, only she won't eat anything an' Dad can't eat much, either.'

'Take me up to him, will you, love?'

He was shocked by his uncle's appearance. Fred looked twenty years older than last time Lucas had seen him. He seemed aware of what was going on around him, however, so Lucas took his hand and said slowly and clearly, 'I'm here now, Uncle, and I'll stay for as long as you need me.'

The relief in the sick man's eyes was wonderful to see.

Lucas went downstairs again and got Belinda to help him make up a bed in the parlour. He'd have to find work here in Hedderby, couldn't see himself being able to go back to London for some time. Wasn't that always the way? As soon as you were happy, fate dealt you a blow. He'd never find a job like the one he'd had in London round here, would have to go back to simple carpentry, which wasn't nearly as interesting once you'd tasted another way of earning a living.

The next day Mr Forrett, owner of the cotton mill where Uncle Fred had worked in the office, called round to see how his former employee was doing. He shook his head when he saw Fred and left his wife with five guineas to help tide her over.

'It's very generous of him,' Aunt Hilda said.

'How many years has he worked at the mill?'

'It must be at least twenty.'

'Five shillings for every year. Not all that generous.'

Hilda looked at the money lying on the table. 'Most employers wouldn't have given us anything.'

He didn't argue with his aunt. What was the use? She was right. Hungerton wouldn't have given anything and would have thrown them out of their cottage. He must ask Hilda later how much the rent was. They'd have to be very careful with money from now on.

Lucas found a job within two days, but it was boring work, even worse than he'd expected. He was given the sorts of tasks an apprentice would usually be doing because Mr Trumble didn't have a lad to do the odd jobs round the place. Once his uncle was better, Lucas intended to start his own business but it took time to build one up from scratch. Even then you got all sorts of small jobs at first until you got a reputation for being a good craftsman.

It was a comedown in the world for a man of his skills. *Where are your fine dreams now?* mocked a voice in his head.

Should he write to his family to let them know where he was? No, better not. They might let the information slip and then Hungerton might try to push him into returning. No, the best thing he could do now was keep quiet and concentrate on helping his uncle and family.

Once or twice he remembered the girl he'd helped on the train. He'd meant to visit her, but hardly had a minute to call his own. She'd be all right, he consoled himself. She had a family to look after her and they weren't poor, from the size of the house.

But he'd like to see her again.

6

Jeremiah moved to Hedderby the week following his visit, as arranged. He had written to apprise Cousin Maria of his time of arrival and ask that the carriage be sent to pick himself and his luggage up at the station.

When he got there, he saw that the private carriage waiting for him had its paintwork somewhat blistered and its interior still smelled of smoke. The servant who'd been playing with the two boys was standing next to it talking to the elderly coachman, but stepped forward when he saw Jeremiah.

'Can I help you with your luggage, sir?'

Jeremiah frowned as they drove off. It seemed extravagant keeping a manservant just to do odd jobs and play with the boys, but he would suspend judgement on that until he saw how the household was run, how much work there was for this Renny fellow to do. He assumed there would be enough money coming in from the engineering works to pay the servants' wages. From the size of its buildings it seemed a fairly large concern.

Their way again took them past the burnt-out building on the main street, but the land had been cleared in the past few days. Well, you'd expect a thriving business to rebuild as quickly as possible. The sight of a fire-ravaged place inevitably brought back bad memories for Jeremiah and he was so sunk in them that when the carriage drew up at the house he didn't at first notice they'd arrived until the carriage door was opened.

Renny popped his head inside. 'Are you all right, sir?'

'Yes.' Jeremiah took a deep breath and banished the memories that wouldn't leave him in peace for long. The front door was again opened before he got there. Did these servants have nothing to do but watch out for visitors?

The housekeeper greeted him. 'Mrs Stott asked me to show you up to your room, sir. She's not very well, I'm afraid, has a feverish cold and has been in bed for the last few days.'

'Has the doctor been called?'

'No, it's just a cold. But she's not recovered yet from all the recent trouble, so I persuaded her to have a proper rest.'

'*You* persuaded her? Is that your place?'

She looked at him sombrely. 'I wasn't trying to presume, sir, but she has no one to care for her and she pushes herself too hard. I've worked here for several years now, so perhaps I'm a bit closer to her than servants would usually be. I'm hoping, and I know she is too, that you won't be wanting to make any changes in the staff.'

How to answer that frank speech? He didn't know so didn't even try. Did none of the servants here know their place? he wondered. The ones at his father's home, admittedly only three of them, were quiet and obedient, never speaking out of turn. Was that better or worse than this woman, who sounded as if she cared deeply for her mistress?

Why did he always question the way things were run? Why could he never accept the status quo? His father had tried hard enough to inculcate him with the same values as himself, but still questions crept into Jeremiah's mind and he was never comfortable unless he could assess a situation and form his own opinions. 'Please show me to my room, Mrs Ibster, and afterwards perhaps I can start getting to know the boys.'

'They're doing their lessons with the governess, sir. Miss

Cavett, she's called. She's been here for quite a few years as well. Very fond of the boys, she is, used to protect them as much as she could before . . .' She broke off without finishing her sentence and moved towards the stairs.

Protect them from their father? he wondered as he followed. Surely a man wouldn't harm his own children? But he didn't pursue the point and ask her to explain herself. It wasn't right to discuss such things with servants.

The housekeeper showed him to a handsome bedroom at the side of the house. 'I hope this will be suitable for you, sir.'

'It looks very comfortable.' And he could see that Mrs Ibster knew her job, because like the rest of the house, the place gleamed with polish and smelled fresh.

'We aired the bed and there's a hot-water bottle in it now, just to make sure, because the room hasn't been used for a while.'

'This wasn't my cousin Athol's room, then?'

'No, sir. That one is still empty. Mrs Stott hasn't been able to face clearing the master's clothes and other stuff out. His old artificial leg is still in the cupboard.' She shuddered. 'Renny says he'll clear it if we wish, but he's not been back long and the boys still take up a lot of his time.'

'Not been back?'

'The master dismissed him for protecting the boys from – seeing something horrible. He loves those boys, Renny does.'

It was out before Jeremiah could stop himself. 'Your master sounds to have been rather difficult.'

Her involuntary shudder was more eloquent than words. 'I don't think it's my place to talk about him, sir, only well, you can't help remembering, can you? Renny could tell you more than anyone else except the mistress. He used to look after Mr Stott until just before . . .'

'Just before what?' He looked at her and came to a decision. 'Please don't start telling me things then stopping. I don't want to gossip unnecessarily but I do need to understand.'

'I was going to say: just before the master started behaving very strangely, sir. Mr Stott locked the mistress in her room for days and the reason he dismissed Renny was for stopping him killing the boys' dog in front of them.' Tears came into her eyes and she swallowed hard, then spread her hands in a helpless gesture. 'It was bad, sir.'

'*Killing the boys' dog!*' He stared at her in astonishment.

'Yes, sir. It had tripped him up. He was a bit clumsy with that artificial leg.'

Jeremiah didn't question her further. If she was telling the truth, his cousin must have had a sadistic nature. What would a scene like that have done to two young boys? He shuddered even to think of it. 'Thank you for telling me. You did the right thing.'

'I hope so. Now, if you'll excuse me, I'll get on with my work. If you don't need anything else, that is? Do you want someone to unpack for you? Only we're a maid short. One of the girls wouldn't stay after the fire.'

'I'd prefer to unpack myself. Afterwards I'll take a look round the house.'

But when the housekeeper had gone downstairs again, he didn't at first do anything because he couldn't get what she'd told him out of his mind. *Killing the boys' dog in front of them?* What sort of man would try to do something as terrible as that?

Shaking his head in bafflement and wondering what other dark secrets he would discover here, Jeremiah began to put away his things as methodically as he did everything else. He was pleased with the size and feel of the room, and relieved to have got away from his father and a town filled with unhappy memories.

But try as he would, he could not prevent his thoughts from dwelling on the picture Mrs Ibster had painted of his cousin. Could Athol Stott really have been that bad?

Another man arrived in Hedderby that same day. He turned up at Linney's unheralded, carrying a flat leather case of the sort used to hold large pieces of paper.

'I'm here to see Mr Beckett. I'm Maitland Trevin, architect. He and I have been in correspondence about building a new theatre of varieties here.'

Carrie, who had answered the door, hitched Abigail higher on her hip, puzzled. 'Was he expecting you?'

'My good woman, kindly tell me whether he's here and if not where he is to be found. I'm a man to whom time is money and I can't waste it in idle chit-chat.'

She stiffened, not liking his tone, and for some reason did not explain that she was Eli's wife. 'He's not here. You can probably find him down at the site.'

'Thank you. And where exactly is the site?'

Carrie gave him directions – well, it was only a matter of walking down the hill and turning right at Market Street – and he left, whistling in a thin, tuneless whine. She stood at the door and watched him go, frowning.

When she went back into the kitchen, Essie asked, 'Who was that?'

'The architect who contacted Eli after the fire. He'd read about it in the *Manchester Guardian*, he said. We wrote back to him and now he's just turned up out of the blue. Strange, that he's come here to see Eli without being asked. I'd not have expected an architect to do that. Would you?'

Essie shrugged. 'I've never met an architect. I've no idea how they work.'

⋆

Well over an hour later Eli came home, accompanied by Mr Trevin. 'This is my wife, Carrie. She's the one who understands drawings and how spaces fit together.'

Mr Trevin blinked in surprise then shook Carrie's hand warmly. 'We've already met. Delighted to see you again, my dear lady. And your charming little daughter.'

Abigail leaned away from him as he tried to pat her cheek. Carrie felt like doing the same. It wasn't just that he'd called her 'my good woman' in a patronising tone earlier and now she had suddenly become 'my dear lady', but there was something about him which she instinctively disliked. But Mr Trevin's visit had obviously put her husband in a better mood, so she suppressed her own feelings.

'Can you come into the parlour with us to look at the sketches Mr Trevin has brought with him?' Eli asked.

'Of course.' She gave Abigail to Gwynna, who was sitting by the kitchen fire, still languid, with a big bruise on her temple, then followed them into the parlour.

Mr Trevin quickly spread out some exquisite drawings of theatres he'd built and by the time they'd studied a few, Carrie had decided to ignore her feeling of antipathy towards him because the drawings spoke for him, said he knew what he was doing. The buildings they showed were very attractive indeed.

'Mr Trevin has had an unexpected cancellation of a commission due to the bankruptcy of a client, so has some time to spare for us as long as we can start work at once and finish here before his next building project is due to start,' Eli explained. 'What do you think, love? Will any of these buildings do? They're already designed, so can be built quite quickly.'

She bent over the drawings, sensing that their visitor was unhappy to have a woman involved so closely in the decision making. Well, let him frown at her. She knew she had the ability to see sketches and turn them to buildings in her mind, yes and picture the spaces inside the buildings, too. 'That one looks the best for us,' she said after she'd gone through them, pulling out the simplest of the sketches.

Mr Trevin looked at her dubiously then turned to her husband. 'And you, sir? Which one do *you* prefer?'

Eli shrugged. 'I agree with my wife, who proved she has more of a feel for that sort of thing than I have when we were building the Pride.'

Carrie leaned forward. 'There's just one thing. We lived above the old pub, so what about living quarters in this theatre?'

He looked down his nose at her as if she'd suggested something outrageous. 'It isn't usual to have a family living in a modern theatre, not a *proper* theatre, that is. And what's more, if you need the place building quickly and for a price you can afford, then you won't want to make big changes to it, will you?'

'Maybe we could find room in the upper storey at the rear or side? There's—'

'Not if you want a proper balcony and space for your backdrops.'

She knew she was right and looked at Eli who only shrugged again.

'We can rent a house for ourselves.' He wiped sweat from his brow. 'After all, it's the theatre that counts now.'

Which wasn't much use, she thought in annoyance.

He stood up abruptly. 'Discuss the details with my wife, Mr Trevin, and I'll do what's necessary to get permission to build the place. I'll have to talk to the people at the Town Hall, who seem to have formulated a lot of rules and regulations about building these days.' He stood up and moved towards the door.

Carrie saw how pale he'd become and wondered if he was

feeling ill. She stifled a sigh. Ill or not, the old Eli wouldn't have left things to her. He might have listened carefully to her opinions but he'd have been involved in every aspect of the building.

Mr Trevin watched Eli walk out then turned back to Carrie, giving her a forced smile. 'Well, let me explain the details of this sketch to you, then, Mrs Beckett.'

'I don't need it explaining. I've got eyes.' She couldn't keep a tart tone out of her voice. 'But I would like to see what the inside would look like. Do you have any other drawings?'

'Are you sure about this one?'

'Of course I am. If those measurements are correct, it'd fit quite nicely on our piece of land with only minor changes.'

Trevin took out his pocket watch, clicked the lid open and squinted at it, then looked at her suspiciously. 'Can you really decide so quickly which music hall you want to have built?'

'Yes. But I'll need to know the price.' She wanted to start things moving, then Eli would be so busy he'd have no time to brood.

'I'll discuss prices with your husband.'

'Can you give me an approximate idea of what it will cost? We only have the insurance money to build it with.'

'Which is?'

She told him.

'Hmm. We may have to make a few modifications to do it for that price, simplify things a little.'

'You can do that?'

'Of course I can.'

'Well, your sketch of the outside looks very attractive. If the inside is as good and we can find a builder who can do it for that price, it all seems very straightforward to me.' It didn't really. She was terrified at the mere thought of so much responsibility, but she wasn't going to show that to *him*.

'In that case, I think I'd better go and fetch the sketches of the interior. Oh, and I have a builder who works with me so we can do the whole job for you much more cheaply than an outsider would. Perhaps I could bring him back with me next time, then we'll hire local men to work under him and his assistants?'

'Yes. But it will still depend on the final cost whether we agree to all this.'

'I can discuss the details with your husband later.'

She didn't say that she'd be involved in those discussions as well. He'd find that out.

She was surprised when Trevin consulted his watch and said he had to go. Surely he should have stayed and discussed costs with Eli? But maybe she was letting her feelings about the man influence her. The sketch had been lovely, exactly the sort of place they wanted, a bit like a theatre they'd visited in Manchester.

She smiled as she went back to reclaim her daughter. She didn't understand how she knew instinctively that the building in that sketch would sit well on their piece of land, she just did, always had been able to picture things inside her head.

When Eli came back he looked a bit brighter. 'I've spoken to the clerk at the Town Hall. If we take our plans in to show him, he'll expedite matters, because the Town Council are very much in favour of our rebuilding quickly. Where's Mr Trevin?'

'He went home to fetch the sketches of the interior. I'm surprised he didn't have them with him. We need to see what that's like before we make our decision, not to mention discussing the cost of building it, though he says he can do that for us to fit in with the money we have available. He has a builder working with him.'

'They can do the whole job for us? That'll make it much easier.'

Eli seemed so much brighter as he began talking of all the tasks that would need to be done. That made her decide to let nothing and no one stop them getting on with the rebuilding. She'd seen women become down in spirits after they'd had babies, but hadn't realised men could feel a similar sort of sadness. Perhaps you didn't notice it with men, since they were usually out at work all day, but Eli was around a lot of the time and although he kept making an effort to be cheerful, he couldn't fool her.

Losing the Pride had knocked the stuffing out of him and she would do anything to help him get better. Even put up with a man like Trevin, one who made her flesh crawl just to be near him.

The following day, Carrie had a chat with Nev and Essie while her husband was out. 'There isn't going to be a place for us to live in the new theatre, so we'd better start looking for a house to rent as well as buying some new furniture and clothes.'

They exchanged glances which said they'd already discussed this.

'Have you thought of living here for a while, love?' Essie asked. 'Until the theatre is rebuilt at least? You could pay us a bit of rent and move down to the rooms we used to let out to visiting performers, then we'd get some income and you'd have people around you to help with little Abigail?'

Carrie hugged her on the spot. 'I hadn't dared hope you could put up with us for so long.'

'Get on with you! We love having you here, don't we, Nev?'

He nodded, beaming at her so that Carrie had no doubt about his feelings. He'd been rather a shy man when he married her mother, but he clearly loved having his step-children around and indeed, had blossomed into a kindly man, who'd probably get even more like his father Raife as he grew older.

'Thank you,' she said warmly. 'I don't even have to ask Eli. I'll accept for both of us.'

As she'd expected, Eli made no objections to staying there. Indeed, he didn't even seem very interested. They moved down to one of the two most expensive rooms that had previously been rented to star performers, while Abigail slept in a smaller room nearby. The big rooms were beautifully furnished and best of all near one of the two bathing rooms. It made life very easy not having to go outside to a privy. She made a mental note to speak to Mr Trevin about putting lavatories into the new building, for artistes, staff and customers. They might as well do the thing properly, with all modern conveniences.

If it hadn't been for her worries about Eli, she'd have been feeling quite happy now, as happy as you could be when you'd lost everything in a fire. But then, she'd never been one to let things get her down.

And she *would* find a way to help Eli. She had to. She wanted them to be as happy as they'd been before the fire, before he changed. She wanted that as desperately as she'd once longed for regular meals and a change of clothing.

Gwynna took a while to recover from Jabez's attack. Essie said it didn't matter that she wasn't paying her way and they could do with a hand here. This wasn't really true, because Carrie was there and she was a hard worker, and Essie had been too soft-hearted to turn off their scrubbing woman, a widow who depended on the money she earned to feed her children, so there were many willing hands and no paying guests to clear up after.

Gradually Gwynna felt her energy and spirits returning. It cheered her up when she received a letter from Mrs Robert, enclosing a reference to say she'd been good at her job and had left only because the family's circumstances had changed. She showed the reference to everyone, proud that Mrs Robert had said such kind things about her.

It was decided that she should take over the daily running of errands. She would rather have worked inside the house, but Essie insisted that the fresh air would do her good. And she did enjoy her outings to Mr Marker's emporium, loving to watch him and his measuring and weighing her purchases with a sure hand. She kept a careful eye out for her family each time she went out but to her great relief didn't see any sign of them.

Today Mrs Marker took her aside after she'd made her purchases. 'I heard you're looking for work as a nursemaid. Is that right?'

'Yes.'

'You soon left your other place.'

She'd worked out what to say. 'They moved away. Mrs Hungerton has given me a reference, though.'

'Ah. Well, I heard yesterday that Mrs Forrett at the mill is looking for a nursemaid. Her other one had to leave suddenly because her mother died and her father needed her. You could go and ask.'

'I thought they were selling the mill and leaving Hedderby.'

'Seems the sale has fallen through. Mrs Forrett was very upset about that.'

Gwynna walked slowly back to Linney's. If she got a job in Hedderby her employers would know about her past, the baby and her family, everything. She wasn't sure anyone here would even want to hire her. But it didn't cost anything to try, did it? She told Essie what she was doing, changed into one of the outfits she'd worn at Hungerton House and walked round to Mill House.

As she passed through the mill yard, two men working on

a dray called out to her, suggestive remarks that made her face flame. It still felt red when she knocked on the front door.

The door was opened by a thin maid who looked tired out. A bad sign, Gwynna thought, and nearly turned away there and then. But that would have been cowardly. 'Could I see Mrs Forrett, please?'

The maid looked at her doubtfully.

'It's about the job of nursemaid. I heard they needed one.'

The girl's face cleared and she smiled at Gwynna. 'Come in. I'm sure she'll see you because she's desperate. Just wait in the kitchen till I tell her.'

From upstairs came the thin sound of a baby crying, a tired unhappy baby, not a lusty roar.

Gwynna sat in the kitchen for ten minutes by the clock on the wall, then the maid came back. 'Mrs Forrett will see you now.'

As they went upstairs, Gwynna stared about her curiously. The house was very dark because it was overshadowed by the mill, and though the furnishings were expensive they seemed so heavy, the colours so dark that they added to the feeling of being shut in, trapped.

'Mrs Forrett is in the nursery,' her guide whispered. 'She can't get the baby to settle today.'

The nursery was on the second floor, up a set of narrow steps covered only with sacking. But the room itself had a big dormer window and felt much more cheerful than the rest of the house.

The woman who greeted Gwynna was puffy looking and seemed half asleep. Her clothes had been thrown on anyhow, her voice was slurred, her words punctuated by sighs and pauses for which there seemed no reason.

'Jenny says you're looking for a job – as a nursemaid. Have you had any – um – experience?'

'Yes, ma'am. I worked for Mrs Robert Hungerton in Sutherclough.'

Mrs Forrett gave a huge yawn. 'Why did you leave?'

'They were leaving Hungerton House and . . .'

The baby began to wail again and Mrs Forrett looked at it helplessly.

Gwynna hesitated then said gently, 'She's got wind. See how she's moving her legs. If you'd let me hold her, I'm sure I could make her more comfortable.'

Mrs Forrett held out her daughter at once and watched as Gwynna laid her over her shoulder, patting her back until the infant let out a loud burp. The crying stopped and the baby let out a tired murmur, snuggling against the newcomer.

'Well, you certainly know how to deal with babies.'

'Yes, ma'am.'

'I'll have to see my husband. He always has to approve new maids. But I desperately need help.' She sighed and rubbed her forehead. 'My other children are grown up. I hadn't expected to have another baby at my age, and Libby cries a lot. It's too much, it really is.'

She stopped speaking to stare into the distance, then blinked and looked at Gwynna as if she didn't know what to do next. After frowning for a moment or two, she said, 'I'll send across to the mill – for my husband and – um – he can speak to you. Could you look after Libby for a few minutes?'

'Of course. Could I change her for you? She's very wet. Have you some clean clouts?'

Mrs Forrett waved her hand vaguely and wandered out, so Gwynna hunted for the baby clouts, finding a pile of dirty ones in a corner, which made her wrinkle her nose in disgust. She talked gently to Libby as she cleaned her little bottom, noting in disapproval the red rash and soreness. Then she rocked the infant in her arms until she fell asleep.

It was a full half hour before heavy footsteps came up the stairs. Gwynna had seen Mr Forrett about town, had heard that he visited a woman in one of the lanes and knew he sometimes pestered the girls who worked in the mill, so was feeling a bit nervous. She didn't want the job if he pestered the maids at home as well.

He stood in the doorway, staring at her. 'My wife says you've got a reference from your last job.'

Gwynna hitched the baby to one side, but Libby didn't stir. She handed the piece of paper to him, watching as he quickly ran his eyes down the page.

He handed it back to her. 'Where are you living at the moment?'

'Linney's. I used to work for them, but they treat me like family now.'

'Well, they're respectable enough.'

She realised suddenly how easily he could find out about her past and decided to tell him. 'I was wet nurse to Mr Linney's daughter when his wife died.'

'*Wet nurse?*'

His voice was much sharper suddenly and her heart sank. She was sure he wouldn't want to employ her now. 'My own baby died.'

'And your husband?'

'I didn't have one, sir. My young man would have married me but he died before he even knew about the baby. Patrick Culshaw, he was called. He died in an accident in your mill.'

Silence, then, 'I remember him. Good worker.'

Mr Forrett stared at her and she couldn't tell what he was thinking.

'What if I wanted to take you to bed, what if I made that a condition of giving you the job?'

She glared at him. 'Then I'd have to find myself another job. I only ever went with my Patrick. I'm not free with my favours.' She laid the baby down in the cot and moved purposefully towards the door.

He chuckled and put out one hand to bar her way.

Her heart began to pound. What did he want?

'I'd not have given you the job if you'd said yes, but I'd have set you up in a house. You're a trim lass. I like them thin, unlike my pudding of a wife.'

'Would you let me pass, please?'

'Don't be so hasty.'

She wondered if she'd have to scream for help.

'Since you're not a girl of easy virtue, I'll hire you, though we won't tell my wife about your past. Let's get it clear from the start, though. I don't employ anyone inside my house who misbehaves.'

'I won't, sir.'

'What were they paying you in your last job?'

She told him.

He pulled a face. 'And what if I offered you less?'

She took another risk. 'I'd not take the job. I'm good at what I do, really good, and I love children. I'll be worth it, I promise you.'

He threw back his head and roared with laughter, then yelled down the stairs, 'Nenny! Come up and meet your new nursemaid.'

There were slow, hesitant footsteps on the stairs and Mrs Forrett drifted into the room. Again, she didn't seem fully aware of what was going on around her and looked at her husband as if expecting to be told.

'She'll do. Hire her,' he said and went downstairs without another glance in Gwynna's direction.

Mrs Forrett promptly burst into tears and it took Gwynna some time to calm her down.

'I'm so *tired*, you see. I've been up half the night with Libby. And now the sale of the mill's fallen through and we have to stay here and I hate it!' She gulped and mopped her eyes. 'When can you start? You couldn't go and bring your things right away, could you?'

'Yes.'

More tears greeted this reply. Normally Gwynna would have put an arm round someone so upset, but she hadn't taken to Mrs Forrett, didn't want to touch her or even stand close to her. Beneath the cloying perfume you could smell unwashed flesh. She hated that sort of smell. Warm water was easily available to someone this rich, so there was no excuse for it.

When she went out into the yard the same young man called out after her.

Mr Forrett stuck his head out of the office and yelled, 'I've told you before not to annoy my maids! If you don't mind your manners you'll be looking for another job. This is our new nursemaid.'

'Sorry, miss.' The man turned back to his work.

Gwynna walked home, pleased to have got another job but wondering what it'd be like to work in a household where the mistress didn't seem very capable. She was so lost in her thoughts that she bumped into someone, bouncing off him so hard that if he hadn't caught hold of her, she'd have fallen. She looked up to thank him and the words died in her throat, because it was the man who'd rescued her on the train. She'd have recognised him anywhere. Such a good-looking man with the kindest smile she'd ever seen. She'd thought about him several times.

'Gwynna!' He smiled down at her. 'I was wondering how you were.'

'Much better and very grateful for your help, but I didn't know how to find you to say thank you.' She blushed, remembering suddenly that he had seen her torn bodice and possibly even her breasts. She still felt herself go hot with shame every time she remembered that.

'I meant to come and see you, but my uncle's had a seizure and I've been helping out. I'm the breadwinner now and had to find a job straight away. He's starting to recover, though we doubt he'll ever be quite the same again.'

'I'm sorry to hear that. Life can be cruel.' She hesitated then said in a rush, 'I don't even know your name.'

'It's Lucas. Lucas Kemp. And you're Gwynna . . . ?' He looked at her questioningly.

'Jones. I'm staying at Linney's at the moment, but I've just got myself a job working as a nursemaid for Mr Forrett at the mill.' She beamed at him. 'I love looking after babies and this little girl is such a darling.'

They didn't stay any longer because Lucas had to get back to work, but all day he kept remembering Gwynna's vivid face. She wasn't exactly pretty, but when she was happy and excited, there was something about her face that he liked very much. He hoped he would see her again. Then he frowned. He usually became tongue-tied when talking to young women he found attractive, but Gwynna was easier to talk to than others. He'd better be careful, though. He couldn't afford to get involved with anyone for years yet.

He was tired of putting off making a home for himself. He'd had to do that when working for Mr Hungerton because if there'd been any hint of him walking out with a young woman, they'd have pushed him into getting wed. But he was a normal man, with a normal desire for a wife and children, and physical frustration sometimes kept him awake at night.

When he got back to the workshop, Mr Trumble started complaining about how long he'd taken to run a simple errand. Lucas had had enough. He leaned on the bench and said slowly and clearly, 'I'm a carpenter not an apprentice, and there's not so much work here that I can't take a minute to greet an old friend while I'm out. If *I* don't complain about running errands, *you* shouldn't complain about how long I take to do them. What's more, if you find my work unsatisfactory, I'll happily go and find myself another job, because I won't put up with being spoken to like that.'

Trumble goggled at him. 'There's no need to take a huff, Kemp. I don't find your work unsatisfactory. I just wondered why you'd taken so long, that's all. I *am* your employer and you should . . .'

Lucas gave him a long, level look and the other shrugged, not bothering to finish his sentence. *Don't find your work unsatisfactory, indeed!* Lucas thought. The work was good and was in fact, far better than Trumble's own slapdash efforts.

'Anyway, there *is* work to be done. Mr Burtell wants some alterations done on his attic. He's got friends coming to stay and they need a partition putting up or something to make a room for the visiting maid. He sent word while you were out.'

'I'll go round at once.' He didn't say he knew Mr Burtell but was pleased to think he'd be seeing the lawyer again.

Jack took one look at him and clapped him on the back. 'So you did return to Hedderby after all.'

'I had to. My uncle's had a seizure and I'm the breadwinner now. But I did spend some time working in London.' He explained what he'd been doing there to a man who was genuinely interested, as no one else had been since he came back.

'That's hard luck, losing such a good opportunity. And you're working for old Trumble now.' Jack grinned. 'He's a surly devil, but he did a good job for me a couple of years ago. He's been trying to sell his business through me for a while, but there haven't been any takers.'

Lucas stared at him in surprise. 'He never told me that when he took me on!' So his job wasn't even secure!

'Close-mouthed as an oyster, he is, and always has been. But I did wonder if you might be interested in buying it?' He smiled. 'We lawyers often sell properties for our clients.'

'How much does he want for it?'

'Three hundred and fifty pounds. It's not just the stock and goodwill, he owns the whole building.'

'Oh.'

'You'd have been interested?'

Lucas nodded. 'Yes, but I can't afford that much.'

Jack raised one eyebrow. 'How much can you afford?'

'Eighty pounds, maybe eighty-five at a pinch. I wasn't looking to buy a whole house, you see, just wanted to set up my own business. I've been saving for it for years.'

Jack looked thoughtful. 'If I might make a suggestion? Talk to your uncle about it. He owns his own house. He might sell it and come in with you if you're going to continue providing for his family.'

'Uncle Fred owns his own house?'

'Yes. I acted for him when he bought it. Vigorous fellow, he was then. I hate to think of an active man like him sitting there, unable to work . . . Life can be cruel. Anyway, come and see what I need doing and tell me what you think about making a room in my attic . . .'

He would, Jeremiah decided, go up to see the boys as soon as he'd unpacked. He particularly wanted to meet their governess. If he was to do his job as guardian properly, he must make sure she was a suitable person to teach them, though really lads of that age should be in school learning to get on with others.

An hour later he had finished unpacking and had rearranged the whole room to his satisfaction. Leaving it, he went upstairs to the second floor, where he assumed the schoolroom would be situated. Pleased to find himself correct in his assumptions, he followed the sound of boys' voices – talking eagerly he noted with approval, as if the subject interested them. He knocked on the door.

'Come in!'

He went in to see a plain-faced woman in dark clothing sitting between the two boys at a table. They all fell silent at the sight of him. 'Please continue what you were doing.'

But when she tried to go on with the lesson, the boys shook their heads in answer to her questions and positively shrank away when he went forward to join them. Surely not his resemblance to their father again?

She looked at him so pleadingly that after studying the things on the table and noting that they were using the sort of schoolbooks you'd expect for boys of this age, he left them to it. He'd speak to her privately about their progress another time.

He'd noticed that the older boy had dark circles under his eyes and there had been fear – yes, it was definitely fear – showing in Isaac's taut body and anxious expression when Jeremiah went near him. He remembered on his previous visit the housekeeper telling him that his cousin Maria had been up during the night because Isaac had nightmares. What exactly were those boys afraid of? Their father was dead now.

He explored the rooms on the ground floor, noting with pleasure that there was a well-stocked bookcase in the rear sitting room. But he found that room oppressive for some reason he couldn't fathom. He discovered a smaller sitting room which contained embroidery materials and a frame containing an exquisite depiction of flowers, almost completed. This was presumably Cousin Maria's private domain. He couldn't resist stroking the embroidery. He loved flowers, though his father said that was wrong. How could it be when flowers were among the most beautiful of God's creations? 'Consider the lily,' he muttered.

There was a dining room full of sombre gleaming furniture but it looked unused, as if no guests had been entertained here for a long time. The smaller breakfast parlour was obviously where the family ate and there was a drawing room at the front of the house where the furniture was arranged stiffly round the edges and there was an unused feel to the place.

From there he went through to the rear of the house, startling the housekeeper, who was in the kitchen helping the cook to chop some vegetables. 'Sorry, Mrs Ibster. I'm just getting to know my way around.' He nodded to the cook.

'Is there anything I can get for you, sir?' she asked.

'Perhaps a cup of tea?'

'Certainly, sir.'

He went out into the back garden and found himself facing the dog. Was this the same one his cousin Athol had tried to kill? It didn't look at all dangerous. Bending, he held out his hand, letting it sniff him, which he'd been told you should do with dogs, and was pleased when it began to wag its tail.

'Are you a good dog?' he asked it, not sure how to get on good terms with dogs because his father had never allowed animals into the house, not even a cat to keep the mice down.

At the sound of his voice the dog wagged its tail even harder and you'd think it was grinning at him. Jeremiah relaxed a little.

'It's taken to you,' a voice said behind him and he turned to see Renny with an empty coal scuttle in his hands.

'It seems a pleasant-natured creature.'

'He is. He's called Migs and he's loyal and intelligent. I make sure the boys look after him properly. That teaches them responsibility as well as a love of their fellow creatures.'

Jeremiah nodded slowly, approving that attitude. 'What exactly are your duties here, Renny?'

'They aren't clear yet now that *he* has gone, but I can turn my hand to most things. I don't like to be idle. People also say I have a gift for healing.' He looked up in the direction of the schoolroom window, his expression suddenly sad. 'Those lads have been sorely hurt and will take a long time to recover. Cruelty casts a long shadow.' He looked back at Jeremiah. 'You've a sadness in you too, sir. It's hard to lose a wife and child. But you'll marry again, be happy again.'

Jeremiah gaped at him, not sure how to take this. The man wasn't surly or impolite, but he was acting as if they were equals. And did he fancy himself a fortune teller as well as a healer? But by the time Jeremiah opened his mouth to deliver a reprimand, Renny had walked away.

As he strolled round the garden, Jeremiah's thoughts turned back to his cousin Maria. Was she really ill or was it an affliction of the nerves? Had there been a grain of truth in Cousin Athol's warning about her nature? He would wait and observe her, always a good tactic in new situations.

Looking round, he breathed in the crisp, chill air with pleasure. He liked Hedderby, the closeness of the moors, the busy, bustling people on the main street, the feeling that the little town was thriving.

But there was something very unhappy about this house, especially that rear room. He wasn't usually fanciful, but he could sense a dark, brooding atmosphere. Was it a legacy of Athol Stott? Was that sort of thing possible? He'd not have even considered it before he came here, but now, he wasn't sure what to think.

7

Gwynna was back at the mill house within the hour. She knocked on the front door because there was no way Raife could get the handcart with her trunk on it round the narrow walkway to the back.

The same maid opened the front door and cheerfully helped them up the stairs with the trunk.

'I'm Jen, general maid here,' she said once Raife had left. 'I got your bed changed but the room really needs a good clean out. Maddy left it in a right mess. She was good with the baby, but she didn't keep things very clean, I'm afraid.' She lowered her voice to a whisper. 'And Mrs Forrett isn't at all good at managing, so things have got worse in the past few days. I've only one pair of hands, after all.'

The nursery smelled sour and Mrs Forrett was asleep in the nursing chair, the baby curled up in the crook of her arm.

That child could have fallen off and hurt herself, Gwynna thought, shocked. She took Libby gently away from her mother and laid her down in the cot. The baby stirred for a moment, then went to sleep again, breathing heavily as if drugged. When Gwynna bent over her she smelled something and sniffed again. Dr Godfrey's Cordial! No mistaking that smell. She hated the stuff, which her mother had given her little sisters sometimes to keep them quiet. Was that what Mrs Forrett had been doing?

Jen had vanished and Gwynna wondered what to do, but

the day was getting on and she knew she couldn't leave the nursery in this state. Nurse Parker had always said cleanliness made for happy, healthy babies and Gwynna had grown used to it in Essie's house too. After a moment's hesitation, she shook her mistress's arm gently.

'What?' Mrs Forrett stirred, yawned and tried to snuggle down in the chair again.

'Please wake up, ma'am. I need to ask you a few things.'

'Are you back already?'

'It's over an hour since I left. I've put Libby down in the cot to finish her sleep but I think I should clear the nursery up a bit, don't you?'

Mrs Forrett heaved herself to her feet and Gwynna took an involuntary step backwards at the unpleasant odour coming from her mistress's body.

'The wet nurse will be here soon. She comes morning and evening. Mr Forrett won't let the baby go to her house, you see.'

'Is there a washerwoman for the baby's clouts?'

'What? Oh, yes. I suppose so. You'll have to ask Cook about that.' Mrs Forrett moved towards the door, yawning again. 'In fact, you can ask Cook and Jen about the other things too. I'm too tired to sort things out. I haven't slept properly since Maddy left. Mr Forrett gets so angry if he's disturbed during the night. You'll have to make sure you stop Libby waking him up. There's some Dr Godfrey's Cordial in the cupboard. That usually sends her off to sleep for a few hours. It's very good. I take it myself too.'

And to Gwynna's amazement her mistress went down the stairs without giving her any real instructions.

After a moment's hesitation, she checked that the baby was all right and then hurried down the back stairs to the kitchen. Cook was frowning and muttering to herself and seemed annoyed to be asked about anything.

'Jen will tell you,' she snapped. 'I've the master's meal to cook and he'll be angry if it's not ready for him. You'll soon learn not to upset him or you'll be out on your ear.'

So Gwynna got herself a ewer of hot water from the boiler at the side of the big stove, filling the boiler up again from the tap above it. Then she began to clean the nursery. As she was carrying up a second ewer of hot water later on, Mr Forrett came into the house and stopped on the landing at the sight of her.

'Sorry, sir. I'm just taking up some water to wash the baby.'

'About time somebody did that.' He vanished into the front bedroom.

She knew by now that the mistress's bedroom was at the back of the house, so the two of them obviously didn't share a bed. Shaking her head at this strange, disorganised household, Gwynna returned to the nursery. She was just finishing bathing Libby when someone came up the stairs and she turned to see a raggedly dressed woman, who was carrying another baby.

'I'm the wet nurse, love. I had to bring him, there was no one to look after him at home. Jen sent me up. I'll just feed Libby, shall I?'

The woman laid her own baby on the floor and set about her task. Gwynna hesitated then asked, 'Shall I wash your baby for you? There's plenty of warm water left from Libby's bath.'

'Don't you mind?'

'Of course not. It's a waste just to throw the water away.'

Tears filled the wet nurse's eyes. 'That'd be lovely. I can't wash him all over very often. I have to fetch the water from the pump and heat it up on the fire.' She sighed and leaned her head back tiredly.

Gwynna began to undress the baby. 'What time do you come in the mornings?'

'When I can, after I've seen my man off to the mill. I feed Mr Forrett's baby then if there's anything left, my Sim gets it. Poor little thing, he's allus hungry.'

'You could give him sops soaked in ordinary milk. He looks old enough to manage that.' Libby too was nearing the age to be weaned, surely?

'I hant got money to buy food for him. My man takes most of it for the booze. If I didn't get a meal here night and morning, I'd not be eating enough myself to make good milk. It's a godsend, this job is.'

Gwynna could understand that.

When the feeding was over, she handed back the newly washed baby and took Libby in her arms. 'Are you going down to the kitchen for your meal now?'

'Yes.'

'Right. I'll come down and see about you getting some sops for your baby.' She felt so guilty that the poor little boy went hungry so that his mother could feed Libby.

'That's kind. Right kind of you, it is.' She didn't seem to expect kindness.

When Gwynna got to bed that night, she was exhausted, but had made a good start on cleaning the nursery. She'd roll up the rug and scrub the whole floor thoroughly the next morning.

In the middle of the night she woke suddenly to hear Libby crying and someone thumping on her bedroom door.

'Can't you hear her, girl?' roared her master.

'Sorry. I was tired out after cleaning everything.' Gwynna pulled a shawl round her shoulders and stumbled into the nursery next to her room.

Mr Forrett lit a candle in there for her from his own, then held his up to stare round. 'You have been working hard!'

'I like to keep things clean. Babies thrive better if you do.'

He looked down at his daughter, his lip twisting down at

one corner as if he didn't like what he saw. 'That one's never thrived. She's either crying or sleeping.'

'I think she's hungry, sir. She needs more than a wet nurse now. Will it be all right if I go down and boil her some milk? I can put a few breadcrumbs in it, see how she takes to it.'

He looked at Gwynna for a minute as if considering what she'd said, then nodded. 'I'll light you down the stairs.'

She was a bit nervous, wondering if he was going to pester her, in spite of what he'd said about the maids in his own house, but he didn't. Indeed, ever since she'd refused his offer, he'd treated her with nothing but respect. 'Could you hold her while I get the kitchen fire burning up, sir?' she asked. 'I need to boil some milk. It's not safe to give it to them otherwise, I've been told.'

He sat down at the table and held his arms out, staring down at the baby in his arms. 'She's an ugly little thing, all puffy like that. My others were much prettier.'

'She will be too once I've worked out what she needs.'

He looked at her and grinned. 'Stop eyeing me as if I'm about to attack you! I don't attack respectable women.'

He watched as she made some sops and fed the baby. When Libby had fallen asleep in her arms, he stood up. 'Come on. I'm tired and want my bed. I'll light you upstairs then we can all get some sleep.'

'I was going to clear up first.'

'Leave it. What do I employ a cook and maid for?'

'They've enough to cope with, sir.'

He stopped and stared at her again. 'Are you telling me I don't employ enough staff?'

She didn't know what to say. Surely it was the mistress's job to deal with the servants?

'Well? Not afraid to talk to me, are you, girl?'

'It's not my place, sir.'

'I know, but that damned wife of mine is no use. You're a

bit young, but you seem to have your head screwed on right. I'll ask Cook about it in the morning.'

'I think she's frightened of you, sir. She may not tell you the truth.'

He roared with laughter. 'Oh, I'll make sure she does. Now, let's get to bed.'

It was a while before Gwynna could get to sleep. She didn't understand her new master at all. Why was he treating her so well? He hadn't laid a finger on her, either. Perhaps he was different at home to at the mill.

But how was she to manage with a mistress who didn't seem to know what she was doing in the house? It would make life difficult, she was sure.

Mr Trevin returned to Hedderby two days later, bringing with him the plans for the interior of the theatre and behaving as officiously as ever with Carrie. He again tried to deal only with Eli, who insisted he'd have to ask Carrie's opinion.

Mr Trevin gave her a thin smile. 'I'll go and examine the site while you two study the plans for the interior of the theatre *together*.'

'You'll not change a man like that,' she said when he'd gone, 'so you'd better deal with him yourself.' She noticed that Eli was looking longingly towards the door, becoming inattentive. 'The plans are as beautifully drawn as the exterior, don't you think?' she prompted, digging her elbow into his side. He made a big effort to concentrate. After discussing some small modifications which Carrie suggested, they waited for the architect to return.

By now Eli's brow was sweaty and he was looking stressed. He heaved a sigh of relief when Mr Trevin returned. 'We'd like to build the Phoenix to your design. My wife knows what we want and she'll go over the plans in detail with you now.'

'Don't you think it'd be better if *you* stayed with us, Mr Beckett?'

'I need to see someone.' He left with no more than a curt nod at Carrie.

She watched him go with a frown. He didn't seem able to concentrate on anything lately, kept walking out of the room in the middle of a conversation. Essie had commented on that only yesterday.

Realising that the architect was waiting for her, Carrie dragged her thoughts back to the music hall and indicated a chair beside her. 'Perhaps you'd like to sit down, Mr Trevin. I made some notes as Eli and I discussed it and . . .'

As they went through them she had the satisfaction of seeing a grudging respect for her skills dawn in his eyes, but he continued to talk to her in that patronising tone of voice that set her teeth on edge.

'I'll – um – go and find Mr Beckett now to discuss the financial arrangements.' He began to gather up the papers.

'My husband has already told you that I can deal with the financial side of things.'

'Very well, then! I shall require a sum of four hundred pounds in advance as earnest of your good intent.'

'*What?* Before you've even started? I can't see any reason for that.'

'That's precisely why I'd rather discuss such matters with your husband. However good you are at keeping the house-hold accounts, my dear lady, it is *he* with whom I'm doing business and *he* who is legally responsible for all your debts.'

She'd had enough of him so slapped one hand down on the papers, pleased to see him jump in shock. 'Go and see him then. He'll only come back and ask me about it.'

'I think you'll find that he and I will quite easily come to an agreement. The masculine mind comprehends business matters rather more easily than the female mind, even one as sharp as yours.'

She glared after him then turned back to the papers. If he hadn't drawn up such exquisite plans she'd have suggested finding another architect. But they were exquisite, so she'd just have to bite her tongue. They'd only be dealing with him for a few months, after all. She could cope with that.

It was some time before Eli came back. 'I paid Trevin the advance.'

'*What?*'

He looked at her. 'He told me you'd sent him to see me so that I could get the money out of the bank.'

'I did no such thing! Eli, you're not thinking straight. Why should we pay him so much money when he hasn't done a thing except bring us some sketches? It's foolish to do that. Why, he could just run away with the money.'

'But he assures me it's the usual thing to make a preliminary payment.'

'Not in any business that I've heard of.'

'Carrie, darling, you haven't had to deal with an architect before.'

She breathed in deeply. 'We'll ask Mr Burtell when he draws up the contract for us.'

'But Trevin and I have just shaken hands on it and agreed that he can start hiring workers to dig the foundations. Surely we don't need a contract? We have the sketches, after all.'

'I don't care how many times you've shaken hands with Trevin, I want a proper contract drawn up. Eli, I lie awake sometimes worrying about how much this is all going to cost. We have to be very careful what we do.'

He sighed. 'But Trevin is coming back tomorrow to start work. He tells me he's found lodgings in a village just down the line and has some men who can start work straight away, the ones who'd have been working on his cancelled job.'

'All the more reason for us to go and see Mr Burtell today,' she repeated.

Eli sighed. 'Very well.'

She watched him relax a little as they went outside, then grow tense again when they went into Mr Burtell's rooms.

The lawyer listened to their tale. 'Perhaps I should speak to Mr Trevin for you tomorrow? I do think Mrs Beckett is right. It's always wise to have a written contract before anything so major is undertaken. What's more, one doesn't usually pay architects in advance.' He frowned. 'Have you checked the theatres this man has built?'

Eli shook his head. 'No. He brought a lot of drawings of them to show us, though, beautiful drawings too, and clever designs. It's obvious that he knows how theatres should be built and has all the points I'd consider necessary, judging from what I've seen elsewhere.'

'Hmm. Still, it's usually sensible to find out more about someone's work before employing them. How did you hear about him?'

'He contacted me after the fire.'

Carrie watched Eli in concern. He seemed very un-comfortable, was fidgeting and running one fingertip round the inside of his collar as if it were too tight, and had stopped paying full attention to the lawyer.

He stood up suddenly. 'I'm sorry. I'm not feeling well. Arrange it with Carrie, will you?'

She watched in concern as he rushed out – there was no other way to describe it – then turned back to the lawyer. Seeing the sympathy in his eyes, she didn't try to hide her worries. 'He hasn't been himself since the fire.'

They discussed the contract then he promised to have it

drawn up by the following morning. 'Send your Mr Trevin to see me and I'll get him to sign it.'

'Thank you. He doesn't like dealing with a woman, I must admit.'

'Then he's a fool. One should judge people by how they act. A person only has to listen to you to realise you understand what you're talking about.' He hesitated, then added, 'And if I were you, I'd go and look at one of his other theatres before you pay out any more money.'

She walked home in a glow, pleased that a respected lawyer thought so highly of her, but underneath that glow was a layer of anxiety. How could she find out where one of Mr Trevin's other theatres was? How persuade Eli to go and look at it?

Her husband wasn't there at Linney's, but came in much later, saying he'd gone for a long walk and the fresh air had made him feel better.

But he didn't look better. And when they went to bed that night, he waited until she'd blown out the candle then said in a low voice, 'I can't seem to think straight since the fire. I don't know what's wrong with me, Carrie. And . . . I'm having nightmares about the fire still.'

'I know, love. I've heard you cry out, woken to find you've got up. I must admit it comes back to me sometimes too.' She shuddered and nestled against him.

'I'm tired now.' He turned away from her and was soon breathing deeply. Yet again he hadn't made love to her.

She'd wanted to discuss the new name of the music hall with him tonight, because she didn't want to change it to the Phoenix. People in the town still talked about the Pride, still sang the song 'Pride of Lancashire', which Raife had written especially for the opening night of the music saloon. Indeed, the tune had become so popular in Hedderby that children sang it as they played in the streets. It would be silly to change the name, in her opinion.

And they definitely ought to go and see one of Trevin's other theatres, should have done so before now.

Jeremiah couldn't for a moment remember where he was when he woke up in a strange bedroom, then he smiled as he realised he was in his new home. A maid tapped on the bedroom door and when he replied, asked if he wanted his hot water bringing up now.

He went down to breakfast looking forward to the day, pleased to find Maria waiting for him at the table. 'Are you feeling better now, Cousin?'

'Yes. I don't usually take to my bed for a mere cold, I assure you. I was just – exhausted.'

Her voice was a little hoarse still and her nose reddened, but she was as neatly dressed as ever, though again not in mourning clothes. He would ask her about that later. It didn't seem respectful, whatever his cousin Athol had been like.

'Could we discuss breakfast arrangements? When Athol ate with me, he wanted a range of dishes kept hot for him. He was a big eater, but that was very wasteful. I don't know your likes and dislikes so I took it upon myself to suggest to Cook that today I ask you what you want to eat and let her know. Then perhaps we can make a more permanent arrangement and you'll be served more quickly.'

'I share your dislike of waste. I'm quite happy to eat anything, eggs, bacon, ham, whatever you normally serve.'

'I eat very lightly, so it's a question of what *you* prefer.'

He wasn't used to choosing food, had been brought up to eat whatever was set before him. However, there was no harm in having what he wanted if he was the only one eating. 'I'm fond of porridge to start my breakfast in winter, with maybe a couple of boiled eggs afterwards or some ham. I'm not a large eater and not fussy either, so we can leave it to your cook, perhaps. Is that enough for her to go on?'

She smiled. 'Yes. I'll just go and tell her.'

'Shouldn't you ring for the maid to pass on the message?'

'They're very busy. One of our maids left after the fire, so we're a person short. I need to hire another but couldn't do it without your permission now.' She left the room and came back a minute later.

He had been sitting worrying about what she said. She must feel very upset to have no authority in what had been her home for years. 'You must hire the staff you need. I'd hoped to leave that side of things in your hands completely.'

'Thank you.'

'Do the boys not eat breakfast with you?' He watched her fiddle with the handle of her teacup as if uncertain what to say.

'My sons are – a little nervous of you so I thought it best to wait until everything has settled down again, till they know you better.'

'I'd rather they joined us from tomorrow onwards. Otherwise how will they get to know me?'

'Could you not wait and—'

'I'd prefer to have them with us.'

'Very well.'

She only picked at her food while Jeremiah enjoyed his, leaving his knife and fork precisely in the middle of his plate when he had finished, his table napkin carefully folded. He didn't force conversation, enjoying the tranquillity of a meal without his father's noisy presence.

He was more aware of her than he liked because he found her an attractive woman. This was completely un-expected. He hadn't really noticed another woman in that way since his wife's death. Maria's features were even, her eyes large and beautiful. As for her dark hair – he didn't know much about women's hair, but you couldn't help noticing that the centre parting, which seemed to be the fashion, made some women look very plain if not downright ugly. On her, it looked just right, emphasising the pure lines of her face. The side hair was looped over her ears and twisted up behind to form part of a bun at the nape of her neck. The bun was large, so she must have very long hair.

He hoped the angry red weal across her cheek would fade. It was a pity to mar such an elegant face. He also hoped she would soon realise that he meant her and her sons no harm and relax more with him. It was hard to make conversation with someone who seemed to regard anything he said with suspicion, who stopped eating to frown and took a long time to answer even the simplest question.

When the meal was over he said, 'On reflection, perhaps the boys can join us for the evening meal tonight? We could eat at whatever time suits their daily routine. I want to get to know them.'

She was still looking unhappy but nodded. 'I'll tell them.'

Jeremiah spent the day going through his cousin Athol's business papers and accounts. Mr Hordle had given him some papers and there were others in a crumpled mess in the desk. He took over the room at the rear of the house to do this task, since it had a roll-top desk in it. He had intended to go and see his cousin Edmund today, but after discovering what a mess the papers were in, he decided it'd be better to do that once he understood the financial situation.

An hour later he admitted to himself that this room was making him feel uneasy. That was foolish, but it felt as if someone was watching him.

After lunch, which he asked to be brought to him on a tray so as not to interrupt his work, he heard children's voices and looked out of the window. The boys were playing with the dog. He stepped back a little, not wanting them to feel they were being spied on, but enjoyed seeing them running round and shouting. They only seemed to do this when Renny was with them, so perhaps for the moment the man was fulfilling an important function in the household. Jeremiah noticed that he restrained them when they got over-excited and that all three treated the dog with kindness. He envied them. He'd have liked to be outside with them throwing the ball for the dog to fetch, teasing the boys, maybe picking up the younger one and tossing him in the air, as he used to do with his daughter. He blinked furiously at the thought of Cassie.

When the governess went outside to call the boys back to their lessons, they complained and behaved like normal boys, begging to take the dog with them, which she rightly refused to allow. A sudden memory of his tiny daughter playing with a kitten made Jeremiah's vision blur for a moment or two, but he regained control of himself and went back to the accounts.

From time to time he glanced out at the garden. Renny kept coming and going, doing a variety of tasks in the walled vegetable garden. It was bare at this season but couldn't have been cleared up properly the previous year, judging by the amount of rubbish carted out of it. The man was not only a hard worker but didn't need direction, which was another good point in his favour.

Chaos was not too strong a word to describe the accounts. A few scrawling entries here and there denoted withdrawals of money from the bank account, seemingly at random. Bits of paper proved to be a mixture of tradesmen's bills, receipts and reminder notes. Was this Cousin Maria's work? Was this why her husband hadn't left her any money?

And yet there were neat pages with lists of household expenses appended every month, all of which balanced to the penny. Who had done those? Surely not the housekeeper?

Nothing was at all clear. He would ask Maria about these papers the next day, but he'd seen her go out on foot a short

time ago, presumably to call on a friend. Yet again she wasn't
wearing mourning. What would people be saying about that?

The evening meal was set for six o'clock to accommodate
the boys. Jeremiah went up just before then to wash and tidy
himself, since he knew he had a tendency to run his fingers
through his hair when concentrating on paperwork.

As he opened his bedroom door to go back downstairs,
he saw Maria shepherding the two boys along the landing.
If ever children radiated extreme reluctance to go somewhere, these two did. He stepped back into his bedroom and
gave them time to get to the dining room before going down
to join them.

When he went in they were sitting stiffly on either side of
the table, with their mother at one end and an empty place
at the other.

'Good evening, Maria. Good evening, Isaac and Benjamin.'
He paused just inside the doorway.

They stared at him and both seemed to shrink away, as
if they expected him to hit them.

'It's usual to reply when someone greets you,' he said
mildly.

Isaac muttered something and looked down at his hands,
while Benjamin seemed about to cry.

'What's wrong?' Jeremiah asked Maria.

'They're – um – not used to you yet.'

'Are they like this with every stranger?'

Her eyes pleaded with him to stop the questioning so he
walked round to his place and sat down. Isaac flinched when
Jeremiah walked behind him, as if he expected to be hit,
which upset him.

There was a tureen of soup steaming in the centre of the
table. Taking off the lid, Jeremiah dipped the ladle in it. A
wonderful savoury aroma of mutton and onions rose from
it. 'This looks delicious. May I serve you, Cousin Maria?'

'Yes, please.' She passed her soup bowl to Isaac to give to him, but when Jeremiah reached out to take it from him, the boy jerked away, again acting as if he was about to be struck.

'What *is* the matter with you?' Jeremiah demanded.

With an inarticulate cry Isaac shoved his chair back and fled from the room.

Benjamin looked from the man at the head of the table to his mother, burst into tears and ran out after his brother.

'What on earth caused that?'

Tears were running down her cheeks. 'You didn't do anything. It's what you *are*.'

'I don't understand.'

'It's the resemblance between you and their father. That upsets them.'

'That's ridiculous. You must have spoiled those boys if they have no more self-control than that. They must be brought down and taught to sit at the table without all this foolishness.'

'Can't you – just leave it for tonight? Please?'

'No.' He stood up and walked out of the room.

Halfway up the stairs she caught up with him, taking hold of his arm to prevent him continuing. 'Jeremiah, stop! You don't understand.'

He lifted her hand gently off his arm. 'You're becoming as hysterical as they are.'

'There's a good reason for—'

But she was talking to empty air.

By the time she caught up with him again, he had reached the schoolroom and flung open the door. The boys were cowering – there was no other word for it – beneath the table. He reached down and tried to haul Isaac out, upon which the boy went hysterical, flailing out with arms and legs.

Maria tried to pull Jeremiah away. At the other side of the table, the governess was on her knees, comforting Benjamin.

'This is *ridiculous!*' Jeremiah shouted, angry now. 'What have you told them about me?'

His words made Maria angry too. He could see the change in her expression. She glared at him and turned back to Isaac, pulling him gently from underneath the table but keeping her body between him and his new guardian. 'I have to show Cousin Jeremiah what happened to you, darling. He doesn't understand.'

The boy was sobbing still, but didn't pull away when she slid off his jacket and unbuttoned his shirt, pulling up his vest to show Jeremiah his back.

What he saw made him feel physically sick. 'Dear God in heaven! How did that happen?'

'Athol did it.'

And suddenly it all fell into place, the weal on her cheek as well. He reached out to touch it without thinking. 'And you got this protecting your son?'

She nodded.

'We have to talk. I'll wait for you downstairs. Don't hurry. Help the boy first. I'm sorry, Isaac. I didn't understand.' He stopped in the doorway to add, 'I promise I won't hurt you. I'm not like your father.'

He went to let Cook know that the boys were upset and the meal would have to be delayed. 'They may want something taken up to the schoolroom later. I'm sure Mrs Stott or Miss Cavett will let you know.'

Her hostile expression made him feel even more guilty.

It was nearly an hour before Maria came down. She hesitated in the doorway of the front parlour, looking so wan he went across and guided her to a chair. 'Come and sit down. Let me pour you a glass of red wine. It can be very strengthening.'

'Thank you.'

He watched her sip the wine then set it down, and doubted

she'd even tasted it. 'Tell me everything. Please. How can I help them if I don't know what I must and must not do?'

She looked down at her hands and unclenched them with a visible effort. In a cool voice, as if she were reciting a lesson, she began to tell him about his cousin, the horrendous injuries Athol had sustained in an explosion, the increasing violence he'd shown towards everyone, including his own sons, and – there was no other word for it – his insanity.

Jeremiah listened with head bowed, sensing that she didn't want to look at him, but when she began sobbing and seemed unable to continue speaking, he could bear it no longer and went to her side, kneeling to put his arm round her shoulders. He had never seen anyone in such agony of spirit.

Except, a voice whispered inside his head, *yourself, when you lost Harriet and little Cassie.*

Maria wept for a long time and he didn't try to stop her, only held her. When she began to calm down she pulled away from him, trying to apologise for breaking down like that, and he let her go at once.

'I think you needed to tell someone,' he said quietly, standing up again. 'And who else is there but me? I am in some sort a cousin, with a responsibility for you and the boys, so it's right that you should turn to me.' What her life with that monster must have been like, he dreaded to contemplate. 'Are Isaac and Benjamin all right?'

'Renny's with them. He seems able to help them more than anyone else can. He tried very hard to help Athol, but my husband was too steeped in evil.' She hesitated, then asked, 'Could you not, perhaps, make me an allowance and leave me to bring my sons up?'

Jeremiah shook his head. 'No, definitely not. I shall, of course, make you a personal allowance, and a generous one, too. It's shameful that you've not been left anything in your own right. I promise you I shan't try to come between you and your sons, but I *am* their guardian and couldn't reconcile it with my conscience to abandon my duties here.'

He walked over to the fire and put on some more coal, waiting till the flames were starting to leap around the new pieces before turning to her again. She was sitting with her head against the chair back, her eyes closed, looking so weary he was startled by a sudden urge to carry her up to bed.

'You must have something to eat or you'll not recover your health,' he said abruptly. 'There was some soup. Shall I tell Cook to heat you a bowlful? You could eat that, surely? Just a light meal. I'm hungry too, now that I come to think of it.'

'I think I'll just go to bed, if you don't mind.'

He opened the door for her, watched her climb the stairs as if they were mountainous, then went to the kitchen.

'Mrs Ibster, your mistress hasn't eaten a thing. I wondered if you could take something up and persuade her to eat. She looks worn out, but how is she to recover if she doesn't have nourishing food? And if I could have something to eat now, please, Cook? Anything will do.'

But as he ate, sitting alone in the dining room, his thoughts were still with the woman upstairs. The boys weren't the only ones to have been sorely hurt by his cousin.

If Renny could help Isaac and Benjamin, the fellow could stay here for as long as he liked, because Jeremiah didn't know where to start. Perhaps it was because Renny radiated simple kindness and honesty that they felt safe with him. You couldn't be afraid of a man with such an open and kindly expression on his face.

Would the boys continue to fear their new guardian? Jeremiah went to look in the mirror, saw a severe face frowning back at him and tried to smile instead. The smile was a poor effort, a temporary lifting of the corners of his lips only, no warmth in his eyes as Renny had. It had been a long time since he'd even tried to smile. Perhaps he'd forgotten how?

His father would say he was being foolish, would tell him to punish the boys. But they'd been savagely hurt by the man who should have cared for them and they didn't need any more punishment. Jeremiah wasn't sure of much in his new life, but he was sure of that.

As for Maria, she needed help too. But would she let him provide it?

8

Gwynna found life at the mill house bewildering. That first morning, when she went down for something to eat, carrying the baby, Cook turned to her with a hostile expression on her face.

'You were down here in the night, weren't you?'

'Yes. Libby was hungry so I made her some sops.'

'You could have cleared the mess up, put the dishes in the scullery at least!'

'The master said I was to get back to bed as quickly as possible so that he could get his sleep.'

Cook rattled a frying pan about. 'You shouldn't have been wandering round the house at night, let alone talking to *him*.'

Gwynna was starting to get angry. 'If I hadn't come down, Libby would have gone on crying.'

'Maddy used to give her Godfrey's Cordial at night. That always put her to sleep.'

'It's got laudanum in it. You shouldn't give that to babies!'

'You're a right know-all, you are,' Cook said sarcastically. 'And how old are you? Nineteen, twenty? You should listen to your elders, you should. We'll all get woken up if you don't go on giving her that cordial. And in future, you just stay out of my kitchen.'

A voice from behind made them both jump. 'Where's my breakfast, Cook? I haven't all day, you know.'

The older woman gasped and turned pale. 'Sorry sir.'

'And Gwynna has my permission to use the kitchen any time she likes. How else is my daughter to get fed?'

'She's only to ask for what she needs, sir.'

'In the middle of the night? Don't be foolish.' He stared at the woman, eyes narrowed. 'You look tired out and you're not usually so grumpy. Do you need more help in the house?'

She gaped at him.

'Well, do you?'

'Yes, sir. If you don't mind, sir.'

'Of course I don't mind! My wife's too – er – busy to find you a maid, so do you want to find someone or shall I?'

'I know a girl who's looking for a job, sir. She's the niece of one of my old friends. I could see if she's still free.'

He nodded. 'Good. Do it. And now get me my breakfast, then feed the new girl.'

When he'd gone Cook stared after him as if she'd seen a ghost. Gwynna didn't say anything but went to stand out of the way, rocking the baby in her arms. The wet nurse arrived just then, so she handed Libby over and went down to get herself something to eat.

'What time does the mistress usually want to see Libby?' she asked as she cleared her plate away.

Cook let out a snort of laughter. 'Never. She only looked after the baby when Maddy left because the master told her to. She stays in her bedroom most of the day and rings for food. She doesn't usually get dressed until evening, ready to eat dinner with *him*.'

Gwynna waited but Cook didn't offer any more information, so she put her plate in the bucket of cold water in the scullery and went back up to the nursery. The kitchen was well run, but the work in the rest of the house seemed to have been skimped.

She spent most of the day either cleaning the nursery and everything in it or playing with Libby. The child looked a little brighter this morning but by midday she began to grizzle, so Gwynna took her down to the kitchen for some more sops. The baby ate everything she was offered.

'I think she's been crying because she was hungry,' Gwynna said. 'Maybe we can start her on other things from next week? She'd only need a spoonful of gravy to soak some bread in at first.'

Cook shrugged. 'There's always food for her in *my* kitchen. The master had no need to say that to me.'

'I can see you're a good cook.'

'How would *you* know that?'

'I worked in a big country house before this. The food there didn't taste as nice as yours.'

'Don't think you can worm your way round me with flattery, young woman.'

'I'm not trying to flatter you. I'm only telling the truth.'

'Hmm.'

Gwynna went upstairs again with a sense of relief. Every time she went down to the kitchen she was on edge in case she upset Cook.

After his talk with Mr Burtell, Lucas went home in a thoughtful mood. When he got there he went to keep his uncle company in the front bedroom until the evening meal was ready. Fred Kemp could now speak after a fashion and was beginning to get some movement back into the side of his body that had been affected by the seizure.

Lucas tried to find cheerful things to talk about, but could only think about the carpenter's business.

His uncle plucked at his arm. 'What's – matter?' he asked slowly and painfully.

Lucas looked at him and saw the same intelligence in the eyes, even if the body was not working properly. On an impulse, he explained about Mr Trumble's business and how he didn't have enough money to buy it.

His uncle was silent, then said, 'Sell this house. All move. All help you.'

Lucas looked at him in shock, so quick had been the decision. 'Are you sure?'

'Yes. Business can keep my family. Been worrying 'bout them. See Mr Burtell, sell house.'

'Should I talk to my aunt first?'

The invalid shook his head. 'I'll tell her. You see Burtell. Tonight.'

So Lucas found himself returning to the lawyer's rooms. He caught him just as he was leaving and asked if it would be possible to sell his uncle's house and buy the carpentry business and house. They went back inside and did the sums together.

'You'd still need a loan, Kemp, and you'd be hard pushed for a while to make payments.'

'I could take on an apprentice – they have to pay you a premium for that, and I'll need the help. But I'm a hard worker. I'm sure I can make a go of it.'

'I'll look into things, then.'

The following day Lucas asked Mr Trumble to sell the workshop to him. To his surprise, the old man scowled at him.

'You won't be able to afford it, a young fellow like you, and I'm not lowering my price.'

'You could lower it a bit. You're asking too much and we both know it. You've been trying to sell the place for a year, though you didn't tell me that when you hired me.'

More scowls then, 'How much can you pay?'

'Mr Burtell said to leave the bargaining to him.'

'Hmm.'

Mr Trumble went out an hour later without saying where

he was going, and came back looking angry and muttering about people trying to cheat a man out of his life's work.

Lucas bit back an angry response and got on with the job. Trumble had said it would do now, but he liked to get every detail right. It was how he had been taught to work by Mr Hungerton's head carpenter and for that he'd always be grateful – though never grateful enough to go back and work on the estate for the rest of his life.

The following afternoon a man came to see Mr Trumble. Later the old man came into the workshop looking smug. 'Shan't need to accept your offer, Kemp. Had a better one last night.'

'Oh? Who from?'

'None of your business.'

When Mr Trumble went out to see a client who owed him money Lucas hesitated, but his family depended on this so he went into the house that adjoined the workshop and had a quick look round. It didn't take him long to find the piece of paper on the mantelpiece.

He read it quickly and fury coursed through him. Mr Hungerton was the man behind the offer and it could only have been made to prevent Lucas from buying, because the landowner had no need whatsoever of a small business like this one and had his own team of estate carpenters. Lucas put the paper back carefully then went round to see Mr Burtell.

'Can we make Trumble a higher offer – on condition he sells to me at once?'

'How will you repay him?'

'Any way I can. I won't be driven back to work for Hungerton, whatever anyone says or does. I'll go down to work in London first. But if I don't get this business so that I can stay here, what is my uncle going to do? That's what worries me.'

The lawyer sat tapping the fingers of his right hand on the desk, then sighed. 'I'm too soft for my own good.'

'I beg your pardon?'

'I'll go into partnership with you.'

'You will?' Lucas couldn't seem to think straight.

'Yes. Send Trumble round to see me. I'll have a contract waiting for him by the time he arrives. He's desperate to sell quickly.'

'I won't be able to pay you back for a long time.'

'I know. But it galls me to see the way some rich men use their money to spoil poor men's lives. You caught me at a good moment. An investment I hadn't expected to prosper paid me back, so for once I have a little money to spare. Oh, and I have a buyer interested in a house like your uncle's, so it'll all work out very neatly.'

Lucas's voice came out thick with emotion. 'I never expected this.'

'No. But I'm sure you won't let me down. I've seen your work and it's excellent.' He grinned suddenly. 'Philanthropy sometimes pays good dividends.'

Back at the workshop Lucas found Mr Trumble waiting for him, angry that the place had been left unattended. 'Never mind that. If you go and see Mr Burtell now, you'll get a higher offer for your business.'

'How can *you* afford that?'

'None of your business. It's the money you're interested in, isn't it?'

'*He's* helping you, isn't he?'

Lucas didn't intend to go into any details. 'If you want the extra money you'll go and sort matters out now and stop asking me questions I don't intend to answer.'

He went back to his work but couldn't settle, not till he knew.

Mr Trumble came back an hour later looking smug. 'Looks like you've got yourself a business, Kemp.'

'Good. How soon can you get out of the house?'

'Next week. I've already bought a cottage near my daughter's. I'm not staying in Hedderby.'

For once Mr Trumble smiled as he worked, though he didn't work very hard.

Lucas went home torn between happiness and worry about the debt he was taking on. As long as nothing went wrong . . .

But it gladdened his heart to see the relief on his uncle's face when he told him the good news, and his aunt wept for joy in the kitchen.

Carrie decided to give Eli something else to think about apart from the rebuilding and discussed it with Essie, Nev and Raife. Together they hatched a plan, which she put to Eli that very afternoon.

'Why don't we hire the church hall and put on concerts there on Saturday nights? People would love it, I'm sure. Women keep stopping me in the street to tell me how much they miss their outings.'

Slowly his face brightened as the idea sank in and he clipped her up in a big hug. 'Good idea.' The hug went on for a long time, as if he needed to be close to her, then he let go of her, stood back and considered it, head on one side. 'We couldn't get the top performers to come here under those conditions, but we could hire some of the local ones, or get a few in from Manchester. And I'm sure Raife would play for us again.

'If someone has a week without an engagement, they'll come like a shot for a day's work. And that would bring a little business to Linney's. I feel guilty that Nev almost rebuilt his whole boarding house to suit our performers, then the fire took away most of his income.'

'He says he has money put aside that'll tide him over till we rebuild. You'd better go and see the Minister straight away. We can't do anything without the hall.'

Eli went off looking happier than she'd seen for a while.

She went to tell Nev and Essie how well their plotting had worked and to give her stepfather an especially big hug. He was a quiet man, shy almost, but he was good with ideas for making money.

The next day Jeremiah decided to go and see the engineering works, of which he was now nominally in charge. He hoped Edmund Stott, who was also a second cousin of his, would continue to manage things there because he knew nothing about making machinery! He sent Renny round with a note to Edmund, asking about the best time to visit, and received an immediate reply scrawled on a scrap of paper decorated with a big blot.

> *Come any time you like. I'm happy to show you round and discuss the business with you. There's a lot to do to bring it up to scratch.*
>
> *E. Stott*

Jeremiah decided to go at ten-thirty, which seemed a reasonable time, because surely the day's work would be well under way by then.

When he stood in the doorway of the engineering works, however, he realised at once that he'd walked into a crisis of some sort. One man was sprawled under a machine which had broken down and a couple of others were standing beside him, passing tools or discussing the problem. Jeremiah turned to the nearest workman. 'I'm looking for Mr Stott.'

'That's him under the machine. Bugger it is, that one. We need a new one, really.'

Jeremiah walked across and waited.

After a few minutes the man underneath poked his head

out again, blinked sweat out of his eyes and grinned. 'Cousin Jeremiah, I presume?'

'Yes. I seem to have chosen a bad time. Shall I come back later?'

'Give me half an hour. You could start going through the accounts and papers while you're waiting. You'll need to see how the business stands financially and I haven't had time to sort that side of things out since Athol died. Wiv, show Mr Channon into the office.' He vanished under the machine again.

An older man came forward and led Jeremiah across to the far corner of the room, where a space was roughly boarded off. 'I'm Renny's brother,' he said, in that frank way people in Hedderby had even when talking to strangers. 'I used to work for Mr Athol Stott, then Mr Edmund took me on here after the fire.' He looked round with a satisfied air. 'I'm his assistant now. Very interesting work it is, too.' With a nod he opened the door and left.

Jeremiah studied the office. Crowded into it were several pieces of furniture: a sloping desk with a half-finished sketch of some machinery on it, one corner curled up, a large desk and some tall cupboards, one door of which was partly open with rolls of paper sticking out. Feeling like an intruder, he sat down behind the desk and began to examine the papers on it, surprised at being invited to do this – though it spoke of honesty, at least, a trait he valued greatly after a lifetime with his father's hypocrisy.

He soon found that the paperwork had been grossly neglected and began automatically to sort things into relevant piles, not stopping till the door opened and Edmund came in, wiping his hands on a bit of sacking.

'Sorry about that. Some of the machinery is very old and held together by luck and persuasion! No, don't get up. I'll sit here. We need to talk.'

For over an hour he spoke about the business and Jeremiah heard in horror how Athol's penny-pinching ways had led to the dangerous explosion in which Athol had lost a leg the previous year.

'We don't work like that now and we never will again if I've any say in the matter,' Edmund wound up. He cocked one eyebrow at his visitor. 'The question is, do I have any say in the matter?'

'I'm hoping you will stay in charge here,' Jeremiah said at once, 'although I'd like to be involved in a minor way, because I must keep an eye on my wards' inheritance. I know nothing about this sort of work, however.'

'In that case, I'll state my terms for staying on.'

There was a shout from outside and he went to peer out of the door, turning with a grimace. 'Another breakdown. It seems a bad day for serious discussions. I could come round to see you after we close down today. We'd not get interrupted then.' He waved one hand at the desk. 'If you want to stay on for a bit and help me with the damned paperwork, you'll be more than welcome. I'm behind with everything, thanks to my cousin's death. I really need a clerk but I didn't like to hire anyone else until the future of the business was settled. What we need most of all here is some new machinery.'

Jeremiah spent the rest of the morning sorting out the papers on the desk, making entries in the account books and gathering together a list of people who owed the company money.

In the end hunger drove him home at two o'clock, but he felt happy with his long morning's work.

He rather thought he'd go back to his own profession eventually, but for the time being he'd concentrate on settling in with his new family and helping get the boys' inheritance in order. He wanted very much for them to consider themselves his family now.

After Jeremiah had finished his belated luncheon, Renny came to speak to him.

'The boys are frightened of you, sir, because you look like their father.'

'Yes, so I discovered yesterday.'

'I think I can help, if you'll let me.'

'Oh?'

'Migs has a brother who looks very like him. I want to take the boys to see the other dog.'

Jeremiah looked at him in puzzlement.

'So that they can see for themselves that two creatures can look alike but not *be* alike.'

'If you think it'll do any good, go ahead.'

'It may take time for them to feel *easy* with you, but we need to make a start. I'll have to interrupt their lessons.'

'It seems more important to help them feel comfortable with me at the moment.' He still felt sick when he thought of Isaac's back and added sadly, 'And to help them recover from the ill-treatment.'

'We can do that, sir.'

'I don't know how.'

'Little by little.'

An hour later, Jeremiah saw Renny and the boys walk past the window – well, Renny was walking and they were skipping about beside him, clearly delighted to be released from the schoolroom. He wished he could go with them.

Work finished somewhat later than usual that night, because Mr Trumble was fussing about completing all the jobs on the books so that he could get the money for them before he left. The only highlight of the day was a chance meeting with Gwynna with whom Lucas had been able to share his good news.

As he walked home along one of the narrow streets that led to his uncle's house, he gradually became aware of a prickling sensation in his neck, an uneasiness, as if someone was watching him or following him.

He stopped, pretending to tie up his shoelace but could see no one behind him. When he started walking again, the feeling persisted so he heeded it. Turning suddenly down an alley he ran towards the main street, hearing footsteps pounding along behind him.

He didn't even try to turn round to see who it was, but ran as fast as he could. When he turned into Market Street, he found himself in the middle of a group of working men, decent fellows by the looks of them.

'Someone's chasing me,' he gasped. 'Can I walk with you a short way?'

They looked at him in surprise then one of them nodded. 'Walk between me and Tommo. I'm Declan Heegan, by the way.'

'Lucas Kemp.'

'Don't turn round, Lucas, but two men have just come out of the alley.'

'Do you know them?'

'No. And I know most fellows in town by sight at least. These two are outsiders, I reckon.' He grinned at Lucas. 'Will we get ourselves some ale now, then we can maybe get a better look at them where it's light?'

There was a chorus of approving grunts as they set off walking. One of the men behind them said, 'They're standing there watching us, Declan lad. Who the hell are they? I've a mind to thump 'em if they don't tend to their own business an' leave me to tend to mine.'

'Don't thump them yet, me boy.'

Lucas felt some sort of explanation was necessary. 'They've probably been sent by Mr Hungerton, who lives south of here. I left his employment when he wanted me to stay there permanently. I'm a carpenter.'

'Would a man of means keep after you?' Declan wondered.

'Oh, yes. He feels he owns his workers body and soul, you see, and I'm good at my trade, if I do say so myself.'

'I do enjoy stopping rich men from bullying poorer ones,' Declan said with relish.

They came to a pub and Lucas hesitated because he had no money to waste on boozing, no taste for it, either.

'Go on in.' Declan gave him a push. 'We'll only be a few minutes. A carpenter can afford one pot of ale, surely?'

The men found a couple of tables and sat down, leaving Lucas and Declan the sole use of one table.

'Are you all Irish?' Lucas asked.

'We are. Who else would drink with low fellows like us but other low fellows?' Declan chuckled. 'But we know how to look after our own and those we call friends.'

The Irish weren't liked by some people, Lucas knew, and trouble did seem to follow them more often than other folk, but these men had protected him tonight and as far as he was concerned, you spoke as you found. 'I'm grateful for your help tonight and I'd be happy to call you friends.'

Declan nodded then began to look thoughtful. 'We can help you tonight, but what if they're waiting for you tomorrow? They have that look to them. Bullies hired to do someone's dirty work. So what are we going to do about it?'

Lucas sighed. 'I don't like fighting, though I can give a good account of myself if I have to. But with Hungerton that could lead to worse and they could charge me with assault. He's got friends of his own class everywhere, like the magistrate in our village back home. If I was jailed for a month or two, who else would employ me? I'd be truly in his power then.'

'Then we'll have to bring the town's new policemen in on it before he does that,' Declan decided. 'They're honest men here in Hedderby – for policemen.'

'How do we do that?'

'I'll send a message to the sergeant. He'll listen.'

Lucas watched as the Irishman beckoned. One of his men was at his side in an instant, attentive, ready to do what he was told. Clearly Declan was the leader of this group. 'Can I buy you a drink?' he asked when the man had hurried away.

'Why not? Will you be joining me?'

'Just the one. Is the beer good here?'

'I wouldn't drink here otherwise.'

Lucas found himself explaining how he'd come to settle in Hedderby.

'So old Trumble's sold out at last? Good riddance to him. He's not a very skilled craftsman. Are you?'

'Yes, I am. I do carving as well as carpentry, when I have time that is, and—'

'Here he is.' Declan stood up. 'Thank you for coming, Sergeant.'

'This isn't the first time you've asked me for help. The others weren't wild-goose chases, so I did as you asked and there are two men waiting outside. Who is it I'm going to catch now?'

Declan introduced Lucas, then explained the situation.

The sergeant studied Lucas, then nodded as if satisfied with what he saw. 'If you'll go out first, Mr Kemp, we'll follow and keep an eye on you.'

Lucas drained his pot, said his farewells loudly and walked outside. One man sitting near the door looked familiar, though he couldn't quite place him. He turned up the hill and where the streets grew narrower, sure enough he heard footsteps echoing his own once more. They speeded up and when he swung round, he found himself facing the same two men. 'Why are you following me?'

'To bring a message that you're wanted back on the estate.'

'I've a job here now.'

'If you don't go back willingly, you'll go unwillingly because you'll be arrested for attacking my friend here.'

'I've attacked no one.'

'Not yet. But I've a fine story for the police after we've finished with you, and Mr Hungerton himself to give me a character reference. Are you sure you won't change your mind?'

Anger filled Lucas. 'You can tell Hungerton I'll never go back to work for him, no matter what he does.'

Before he'd even finished speaking they both ran at him, trying to shove him down on the ground, kicking as well as punching.

A whistle blew nearby and three men came out of the darkness, two wearing the uniform of Hedderby's new police force. They hauled the attackers off Lucas and kept hold of them.

'You're under arrest,' the sergeant told them.

'What for?'

'Brawling.'

'It was him as started it.' One of them pointed to Lucas. 'He attacked my friend and I only—'

'We were listening to what you said, watching too. He did nothing. *You* attacked him for no reason.'

Suddenly the two men shoved away the policemen and tried to make a run for it, but Declan and his friends moved out of the shadows, barring their way, smiling.

One man shrank visibly at the sight of Declan and whispered something to his companion, after which they let the policemen take them away. Some of the Irishmen followed, but Declan and the sergeant stayed behind.

'There you are, Sergeant. Did I not tell you there were troublemakers in town?'

'You did. Make sure you keep on telling me about such things and don't go back to dealing with them yourself.'

'I've moved past that, Sergeant, as you well know. A man with a famous brother has to make something of himself, does he not? Pity I've not got a voice like his. Singing's a much easier way of making a living than working with your hands.'

The sergeant walked away and Declan clapped Lucas on the shoulder. 'You'll be safe from those two, at least.'

'Yes. I'm grateful to you.'

'I'll maybe come by and see what you're making in that workshop of yours.'

'You'll be welcome any time.'

'You're not married?'

'No. I've my uncle and his family to support. He had a seizure.'

Declan snapped his fingers. 'Fred Kemp. You're his nephew. He's a decent fellow.'

'Yes.' Lucas watched his new friend wave, then melt away into the darkness. He didn't linger, walking home briskly.

He didn't mention the attack to his family because his aunt had enough to worry about. He explained the bruises on his knuckles by saying he'd had a pile of wood fall on him, but could see that his uncle knew better. As he ate his tea he wondered about the Irishman. Declan had spoken easily, smiled a lot, but behind that smile was power. He was a big fellow, looked as if he could handle himself. You wouldn't want to get on the wrong side of him. And now that Lucas came to think of it, one of the attackers had recognised Declan and gone with the police rather than confront him. So he must have a name in the town.

The sergeant was an imposing figure of a man, too, but even he had treated the Irishman with respect, no not exactly respect but wariness.

Was there no length to which Mr Hungerton would not go to get his own way? Surely the man could find someone else to restore the fancy carved railings on his gallery? Or was this just spite?

And what about Lucas's parents and brother? Would they also suffer because he'd upset Hungerton?

As if he didn't have enough to worry about with his new business and his debts!

What he needed now was to find himself an apprentice and get on with earning some money.

9

'We're going to see Migs' brother,' Renny said quietly as he and the two boys walked towards the outskirts of the town.

'Are we getting another dog?' Benjamin asked at once.

'No. I want to show you something.'

When they came to the house, he knocked on the door and his friend's wife opened it.

'Jimkin's in the back garden. Be careful with him, Renny. He's nervous of strangers.'

He took the boys out to the back doorstep. 'Don't move from there.'

As he stepped forward a dog that was almost identical to their own appeared and began growling at him. He talked to it gently and it stopped baring its teeth, but it wouldn't come to him.

He turned to the boys. 'Well? What do you think of Jimkin? He looks like Migs, doesn't he?'

'He's not as friendly, though, not at all like our Migsy-Pigsy.'

'No, he isn't. So two creatures can look alike and not be alike. Don't forget that when you're dealing with your cousin Jeremiah.' He didn't wait for an answer. 'Now, let's go for a walk on the tops. I feel like stretching my legs.'

The boys ran and played for a while till both had rosy cheeks and were breathless, then he called them back. 'We need to go home again now.' As they walked down towards the town, he asked quietly, 'Why won't you eat meals with your cousin?'

Isaac stopped and scowled at him. 'Because I don't like him.'

Benjamin, as usual, echoed his brother. 'I don't either.'

'Why not?'

'He looks like my father.'

'That's not fair to him. You haven't even given him a chance to show you what he's like. Migs likes him, and dogs can always tell about a person. Migs didn't like your father, though.'

The boys started walking again, but didn't speak. Isaac had a little furrow on his forehead which meant he was thinking, so Renny didn't say any more. He delivered them back to their governess, hoping his little lesson would gradually sink in. He didn't think he'd misjudged Jeremiah Channon, because he didn't usually misjudge people. Those boys needed a kind man to wipe away their bad memories.

He went back to work in the garden, which needed a lot of attention. He wanted a beautiful display of flowers this year, to gladden the hearts and cheer up everyone in what had previously been one of the unhappiest households he'd ever known.

When the rain drove him indoors, he went to see how he could help Mrs Ibster because he liked to keep busy. But as he moved about the house, his thoughts were on the back room, where evil still seemed to linger, and on Mr Channon, who kept himself so tightly closed to others that Renny worried about him. It wasn't good to keep your feelings shut up inside yourself that way. Perhaps he'd be able to help the man, once he got to know him better. He didn't like to see an unhappy soul.

A smile crossed Renny's face. Or perhaps Mrs Stott would be able to help Mr Channon . . .

It soon became plain that her new charge needed fresh air and since the house stood on one side of the mill yard, with no garden, this presented a problem. In the end, Gwynna nerved herself to make a suggestion to the master, waiting in the hall to catch him when he came in from the mill.

'Please, sir.'

He scowled at her. 'I'm sharp set and wanting my food. Tell me what you want quickly, lass.'

'I was wondering if we could get a stick wagon made for Libby so that I could take her out for fresh air on fine days. It's not good for a child to be kept indoors all the time and she's a bit heavy to carry very far.'

'What the hell's a stick wagon?'

'It's a little carriage for children who can't walk yet. I know rich people don't usually use them, but I thought it'd be just the thing for me to take Libby out in.'

'Tell me what they're like.'

Gwynna tried to explain that it was like a cage on wheels, without a top, and children sat or stood in it while you pulled it along. 'Any carpenter would know how to make one, sir. Folk knock them together from all sorts of bits and pieces of wood.'

'Well, my mill carpenter's busy at the moment, so I'll need to find someone else to make it. You'll have to wait until I'm less busy.' He turned away.

'Sir?'

He turned back impatiently. 'What now?'

'I know a carpenter who could do it.'

'Oh, you do, do you? Your young man, is he?'

'No, sir, just someone I know. He's started a business here in Hedderby, bought Mr Trumble out.'

'I hope he's better than Trumble.'

'Lucas Kemp is a really good carpenter, sir.'

'Send him round to see me tomorrow, then. He's to come at ten sharp, mind. I'll speak to him while I'm having my cup of tea, then make up my mind.'

'Yes, sir. I'll go round and see him later.' But in one way she wished she didn't have to see Lucas. Being with him made her heart beat faster, a bit like it had with Patrick, only with Lucas the feeling was much stronger. He was a large man but he didn't seem threatening as some big men did, because there was a gentleness to him and his kindness showed in his face and eyes. She valued that in anyone. She liked how he looked, too, his fresh, open face with the brown hair that always looked as if the sun had gilded it, and she liked the way he talked to her, listening as if he was really interested in what she said.

Oh dear! What was she doing thinking about him like this? She liked him far too much for her own good. He had a family to support and she couldn't afford anyone to say she was seeing another fellow because she wanted desperately to make a success of this job, to make Nev and Essie proud of her. It hadn't been her fault Mr Hungerton had dismissed her, but it still didn't look good to have been thrown out of a job.

Lucas was surprised when Gwynna came into his workshop carrying a baby. She was out of breath.

'Have you been running, lass?'

'No, Libby's just at that age where she's a bit heavy to carry round.' She stared at him. 'What have you done to your head?'

He knew she'd understand because she too had worked for old Hungerton, so he explained what had happened.

'You don't think he'll send someone after me as well, do you?'

There was a little anxious catch to her voice which touched him. 'Shouldn't think so. He'll have forgotten about you by now. He wants me to do some fancy work for him.'

She didn't seem convinced, but there was nothing gained

by speculation, so he changed the subject and smiled at the child, who looked puffy and pale, unlike her rosy-cheeked nursemaid. 'What can I do for you?'

'My master wants a stick wagon making for Libby, so that I can take her out and about more.'

'I can do that.'

'He wants to see you about it tomorrow at ten sharp at the mill office.'

When she'd gone Lucas got out a piece of paper and one of his precious pencils. They weren't cheap but there was nothing like them for drawing sketches, as he'd found when working for Mr Hungerton. He'd bought two pencils only a few days ago because it always helped when customers could see a rough picture of what he was talking about. He drew a little stick wagon then sat thinking about it. He could make one easily enough, knock it up out of offcuts, but he didn't think Mr Forrett would want his daughter sitting in straw, which was usually placed in the bottom. Maybe the design could be improved, though it'd cost more to do something fancier. Still, the mill owner wasn't short of a bob or two.

The following morning Lucas took his sketches with him and showed Forrett what a stick wagon usually looked like, then produced his own design, a smaller wagon designed for one occupant only. It had a bench seat in it and a strap to hold a small child safe, but still had the wooden slats round the edges. The big difference was that it was a device made to push, not pull. He'd been inspired by a wheelbarrow, but of course he didn't mention that.

Forrett studied the design and looked at Lucas with dawning respect. 'Clever. You wouldn't rather work for me in the mill, would you? The fellow who does my carpentry now does what I or my overlooker tell him, but he's never come up with a new idea on his own.'

'No, thank you. I appreciate the offer, but I couldn't stand the noise and being shut up all day. If you ever want anything doing round the house, though, or small pieces making for the mill, I'm your man.'

'Hmm. Well, do me this fancy stick wagon, then, and put a bit of carving on it like you've drawn. That new nurse-maid told me about you. She's another who has her head screwed on right.' He stared at Lucas. 'Don't come courting her, though. I need her to look after my daughter.'

'I'm not likely to go courting anyone. I've my uncle and his family to support and a new business to get going.'

As he was walking home, Lucas realised with a jolt of surprise that he'd like to get to know Gwynna better. He always felt comfortable with her.

Ironic, wasn't it? He'd stopped working for Hungerton because he didn't want to marry. And now that he was inter-ested in a young woman, he didn't dare do anything about it because he couldn't afford to take on extra responsibilities.

Maria had spent the whole day trying to persuade herself to clear out Athol's room, and she even got as far as the door once. But when she opened it, she felt a darkness surround her and took only two steps inside before turning round and fleeing.

It felt as if Athol was still there!

On the landing she bumped into Jeremiah and stopped with a gasp, pressing one hand to her racing heart. 'Sorry.'

'Did something upset you?'

She looked back over her shoulder and shivered. 'I need to clear out my husband's bedroom, but I can't bring myself to do so. I can't even bear to go inside. It's as if he's still there.'

'I could do it for you.'

'I *ought* to be the one to do it.'

'Let me.'

She hesitated, feeling guilty, then nodded. 'Thank you. I'm sure Renny would be happy to help you.'

Jeremiah went to look inside the room and even to him it felt full of anger and evil. He wasn't usually a fanciful man but he could understand why Maria couldn't bring herself to come here. He went to find Renny, who was sitting in the kitchen, his hair still wet from a sudden shower.

'Are you busy?'

Renny shook his head.

'My cousin would like her husband's room cleared. Would you help me?'

'Yes.' Renny stood up and the two men went upstairs again.

The feeling inside the room was just as bad and Jeremiah looked round, half expecting to find someone there with them.

'The evil still lingers.' Renny studied the room with a frown.

Jeremiah didn't reply, couldn't, because he was finding it difficult to breathe in here. 'I think we need to open the windows,' he said. 'It seems very – stuffy.'

Renny nodded and flung both windows wide, though the wind immediately began sending showers of droplets inside. 'He's not resting easy,' he said.

'I don't believe in ghosts,' Jeremiah replied automatically.

'They'll come whether you believe in them or not.' Renny turned to survey the room. 'I think his things should be burned. They'll do no one any good.'

'Did he have any jewellery?'

'There was a ring and a gold pocket watch. They must have burned with him at the Pride because he always wore them. He had other pieces from his father, but he didn't wear them, so perhaps they won't be tainted.'

Jeremiah opened his mouth to contradict the idea that such objects could be tainted by their wearer then shut it again. In this bleak and unhappy space, anything seemed possible.

Renny walked across to one cupboard and pulled out an artificial leg. 'This was his spare one. It should go first. I've been burning some garden stuff. If the bonfire hasn't gone out, I'll throw some lamp oil on it and burn this straight away.'

And Jeremiah couldn't for the life of him do anything but nod, because the leg made him shudder and he definitely didn't want to touch it.

When Renny had taken the thing away, Jeremiah forced himself to open the wardrobe and start pulling out the clothes. Once he thought he heard mocking laughter and swung round, but he was alone. So as he worked he began to murmur the Lord's Prayer under his breath. He felt ashamed of his weakness, but couldn't bring himself to stop praying.

It seemed a long time until Renny returned.

'It's burnt.' He looked across the room and added, 'And your bravery does you credit. If we hurry with these, we can burn the other things before dusk falls. It's stopped raining now. We can leave the rest of the room until tomorrow and then decide what to do about the furniture.'

Jeremiah nodded.

'There is goodness in the world as well as evil,' Renny said quietly as they worked. 'Some people call it God, others use different names. This goodness can counteract evil if we let it.'

Jeremiah looked at the man who was, after all, only a servant, but who was definitely in charge at the moment. He didn't say anything, just nodded and picked up a big pile of clothing. Renny did the same.

When they went out they passed Maria, who drew back when she saw what they were carrying.

'We're burning everything, ma'am,' Renny said gently. 'Best way.'

'Yes.' She backed away, looking as if she was near fainting.

He wasn't the only one to feel the strangeness, Jeremiah thought. It was as if evil had taken on a life of its own here.

He didn't like this house, didn't like it at all. Perhaps they should all move somewhere and make a new start. That might be best for those lads.

10

The following afternoon Renny let the boys play out until they were pleasantly tired, then took them to the kitchen to find food for Migs. 'Isn't it about time you started eating your evening meals with your mother again?'

'I don't like to sit with him. He looks so like my father, Renny.'

'So will you when you grow older.'

Isaac looked at him in horror.

Renny laid one hand on each boy's shoulder. 'Remember Migs' brother? How different he was, though he looked like him? It's what's inside a person that matters, not what they look like.'

They avoided his eyes and said nothing.

'I'm sorry you won't give your cousin a chance to show you what he's like. You're not usually so unfair.' He didn't press the point. He'd wait a day or two to let his message sink in, then try again. After the boys had gone back to their lessons he explained to Mrs Stott what he was doing and asked her not to force the boys to eat downstairs till they were ready.

'What do I say to Cousin Jeremiah?'

'The truth. He's a reasonable man.'

So Maria found herself dining alone with Jeremiah. She found it hard to get him talking about anything personal, but he seemed happy to talk about his work, explaining the way he'd designed houses to incorporate modern devices like gas lighting and a bathroom. 'This house is very old-fashioned. The kitchen needs complete redesigning because it's very inefficient.'

'Cook doesn't seem to mind.'

'There are other problems too. Have you ever thought of moving?'

She stared at him in surprise. 'Moving?'

'Yes. Making a new start.'

'If only we could! But I don't think there's enough money. Edmund says the works needs new machinery and there won't be much to spare for quite a while.'

Jeremiah didn't press the point. He had the information he needed. If she had felt that this place was her home, been happy here, he would have found some way to make the house more comfortable. But she didn't even like it.

Nor did he. It was another thing he would have to deal with.

Gwynna took Libby out for a walk in her new wagon, smiling to see how much the child was enjoying the outing. Libby kept gurgling, pointing and waving her chubby little hands at all the sights. Gwynna stopped the wagon and stared at the excited child. Perhaps she hadn't been out much with her other nursemaid. She had certainly been pale enough when Gwynna first started working there.

As they walked past Barley Lane she stopped to admire the new sign: *Lucas Kemp, Carpenter and Joiner.*

Suddenly a woman lurched round the corner and Gwynna's heart began to flutter with anxiety. She turned the wagon round, trying to get away without being recognised but it was too late. The woman had seen her and screeched loudly in surprise as she ran across the road.

'Gwynna? Our Gwynna?'

'Hello, Mam. How are you all?'

'How d'you think we are when the daughter who should be helping us in our old age ups and leaves? What are you doing back in Hedderby?' She looked down at the little wagon, fingering the shiny top rail.

'I've got a new job here. I'm sorry but I can't stop to chat, I have to get on.'

Swaying and reeking of gin, her mother blocked her way, one hand firmly gripping the top of the wagon now. 'Think you're better than us now, don't you? Can't even stop to talk to your own mother.'

'I'm working, Mam. I have to take Libby out for a walk.'

'I don't call looking after a spoilt little brat working.' Mrs Jones leaned into the little wagon to poke the child with one dirty fingertip, then poke again, hard enough to make Libby's face pucker up with dismay.

Gwynna tried to push her mother away. 'Don't! She's clean and your hands are dirty.'

But Mrs Jones was in an argumentative mood and shoved back so hard that her daughter staggered backwards, letting go of the wagon handle, which her mother immediately grabbed. When Gwynna tried to take it back, her mother laughed, rocking it about roughly so that the child started crying in fright.

'I allus were stronger than you. Puny you are, born weak an' allus will be weak.'

A shadow fell across them and a deep voice asked, 'Is this woman annoying you, Gwynna?'

She looked up at Lucas and couldn't stop tears of humiliation from filling her eyes. 'Yes, she is.'

He turned back to the drunken woman. 'Go away and leave her alone.'

'I'm her mother an' I'll talk to her whenever I want.'

He looked at Gwynna in such surprise she could feel herself going red with humiliation.

'She *is* my mother, but I don't have anything to do with her if I can help it. You can see what she's like, drunk as usual.'

'Who are you calling drunk? I've only had a sip or two for my rheumatiz.'

Libby was howling lustily now and Gwynna bent over the wagon, speaking in a soothing voice to the baby.

Lucas pulled Mrs Jones back as she tried to paw her daughter. 'I said: leave her alone.'

The woman spat at his feet and reeled away. 'I'll find her again. See if I don't. Thinks she's too proud to talk to me these days. Well, I'm not too proud to talk to her. I'm going to find out where she works and call in to visit her. See what those fine employers think of their new nursemaid then!' She staggered away, laughing.

Gwynna couldn't hold back her tears. 'She'll do it too. She enjoys causing trouble. I suppose she's hoping to get money out of me.'

He looked at her in sympathy. 'If I see her pestering you, I'll stop her.'

'Thanks.' But she knew he wouldn't be there most of the time. Her mother would lie in wait for her now she knew Gwynna was back in Hedderby. Or, worse still, turn up at Mill House, too drunk to care who she offended.

'I've been dreading meeting her,' she confessed, fumbling for her handkerchief and mopping her eyes. 'I'd better tell Mr Forrett about this before someone else does.' She tried to smile at him. 'It's a lovely little wagon you've made, really easy to push. A lady stopped me in the street to ask me where I got it. I told her from Kemp's, the new carpenter's in Barley Lane, so you may have a new customer.'

The baby continued to roar lustily. 'I'd – um – better get on now. She's getting hungry. All right, Libby love. We're going home.'

She walked off and Lucas stood watching her, admiring her slender figure and neat appearance. It'd be a real shame if her mother spoiled this job for her.

He went back into his new home, where they'd all settled down quickly. There were advantages to having his aunt there to run the house for him because she was a very capable housewife. He'd put up a few new shelves for her in the kitchen and fixed the tap on the cistern of the stove. Other improvements would have to wait.

His main need now was to drum up as much custom as possible.

As Lucas was locking up for the night, he heard a faint scuffling noise that could have been a small animal. It came from the wood store behind the workshop, a place in sore need of a good clear out. Perhaps there was a nest of rats in there? No, he'd have seen the droppings. He pretended to lock the door that led from the workshop into the house, then crept across to listen at the wood store door, shielding the candle beneath his coat and hoping the faint light that escaped wouldn't betray him.

And as he stood there he heard the sound again, followed by what was unmistakably a sigh. It was a person, then, not an animal. But what was anyone doing in the wood store?

Surely even Hungerton wouldn't burn his home and business down? The tales he'd heard of the big fire that had destroyed the music saloon had made him more than usually wary of the risks of fires, so once he'd got rid of the intruder, he'd make sure no one else could get into his premises.

If he hadn't had good hearing, he'd not have caught the sound of the shavings on the floor rustling and crackling faintly as someone crept towards him. The door opened and a figure crept out, a very small figure. He reached out and caught the lad by the back of his jacket with one hand while raising the candle with the other to see better. The garment the child was wearing was so thin it tore in his hands and he dropped the candle to grab the nearest arm, holding on tightly as he stamped out the glow that had started in the sawdust.

It was all too easy for a man of his size to keep hold of the intruder, who couldn't have been more than seven or eight years old and who was pitifully thin. But when the boy bit him, he cuffed the lad on the side of the head and slung him over his shoulder. After checking to make sure there were no glowing embers left, he picked up the candlestick holder and the candle and strode across the workshop to the house.

The child had stopped struggling and suffered him to do what he would, so he went into the kitchen, slid the small body down and stood the boy on the rug.

'Look what I found in the wood store.'

His aunt Hilda stopped stirring her pan and turned round. 'Eh, he's young to be a thief!'

'I ain't a thief!'

'What were you doing in my wood store, then?' Lucas kept his eyes on his captive in case he tried to escape, but the child was shivering and holding his hands out to the fire. 'Well?'

'I been sleeping there all winter. *He* don't notice an' I haven't done no harm.'

'He's very dirty,' Belinda said, keeping her distance and wrinkling her nose at the smell of the lad.

'He's very thin, poor thing,' Aunt Hilda said.

'I used to eat the food they threw out at the back of the music saloon, lovely stuff some of it was,' the boy informed them, 'an' I slep' there too sometimes. But when it burned down it got harder to find food.'

The lad had what Lucas thought of as a famine face on

top of that stick-like body. You couldn't mistake the look, which was the result of a long period of not eating enough. 'Where are your family?'

'Only had me mother an' she died last summer. I ain't going into the workhouse, though! They put you to work in the mill and it's bad in there, worse than being on the streets.'

'You've been looking after yourself all that time?'

He nodded. 'I run errands and do little jobs for people. I'm managing all right.'

Lucas looked across at his aunt. 'It seems to me the first thing to do is feed him. Then we'll decide what to do with him.' But he already knew. He was soft about young waifs like this one, had been all his life, but even more so since they'd found a little lad frozen to death the previous winter in one of Mr Hungerton's sheds.

The boy stared at him unwinkingly. 'What do I have to do for it?'

'You don't have to do anything. I'm feeding you because you're hungry and we have some food to spare. Belinda, fetch a stool over. He can sit next to me.'

When a plate was set before him, the child began stuffing the food into his mouth and gulping it down, as if afraid someone might take it away again.

Lucas reached out to still the nearest claw of a hand. 'Slow down. It's not going to run away and no one's going to take it from you. If you gobble it like that, it might make you sick, which would be a waste.' He could see his nieces staring in horrified fascination. His aunt shook her head fondly at him then turned to help her husband to eat.

But his uncle Fred smiled at him across the table with that gentle, newly lopsided smile. Lucas knew that he understood and approved of this act of charity.

When they'd all finished eating the urchin sighed in pleasure. 'I've not et like that for a long time. Thanks, mister.'

'You're welcome.' Lucas looked at his uncle again, then said it. 'I'm in need of a lad to help in the workshop. Do you want a job? I can't pay you anything but I'll make sure you have warm clothes, somewhere to sleep and you'll eat well.'

His aunt gasped, Belinda made a scornful noise.

The boy sat utterly still. 'Me?'

'Why not?'

The eyes that had stared at him with an old man's world-weary gaze suddenly turned into a child's eyes and filled up with tears. All the boy could manage was a nod and a gulp.

Uncle Fred had over-bright eyes too.

'What's your name?' Lucas asked.

'Joe.'

'Do you have another name?'

He shook his head.

'Welcome to Kemp's, Joe. You can sleep down here on the rug by the fire for the time being.'

The lad beamed at him as if he'd been offered a fortune.

His aunt said, 'He'll have to have a wash before he does anything else.'

Joe's smile faded a little.

'We all keep clean here,' she said firmly, 'so if you want to stay, you must too.'

Lucas still needed to find himself an apprentice because Joe was neither old enough nor strong enough to do what was necessary. But before he could start looking, a lad turned up.

'Are you Mr Kemp?'

'I am.'

'Do you need an apprentice?'

'I do. How did you know?'

The lad grinned. 'I was just hoping. I want to be a proper

carpenter, you see, so when Gwynna said you'd taken over from Mr Trumble, I thought I'd give it a try.'

'What do your parents think of that?'

'They're both dead, but my stepfather thinks it's a good idea.'

'Can he afford the money for the premium?' One act of charity Lucas could afford but he needed the money an apprentice would pay to learn his trade.

'He said he'd find it if I found someone to take me on. Our Gwynna showed me the stick wagon you made for Mr Forrett and I liked it. I've not seen one like that before.'

'Tell me about yourself, starting with your name.'

'I'm Ted Preston and my stepfather's Nev Linney. I've been working with wood for years now, with my friend's dad, only he can't take me on as his apprentice because he's got his own son to train. So I have to find someone else to take me.'

'Come and show me how you saw a piece of wood,' Lucas said. He watched the boy and nodded approvingly, then gave him a hammer and some nails and told him to hammer them into an old piece of wood. The lad did it easily, not bending any of the nails.

'Your friend's dad has taught you well, Ted. You'd better bring your stepfather along to see me.'

He smiled as he watched the lad hurry away. He liked to see enthusiasm in apprentices. In fact, he liked teaching the young and had done quite a bit of it back on the estate. He turned round and saw Joe peeping out of the wood store, scowling in the direction of the door.

'You won't need me if you've got him,' the waif announced.

'Oh yes, I will. You aren't old enough to be an apprentice. You'll be the errand boy, but you'll also be in charge of sweeping up – we need to keep this floor clean at all times – you'll be doing a dozen different jobs to save us the trouble and one day, if you work very hard, I may teach you to be a proper carpenter. You'll also be helping my aunt in the kitchen as well, doing anything she needs. We definitely need you here.'

The scowl didn't quite vanish but Joe's expression grew a little less suspicious.

Lucas grinned. He was going to enjoy having the lads around. And he had two more jobs booked, so things were starting off well. They were only small jobs, though. He'd need a lot more work than that to pay off his debts – and support his new dependant.

II

Things were going from bad to worse for Gwynna. It seemed no sooner did she go out for a walk than her mother appeared. She hadn't told Mr Forrett yet about this because she was worried he'd dismiss her. But if it went on she'd have no choice because her mother had made a scene last time and people had stared.

The reason for the harassment soon became obvious. 'I need some money an' I need it now,' Mrs Jones said the next day, having chosen her spot well for accosting her daughter.

'I don't have any. I don't get paid until the end of the quarter.'

'There must be some coins lying round in a rich person's house. You can easy pick up one or two for y'r poor old parents.'

Gwynna stared at her in horror. 'I wouldn't *steal*!' She tried to push past her mother, but as she stepped backwards she bumped into someone and turned to find her father hemming her in from the other side. 'I mean it! I'd give up my job before I'd steal!' she cried. 'Let me past!'

A gentleman who had stopped at the sight of someone in trouble came forward. 'You two let that young woman go at once.'

Gwynna's parents hesitated then backed away, but their expressions said they'd catch her again.

'Thank you so much, sir. I was getting a bit frightened there.'

'I'll walk back to Market Street with you. You'd better stay where there are other people in future.'

'I'm really grateful.'

She walked back to Mill House feeling as if the sky had fallen in on her head. How was she to persuade them to leave her alone? And why was her father not at work? If he'd lost his job again they'd be even more of a nuisance, because they'd be desperate to obtain money for their drinking.

There was no getting away from it now. She'd have to tell Mr Forrett and the sooner the better.

She waited till he came in from the mill for lunch. 'Can I speak to you, please, sir?'

'After I've eaten. I'll send for you.'

'Yes, sir.'

Jen panted up the stairs to the nursery half an hour later. 'He says you can go down to see him now and I've to mind Libby. Eh, she's looking bonny lately, getting a bit of colour in her cheeks. You've worked wonders with her, you really have.'

Gwynna walked downstairs, feeling as if she were going to be executed.

'There you are. I haven't all day, so spit it out. What's the matter?'

She explained.

He stared at her solemnly. 'Is that all?'

'All?'

'Yes, all. I didn't realise you were old Bill Jones's daughter. He used to be a good worker once, till he got on the drink. I'll send someone to fetch him in and have a word with him. He won't bother you again.'

She felt so faint with relief that she had to clutch a chair back.

Forrett laughed. 'I'm glad to see Libby looking so well. You obviously know your job.'

'I had to help with my sisters at home, sir, and when I worked for Mr Hungerton Nurse Parker taught me a lot more about the *proper* way to look after young children.'

He looked thoughtful then said, 'Don't mention the little problem of your parents to my wife because she'll be annoyed. She's not always very reasonable, I'm afraid. Still hasn't recovered properly from having a child. It always makes her weepy for months. It's taking longer than usual this time, though, for her to get back to normal.'

'I won't say a word about them, sir.' How could she when Mrs Forrett never came near her and Libby?

'Now, if there's nothing else worrying you, leave me to drink another cup of tea in peace and get back to your work.'

'Thank you, Mr Forrett. I can't tell you how grateful I am.'

'Just keep looking after my daughter properly, that's all I ask.'

Gwynna felt quite giddy with relief as she walked back to the kitchen, where Jen and Cook were working together, smiling and chatting. 'You two look happy.'

'The new maid's starting tomorrow, that's why,' Jen said. 'It'll be good to have an extra pair of hands to help out, won't it? I hope she's nice.'

'What's she called?'

'Betty, I think. Don't know her second name.'

Gwynna too hoped this Betty would be nice. It made such a difference if all the servants got on well.

Jeremiah was glad he'd been able to help the young woman in distress. It hadn't escaped his notice that the two people who'd stopped her were both the worse for drink, early in the day though it was. He wondered if there was much drunkenness in the town. He hated to see people in that condition, especially those whose families needed the money for food. He wouldn't go as far as his father and advocate complete abstention, but he did believe in doing something about the problem. When he'd got settled in here, he'd offer his help to the Minister, whose sermon last Sunday had been very interesting.

That evening as they sat waiting for their evening meal to be served, he suggested to Maria that they try taking the boys to church on Sunday. He watched doubt etch itself in her face, then said gently, 'They need to start leading a more normal life. I noticed that none of you went to church last Sunday.'

'I couldn't face it. Athol was so hated in the town that people cross the street to avoid me now. They don't want anything to do with us. The boys are terrified to go out alone. Other children can be so cruel.'

Jeremiah considered these statements for a few seconds while the maid brought in a tureen of soup. 'You do go out, though. To call on friends, I think.'

Maria hesitated then decided to tell him the truth. 'Only one old friend who used to know my aunt. The other ladies I used to see – well, I've called on them in the past week, but their maids tell me they're out when I know they're not.' Her voice wobbled as she added, 'I've seen other ladies admitted to the same houses even before I've had time to walk round the corner.'

'That must be hurtful.'

She nodded.

'Perhaps if you wore mourning as people expect, they might—?'

'No! I won't go into mourning for him. *I won't!* I'm glad he's dead. If he hadn't been killed I might have had to kill him myself, to save the boys.' She realised what she had just revealed and clapped one hand over her mouth, then whispered, 'I've not told anyone else that.'

'You intended to kill him?' He stared at her in shock.

Her voice grew fierce. 'Only if I had no alternative. You saw what he did to Isaac's back. What might he have done to them next? A father has such power over his children and who else but me was there to stop him? I knew Edmund would look after the boys if – if it came to the worst.'

He looked at her, thin and fragile looking, yet courageous as a vixen defending her cubs. 'Things must have been very bad to drive you to that point.'

She nodded, unable to speak for a moment or two as the memories flooded back, then she had to ask, 'You don't – despise me for it?'

'No. The more I hear about my late cousin the more I wonder how you survived for so long married to him.'

She gave a scornful laugh and suddenly more confidences poured out, things she had told no one else. 'I survived because I learned to be very meek and colourless, whatever he did to me. He enjoyed seeing me weep, so I learned not to. The only time I ever begged him for something was when he whipped Isaac and I asked him to stop. He just laughed at me so I threw myself between them.' She fingered her cheek. 'He could have stopped the whip before it hit me, but he didn't. He meant to mark me. He enjoyed hurting people.'

When Jeremiah made a sympathetic noise, she went on in another rush of words, 'After Benjamin was born I got the doctor to tell Athol that having another child would kill me. He didn't come near me in that way from then on. It was – the greatest relief you could ever imagine. He taunted me, said I wasn't a real woman any longer, so it was no loss to him not to have me in his bed. He said he could find plenty of other women to serve his needs but as long as I brought up his children properly, he would put up with my presence in his house.

'At one time he was proud of having fathered two sons, you see, but as they grew older and turned out to be rather gentle boys, he began to despise them.' She paused to draw breath, horrified by how much she had revealed. 'Well, that's all in the past now.' It had been a great relief to tell someone, though. She'd been alone for so long. After fighting for control, she took a spoonful of soup and changed the subject. 'Tell me about yourself, Cousin Jeremiah. I know nothing about your branch of the family. Do you have any brothers and sisters?'

'No, I'm an only son.'

'And you never married?'

He hesitated then said, 'Yes, but my wife was killed.'

'I'm sorry. What a pity you didn't have children!'

He couldn't speak for a minute or two, but knew if his parents came to visit, as they were bound to one day, they'd say something. Best get it over with, he told himself. 'We did have a child, a daughter. She and her mother were both killed at the same time.'

Maria looked at him in consternation. 'Oh, Jeremiah, I'm so sorry. I didn't mean to reopen old wounds.'

He blinked and to his horror, could feel tears welling in his eyes, so pushed his chair back and moved towards the window, staring out into the darkness and surreptitiously flicking away a tear that escaped and rolled down his cheek. Now it was his turn to struggle to control himself and he was finding it difficult.

'There's no shame to weeping for the loss of loved ones,' she said gently from behind him. And for one moment her hand rested on his shoulder, light as a butterfly.

He wished she'd left it there. Its warmth was comforting. He could feel her still standing close to him, was glad of that. 'I don't usually tell people. I find it better to keep the past in the past.'

'Not if it was a happy time, surely? I had a sister who died when she was fifteen. She was so lively and full of life, then she fell ill and was gone within two days. I couldn't accept that for a long time then I began to remember the happy times, to be glad I'd once had her.'

He shook his head and felt her touch his arm, only this time her hand stayed there, a small patch of warmth in the chill that had enveloped him since Harriet and Cassie died. He had a sudden urge to turn round and pull her to him, to take comfort from the remembered softness of a woman's body. Her voice was low and musical when it wasn't thick with tears. Everything about her seemed – womanly.

'How long since it happened?' she asked.

'Two years.'

'You must have loved her very much to be grieving still, Jeremiah.'

More confidences leaked out. 'I didn't love her and that makes it worse.' When he dared raise one hand to lay it over Maria's, she didn't pull away but clasped his as if she understood his need to be touched.

'Harriet and I married because it was considered suitable by our families. Her people were members of our church, among the few my father totally approved of because her father was nearly as strict as mine. I didn't really want to marry her, but I did want a home and family of my own. I soon found out she was rather stupid and I grew bored by her endless prattle about nothing. I could have been kinder, not spoken to her so sharply, and deeply regret that now. She died bravely, trying to save our daughter's life. I honour her for that. The house caught fire, you see, and the governess was downstairs at the time. My daughter was trapped on the second floor, must have overturned a lamp. Harriet rushed through the flames to find her but couldn't get back down. And there were bars on the nursery windows, so although she broke the glass, no one could get them out in time.'

He let go of Maria's hand, unsettled by his desire to cling to it. 'Ironic, isn't it, that we both lost our spouses in fires?'

'Yours was a tragic accident. Athol fully deserved what happened to him.'

'Our fire was an accident that could have been avoided. If you don't mind, we'll have those bars removed from the schoolroom and nursery windows this very week. I can't bear the things.'

She nodded and as he dashed one hand across his eyes, she went back to the table and took her place there, not looking at him, fussing with her napkin to give him time to pull himself together.

There was silence behind her for a minute or two then he said in a tight voice, 'I must beg your pardon for my unseemly display of emotion.'

'There's nothing unseemly about weeping for the loss of a child. I weep still for what Athol did to Isaac, not only the beating, but the way he terrified both boys. I pray that I can help my sons to recover from having a father like that.'

Jeremiah walked across to join her at the table, stopping beside her chair to say quietly, 'If I can help you bring up your sons then my life will have some meaning again.'

She nodded. 'It will be good for them to have a decent man to set an example of how to live.'

He was touched by this compliment but it made him feel emotional again, so he said in a voice thickened by unshed tears, 'I find I'm not hungry tonight and I have a headache. I beg you to excuse me.' He didn't wait for her answer but swung round and left the room, running lightly up the stairs to his bedroom.

Maria listened to the door open and shut above her and realised suddenly that she'd stopped worrying that he resembled Athol, stopped even noticing that, because Jeremiah was very different. The way he moved, so quietly and gracefully, and the way he spoke, in that calm, controlled voice. Everything about him had been moderate and restrained – until tonight.

She forgot about the food as she thought about what he'd told her, and what she had told him. He was, she decided, a man in great mental pain. What she couldn't understand was why Athol had chosen him as guardian for the boys.

Jeremiah was right about one thing, though. She must conquer her cowardice and start going out and about again, for the boys' sake. Even if some ladies in the town did shun her, there was no reason not to take the air, go to the shops, behave normally. She could take the boys for walks, too. They'd be safe enough with her.

She'd had a poor appetite for a long time but forced herself to eat because she had to build up her strength again.

She felt differently about the future now. Jeremiah wasn't doing what Athol had hoped for.

It was only as she was slipping into sleep that she recognised what the new feeling was that was filling her with gentle warmth. Hope.

The architect got the building work on the theatre started on the Monday with a lot of hand waving and gesticulating. His foreman had hired local men to dig the foundations and they shovelled away the layer of loose blackened soil to get to the heavier layers beneath. In some parts they left the old foundations in place because the architect said they were still strong enough to use.

Eli had a word with Mr Trevin, then watched the men digging with a sense of envy. He longed to pick up a spade himself and work with them till he was exhausted. Maybe that would drive away the darkness that had been clouding his thoughts and feelings since the fire. But it probably wouldn't do any good. He'd tried going for long walks until he was almost too tired to put one foot in front of the other and that hadn't helped him sleep properly.

Last night, yet again, he'd lain awake for a long time,

envious of Carrie who was breathing peacefully at his side. But no sooner did he begin to doze than the flames rose around him and he came fully awake with a jerk, unable to breathe, burning, burning . . . He had to get up when that happened, stumble downstairs and hurry outside, where he could gulp in great breaths of cold night air. There at least he could breathe properly.

Only when he was so exhausted that everything was a blur around him could he snatch a few hours' sleep.

Carrie was worrying about him, he could see it in her eyes. She watched him when she thought he wasn't looking, and had begged him to talk to her about it. But even with her, he couldn't face describing the horrors he kept experiencing again and again.

The trouble was, it had started to happen during the daytime now, because he was so tired that sometimes he was almost asleep on his feet. If he relaxed for even a minute on such days, the flames and smoke gathered around him and he could hardly see straight, had to make excuses to get outside quickly.

It was a while before he could tear himself away from the messy building site, because it was both a pain and a pleasure to see the work start, hear the men joke with one another and see the piles of dirt grow. But he had to see the Minister about hiring the church hall, so when the town hall clock struck ten he forced himself to walk along Market Street to the church.

It was a delicate negotiation and at first he was able to lose himself in the old pleasures of bargaining, then suddenly his mind fogged over. He faltered to a stop, couldn't think straight, had to get outside. When he looked at the Minister he realised the man was speaking, but he couldn't make out the words because the flames were crackling too loudly inside his head.

Only when he was standing in the doorway, gulping in big breaths of air, did he start to think straight again. Then he became aware of someone standing beside him and turned to face the Minister.

'It's all right. I do understand. I've seen men haunted by tragedy before. It *will* pass, Mr Beckett, I promise you. I'll mention you in my prayers every day and if you should want someone to talk to . . .'

'Thank you. I'll – remember that. It's the memories, you see, of being trapped inside a burning building, of not being able to help my wife. I can't get that out of my mind.' Eli snapped his mouth shut, concentrating on the fresh, cold air he was breathing in – the colder the better.

Only when he felt he had himself under control did he turn back to the Minister and even then he didn't want to go back inside to the cluttered study. 'You were saying?'

'I was speaking about the hall. Maybe we should walk along there now to finish our discussion? You'll need to study the place in detail and perhaps you'll feel better in a bigger space?'

Eli shrugged. He didn't feel really comfortable anywhere these days. 'You won't – tell anyone.'

'Of course not. What does your wife think?' There was silence, then the Minister said softly, 'You ought to confide in her, at least.'

'Can't – talk about it.'

'Come with me to the church hall, then. We're in need of funds for our work among the poor of this parish, so the money you're offering for the use of the hall will be very useful indeed. The Lord works in mysterious ways to supply our needs, does he not?'

Eli let the Minister's gentle voice flow past his ears, drawing comfort from the sound of it but not really taking in the words or their meaning. By the time they got to the hall, he had recovered enough to negotiate terms and conditions. Sadly, there was to be no alcohol sold there, because of the church's campaign against drunkenness, Mr Nopps was adamant about that, but Eli could still sell lemonade, gooseberry cordial, cups of tea, little cakes perhaps. You could make a profit from anything if you went about it efficiently.

He went home feeling slightly better because at least he had managed to do something without Carrie's help. But for all that Linney's was a big house, it seemed to close too tightly around him when he went inside and it was hard to keep his mind on the detailed planning they needed to do for the decoration of the new music hall.

Ted turned up at Lucas's workshop with a plump older man in tow. 'Mr Kemp, this is my stepfather, Mr Linney.'

It did Lucas's heart good to see the lad's bright, hopeful expression. He turned to shake the man's hand. 'Won't you sit down? I presume you're interested in an apprenticeship for your son?'

'Yes. Our Ted's allus liked making things out of wood. And it's a good, solid trade, carpentry is.'

Lucas explained the terms and conditions, the cost and the tools needed. Mr Linney nodded and agreed to do whatever was required. It wasn't long before the apprenticeship was sealed with a handshake. 'We'll need to see Mr Burtell to draw up a contract. Five years it'll take, young Ted. How old will you be then?'

'Eh, I'll be eighteen, going on nineteen.' Ted rolled his eyes as if the thought horrified him.

Both men tried to hide their amusement. That might seem old to Ted, but they both knew how young and inexperienced most 'men' of that age were.

12

It was a bright, sunny morning, if cold, and Jeremiah was tempted out for a stroll. He was gradually getting to know the patterns of the streets by methodically walking up and down them till the town's layout was imprinted in his mind. It was a quirk of his to need that understanding of his surroundings.

Some of the buildings caught his interest, especially the Methodist church, which was in the Greek style, with pillars and pure classical lines. It was the first time he'd been truly interested in anything architectural for two years. Was that a good sign? He couldn't tell but he had a faint hope that it might be.

Today he paused opposite the burned-out music saloon, where work had recently started, and watched a group of men busily digging up the ground, presumably to extend the cellars, which you'd need to do in a modern theatre of any sort. Interested, he crossed the street, braving the muddy footpath to study the layout in more detail.

As he stood there a pompous little man came over to him. 'Good morning to you, sir. I see you're interested in our venture. It's a smaller theatre than I usually design but still, every building must be the best that one can create.'

Jeremiah nodded and made a non-committal sound in his throat.

Thus encouraged, the man began pointing out where things would go, speaking in a patronising tone, as if the newcomer was bound to be lost in wonder at what he was doing.

When Jeremiah didn't respond with the display of admiration that was clearly expected, the man let out a sniff of annoyance and said, 'Well, I must get on. We've a lot of work to get through if we're to build this theatre in four months.'

Jeremiah walked on, shocked to the core. Four months! How could they possibly build something as big as a theatre in that time? Well, they couldn't, not properly. Even with the excellent craftsmen he'd used regularly over the years, he couldn't have managed that for a large house, let alone a theatre. It was one of his skills, finding men who had a real flair for what they did and working with them to produce something you could be proud of, something that would last. He believed he recognised a similar flair in Edmund Stott, because the men at the engineering works seemed to toil willingly without anyone needing to stand over them and keep them at it.

When he got home the boys were at their lessons and Maria was not in any of the main rooms. He felt disappointed because he'd been looking forward to asking her about the theatre, finding out more about what it had been like before. After fidgeting around for half an hour, picking up books and putting them down, rustling the newspaper in front of him but not seeing the print clearly, he went out again, this time to the engineering works to ask a few more questions about the accounts.

Men called out his name in greeting this time and there were no signs of any crisis. He found Edmund Stott sitting at the desk in the office, staring at a pile of papers with every sign of loathing.

Jeremiah cleared his throat because his cousin hadn't even noticed him standing in the doorway. 'Do you need any help?'

Edmund looked up, his face brightening as he got to his

feet and came across to shake hands. 'Indeed I do. I'm trying to sort out the accounts and work on a financial plan for buying into the firm, and the two don't seem to mix in my head.'

'Why don't you let me deal with the accounts, then? That's something I find easy.' He hesitated, then added, 'I'll take your word for how much money will be fair to buy a half share in the engineering works. If you work that out and explain your figures to me, we'll put it in train immediately.' This offer surprised him, because he didn't usually trust people so easily. But he did trust this cousin, for some reason.

The two men worked in silence for an hour then Edmund sighed and leaned back to stretch his arms above his head. 'How's it going?'

'Nearly finished. It seems to me your creditors have been allowed too much leeway. I wouldn't have given them more than thirty days for payment of bills.'

'I know that's how I *should* do it, but some of them have endured difficult times in the past few years, so I haven't pressed them too hard for payment.' He got up and went to lean over Jeremiah's shoulder, sorting through the nearest pile of papers and explaining which firms he'd allowed time to pay and which could be expected to pay within the month.

Jeremiah could tell that Edmund knew his business and customers, even if he didn't keep up with the accounts as he ought to. He scribbled down a few details about each customer as the other talked. 'You need a clerk to do this.'

'I know. But Athol wouldn't let me hire anyone else and I didn't like to take anyone on until I'd spoken to you.' He looked through the inner windows of the office at the shop floor. 'Oh, there's Robbie. You didn't meet him the other day. He's in tutelage to me, training to be an engineer. Came from the shop floor but has a real talent for engineering, so I waived the tutelage fees.' He went to stick his head out of the door and yell, 'Robbie, come and meet Mr Channon.' As the man, who was bent over a machine, pointing and gesticulating, held up his fingers to signify five minutes, Edmund went back to explain, 'He's one of the Prestons. His sister Carrie is married to Eli Beckett, the man who owned the music saloon.'

'They've started digging out the cellars.'

'Oh, good! We're all missing having a music saloon, though I gather this one is to be a proper theatre. Strange how much we're missing it, when three years ago we didn't have any entertainment like that. I've taken my wife to shows a few times. I enjoy the animal acts most, but she liked the singers.'

'I've never seen a show of that sort.'

'You sound as if you disapprove.'

'Doesn't it encourage working men to spend money they can ill afford on drink and – and frivolity?'

Edmund raised one eyebrow. 'No. It gives them a treat they well deserve after a hard week's work. I'd forgotten that your family is rather – um – strict about religion, because *you* don't lard your conversation with it. But I do assure you that the Pride was just that, a place of entertainment which the whole town could be proud of. No loose women were allowed inside the doors and no drunkenness was permitted among patrons, either. It was very efficiently run. Beckett seems lost without it, he's not looking at all well.'

There was a moment of constraint. Jeremiah knew that his father had a bad reputation in the family. They didn't associate with any of their relatives nowadays because his father had quarrelled with them all, insisting they were lax and godless. 'My father can be very extreme in his views, I'm afraid. But I hope I'm not as . . . as . . .'

'Narrow-minded?' Edmund cocked one eyebrow at him and grinned.

'I suppose you could call him that.' It occurred to Jeremiah that he too had been narrow-minded, judging things he'd never experienced, like the music saloon. Perhaps it was a good thing he'd left his old life and started a new one. He didn't want to turn as sour and bitter about the world as his father had. He realised his cousin was speaking and forced himself to pay attention.

'I'm sorry. It was rude of me to speak about your father that way. But I didn't like to hear you speak slightingly of the Pride. It took men *away* from heavy drinking, actually.'

'I haven't taken offence. And my father has grown even more difficult since he had a seizure, so if he comes to visit I pray *you* won't take offence at the things he'll say. I must warn Maria about that.'

'How is she? I haven't seen her for a few days. Faith was wondering if you would like to bring her and the boys out to visit us on Sunday and eat a midday meal with us? It's a pleasant walk to Out Rawby, which is a very small village to the north-east of Hedderby – well, its more a hamlet than a village really.'

'That's very kind of you. I'll ask her and then confirm that we're coming.'

'Is she coping all right?'

'She's coping better than she was, now that she's not as afraid for the boys.' The two men's eyes met and Jeremiah added softly, 'I've made it plain that I don't intend to deal harshly with them – or her. From the sounds of it, her life with our cousin was very difficult.'

'That's putting it mildly. I'd call it a living hell. I stayed with them for a while and if you'd seen how scornfully he spoke to her, how he treated her . . . I don't know how she survived. Well, at least she's free of him now. Are you going to stay on here permanently?'

'Yes. I take my responsibility towards those boys very seriously indeed. Children are important.'

'I was sorry to hear about your own loss. I didn't feel on good enough terms to write to you, but I truly sympathised. I know how I'd feel if anything happened to Faith and my two little terrors.'

'Yes.' Jeremiah quickly changed the subject. It was not until he was walking home that he admitted it to himself: the only person he had been able to discuss his loss with was Maria. She understood serious troubles as people who'd led normal, happy lives never could. He both liked *and* respected her.

On the way back he passed a carpenter's workshop. He stopped, hesitated, then went inside. Time he started getting to know the local tradesmen, just in case . . . He didn't finish that thought, didn't dare hope for too much yet, but the future was starting to look brighter.

A man he presumed to be the owner was working on a small child's conveyance, but it was like no stick wagon Jeremiah had ever seen.

'Could you wait a moment, sir? This is the tricky bit while the glue is still hot.'

Jeremiah stood back, understanding perfectly well what the task involved because he enjoyed working with wood when he had time. The piece was well built, he could see, with all the joints fitting perfectly. 'I've not seen that design before.'

'It's one of my own.' Lucas stood up. 'I made one like this and someone saw it in the street, so ordered another from me. There. It's safe to leave now. Clear those things away, Ted. How can I help you, sir? I'm Lucas Kemp, the new owner, but I'll not offer my hand because it's sticky.'

Jeremiah introduced himself and explained about the schoolroom bars and how the woodwork would need making good when they were removed.

'I can come round to look at them straight away, if you like, once I've cleaned myself up. Since I've only just bought this business I'm not too busy yet.'

'I'm sure you will be when people see how well you work.'

He looked at Jeremiah in surprise. 'How can you know that? I'm a stranger to the town.'

'I'm a stranger too, but I'm an architect. I used to specialise in designing and building family houses. I've dealt with many tradesmen. It's usually apparent quite quickly whether men know their trade or not. I've just seen a piece you've designed and watched you working on it. That was enough to tell me how good you are.'

'Thank you.' Lucas rubbed the glue off his hands with sawdust, then went to wash them. He put a notebook and pencil in his pocket and told Ted to keep an eye on the work-shop and to fetch his aunt if someone came in wanting a job done, then walked back to his new customer's house.

In the schoolroom Jeremiah gave the boys a smile, which they didn't return, then explained to the governess what he was doing. He was aware of the lads watching wide-eyed as the job was discussed.

'I could come round tomorrow if that's convenient, Miss Cavett,' Lucas told the governess.

'Oh yes. Yes, of course.'

'The sooner the better,' Jeremiah said. 'I disapprove of such bars. Children should not be brought up in cages.' He turned to the boys. 'I dare say you'll enjoy watching Mr Kemp work, if Miss Cavett doesn't mind? I think every boy should learn how tools are used and I'm hoping you'll help me with a few jobs around the house later.' He didn't wait for an answer but led the way out and, as they walked down the stairs, he said quietly, 'The boys are still nervous of strangers, especially men. Their father didn't treat them kindly, you see.'

'I've heard about him.'

'I suppose it's common knowledge.'

'I'm afraid so. The fire and everything connected with it

is still a matter of great interest in the town. People are angry at losing their music saloon.'

'Well, we'll see you tomorrow.' Jeremiah stood at the door and watched the carpenter stride away, then went inside, wondering yet again how he was to win his wards' confidence.

When she took Libby out for her mid-morning walk, Gwynna saw Lucas turn off Market Street and stride up the hill, followed by Ted carrying a canvas bag. That lad had always wanted to be a carpenter, used to talk about it when they all lived at Linney's. She was glad he'd got his wish. She sighed and stopped walking till the two had vanished from sight, then got angry with herself. It was stupid to keep dreaming about Lucas Kemp. A man like him wouldn't think of her in that way. He owned his own business, which put him way beyond her reach. Men like that married someone from another family in trade, not a girl from the slums.

She blinked in shock. Married? What on earth was she thinking like that for – and about a man she hardly knew? She'd sworn never to marry.

But that was before you met Lucas Kemp, a little voice whispered inside her head. She tried to push the thought away, but it wouldn't be pushed. He was so tall and had such a warm smile . . .

She felt a dampness on her cheek. It was going to rain soon so she decided to cut the walk short. There was no sign of her parents today, to her great relief. Had Mr Forrett spoken to them already? She got back to the house in time to meet the new maid.

Betty was short and stocky, and her expression wasn't friendly. She nodded to Gwynna when introduced but made no attempt to get into conversation.

'Jen will show you your room, Betty,' Cook said, her

attention more on the pan simmering on the stove than on the three young women. 'Before you do that, Jen love, go and ask the yard men in to carry her trunk upstairs for us.'

Jen hurried outside and returned with two men, then the four of them vanished up the stairs.

'Can I get Libby something to drink before we go up?' Gwynna asked.

'Of course you can, love.'

She hid a smile as she heated some milk, because Cook now seemed to accept her completely. Nurse Parker had always said milk must be boiled before you gave it to young children, water too. She knew Cook thought this too fussy, but she wasn't going to give in about it. After all, look at how Libby was thriving now. She was proud of that.

As she was carrying the child upstairs she passed the mistress, who was up and dressed today, but still had that faint, fretful expression on her face. What did *she* have to be miserable about?

'Ah, there you are. How is she?' Mrs Forrett peered at her daughter but made no attempt to take her and give her a cuddle. 'Yes, I see she's coming on nicely now, and thank goodness she's stopped crying so much. It used to make my head ache.' She sighed as if she had the troubles of the world on her shoulders and drifted off down the stairs.

Gwynna watched her go. It was the first time Mrs Forrett had been near her daughter for days yet she'd made no attempt to hold her. How could a mother be so indifferent to her own child? Why, even Mr Forrett had started coming up to the nursery when he came home from the mill to jiggle his daughter about, give her smacking big kisses, and ask about her progress. Gwynna felt on edge the whole time he was there, because his sharp eyes didn't miss a thing, but he never treated her with anything except respect. Maybe what he'd told her was right: if you were respectable and worked in his house, you were safe.

The new maid was unpacking, the door of her attic bedroom open. She turned, saw who had come up to the attic floor and deliberately turned her back, not even nodding in greeting.

Why was she so unfriendly? Gwynna wondered. Something else niggled at her all the time she was changing Libby: why did she keep thinking she'd met Betty before? She was sure she hadn't, yet felt as if there was something familiar about the other maid's face.

Carrie and Eli went down to the site just before it grew dark, wanting to see how the work was getting on. The old cellar had just been opened up again now and to their surprise some bottles of wine and spirits were being removed. As they watched from a distance the foreman put them into a bag.

'I didn't think anything would survive.' Eli watched in amazement as the man closed the bag and picked it up. He walked quickly forward. 'What are you doing with those?'

'Oh, just going to throw them away, sir.'

'I'll do that. They may be all right.'

'I don't think so, sir.'

Eli glared at him. 'It's for me to judge that. There were some tools in the cellar as well. Where are they?'

The man was scowling and for a moment their eyes met, then he looked away. 'I've got them over there.'

Again they were in a bag, ready to be taken away presumably.

'I'll take those as well. And in future, if you find anything, see me about it.'

The man nodded and walked away, leaving them alone on the site.

Carrie shivered. 'I don't like the way it all looks at the moment, just a series of holes and piles of muck.'

'He's getting on with it, though. You have to give him that. And it'll be good to have a big new cellar under the stage for storage.'

She nodded and continued to study the place.

'Trevin knows what he's doing,' Eli muttered, sounding as if he was trying to convince himself as well as her.

'Yes, I suppose so.' She had no reason for her instinctive mistrust of the man, but still it lingered, colouring her feelings towards him and what he was doing. She tried to think of something cheerful to say. 'I can't wait to have the Pride open again, with shows and performers and bright lights. I love to hear you introducing the acts. You have such a nice loud voice.'

'We're calling it the Phoenix, not the Pride. Remember?'

'You can call it what you want, but people in the town call it the Pride still.' She looked at him in mingled exasperation and worry. 'What's wrong, Eli?'

'I may be starting a cold. I feel all shivery.'

She knew he wasn't telling her the truth.

They walked back to Linney's but when they got to the door, Eli hesitated. 'I'll just – go for a walk, I think. I'm getting twitchy for lack of an occupation.'

She'd had enough of this chopping and changing, so she grabbed his arm. 'Eli?'

There was a question in her voice, a question he didn't want to answer. He tried to pull away, but she kept a tight hold of his arm. 'Eli, what's wrong? Please tell me.'

'I can't – talk about it.'

'You have to. How can I help you if I don't know what's upsetting you? Since the fire you keep avoiding me, slipping out of the house on the silliest excuses, and you're not even helping much with the rebuilding, but leaving most of the planning to me. We can't go on like this.'

She heard him swallow hard, a sound perilously close to

a sob and flung her arms round him. 'I'm not moving from here till you tell me what's wrong.'

He could have shaken her off, he knew. She was a tall woman but he was far stronger than she was. But he didn't because she was right. He did need to tell her. 'Not here. We'll go for a walk.'

It was cold, they hadn't had their evening meal and she was trying to hide the fact that she was shivering, but she linked her arm in his without hesitation. 'All right. Come on, love.'

It wasn't till they were out of the town, standing looking down on the rows of new street lamps, that he began to talk, telling her about the nightmares he was having, night and day now, and about the roaring, crackling flames that seemed to fill his head so often.

She hugged him close. 'Oh, Eli, why didn't you tell me before? Did you think I wouldn't know something was wrong?'

'Couldn't tell you. Makes it worse to talk about it.'

'Have you seen Dr Pipperday?'

'No.'

'Why not?'

'I don't want to talk about it, not to anyone. I just want it to go away!'

She threaded her arm in his again. 'Well, I think you've made a good step forward by telling me about it. Let's go back now. I'm chilled to the bone. We'll find some way to help you, Eli love. Or maybe it'll just fade gradually.'

'Maybe.'

But that night he had the worst nightmare ever, in which he saw Carrie burning, her face melting like candle wax. He woke the whole household when he screamed her name and it was some time before he could calm down. He felt embarrassed that he'd disturbed everyone, but Carrie went to the door and spoke to Nev quietly, then the others went back to bed.

Was he going mad? He sometimes thought so. Perhaps he should see a doctor?

But when he went round to Dr Pipperday's house the following day, waiting till the street was clear to slip along the garden path, it was to find that the doctor and his wife had gone to London for a few days. The maid who answered the door suggested he see Dr Barlow, but he couldn't do that. The town's other doctor treated everyone except his rich patients as if they were stupid, speaking to them more loudly and slowly than usual, and not hiding his scorn about their problems. Poorer people only went to Dr Barlow in dire emergencies.

On his way home Eli went to visit the building site again and ignored the foreman's scowl. He noticed a tall man standing on the other side of the street frowning at it as if he didn't like what he saw and out of sheer curiosity made his way across to join him. For a moment he hesitated because the man suddenly reminded him of Athol Stott, which was foolish. Eh, he was getting more stupid by the day. He needed to pull himself together, he did indeed. 'It's going to look even better than the old music saloon,' he said by way of an introduction.

The man turned to him. 'I never saw that, so I can't pass an opinion. Are you connected with it, sir?'

'Yes. I'm the owner – well, my cousin owns a share as well, but she's a singer and doesn't visit here very often.'

'Who's the architect you're using?'

'Maitland Trevin.'

'Oh?'

'He's from London and he's built a lot of theatres.'

'I'm afraid I've never heard of him.'

Eli looked at him. 'Well, not many people know much about architects. I didn't before this.'

'Yes, but I'm an architect too, so I'd have expected . . . Well, I don't suppose it matters. If he's done as many theatres as you say, he must know what he's doing.'

Eli knew a moment's unease but dismissed his worries. He was being foolish again, his lack of sleep making him grumpy. For a moment or two the two men continued to stare at the mess, with several labourers digging and wheeling barrows of muck out of the new cellar. 'Why do you ask about Trevin? Is there something wrong with the place?'

'No. I was wondering when they're going to start on the brickwork to shore up the walls of the cellars. That'll need doing carefully with such large cellars.' He held out one hand. 'I'm Jeremiah Channon. I've just moved to live in Hedderby.'

'Eli Beckett.'

They stood side by side staring across the road.

'My wife and I are looking forward to having our business back again. Four months, Trevin says.'

'That's very quick. Um – is he a short, plump man?'

'Yes.'

'I was talking to him the other day.' Jeremiah hesitated. 'Perhaps I spoke out of turn. He seemed to expect me to – to marvel at it, but I've seen quite a lot of building sites and this is the stage I like least. I usually build houses, not theatres, but I've built some big places with huge cellars.'

'The principles would be the same, surely?'

'Yes.'

Eli suddenly decided to ask about something that had started to worry him, since Trevin was talking about him making another payment soon, something to do with 'work in progress' and 'first stage of plans carried out'. He took a deep breath and said, 'Would you mind my asking you something? Would you expect a client to pay money before the building was completed?'

'Certainly not.' Jeremiah looked at him. 'Did he ask for money in advance?'

'Yes.'

'Hmm. I dare say he's all right, but one can't be too careful and this is a big job. You might like to check out the other places he's built.' With a farewell nod he walked away.

'Wait! Would you tell me where I can contact you in case I need to ask your advice?'

The other man hesitated, looked across at the building site again, then said, 'I'm living in what was Athol Stott's house. I'm a distant relative and I'm his sons' guardian. I'm told I resemble him physically, though I can assure you that I'm not like him in any other way.'

Eli stared at him, head on one side. 'The resemblance isn't that great, actually. You've got sane eyes and you speak civilly. Stott had a wild look to him and seemed to hate the world.'

Jeremiah inclined his head. 'Thank you for that. I'm finding that some people seem to mistrust me because of the resemblance.'

Eli stayed for a few minutes longer watching the men work, then made his way home, worried now about the building. He should have checked out Trevin's credentials, not relied on a few sketches, however beautiful they were.

If only he could sleep properly for a few nights, he'd be able to think more clearly, act decisively like he used to.

But it wouldn't take much effort to go and look at the theatres Trevin said he'd built, would it? Carrie had been going on about it for a while now. That at least he could do.

Feeling better than he had for days, he began to walk faster.

13

Lucas looked up as someone entered the workshop. The man had his hat pulled low over his forehead and a scarf wound round his neck hid his features. Tensing, Lucas looked round for something to defend himself with. Then the man raised one hand to unwind the scarf and he saw that it was an old man's hand, wrinkled, covered with age spots. As the scarf was removed he was astonished to see Hungerton's land agent. 'Mr Lester! What on earth are you doing in Hedderby?'

His visitor looked round. 'Are we alone?'

'Except for my apprentice.'

'Could you send him away and lock the outer door, do you think? I need to talk to you privately.'

'Yes, of course.' Lucas sent Ted and Joe into the house and told them not to come out until he fetched them. Then he locked the outer door, feeling rather foolish to be acting so secretively. When he turned round, he saw that Lester had taken off his hat and was holding it by the brim, turning it round and round in his hands, staring down at it.

'I'm still not sure whether I should have come or not, but I felt I needed to warn you.'

'About what?'

'Mr Hungerton. I fear he's plotting violence against you and is trying to ruin your reputation so that your business will fail. He's crowing because you're short of money and will soon lose everything.'

'How the hell does he know that?'

'He pays men to come here and talk to people, women too.'

Lucas slammed down one hand on the bench. 'Why will the man not leave me alone? Haven't I shown him that I won't work for him again? Does he think he's the right to ruin people's lives to suit his whims?'

'I fear he does feel like that. He's nearly eighty now, you know, born in another age where rich men could do what they pleased. As he's grown older he's become very intransigent about getting his own way. One son has left home rather than bend to his wishes and the other son avoids him as much as possible. Mr Hungerton has got it into his mind that to let you win will show weakness. And to add to the problem, we still haven't found another carpenter with your skills to do the carving. That's angering him because he wants to leave the house to his son in perfect condition. I can understand that, a little.'

'Well, I damned well can't!'

'I – um – ventured to remonstrate with him, said I didn't wish to be involved in such activities and he dismissed me.'

'I'm sorry to hear that. You've worked hard for him.'

Lester gave him a tight smile. 'I was planning to leave anyway. I've been careful with my money and intend to spend my declining years at leisure. My wife and I are going to live in the south of England near our eldest son. But I couldn't reconcile it with my conscience not to warn you before I left about what Hungerton is doing. I've allowed him to ride roughshod over too many people and I'm feeling guilty about that. That sits heavily on my conscience.'

'I'm grateful for the warning, but I don't see how I can stop him.'

'Perhaps you could sell this business and move away from Lancashire?'

'I'll not run away!'

'Well, it's up to you, but at least I've warned you now.' He put the hat on again and began to wind the scarf round his neck so that his features were once more concealed.

'Have you left his employment yet, Mr Lester?'

'No. Not for another two more weeks.'

'If you see or hear anything else, could you let me know?'

Lester thought about this then shook his head. 'I don't want to put anything down in writing. I'm somewhat nervous of incurring his enmity towards myself and my family, which is why I don't want anyone to recognise me today.' He walked across to the door and waited until Lucas unlocked it. 'You'd really ought to consider selling up and leaving, emigrating even. He has friends in high places, and not just in Lancashire.'

'This business has been bought partly with my uncle's life savings. He and his family are dependent on me now, and I *won't* let them down. But I thank you for coming.' Lucas opened the door and stared down the rain-swept street. 'No one around.'

'I wish you well.' Lester slipped outside, walking quickly away, once again muffled up and unrecognisable.

Lucas went inside. Was Hungerton becoming foolish in his old age as people did sometimes? Why had no one stopped him from treating people so badly? Surely Mr Selwyn could have done something?

At this rate he'd never be able to go and visit his parents and brother. He didn't even dare write to them. He wasn't very close to them but they were his family, and that mattered.

Even though Alfred Lester had to go into Manchester to complete the business that had given him an excuse for getting away from the estate for the day, he got back earlier than expected. To his amazement he found Selwyn Hungerton going through the drawers in his office. 'May I ask what you're looking for?'

Selwyn looked up. 'Oh. You're back. Sorry about this, but my father wants me to check everything before you leave. He's being totally unreasonable and we all know that you've served the family honestly all these years, but you know what he's like. I hope you'll not take it amiss.'

Anger at this insult to his integrity boiled up in Lester. 'I do take it amiss, very much so. If that's how things stand I shall leave tomorrow and you can be sure I won't touch these things again.' He flicked one hand scornfully towards the desk then moved forward to stand with his hands on the desk, leaning forward. 'But before I go, I intend to tell you a few things about your father that you won't find written down on these papers. You should know what you'll have to contend with, you and whoever is foolish enough to take over the job . . .'

Jeremiah's heart sank when Mrs Ibster handed him the letters and he saw, sitting on top of the pile, a piece of paper folded and sealed in the old way, instead of protected by an envelope. His father's cramped handwriting was easy to recognise.

Maria looked across the table at him. 'Is something wrong?'

'No.' Then honesty compelled him to amend that. 'I mean, yes. This is from my father. Would you mind if I opened it immediately? It's bad manners but I'd rather know the worst. I should have told you before that my father is a religious bigot of the most extreme persuasion. He is not easy to get on with. In fact, he makes life very uncomfortable for all those around him, and he's got worse since he had a seizure.'

'Aaah!'

He looked up in puzzlement at her triumphant tone.

'That's why Athol named you as the boys' guardian,' she

explained. 'He thought you'd be like your father and make our lives uncomfortable.'

It was out before he could stop himself. 'And do I?'

'No. You've been very kind to us, or as kind as the boys will allow.'

Jeremiah could feel himself flushing because he wasn't used to compliments, so he bent his head to slip his knife under the lump of sealing wax and unfold the paper. When he'd read it he closed his eyes for a moment and sighed.

'Is something wrong?'

'Yes. He's coming to visit us. Today!' He saw her surprise and couldn't keep the bitterness from his voice. 'That's how he checks up on people. Usually he gives no warning of what he's going to do, so I suppose we ought to be grateful for an hour or two's notice. His train arrives just after ten this morning.'

'Then as soon as we've finished breakfast I'd better warn Mrs Ibster.' She hesitated. 'What about the boys?'

'I don't know what to do about them. I can hardly prevent him from meeting them, but I know he'll be sharp with them. Just as I was feeling they were growing more comfortable with me, too.'

'If you'll be advised by me . . .'

'Yes, of course.'

'You should take the boys into your confidence, and perhaps Renny too. Tell them the truth. And if you'll give me permission, I'll tell Mrs Ibster what to expect as well.'

So after breakfast, when the boys went outside to feed their dog, Jeremiah followed them. Migs, having polished the plate so that not a scrap of food was left, came racing across to meet him, tail wagging furiously. He bent to pat the animal, of which he was growing fond and which seemed to like him too.

'Boys, I need to tell you something and . . . well, to ask

your help,' he began and stopped, uncertain how to continue. 'I know it's cold but could we sit on the bench over there for a few minutes? Perhaps you'll stay with us too, Renny, so that you'll know what's going on?'

The man nodded and they all went across to the bench, the boys sitting pressed together with a big gap between them and Jeremiah, Renny leaning against a nearby tree trunk.

'I had a letter from my father to say he's coming to visit us today,' Jeremiah began, paused then went on to explain what his father was like.

'Does he hit people?' Isaac asked suddenly.

'No. But he shouts at them and makes them feel uncomfortable. I'm sorry that he'll be spoiling our day, but I can't stop him coming because he's an old man and not well.'

They stared at him solemnly.

'Why are you telling us?' Isaac said at last. 'What do you want us to do?'

And there Jeremiah was stumped. How did you prepare children for a man like his father? So he told them the absolute truth. 'I don't know what you should do. He'll be bad-tempered whatever we say or do. I just – wanted to warn you – didn't want you to get upset.'

'They'll understand your difficulties with your father, sir,' Renny said gently. 'Their own father wasn't easy, either.'

'I don't think he'll expect you to eat luncheon with us. He believes children should be kept out of sight till they're older. But he's bound to want to meet you.'

'They'll be polite to him, I'm sure,' Renny said when the boys sat frowning.

Jeremiah turned to the servant. 'Perhaps you'll tell Miss Cavett about the visit for me, Renny? And tell her that whatever he says, I'm pleased with her work here and shall be making no changes.' As he walked away he realised with surprise how much he had come to trust Renny.

When their cousin had gone indoors again, Isaac said thoughtfully, 'He's a bit frightened of his father, isn't he?'

Renny nodded. 'Not frightened, but nervous perhaps.'

'I don't want a nasty man coming here and spoiling things,' Benjamin said suddenly. 'Things are nicer since Cousin Jeremiah came. He lets us do all sorts of things and he doesn't shout at us.'

'I told you he wasn't like your father.' Then Renny's face grew solemn. 'I think after today it'd be kind of you to eat breakfast and tea with your mother and Jeremiah.'

Isaac swung one leg out and in, kicking at the leg of the bench with the back of his shoe. 'I suppose so.'

Jen came up to tell Gwynna to take Libby down to see her father. The baby had been bathed and was dressed in her night things, so was looking very angelic and she felt proud of her charge as she carried her down.

As usual he took Libby from her and the baby was so used to him now that she gurgled and waved her hands with pleasure. 'Who's Daddy's little girl, then?'

Behind him Mrs Forrett was looking sour-faced. 'You never used to have the other girls brought down.'

'I must have mellowed in my old age.' He smiled down at his daughter. 'Besides, now that she's thriving, this one is the prettiest of them all, not to mention the sunniest natured. The others take after you, always complaining, and I pity their husbands. This one reminds me of my little sister.' He looked across at Gwynna. 'Leave her with me, lass. I'll let you know when I've played with her enough.'

'Um, sir . . .'

'Yes?'

'If you please, could you not joggle her around too much? She's not long been fed and it makes her spit up her food.'

'All right. How's the wet nurse going?'

Gwynna hesitated. 'I think her milk is drying up, sir, and anyway, Libby is old enough to be weaned now. Only . . .'

'Only what?'

'The wet nurse uses the money you give her to feed her own children, though her husband sometimes takes it, and the only food she gets herself is what you give her here.'

'Are you asking me to become a *philanthropist?*'

Gwynna took a step backwards. 'Sorry, sir.'

'Wait! What did you want me to do about the wet nurse?'

'You could employ her as a scrubbing woman instead and give her food instead of money so that her husband can't spend her wages on drink.'

He rolled his eyes and spoke to the ceiling, 'She *does* want me to become a damned philanthropist.' Then he began to chuckle.

'You may leave us now, girl,' Mrs Forrett said icily as her husband continued to laugh. 'And don't forget your place again. It's not up to you to tell your betters what to do.'

Gwynna backed out hurriedly. She was too soft-hearted, she knew. But the wet nurse talked to her while she was feeding Libby, and she couldn't help feeling sorry for the poor woman.

Lost in thought she went upstairs so slowly her feet made almost no noise. When she heard a sound from the maids' bedrooms, she frowned. Who could be up there at this time of day? She crept along the corridor and saw that the door to her own room was wide open when she knew she'd closed it earlier. As she peered round the door frame she let out an exclamation of shock as she saw Betty going through her drawers and rushed inside to pull the other away from them. 'How *dare* you go through my things? What do you think you're doing?'

Betty smirked, not seeming in the least put out at being caught like this. 'I dare do anything because if you don't do what I say from now on, I'll tell the master about the baby you once had. You're rubbish, you are, shouldn't be employed in a decent household.'

Someone else had called her that. Suddenly Gwynna recognised why Betty looked so familiar. 'You're Jabez's sister!'

The other gaped at her. 'How did you know that?'

'You look like him.' She moved forward and snatched her petticoat from Betty. 'What are you doing this for?'

Betty quickly recovered her confidence in her own power. 'Mr Hungerton got me this job, wanted me to keep an eye on what you're doing. He's angry that Mr Robert's wife gave you a reference. I'm going to let him know you're up to your old tricks, fooling people, making them think you're respectable when all the time you're nothing but a slut. He'll probably tell Mr Forrett to dismiss you, then *I* can get your job. I've always wanted to be a nursemaid because it's the easiest job in the house.'

'Get out of my room and don't interfere with my things again.'

'Don't you order me around! I can't believe someone like you is working in a decent household, but you won't last, I promise you that.'

'I'm not a slut, whatever you say! I only ever went with the fellow I was going to marry.' Gwynna took her by surprise, pulling her away from the drawers. 'And don't *dare* go through my things again. What do you think you'll find there?'

'Things you've stolen from the mistress, probably.'

Gwynna shoved her out through the door so violently she fell over.

'I'll get back at you for that!' Betty yelled as she stood up.

Forrett, who'd been about to return his daughter to her nurse, tiptoed back down again with the sleepy infant, wondering what to do about this. Who was this Hungerton to interfere in other people's affairs? By hell, he'd soon find out! He went down to the first floor and yelled up the stairs, 'Gwynna! Come and get Libby!'

The baby stirred in his arms. He looked down at his daughter and remembered the wan, sickly little infant that his wife had drugged with that damned cordial which she still took every day 'for her nerves'. It was thanks to Gwynna that Libby was looking so well and bonny, and he'd not forget that. What's more, he'd seen no sign of her having loose morals. When she walked across the mill yard she didn't look sideways at the men and she dressed modestly. And she had been adopted as family by Nev Linney. He had a lot of respect for Nev.

So all in all, Gwynna had a lot more to recommend her than Betty, who was a lumpy creature, always frowning about the place.

Then Forrett grinned. It'd be amusing to find out exactly what the new maid was up to before he dealt with the situation. A man needed something to cheer him up when he was married to a whining woman.

A few days after Mr Lester's visit Lucas got a message to say that a customer had changed his mind about the work he'd arranged to have done. Lucas couldn't understand why and since he'd already bought the wood for the job, this late cancellation left him in an awkward situation.

He went into the house to get a cup of tea.

'What's wrong, lad?'

His uncle's voice seemed to get clearer by the day and he was starting to move more easily as well. Lucas looked at him, not wanting to burden Fred with his own troubles – except that it would affect his uncle and family as well if things continued to go badly. So he explained about Mr

Lester's visit and warning, about the way he'd been attacked in the street, the feeling he still got sometimes that he was being watched.

'And then today Mr Traynor sent to let me know he'd changed his mind about the work he wanted done on his summer house. His wife wants it done before the warmer weather because parts of the woodwork are so rotten it's not safe for the children to play in. That can only mean he's giving the job to someone else. And I've already bought the wood, had it delivered to his house yesterday.'

There was silence, then Fred said, 'I'm sorry to hear that, lad. You'll have to get a carrier to bring the wood back here for you. Perhaps you could make more of those baby wagons with it to keep yourself busy. Unless I miss my mark, you're going to get steady sales of those.'

Lucas didn't say that he didn't want to spend his life making stick wagons. As he was leaving to organise a carrier, his uncle said casually, 'Oh, nearly forgot. Can Joe run an errand for me later?'

'Yes, of course.'

'And I was thinking . . . I'm getting better every day. Maybe I could start helping you, sanding stuff down maybe, minding the shop, doing the accounts? I'm good with money and figures after working in the mill office for so long.'

'Are you sure you're well enough?'

'Yes. Dr Pipperday's back from London and he popped in to see me yesterday. He says the more I do, as long as I take it gradually and don't tire myself out, the stronger I'll get. Some men who've had a seizure recover fully, he says. I never knew that. I thought I was done for, but he gives me hope.' His voice broke on the last word.

Lucas laid his hand on his uncle's shoulder and gave it a quick squeeze. 'If anyone deserves to recover, you do.'

Fred smiled at him. 'You're a good lad. I'm grateful for

what you've done. I know you gave up a job you liked to come back and help us. I'll make it up to you one day, see if I don't.'

It cheered Lucas up to have someone as wise as his uncle to talk to, it really did. He walked out whistling, feeling more confident that he'd work things out.

At the nearest carrier's yard, he found the owner there, washing down his wagon.

'Can you do a small job for me?' Lucas explained what had happened and saw the man's face change.

'Look, lad, I'll tell you this for your uncle's sake, but don't let on you heard it from me. Tradesmen around the town have been warned not to have any dealings with you. One of my friends told the fellows who warned him to mind their own damned business. That evening some of his windows were broken and his daughter was attacked on her way home from work. He passed the word about what had happened and well, we none of us need that sort of trouble, especially now when we're just getting on our feet again after some lean times. I'm sorry, lad, more sorry than I can say, but I daren't risk my family.'

Lucas walked out, sick to his soul.

His uncle sat in grim silence as he explained what had happened. And this time he had no suggestion to make.

Later that morning Mr Traynor sent a note offering to buy the wood from him – at half the price he'd paid for it.

Lucas glared at the man who'd brought the message. 'Tell Mr Traynor, I'll burn the wood myself before I give it to him for that price.'

The man shuffled his feet, looking uncomfortable. 'If you won't sell it to him, I'm to tell you that he wants it out of the garden within the day.'

'I'll come for it tomorrow. And think on, if any of it goes missing, I'll be reporting the theft! I know *exactly* how many pieces were delivered.' He wasn't sure how he'd remove the wood but he was determined not to be cheated like this. He spent the rest of the day going round to see the other carriers and getting the same response, then trying to borrow a cart or even a hand cart.

That evening there was a knock on the door. Lucas armed himself with a piece of wood before he opened it, feeling relief run through him when he saw Declan Heegan leaning against the doorpost, grinning at him. Two of his men were standing either side of him facing outwards as if to keep an eye on the street.

Declan jerked his head towards the chunk of wood. 'That's a fine way to greet a visitor!'

'There are people causing trouble for me. It pays to be careful, especially after dark.'

'I've been hearing about your problems and I too have been warned not to deal with you.' He grinned. 'I never did like being told what to do, though, and I threw the fellow out. I thought I'd come and have a chat about what's going on. Would you not be inviting a friend in?'

Lucas stepped back. 'Better come and talk in the workshop tonight, so that we can be private.'

'You'll maybe want to bring your uncle in on this. I hear he's getting better and Fred Kemp never was a fool.'

'You know him?'

'I've dealt with him once or twice when I was doing work for Mr Forrett. He's an honest man, doesn't look down on us Irish. I was sorry to hear that he'd had a seizure.'

He followed Lucas inside and waited until Fred was installed on a bench in the workshop before speaking. 'Right then. I've heard about the warnings people have received not to deal with you, also that you need a load of wood removing from Traynor's back garden.' He cocked one eyebrow.

Lucas nodded. 'Except that no one will remove it for me.'

'I will.'

'Oh? I didn't know you were a carrier.'

'I can always get hold of a cart if I want one.'

'Why should you help me?'

Declan grinned. 'I'd be helping us both. I don't like bullies coming into *my* town and telling people what to do and what not to do. My family left Ireland to escape landlords who treated us like slaves and I don't want that sort of thing starting up here. Nor do I want a gang of bullies frightening folk in *my* town. I've a wife and children, a mother, aunts who walk the streets and I'll see them all safe.'

'That's very public spirited of you,' Lucas said.

'No, it's self-interest. I want the freedom to go my own way too.' He chuckled. 'And mostly I stay inside the law these days.'

'Who's doing this, Declan lad?' Fred asked.

'Someone from out of town. There are hints that you've upset a very rich man who'll spare no effort to put you in your place.'

'It's Hungerton, of course. I did two things to upset him: refused to marry and settle down on his estate, and bested him when he tried to trick me into staying by having me arrested for theft.'

'Is that all? I thought you must have ravished his daughter at the very least.' There was silence, then Declan said, 'Well? Do I have a job?'

'How much are you charging?'

'Nothing this time, though I'd be grateful if you'd use my cousin's services whenever you can afterwards. It's his cart, you see.'

'Would I be getting out of the frying pan into the fire?' Lucas wondered.

Declan grinned. 'No. You'll find him a good carrier, charging no more than anyone else.'

Lucas stuck his hand out. His uncle did the same afterwards.

When Declan had left, Fred smiled at Lucas. 'He's all right, that one. Bit of a rogue when he was younger, but now he's anxious to do well and not let his brother shine him down too much. His wife's a whiner, though. I feel sorry for him married to her. I hear she never stops nagging and complaining. He doesn't stay at home much in the evenings.'

'Sounds like my brother's wife, who was picked out for him by Hungerton.' He went across to help his uncle back into the house.

His aunt looked from one to the other anxiously.

'We've found someone to carry the wood for us,' Lucas explained and saw the relief on her face. She'd lost a lot of weight since her husband's seizure and he knew she still worried about the future.

So did he, even more now.

He lay awake for a long time that night, wondering how he could hold out against such a powerful man. Gwynna too had fallen foul of Hungerton. He didn't want her getting hurt.

He made himself more comfortable and his thoughts turned to her now, not his own worries. He really liked her, as he hadn't liked any other young woman he'd ever met. She didn't pretend, or giggle or try to flirt with him. And to see the fond way she looked at that baby made you realise what a good heart she had.

He fell asleep still thinking about her, wondering if he dared do something about his feelings.

14

Jeremiah took the carriage to the station to meet his father's train, leaving the house with a grim certitude that this was going to be an unpleasant experience. His feeling of duty to his father was already in conflict with his desire to protect Maria and her sons.

His parents got off the train, his father stiffly, his mother easily. Well, she was much younger than him. She started fluffing out her skirts and feeling her bonnet to make sure it was straight. As usual she was dressed in dark, plain clothes, though he suspected that she'd have dressed more fashionably if it weren't for her husband's prejudices against 'bedizened hussies'.

He went forward to meet them. 'How are you?' He couldn't force himself to say it was good to see his father because it wasn't. Indeed, he was surprised at how much a stranger he felt to the old man now. It was as if he was seeing him with an even more critical eye than usual – pinch-faced, lips tightly pursed as his gaze darted from side to side. And cowed was the only word to describe Jeremiah's poor little mother. 'I have the carriage waiting, if you'll come this way.'

Once they were sitting inside it, he braced himself to do something he'd decided was necessary in view of his father's strong opinions about certain things. 'I've told the coachman not to drive off until I give him the signal because there's something I need to tell you before we go back to the house.'

Sitting next to his mother and opposite his father, he gave

them a brief outline of what Athol Stott had done, how his cousin had met his end.

Even his father seemed lost for words for a moment or two, then he muttered something about 'the Devil's work'.

'You'll understand, therefore, that Cousin Maria doesn't wish to speak of her late husband and isn't wearing mourning.'

'*Not wearing mourning!*' His father's tone was scandalised. 'She must be a hard-faced woman to dress in colours and her so recently widowed.'

'I've just explained why.'

'Nonetheless, the man was her husband, whom she took for better or worse, making her vows in front of the Lord. She has a duty to behave in a seemly fashion, if only for your sake, and so I shall tell her.'

'I don't wish you to do that, Father. It's none of your business what she wears.'

'It's every God-fearing person's business to speak out against wrong-doing.'

Jeremiah leaned forward. 'I'm not taking you home until I have your word that you won't harangue her about this. And what's more, should you upset her in any way, I shall ask you to leave the house at once.' He saw his father's eyes kindle with indignation and added, 'I shall escort you back to the railway station forcibly, if necessary.'

Mr Channon gasped in outrage. 'You dare to speak to your own father that way!' Suspicion crawled across his face. 'Has the woman snared you in her toils? Swear to me that she hasn't.'

He felt his mother nudge him, but Jeremiah had done with jumping through verbal hoops to keep the peace with his father. 'That's a ridiculous accusation. I've only just met her and she's newly widowed. *She* behaves at all times in a quiet, modest manner. What's more, you should know *me*, your own son, better than to accuse me of such a thing.'

But his father's words echoed in Jeremiah's mind and would not go away because he did find Maria attractive. Very. What was wrong with that? He rapped on the roof of the carriage.

At the house Jeremiah helped his parents out, offered his arm to his mother and walked down the path slowly, accommodating his pace to his father's awkward, shuffling limp. The door opened and Mrs Ibster stood there, the very picture of a good housekeeper in her frilled cap and apron.

'Shall I take your outer clothing, Mrs Channon? Mr Channon? Mrs Stott is waiting for you in the drawing room.'

'And the boys?' Jeremiah asked.

'They're upstairs doing their lessons, sir, but Miss Cavett will bring them down to meet your parents when you send word.'

'Thank you.' He led the way to the drawing room, which they didn't normally use because Maria had invited him to sit with her in her small sitting room in the evenings, a room he much preferred. This place smelled of polish and that indefinable scent of disuse, and he knew it was fanciful, but it seemed as if some angry spirit still lingered here, though more faintly than in the back room. 'Mother, Father, this is Cousin Maria.'

She was standing in front of the fire, a slender figure in grey, and she looked so vulnerable that Jeremiah wanted to take his father's arm and pull him out of the house now, before he could upset her.

She came forward to greet them in her usual quiet way, taking a seat next to Mrs Channon on the sofa as they waited for Mrs Ibster to bring in a tea tray.

Conversation was laboured and when the tea tray was brought in, his father's expression became sour as he studied its contents. 'You eat lavishly between meals, Cousin,' he declared. 'You should watch the pennies and discourage extravagance. I had my doubts about that housekeeper of yours when I saw the frills on her cap and apron.'

Maria blinked in shock at this accusation and glanced across at Jeremiah, as if uncertain how to counter it.

He rolled his eyes to indicate how ridiculous he considered this, then turned to his father. 'Mrs Ibster has been with our cousin for many years, Father, through some troubled times, and she's an admirable housekeeper.'

'The scones are very light,' his mother put in, her voice fluting nervously. 'So you must have a good cook, too.'

'We do,' Maria said.

'A cook-housekeeper is all a family needs,' his father snapped then looked round. 'This is a far larger house than I expected. I should like to see over it.'

The more he could keep his father away from Maria the better, Jeremiah decided. 'I'll take you round as soon as you've finished your cup of tea, Father, and we'll leave the ladies to chat.'

Luckily his father could only walk slowly, so the tour of the house and garden took some time. Jeremiah listened patiently to instructions on how to save money, prevent servants from being extravagant, watching as a sour old man searched for things to criticise. He felt detached from his father, sorry for someone who was so unhappy inside.

Inevitably they made their way up to the second floor and the schoolroom. The door opened to a picture of orderly behaviour, with the two boys sitting writing, one on either side of the governess.

'Extravagant to keep a governess when I dare say there's a perfectly good school in the town,' his father announced, with his usual disregard of anyone's feelings.

Isaac looked up, his expression anxious, so Jeremiah winked at him. The boy blinked in surprise then gave him a quick, shy smile before bending to his work again.

His father immediately began to question the boys about their church-going and study of the Bible. Jeremiah interrupted smoothly to talk about the church, making it sound as if they attended every Sunday. He looked at the schoolroom clock and noted with relief how much time had passed. 'It's nearly time for luncheon. Perhaps we should rejoin the ladies now, Father?'

He turned at the door and gave the boys and their governess another wink before following the old man slowly down the stairs.

When they were all moving into the dining room Maria whispered, 'How did it go?'

'As well as could be expected.' He smiled at her, saw his mother looking at them and guessed that she had noticed his attraction to Maria.

The visit seemed to be going well until his father began to question Maria about how many times they went to church on Sundays. It was a trick the old man had for catching people out, asking the same thing of more than one person.

Before Jeremiah could intervene, Maria said, 'I haven't been to church yet since my husband died, except for the funeral, of course.'

'*What?*' Mr Channon turned to Jeremiah. 'You spoke about church as if you went every Sunday. She *has* corrupted you. The wife of a sinful man like that must be full of wickedness. You must send her away at once before those boys lose their very souls.'

Spittle was running out of one side of his mouth as he thumped the table and began to rant about the Lord's will.

Not even listening to what his father was saying, Jeremiah left his place and went round to Maria. 'I'm sorry for the way he's behaving. Please believe that I don't agree with anything he's saying. I suggest you retire to your sitting room and leave me to deal with him. You don't deserve to be treated like this in your own home and I won't have it.'

His mother looked at him in sheer terror.

As Maria stood up, Jeremiah offered her his arm, intending to lead her out of the room, but his father stepped into their path.

'Get away from her, son. *He that toucheth pitch shall be defiled therewith.* Get away, I say!'

Jeremiah had never seen his father so agitated about nothing and felt even sorrier for his mother, who was staring fixedly down at her plate with tears running down her cheeks. He let go of Maria and moved his father aside, not without a struggle. 'Please leave us, Cousin. I'll deal with this.'

Maria moved to the door, looked back at the older woman, who had a handkerchief to her eyes and whose shoulders were shaking with sobs. 'Goodbye Mrs Channon. I'm sorry your visit has ended like this. I hope to meet you again in happier times.' With great dignity she left the room.

Jeremiah let go of his father. 'We'll finish the meal then I'll take you to the station.'

'You'll listen to me first. You're my only son and I'll not have you associating with *that woman* any longer.' Mr Channon subsided suddenly into a chair, one hand pressed against his chest, his face ashen. He was panting slightly.

Jeremiah went across to his mother. 'I'm sorry, but I can't let him hurt her like that. She had enough to bear from her late husband. Her life with him was truly hell on earth.'

'Poor woman,' she said aloud, then rapidly whispered. 'Your father had hoped to make a match for you with the daughter of a newcomer to our church, came mainly to discuss that today. But he can see, we both can, that you're fond of Maria. The way you look at her is . . . well, your feelings show. And I like her too.' She sighed and looked at her husband. 'He's getting more difficult than ever, doesn't like to be thwarted in anything. I miss you, son, but I'm glad you at least got away.'

He bent to kiss her cheek, wishing she could get away, too.

'What are you two whispering about?'

'We're worrying about your health, Father. You look pale. Let me get you a glass of water.'

Mr Channon gradually got his colour back but didn't eat much of the excellent meal. When the dessert dishes had been removed he looked at his son and said in a voice that scraped harshly, 'If you won't send her away, then I insist *you* come home and leave that woman to bring up her sons on her own. You can keep an eye on the accounts, make sure she doesn't waste the boys' inheritance, but if you're not going to change how she behaves, there's no point in you staying here.'

'I'm needed here and I want to stay. I've grown fond of the boys already and I have a responsibility towards them. What's more, I've decided to open a new practice in Hedderby.'

'If you have so little regard for filial obedience . . .'

Jeremiah interrupted before his father could say anything irremediable. 'I'm four and thirty years old. I think I can be trusted to manage my own life.'

There was a long, fraught silence, then Mr Channon said. 'I shall continue to pray for you, but I forbid you to return to my house until you have come to your senses.'

It was his mother Jeremiah looked at as he said, 'I deeply regret that.'

'Then abjure this woman!'

'No.'

For a moment the two men glared at one another, then Jeremiah sighed and said, 'Since we can't agree, I think you'd better leave. There's a train at two o'clock. I'll ring for the carriage.'

His father hesitated then pressed his hand to his chest again and inclined his head.

Mrs Channon stood up and went to kiss her son on the cheek, shaking her head as if helpless and unhappy with the situation.

No one spoke as they drove to the station. As Jeremiah helped his father into a carriage, Mr Channon turned a look of burning reproach on him then began to ease himself down on his seat.

'Let me know if you need any help,' Jeremiah whispered as he embraced his mother. 'He doesn't look well.'

'He isn't, but he won't give in to his weakness.'

'It's hard on you.'

With a slight shrug of the shoulders, she settled back in her place as her son closed the door of the compartment and stepped back away from the train.

The visit had been as bad as he'd feared, Jeremiah thought as he was driven back. Why had he put up with his father's domineering behaviour for so long? Why had he not rebelled before?

When he got home, he went straight to Maria's sitting room. 'Have you a moment?'

'Of course.' She put down her embroidery.

'I want to apologise to you.'

'*You* have nothing to apologise for, Jeremiah. You stood up for me and I'm grateful for that, though I'm sad to come between you and your parents.'

'It's only my father. My mother says little, but I know she's embarrassed by him too. It turns out he's decided it's time I remarry and wanted to suggest a match to me.'

'Oh?'

'He did that once before and I was unhappy in my marriage. I shan't allow him to choose me another wife.' Was it his imagination or did a look of relief flit across her face? 'If I ever marry again, it'll be for love.'

'I shall *never* marry again.' She shuddered at the thought.

'You shouldn't say that. You know other men aren't like Athol. You're still recovering from an unhappy union, but one day you might meet someone you could love, someone who'd be a kind and caring father to your sons.'

She looked across at him with a slight frown creasing her forehead, but didn't reply and he didn't press her. He hoped he'd planted a seed in her mind because today had shown him that he couldn't ask anything more from life than to love and protect this woman. She'd given him no encouragement, kept her feelings to herself, but he felt she liked him. Perhaps that could grow into something more enduring.

He needed time to get used to his feelings and she needed time to recover from her unhappy marriage, so he wouldn't say anything yet. Smiling at her, he left the room, going into the library at the rear to continue working through the papers in the desk. But the feeling of anger and evil was even stronger here today so he soon gave up trying and went out into the garden instead.

Migs came trotting over to join him and dropped a ball at his feet, sitting grinning at him, with several inches of pink tongue hanging out of the side of his mouth.

Jeremiah picked up the ball and threw it. Migs brought it back again and dropped it, wagging hopefully.

From the schoolroom window the boys watched their guardian play, smiling to see their pet enjoying his company.

Isaac looked at his governess. 'Renny says animals can always tell what a person's really like.'

'He's right.' She looked down at Mr Channon and then sideways at her charges. She was pleased that they were losing their fear of their new guardian, who was a kind man, one who treated her always with great respect. He was good-looking too, though in a stern way because he didn't smile often enough. She sighed. What was she doing, thinking of him when it was obvious he was starting to grow fond of

Mrs Stott? A lowly governess had no right to grow fond of anyone.

Maria, who had gone into the kitchen to speak to Cook, was also watching Jeremiah play with the dog. How had he grown into such a kind man with a father like that? she wondered. He was quiet, too, though his father was a loud, angry person. She smiled in sympathy as Jeremiah's normally solemn face relaxed into a smile and Migs gambolled around him. How had she ever thought he looked like Athol? He was nothing like her husband, in looks or deeds.

Jeremiah had told her once that he'd never had a dog and now that she'd met his father, she could see that he must have had a very bleak upbringing. Perhaps that was why he was so understanding with Isaac and Benjamin.

Her eyes misted as she thought about them. Whatever she'd suffered in her marriage, it had brought her two fine sons, while poor Jeremiah had lost his only child. How deep a sorrow must that be for him?

She didn't move from the window until he came inside again and felt herself flushing slightly as Cook gave her a knowing smile. She finished discussing the next few days' meals then returned to her sitting room. Even as she took up her embroidery, she found herself smiling and thinking of the way Jeremiah's hair had become untidy as he played with the dog, making him look younger, even less like Athol.

Eli went to look for the sketch of the music hall that Trevin had shown them. He was sure it had been rolled up and left in the front parlour. He moved the furniture, wondering if it had fallen beneath something. But there was no sign of it.

Carrie came in and stared at the mess he'd made of the normally tidy room. 'What are you looking for?'

'Trevin's sketch.'

'He came to ask for it back a couple of days ago. I thought we'd finished with it, so I let him have it. Is there something you wanted to check?'

'Yes. Where the other music hall was built. I can't remember.'

She frowned. 'Was it Halifax? No, I think that was the bigger hall we liked as well, only we couldn't fit it on our site. Was it Rochdale? Yes, I think it was. Why do you ask?'

'I met a fellow in town who's an architect and he was looking at the site. He hadn't heard of Trevin and asked me if I'd checked his work.' Eli ran one hand through his hair. 'For some reason, I couldn't get his suggestion out of my mind. I should have done that, shouldn't I? I think you've mentioned it too. But I'm so tired most of the time I can't seem to think straight. But I thought I'd go and look at one of the places Trevin built.'

She was delighted to see some signs of the old Eli surfacing so she didn't let herself get angry that he'd taken the architect's suggestion more seriously than hers. 'Good idea. I'll ask Essie to mind Abigail so that I can come with you. It'll do us both good to get away.' When he smiled at her, she hugged him close and they just stood there for a minute or two.

'I don't know what I'd do without you,' he said huskily from somewhere near her ear.

'You're not going to get a chance to try.'

He pushed her to arm's length and smiled lovingly at her. 'My bonny lass.'

'Oh, Eli.' And then she had to hug him again.

When they pulled apart he spoke with something of his old crispness. 'I'll go and find out about trains. We'll go early to give ourselves time for a good look round and we'll talk to the owners if we can about how well the building went, if Trevin really did build a place so quickly. And Carrie – don't tell anyone outside the family where we're going, what we're doing. We'll keep this to ourselves for the moment, eh?'

They set off at eight the following morning. Eli was as tired as ever and nodded off on the train, jerking awake suddenly with a gasp, then turning as he felt Carrie's hand on his arm.

'It's all right, love.'

She reached out to hold his hand and he clung to her as the nightmare receded, then gave her a shamefaced smile. 'Same dream. You're trapped by flames. Can't get to you. It's . . .' He shuddered, unable to find words strong enough to express how he'd felt at losing her.

They had to change trains, finishing their journey on the Lanky, as the Lancashire and Yorkshire railway was familiarly known. Getting out at the station they walked down towards the town centre, a broad space around the river, which was a reddish colour that day.

A passer-by saw them staring at the water and laughed. 'It's the dye works upstream a bit. The colour changes every day or two. Meks life interestin'.' He chuckled and was about to walk on when Eli stopped him.

'Could you tell us where the music hall is?'

'The what?'

'The music hall. Or perhaps you call it a music saloon, though it's a bit big for that, surely. A theatre.'

'Nay, I know nowt about any music hall. But there's a theatre in Toad Lane.'

'Can you tell us how to get there?'

They followed his directions, but the theatre was nothing like the sketch.

They asked several passers-by about a music hall, but received only blank stares and shakes of the head.

'We must have been mistaken,' Eli said at last. 'It must be in some other town.'

Carrie shook her head. 'It wasn't. I can remember quite clearly seeing the word "Rochdale" on the bottom right hand corner of the sketch.'

'You must be thinking about another sketch. I'll ask Trevin tomorrow where the other music hall was built.'

She didn't say anything, but the more she thought about it the more certain she was that Trevin had said one like it had been built in Rochdale. When they were pulling into Hedderby, she clutched Eli's arm and said urgently, 'Don't tell him we went to Rochdale. He'll take a huff, for sure, and he's hard enough to deal with already.'

'I'm not stupid, love. Leave it to me.'

15

Gwynna looked out of the nursery window to see Betty talking earnestly to a man behind the sheds at the rear of the house. Both of them were hidden from those in the yard but she could see them clearly from up here. The man had his back to her, but as she watched he patted Betty on the shoulder, pulled his hat down, slipping out by a side gate which the maid locked behind him.

She couldn't see him well enough to make out his features, but he looked familiar. As she got Libby ready for an outing she wished it'd rain, because she was afraid of meeting her parents again.

Mrs Forrett came to the door of the parlour as Gwynna carried the baby downstairs and looked at her sourly. 'Make sure you don't leave her anywhere on her own.'

'Of course I won't. I wouldn't!'

'You can never tell with people like you. And don't go into the back streets. *You* may feel at home there, but they're filthy and no place for *my* child.'

Gwynna was stunned at this unwarranted attack and wondered what had caused it? Normally, Mrs Forrett took little interest in either her or the baby. Keeping tight control of her anger, she said, 'No, Mrs Forrett.' She went through the kitchen to the rear storeroom where they kept the stick wagon, sat Libby in it and buckled the leather strap round the child's waist. How sensible of Lucas to put in this strap! You couldn't be too careful with babies.

At the mill gates the overlooker was talking to a drayman, whose cart had blocked the way out. The overlooker was standing in front of the smaller gate to one side. He stopped talking but didn't move, running his eyes up and down her body in a way she hated.

'Going out?' he asked.

'Yes. Can you let me pass, please?'

'In a minute. It doesn't hurt to say hello to someone, especially when you work so near to that person.'

Forrett came out of the office, saw what was happening and joined them. 'I've told you before, Benting, to keep away from my servants. I don't employ that sort of girl in my house.'

Benting gave a sneering laugh. 'Don't you, though? Then you've made a mistake with this one. We all know she bore a baby out of wedlock and—'

Forrett reached out and grabbed his overlooker by the front of his shirt. 'I know about Gwynna's past and I know how it happened. Don't forget that Patrick worked here. What I'm wondering is why *you* are taking an interest in spreading gossip about her.'

Benting shrugged. 'I just thought you should know.'

'She told me herself before I took her on.'

'Clever bitch, isn't she? Be careful she's not too clever.'

'Enough!' Forrett's sharp tone was backed up by a jerk of his head that said his overlooker had better get back to work, then he turned to look at Gwynna, his expression thoughtful. After a moment he bent towards his daughter and let her play with his fingers for a minute or two, murmuring endearments to her.

'Well, I'd better get on.' He kissed Libby then stood up, his smile fading. 'Take yourself off now, lass. I'll make sure Jack Benting doesn't bother you again.'

'Thank you, Mr Forrett. I'm grateful.'

'And you've no need to worry about your parents, either. I've sent word they're to stay away from you.'

She let out a shuddering sigh of relief. Before she could thank him he'd gone striding back into the office, so she went out of the gate and began pushing the wagon slowly up and down the main street. In spite of what Mr Forrett had said, she kept an eye out for her parents, though they didn't usually come into the centre of the town and they certainly didn't shop at places like Mr Marker's Emporium.

She looked across at the messy space where the Pride had once stood. There were deep holes and piles of the muck dug out of them piled up everywhere around the holes. The street would look very grand when the new music hall was finished. Judging by the size of those holes, the cellars were going to be enormous. Carrie said they would be needed to store the equipment, but Gwynna couldn't picture what sort of equipment a theatre would need.

When they got back to Mill House, Libby was hungry and was grizzling, so Gwynna asked Cook for some warm milk and porridge for the child. Cook sniffed and said it was all right for some, giving orders like their betters. Gwynna stared at her in shock, because the woman had been much friendlier lately.

'I wasn't trying to order you around, Cook, but Libby's hungry and you don't usually like other people doing things in your kitchen. I'll make the porridge myself if you want, though.'

'That you'll not. It's Betty's job and she'll do it. The lazy young besom is always trying to wriggle out of work.'

Gwynna would far rather have made the porridge herself than leave it to Betty but didn't dare protest.

When the other maid brought up a lumpy mess, Gwynna stared at it in disgust. 'How do you expect the child to eat that, let alone thrive on it? Can't you make porridge properly?'

Betty shrugged. 'They'll eat anything, babies will.'

As Gwynna put a spoonful in the baby's mouth, Libby grimaced and spat the food out again, so she tasted it herself, shocked to find it'd been made with sour milk. Carrying Libby on one arm and holding the bowl in her hand, she went back down to the kitchen.

'What do you think you're doing, Betty?' she demanded.

'Don't know what you mean.'

Cook turned round. 'What's up now?'

'She's made this with sour milk.'

'It wasn't!' Betty protested, but she flushed and looked a bit ashamed. 'She didn't eat it, did she?'

'Of course she didn't. It tastes awful.' Gwynna plonked the bowl down in front of Cook.

'I didn't realise.'

Gwynna could see that Betty was lying.

Before the older woman could touch the bowl, Betty grabbed it, pretending to miss and sending it flying to smash on the floor.

'I'd rather make Libby's food myself, Cook,' Gwynna begged. 'You can see what a mess *she* made of the porridge.'

'I'll make you some.' Cook took a pan from the rack and poured some milk in it, setting it on the stove. 'Go and start washing them dishes and pans, Betty. And bring me in that sour milk so that we can throw it away.' When the girl had gone into the scullery, shooting an angry glance at Gwynna as she passed, Cook said gruffly, 'I'd watch my back if I were you.'

'What do you mean?'

She glanced over her shoulder and lowered her voice. 'She's making up to the mistress, who likes a bit of flattery. I'll see Betty doesn't interfere with Libby's food again, but you'd better eat your meals down here from now on because I don't know what might happen to the food on the way upstairs.' She fell silent as Betty stuck her head through the door.

'I need some more scouring sand, Cook.'

'Go and get some, then. You know where it's kept. And where's that sour milk?'

'Sorry, Cook. I must have tipped it away.'

The older woman shook her head and concentrated on the porridge. 'I've some stewed apple left. Shall I mash a bit and put it on the porridge?'

'That'd be lovely, Cook.' Gwynna waited until the food was ready and took it upstairs herself. She was beginning to worry about her future here. Mr Forrett had looked at her strangely this morning, Betty was up to something and her mistress had definitely taken against her.

She'd tread very carefully from now on, but she was beginning to think that if you made one mistake in life, people held it against you for ever.

Declan and one of his men brought the wood round to Lucas's workshop midway through the morning. He was sporting a big bruise on the chin and his companion had a puffy lip.

Lucas looked at them in surprise. 'What happened?'

'Couple of fellows tried to stop us getting the wood.'

'Mr Traynor?'

'No. He wasn't there and if his wife was in, she didn't come outside, even after we'd chased away the divvils who attacked us.' He cocked one eyebrow at Lucas. 'Your friend Hungerton's behind this as well, I suppose?'

'Who else could it be?'

Lucas felt very depressed as he helped them stack the wood and then got on with his work. How could you hold out against a man with so much money to spend on getting his revenge? And what would his former employer try next?

★

Selwyn Hungerton was asking himself the same question as he walked back from the stables after his morning ride. Suddenly, just as he was turning a corner, he saw his father ahead of him. The old man glanced round furtively and disappeared behind the harness room. Puzzled, Selwyn followed, stepping into the nearby shrubbery to avoid being seen. Peering from behind two bushes, he saw his father talking to Jabez, then giving him some money. The former groom had recently been appointed as personal outdoor servant to 'the master', a job which seemed to involve him being away quite often. Money was also passed to Jabez's rough-looking companion – quite a lot of money.

What the hell was his father paying for? Selwyn crept closer and what he overheard made him feel disgusted. It wasn't just Kemp who had upset the old man, apparently, but the nursemaid his father had dismissed.

It seemed the lass had found herself another job and his father was not only planning to get her dismissed but to send her back to where she and whores like her belonged – the lowest gutters. Selwyn remembered Gwynna, who hadn't seemed a bad 'un to him, and remembered also that it was his daughter Jane who'd got her dismissed. That child was turning into a damned busybody, always poking her nose into things that didn't concern her. He'd caught her going through his drawers only the other day, and had boxed her ears for her.

Lester had been right. Selwyn hadn't wanted to believe their former land agent when he'd listed some of the things his father had done over the years, but he did now. And it not only made him feel dashed uncomfortable, but worried him. What would happen if news of such doings got out, especially these latest plans the three were discussing now? What if his father was caught and arrested? Think of the scandal.

Only what was Selwyn to do about it? You couldn't talk to his father lately.

He crept away before they saw him, walking on through the shrubbery towards the house. He paused for a moment as he tried to put things together in his mind. Jabez was obviously the middle-man who carried out his father's plans. Selwyn had always disliked the man, but his father set a lot of store on employing staff from families on the estate.

Jabez wasn't the only employee whom Selwyn mistrusted. The new land agent who had recently been appointed by his father without reference to his son's wishes was a surly fellow, who had put up rents and was treating the tenants badly when they had difficulty paying. One family had been thrown out of their cottage already and they were good people, too. Selwyn had protested to his father about that, but had been told to mind his own business.

Only it was his business if his father brought the Hungerton name into disrepute. And anyway, he was the heir, wasn't he? His father was nearing eighty and might be supposed to have only a year or two to live, so it'd soon be on Selwyn's shoulders. The old man had run mad. That was the only possible explanation. What did it matter if one carpenter left the estate? Kemp could be replaced easily enough. And to hound a poor lass who'd no doubt had a hard life and was now trying to better herself wasn't the act of a gentleman.

He heard someone screeching with laughter, not happy laughter, but the sort that meant a female was getting the better of someone. Looking through the foliage towards the house, he saw his daughter evading the governess, refusing to go back indoors and mocking the poor woman. He strode out of the shrubbery just as Jane ran towards it and caught hold of her.

At first she fought him viciously, biting his hand and

kicking him. Then she suddenly realised who was holding her and froze. 'Father!'

He clipped her round the ears.

'Ow!'

'What the hell do you think you're doing, Jane? Stand there and don't move till I give you permission, or I'll tan your backside for you till you can't sit down.' He sucked his hand, which was stinging where she'd bitten him.

'Sorry, Father. I was just playing.'

The governess came panting up to join them. 'She wasn't playing, sir, she was misbehaving again. I'm not used to such a – a *hellion* and I won't put up with it any longer. After I remonstrated with her yesterday, she went to your father and pretended I'd hit her, so he threatened to dismiss me. Only he'll not have the opportunity because I'm hereby giving you my notice, to take effect immediately. You may pay me for the time I've worked or not, as you choose. *That* is up to your conscience. I'm going to start packing this very minute and I'd be obliged if you'd tell someone to drive me to the station.' She turned and marched towards the house, her back rigid.

Jane giggled. 'Good riddance. She's a stuffy old thing.'

Selwyn shook his daughter hard and kept hold of her as she squealed and tried to wriggle out of his grasp. 'She was your governess and you were behaving like a gutter child. Well, you'll regret what you've done, I'll make sure of that.' He saw that she didn't believe him but didn't tell her what he intended to do. When he let go of her she ran off down the side of the house.

This was the third governess Jane had got rid of in the past twelve months. The child was running wild and his father encouraged her. It had to stop.

It was his wife's job to keep an eye on her, but Anthea said she couldn't control Jane and since she was expecting her third baby in a few weeks, they should spare her such upsets, they really should.

Nurse had taken him aside only yesterday to ask him to do something about Miss Jane, who was bullying her little brother, pinching him black and blue if you took your eyes off him for a minute.

It was no wonder Selwyn preferred to spend his time out riding or visiting friends who lived in places further south, where the terrain was better for hunting and there wasn't a complaining woman and a bullying father making his life miserable. When he inherited the estate, he was going to sell it and buy a place nearer his friends, though he hadn't told anyone that yet. If his father knew, he'd probably disinherit him.

It was no wonder his brother had quarrelled with their father and left home. Come to think of it, Margaret had warned him about Jane as well.

Well, he'd had *enough*. It was time to do something and by hell, he was going to do it. First he'd deal with his daughter then he'd turn his attention to his father.

Determination humming through him, Selwyn walked across to the house and went to find the gentleman's magazine in which he'd seen the advertisement.

The morning following his father's visit, Jeremiah stopped short in the doorway of the dining room. There were three people sitting at the breakfast table waiting for him, all looking slightly anxious. He smiled at them. 'How nice to have breakfast together. Thank you for joining us, boys.' He went to take his place at the head of the table.

Maria looked along the table at him and smiled uncertainly. 'Perhaps you'd say grace?'

He did so, making it brief, then waited as she rang the bell.

Mrs Ibster and the maid brought in several covered dishes and set them in the middle of the table.

'I thought it would be better if we served ourselves,' Maria said, looking at him uncertainly.

Her voice wobbled, betraying her nervousness, and Jeremiah had a sudden urge to hug her and assure her that it would be perfectly all right. 'What have we got here?' he said instead, which was a stupid remark but gave him the opportunity to lift the lids and inspect the contents of the dishes. 'May I help you to something, Cousin Maria?'

When he'd served everyone and covered up the dishes again, Maria took up her knife and fork and the boys did the same.

Jeremiah sought desperately for something to say, preferably something that wasn't a mere platitude, but nothing came to mind. What he really wanted to do was apologise to all three of them for his father's behaviour the previous day. Then he realised that he had fared better with the boys by being honest about the old man, so decided to do so. 'I'm sorry about yesterday, boys,' he said. 'If I could have prevented my father from coming here, I would have done.'

'He shouts a lot,' Benjamin said. 'We heard him even up in the schoolroom.'

'He always has shouted a lot.'

'When you were a boy, did he hit you?' Isaac asked.

Jeremiah heard Maria's quick intake of breath. 'No. But he punished me in other ways, mainly by locking me in my room or making me pray on my knees for hours. I was always afraid of upsetting him.'

They nodded gravely and began to eat.

'Why did your father come here?' Isaac asked a short time later. '*He* isn't our guardian, you are.'

'He wanted to talk to me about something. Only I wouldn't do what he wanted.'

'Is that why he shouted?'

Jeremiah nodded.

They continued to eat in silence until Maria said, 'I liked your mother, Cousin Jeremiah.'

'I like her too. She has an uncomfortable life with my father and I feel sorry for her, but there's nothing I can do about that.' He put a forkful of ham into his mouth and chewed it thoughtfully, then risked broaching an idea that had occurred to him a few days previously. 'I wondered if you three would like an outing to Manchester? I have some friends there whom I visit regularly. I haven't seen them for a while, but I think you'd like my friend's wife, Maria. They have a son and daughter about the same age as you two lads and they have a dog as well.'

Three pairs of eyes were staring at him as if they didn't understand what they were hearing.

'Have I said something wrong?' he asked in bewilderment. 'Only it's nice sometimes to go out for the day so I just thought . . . but it's all right if you don't want to come with me.'

'I'd like it very much,' Maria said. 'I can't remember the last time I went anywhere, and the boys have never ridden on a train.'

He looked at her in surprise.

'Their father didn't like us to go away from home,' she said quietly, then turned to her sons. 'What do you think, boys? Would you like an outing?'

The silence dragged on for a long time as Isaac frowned down at his plate and Benjamin looked at his brother for guidance. When this wasn't forthcoming, the younger boy said suddenly, 'I'd like to go on a train.'

Isaac looked at his guardian as if trying to understand what lay behind the invitation, then at his mother, who nodded encouragingly. He shrugged. 'I suppose we could go.'

Jeremiah filtered out the breath he'd been holding. 'We can go any Saturday, whenever your mother thinks best.'

'Next weekend is too soon,' she said. 'Perhaps the weekend after? That'll give you time to write to your friends and make sure it's all right if we come with you. And I'd like to get some new clothes made for the boys, if that's all right.' She looked down at her own dress. 'Do you think they'd be offended that I'm not wearing black?'

'No. They don't get upset easily. Andrew is a gentle giant, another architect, and Sissy is always great fun to be with. She's a happy soul and her children take after her.'

'You need some new clothes, too, Mother,' Isaac said suddenly. 'You've had that dress for years.'

'Good idea! I'll leave you to organise that, Cousin Maria.' Jeremiah saw Benjamin eyeing the serving dishes again. 'Do you want another helping? There's plenty.'

The boy nodded.

He glanced at Isaac's plate. The food had hardly been touched. He didn't comment on that, but chatted about Migs and suggested buying him a new ball. Isaac ate a few more mouthfuls, then pushed the remainder to one side of his plate, hiding it under the knife and fork as if he expected to be reprimanded. Jeremiah saw Maria's eyes go from her son to the plate and that anxious look come into them again, so gave her a quick smile to let her know he didn't intend to comment.

He was settling to work in the back room, still hating the feel of the place, when there was a knock on the door. 'Come!'

Maria stepped into the room, staying by the door. 'I won't disturb you for long. I just wanted to thank you.'

'What for?'

'Being so kind to the boys.'

He smiled ruefully. 'I'm feeling my way, still considering every remark before I let it out. I'm glad you think I'm doing all right, but it's partly due to Renny giving me advice.'

'You're doing wonderfully. In fact, I still can't get used to it, how easy life is with you.'

For a few moments they stood motionless, their eyes meeting, warmth creeping into both their faces, then she turned to leave.

He didn't try to stop her. But after the door had closed on her he turned round, to be met by such a feeling of fury that he took an involuntary step backwards. A paper blew off the desk and the fire roared up in the grate.

He fumbled behind him for the door handle, turned it and left the room in a hurry, making his way out into the garden, where he gulped in great breaths of fresh air.

'Is something wrong, Mr Channon?'

He turned to see Renny looking at him anxiously and blurted out what was on his mind. 'Do you believe in ghosts?'

Renny nodded.

'Do you think it's possible that *he*, Athol Stott, is haunting the house?'

'Have you seen him, sir?'

Jeremiah shivered. 'No. But I've felt such anger and hatred in that back room. And just now, the papers blew about for no reason.'

Renny frowned. 'That's where he used to sit. I hadn't realised that the presence was quite so strong because I don't go in there now. May I see how it feels, sir?'

Jeremiah nodded and hesitated, then followed the other man back into the house, feeling reluctant to go into the room again. He wasn't usually a coward.

The papers from the desk were scattered everywhere and a red hot coal had fallen from the fire, to lie smouldering on the rug.

'This is dangerous!' Jeremiah said involuntarily. 'And there was no way that coal could have fallen so far from the fire.'

Renny turned to give him one of those cool stares. 'If you'll trust me with this, I'll see what I can do. In the meantime, perhaps you could work somewhere else? There's a spare bedroom next to yours. Don't use *his* old bedroom. I'll bring your things upstairs. Better you don't come into this room again for a while, or let the others in.'

When he thought about it later, Jeremiah couldn't believe he'd acted so foolishly. Ghosts, indeed! He marched downstairs again, determined to confront his fears.

But he had only to open the door of that room to realise there was something dark and dangerous inside it. He closed it again hastily.

16

As she was waiting to rinse out some of Libby's clouts in the scullery, Gwynna heard a knock at the kitchen door.

'Will you see who that is?' Cook asked. 'I've got mucky hands and I don't know where that Betty's got to.'

Gwynna found Lucas standing there and couldn't help smiling at him. Then she noticed a lad hovering behind him. 'Hello, Ted!'

'We've a small job to do for Mr Forrett.' Lucas smiled back at her so warmly she felt as if the sun was shining more brightly and Ted grinned at her, hefting a bag of tools in his hand as if to emphasise why he was there.

Someone shoved Gwynna aside so roughly she bumped her elbow against the wall and Betty planted herself in the doorway, scowling at Lucas. 'What do *you* want here?'

He looked at her in surprise. 'I might ask the same of you.'

'I work here.'

As she started to close the door in his face, he put out his arm to stop her. 'Hold on a minute. Mr Forrett sent for me. I just passed him in the yard and he told me to come into the kitchen and wait for him here. Oh, and to tell Cook he'll be wanting his tea in five minutes.'

She let out a snort of irritation. 'I suppose you'd better come in then, but wipe your feet properly.'

Gwynna stared to hear Betty speak so curtly and was even more surprised when the other girl led the way into the kitchen and stood there with her arms folded, as if on guard.

When she didn't explain the newcomers' presence there, Gwynna took it upon herself to say, 'Mr Forrett's told Mr Kemp to wait for him in the kitchen, Cook. He's come to do a job for the master.'

'You can sit over there.' Cook pointed to a chair set against the wall and Lucas took it, Ted standing beside his master.

As Gwynna went across to make sure Libby was securely tied to one of the other chairs, Lucas said, 'I could make you a baby chair that'd hold her more safely than that.'

'We don't need any suggestions from you,' Betty snapped.

'What suggestion did you make, Kemp?' Mr Forrett stepped into the room. 'And I'll thank you to get about your business, Betty, and to keep your nose out of what doesn't concern you. You're not running this house, *I* am.'

She flounced out of the room and Cook closed her eyes for a minute.

'Is she a good worker, Cook?' Forrett asked.

'She does all right, I suppose. The mistress likes her.'

He grinned. 'Ah. She'll be asking me for a lady's maid again at this rate.' He looked thoughtful. 'Might be the best for everyone.' He stood for a moment, then turned back to Lucas. 'Right, Kemp, let me show you what I want doing, then you can tell me about this baby chair of yours.' He led the way up the stairs.

Cook watched them go, then turned to Gwynna. 'The master's had to be mistress as well as master in the past few years and he does things his own way. You never know what he'll tell you to do next, but you're all right as long as you do it.' She turned back to her cooking and when Betty came back with a request from her mistress for a cup of tea, told her to prepare it herself.

Gwynna took her charge back upstairs. This wasn't a day for a walk, with a chill wind blowing and showers knifing down at regular intervals. She got out some toys she'd made herself and some wooden building bricks Mr Forrett had brought home one day, setting Libby on a blanket on the floor to play with them. It wouldn't be long before the baby was crawling, then she'd suggest getting a gate fitted across the top of the stairs. 'Eh, you're a bonny little thing!'

Without thinking Gwynna plumped down on the rug and smacked a kiss on Libby's cheek, then began to play with her.

Forrett, who had been watching them from the corridor, smiled and went back down the stairs, leaving the carpenter to put locks on the maids' rooms. As he reached his wife's bedroom the door opened.

'I thought it was you. Can you spare me a minute, James?'

He stopped. 'Is it important, Nenny? That mill doesn't run itself, you know.'

'*I* think it's important.'

'All right. Make it quick.' He followed her into the over-heated room, folded his arms and leaned against the door. 'Well, what is it?'

'I was wondering if you could see your way to hiring me a lady's maid. Now that I'm better, I'd like to go out and visit my friends, but I need to dress better. And for that I need a maid – as I've told you before. Only you never listen to me, never care that I—'

He'd been studying her, eyes narrowed, but when she started on her old complaints, he cut her off short. 'I might agree to it if it gets you out of the house and you stop taking that damned cordial of yours.'

She looked at him in shock.

'Don't think I don't know you've been getting that girl to buy it for you.'

'It makes me feel so much calmer, James. Please, I *need* it.'

'Then let's agree that I'll keep the cordial and give you

one dose in the morning and one in the evening – though that's all you'll get. If we can agree on that, you can have your maid.'

Her face brightened.

'I'll contact the agency and see if they can find you one who won't turn up her nose at us like that starched-up creature you hired after our Melly was born.'

'Um – I was thinking of asking Betty to do it.'

'Betty, eh? What does an ugly piece like her know about being a lady's maid?'

'Not much, I admit, but she's very willing. I'd far rather train someone myself, James.'

'All right. Give me your bottle of cordial and I'll go down and see the girl myself.'

'I'll bring it down to you in a minute.'

He laughed and strode across to her bookshelf, taking out some books from the bottom shelf and removing a dark glass bottle from behind them. 'You'll have to get up earlier in the day to best me, Nenny, as you should know by now.'

He went downstairs, whistling loudly, and found Betty standing in the hall, a feather duster in her hand. 'Come into the parlour for a minute.'

She followed him, looking apprehensive.

'My wife wants a lady's maid and she wants *you*. I'll agree to it on certain conditions.' He shook the bottle at her. 'One, you don't buy her any more of this stuff. If you do, you'll be out on your ear. I'll get the cordial and I'll dole out her dose from now on. You can fetch it from me each morning and evening.'

'Yes, sir.'

'And secondly, you are to leave Gwynna alone.'

'I don't know what you mean, sir.'

'Oh yes, you do. And you'll not last long in this house if you underestimate me. Not much gets past me.' He leaned forward and said very slowly and emphatically, 'I'm master here and them as don't obey my orders don't stay. You must decide who you want to work for now, mustn't you? Oh, and I'll give you a rise to twenty-five pounds a year if you prove you can do the job of lady's maid.'

She swallowed hard.

'Well, what's it to be?'

'I'd like the job, sir, and I'll do my very best to please.'

'Aye, well make sure you please *me* first of all because I'm the one as pays the wages here.'

When he'd gone she hugged herself and spun round, thrilled to have got the thing she'd been angling for. Then she stopped and began to frown. This was a good chance for her, the best she was ever likely to have, and she didn't want to lose the job. She daren't risk getting on the wrong side of Mr Forrett – who would? – but she didn't want to get on the wrong side of her brother, either. Or Mr Hungerton. Particularly Mr Hungerton.

Carrie confronted Eli after breakfast. 'You haven't arranged any music evenings at the church hall yet. Have you given up on the idea?'

He shook his head. 'No. But I don't seem to be good at pulling the details together like I used to. I start something, have to go out for a breath of fresh air, then I can't seem to get going properly again.'

'Why don't we do it together? I don't know why you haven't included me in it anyway. I'm fretting for lack of something to do. I don't think I was cut out to be a mother and housekeeper – I had enough of that when I was bringing up my brothers and sisters – and anyway, Essie's so efficient that she doesn't really need me here.'

He hesitated, looked down at his feet and confessed, 'I still keep trying to hide from you how badly I'm doing things.'

She looked out of the window, knowing he was better out of doors. 'Let's go for a walk and talk it through.'

He pulled her to him for a crushing hug. 'There's no man as lucky as me when it comes to a wife.'

She raised one hand to push away a lock of hair that had fallen on his forehead. 'Maybe it's because I love you.'

When he kissed her, for a moment it was as if she had the old Eli back and she clung to him, desperate to keep him. But then he pushed her away and went to get their outdoor things.

The walk was a stroke of genius, she decided as they strode up a lane that led to the edge of the moors. He definitely didn't get as agitated when he was out of doors. They discussed the music evening in great detail, stopping from time to time for her to pull out a notebook and write down the details. She had to ask him to use his pocket knife to sharpen her pencil twice. By the time they got back she had several pages of notes.

It still filled her with wonder that she could read and write so easily now. As the eldest of ten, she'd not had much schooling, since her slapdash mother couldn't afford the school pence and needed her at home. But since she married, Carrie had seized every opportunity to learn. She didn't even care what she learned, just as long as she was filling her hungry mind with knowledge.

It was decided that the first music evening was to be held on the Saturday of the following week and admission would be by ticket only. Raife would handle ticket sales at the side door of Linney's and perhaps Mr Marker would sell tickets at his emporium.

'We can call on him tonight when we go to look at the site,' Carrie said, because they went to inspect progress every day.

That evening they found the bricklayers had started work on the walls that supported the sides of the cellars.

'Trevin's getting things done quickly,' Eli said admiringly. 'He wasn't lying about that, at any rate.'

When they went across the street to the emporium, Mr Marker came to serve them himself. 'I shall be delighted to be of assistance,' he assured them when they asked about selling tickets.

'As a thank you, perhaps you and your family would attend the performance as our guests?' Eli asked, knowing how much the Markers had enjoyed the music saloon.

'It will be our pleasure.'

As they walked out of the shop, Eli noticed a tall, thin figure standing at the edge of the site, studying what had been done. 'That's the architect fellow I told you about. Let's go and have a word with him.'

They walked quickly back along the street and Eli introduced Carrie, then nodded towards the site. 'It's coming on nicely, isn't it?'

'I suppose so.'

Carrie saw Mr Channon's frown, heard the uncertainty in his voice. 'But . . . ?' she prompted.

He looked at her. 'But, Mrs Beckett, I would have had a double wall to support the sides of the cellar, and two lots of pillars in the middle, not one, to support the stage.' He gave her a wry smile. 'I like to be very sure indeed that the building will not fall down.'

'You think Trevin's skimping?' she asked, turning to stare at the big hole again.

'He must have done the calculations for a building this size, but I'm a little – doubtful.' He spread his hands in a helpless gesture. 'You must ask him. I really shouldn't be discussing this with you.'

'I'd be grateful if you did. We know so little about what is needed.'

But he shook his head. 'I'm afraid it would be

unprofessional of me to continue this discussion. I'd better be getting back.' He tipped his hat to her, nodded to Eli and walked off briskly along the street.

'You'll have to ask Trevin about those cellar walls,' Carrie said as they walked back to Linney's.

'*I'll* have to ask him? We'll do that together, surely?'

She knew why he was saying that, but she shook her head. 'Trevin hates discussing things with me, always gets on his high horse. I'm sure you'll do better if you speak to him on your own.'

'I'll go and see that site foreman of his tomorrow and find out when Trevin's coming for a visit.'

But that night Eli's nightmares were so bad that she insisted he take some of the drops Dr Pipperday had given him to help him sleep, but which he hated because he said they left him with a thick head the next day.

By the time he woke up and got ready, it was afternoon and Trevin had been and gone.

'Maybe I could help you, sir?' the foreman asked.

'I was wondering how you calculate the strength of the retaining walls for the cellar. One thickness of bricks doesn't seem enough to me.'

The man smiled. 'I think you can leave that sort of thing to Mr Trevin. He's had a lot of experience at building.'

'You've been with him a while, have you?'

'Yes. He knows what he's doing.'

'He built a theatre a bit like this in Rochdale, I think he said.'

'No, it was in Meldon.' His voice became mocking. 'And it's still standing.'

'That's very reassuring.'

'There you are,' Eli said to Carrie as they walked away. 'The foreman's been with him for some time and he says Trevin knows what he's doing.' He grinned at her. 'But best of all,

I found out where the other theatre is. Not Rochdale, Meldon.'

'We'll go there and check it out, then. I'll feel a lot better when I've seen one he's built.'

As Gwynna was walking up and down Market Street pushing Libby in the wagon, a man bumped against her so hard he sent her staggering into the road right into the path of a cart drawn by two huge horses. If a passer-by hadn't caught hold of her skirt and dragged her back on to the pavement she shuddered to think what would have happened to her and the baby.

'Eh, lass, are you all right?'

'Yes, thank you. I'm grateful for your help.'

The man turned round to stare along the street. 'That fellow wasn't looking where he was going. He's run off now or I'd have given him a piece of my mind, I would that.'

She knew it was no accident; she'd been pushed deliberately and by someone who wanted to harm her, who didn't even care that the baby might have been hurt too.

As she set off again, she heard footsteps behind her and turned to see Joe, the orphan Lucas had taken in.

'That fellow went up to the Black Bear.' He fell in step beside her. 'I followed him, but I didn't go inside the pub or he'd have seen me.'

'I didn't notice you running after him.'

'I didn't want folk to notice me.' He looked down at the baby. 'My mam had a baby once, but it died. This one's nice and fat, isn't it?'

'Yes, she is.'

'I'd better get back now. Been doing an errand for Mr Kemp.'

Within seconds he'd vanished from sight, a slight figure easily lost among the people who crowded the pavements in the centre of town at busy times of day.

She decided not to tell Mr Forrett about the near fall this time. If he thought she couldn't look after Libby, he might sack her. And after all, it might have been an accident that the man pushed her.

But in her heart she knew it hadn't been and she couldn't help wondering if it was Mr Hungerton behind it and if so, what he would do next. Was he trying to drive her away from Hedderby? She couldn't understand why he was pursuing her.

What worried her most was whether he'd try to hurt her friends to get at her. She shivered at the mere thought of that, because if he did start on Nev and Essie, she'd have to leave, just have to. She couldn't think where she'd go, though, how she'd live.

Joe slipped into the workshop and handed a piece of paper to Lucas, who read the note quickly and smiled at his diminutive helper. 'Good lad.'

'I saw that lass while I were out, the one you like.'

Surprised, Lucas stared at Joe, who stared solemnly back. 'Oh? Which lass would that be?'

'Gwynna. I like her too. She's got a nice smile an' the baby's nice too.' He fiddled with a pile of sawdust, pushing it round with his foot. 'A fellow shoved her into the road today an' if another fellow hadn't of grabbed her skirt an' pulled her back, she'd've fell under a cart.'

'*What?*'

'I seed the fellow do it. Wasn't an accident.'

'Who was it?'

Joe shrugged his shoulders. 'Don't know. But I followed him for a bit an' he went into the Black Bear.'

'Gwynna wasn't hurt?'

'No. I went back an' she were a bit pale, but she weren't hurt.'

'You did well, Joe.'

The urchin grinned. 'Folk don't notice lads like me. I see a lot of things, I do.'

'If you see that fellow again, tell me.'

'I will. Can I make summat with wood today?'

'No, but you can sand down a piece for me, and watch me and Ted. You're too little to do the heavy work yet, but you can learn a lot from watching and doing the little jobs.'

'Aw right.'

Lucas kept an eye on the lad, who had settled easily into the household, always cheerful, always willing to lend a hand – and everlastingly hungry, as if he was making up for the lean year he'd spent fending for himself on the streets. Joe followed Ted around whenever he could, modelling himself on the older boy, hanging on the other's every word. And Ted, who only had younger sisters not brothers, seemed to enjoy the lad's company and near hero worship.

Life would be so pleasant, Lucas thought with a sigh, if he wasn't short of work. People who had talked about jobs now crossed the street to avoid him, hardly anyone came to enquire about the cost of doing something and if it hadn't been for the baby wagons he was making – and now the baby chair for Forrett – he'd have had nothing coming in. He was worried that people would stop buying his stick wagons, but the last woman who'd bought one had said they were a godsend and she'd told her friends about them.

He didn't go out after dark on his own – well, there was only the pub to go to and he'd never been a boozer, besides needing to watch every penny. But you could have trouble at home as well as outside. Last night a stone had been thrown through the window of one of the bedrooms, waking everyone and frightening his two cousins. His aunt said she'd been jostled at the market by some rough fellow, who had made her spill things from her basket. The lout had trodden on her onions and potatoes, damaging them, and she was sure he'd done that on purpose.

He might have done worse if one of the stall holders hadn't come to her aid. The man had helped her to pick the things up, a nice Irish fellow he was. Some might not like the Irish, but she spoke as she found and all she knew was this one had been of great assistance to her.

It was Hungerton behind all these little annoyances, Lucas had no doubt. But how to deal with it baffled him. You couldn't accuse a rich landowner of wrong-doing without proof and even then you'd be lucky to get a magistrate to punish someone like Hungerton.

He lay awake at night now worrying about what would happen next – to him and to Gwynna.

That same evening someone knocked on the workshop door just as Lucas was finishing for the night.

'Your aunt all right after her fright at the market?'

Lucas put down the hammer he'd picked up for protection. 'Yes. Thanks to some kind Irish fellow.'

Declan grinned. 'Me brother Michael.' He wandered round the workshop, picking things up then putting them down again till he came to a piece of carving Lucas worked on sometimes in the evenings. He let out a long, low whistle. 'You do this?'

'Yes. It was one of the reasons Hungerton didn't want me to leave.'

'It's good.'

'Thanks.' Lucas waited but Declan was still studying the carving.

Eventually the Irishman looked up. 'I'll get my friends to keep an eye on your aunt when she goes to market. It'd be appreciated if she bought from the Irish in return, and maybe stopped to have a word with my mother, who hasn't many friends in this town outside our own circle. I'll tell Michael to introduce her and Mam.'

'Thanks. I'm sure Aunt Hilda will be happy to meet your mother.'

Declan picked up the piece of carving again. 'Can I borrow this for a day or two?'

'It isn't finished.'

'Doesn't matter. I want to show it to someone.'

He didn't explain so Lucas didn't ask him why. He felt Declan Heegan meant well by him, but as much for his own reasons as to help Lucas. He now knew that Declan was very much a man to be respected in the poorer quarters.

At the moment, any help was welcome because if this went on for much longer, ruin would be staring the Kemp family in the face. 'You're a good friend,' he said quietly.

Declan clapped him on the shoulder. 'You can't have too many friends. Come and have a drink with me and the lads tonight. It won't hurt for you to get known by sight. I'll call for you at eight o'clock.' His smile widened, 'And I'll see you safely home again after, so tell that nice aunt of yours not to worry.'

'All right. Thanks. But only one.'

Declan's expression was gentle. 'Money tight, is it?'

'Getting tight.'

17

The windows of the church hall shone brightly in the chill but fine evening, beckoning people to enter. And they did. Every single seat had been booked in advance and people had to be turned away at the door, disappointment etching itself on their faces.

This was what he was working for, Eli thought as he watched the cheerful crowd filing in, giving people pleasure. In a world full of toil and sorrow it was a worthwhile thing to do with one's life, surely?

When he went inside he found he could keep his demons at bay because the place was brightly lit and full of smiling people. He went to join the performers in the small rooms to one side where the ladies of the parish arranged their flowers or provided cups of tea for the evening classes which were very popular among working people wanting to better themselves.

Carrie was talking to the Minister and both of them turned to smile at him. He could see that her eyes were watchful behind that smile so he squeezed her arm and when Mr Nopps' attention was distracted, whispered, 'I'm all right, love.'

'You sure?'

'Yes. It cheers you up to see them, doesn't it?' He waved one hand towards the door, to indicate the room full of people.

When it came time for him to take his place as Chairman,

he moved forward confidently down the side of the room towards a table at the front. The small stage was only two feet high and had neither curtains nor scenery, just a couple of potted plants borrowed from Essie. From the floor at the other side of it, Raife and three other musicians smiled at him.

Eli's confidence wavered for a minute and he felt a shiver of nervousness run through him. Would he suddenly panic in front of all these people and shame himself by having to run outside? But by the time he had bowed his thanks to a crowd who'd stood up and applauded him all the way, he had forgotten his nerves.

He raised his voice to send it booming down the hall. 'Good evening, ladies and gentlemen.'

As they had done at the Pride they chorused, 'Good evening, Mr Chairman.'

That brought a lump to his throat and he had to swallow hard before he could continue. 'Welcome to our temporary music saloon, for which we have to thank Mr Nopps.' He gestured towards the Minister.

They cheered Mr Nopps too.

They clapped the first act loudly, both before and after the brother and sister started their duet. They were clearly in a mood to be pleased.

Lucas, who'd bought tickets for his two young cousins and himself, let his cares slide away and lost himself in the simple pleasure of listening to the music, joining in the sing-songs, marvelling at a particularly intelligent dog which did everything but speak, and laughing heartily at the comedian. He wished he could have brought Gwynna here tonight, because she'd been looking faintly anxious lately, as if something was worrying her, but of course it'd tell the world he was courting her if he did that.

Well? a small voice asked in his head. *And why not court her?*

No need to get married till you can afford it. She'll understand that.

He sat very still for a moment or two as he digested that thought, then tried to push it away, as he had once or twice before. But it wouldn't be pushed. In the pauses between acts, he kept thinking of her, wishing she was there.

The concert passed all too swiftly and when the audience had at last finished cheering and singing 'The Pride of Lancashire', people began to filter reluctantly out, walking home in small groups by the light of the new gas street lamps, which cast out circles of pale gold light to challenge the darkness.

Arm-in-arm with his cousins Lucas walked home, not forgetting the risk he was taking in going out after dark, but with a feeling that there would be enough people still out in the streets to keep him safe.

Then Declan stepped out from the shadows and said softly, 'We'll walk with you.'

All the worries came pouring back, but mindful of the two girls he was escorting home, Lucas held his questions till Belinda and Peggy had gone inside. 'Tell my aunt I'll join you in a minute,' he told them, then turned to his companion. 'What happened?'

'Nothing. But they'd planned something.' Declan tugged his arm and walked him round to the side of the workshop, pointing to a door that someone had tried to force, a door that Lucas had carefully reinforced. 'Young Joe stopped that.'

'*Joe did?*'

Declan nodded. 'Don't underestimate that lad. He's young but he learned how to survive the hard way. He slipped over the back fence when he heard noises and came to the pub to get me.'

Lucas sagged against the wall, feeling helpless. 'I might

just as well sell up and move away. Hungerton's not going to stop hounding me, is he?'

'Not unless we make him stop. Don't you think it's time *you* did something instead of letting him keep attacking you?'

'My parents and brother are his tenants. I'm afraid he'll turn them out if I fight back.'

Declan cursed softly under his breath. 'They always have some hold on you, don't they, rich sods like him? Well, me and my mates will continue to keep an eye on you till we think of something.'

'I'm grateful.' Lucas took a deep breath and added, 'I'm not going to hold back for much longer, in spite of my family. I can't bear to give in to bullies, even when they're rich and powerful.'

Declan clapped him on the shoulders. 'Good man. Now, I've been thinking about the safety of your uncle and his family. I know a fellow who's paying for lodgings and trying hard to save his money to bring his family across from Ireland. If you give him free board and just let him pay for food, you'll find him quiet and helpful in case of trouble.'

'Send him round.'

Lucas went inside and found the opportunity to thank Joe, who grinned at him and carried on eating a piece of cake.

The next day he told his uncle and aunt about their lodger and why they needed him. His aunt stared at him in horror and his uncle smacked his good hand down on the arm of his chair, muttering something about 'no damn use'.

Lucas went over to him and laid one hand on the older man's shoulder, giving it a quick squeeze. 'I'm hale and hearty, but I'm no use against Hungerton, either. It's brains that'll keep us safe and your brain's as good as it ever was.'

A space was found in the attics and a taciturn man called Cavan O'Guire came to live with them, paying only for his food. He told them he was saving to bring his parents, brothers and sisters, and his sweetheart across from Ireland, so was glad of cheap lodgings.

'And if anyone tries to disturb us, I'll make sure they learn a good lesson, so I will.'

But this was only a temporary measure, Lucas knew. He had to find some way to stop Hungerton doing this. Only how?

He woke suddenly in the middle of the night, realising there was one person he could consult – the lawyer who'd helped him before. At the very least, it'd be worth keeping Mr Burtell informed about what was going on, in case of further trouble, and perhaps he would think of something they could legally do to end this persecution.

Perhaps.

Lucas didn't feel confident about that.

Gwynna found life a lot easier once Betty became Mrs Forrett's personal maid, though the other girl still acted in a faintly hostile way. She spent most of the day either in attendance on her mistress or looking after Mrs Forrett's clothes, a job she seemed to love. Another housemaid was hired, an older woman who was neither friendly nor hostile. She got on with her work, seeming to hate all dirt with a passion, and kept herself to herself, going to bed as soon as her work was over, saying she 'loved a good, warm bed'. The house settled down into a new routine.

Betty had to go into town regularly on errands for her mistress and Gwynna saw her sometimes, walking round with her nose in the air as if she was better than other folk. One day a man stepped out of an alley to stand in front of Betty, and Gwynna stopped in shock. *Jabez*. Here in Hedderby. She moved behind a cart and watched as he began to speak, waving his arms about angrily, his face going red. Betty kept shaking her head.

When he took hold of her arm and tried to pull her into the alley, Betty screamed for help and Jabez ran off. A woman who'd been passing by put her arm round Betty and a man stood at the end of the alley, looking vexed.

What was going on? Was Jabez the one making trouble for her and Lucas? From what she'd seen, Betty was refusing to do something for him. Wasn't she working for Mr Hungerton any more, then?

Intrigued, Gwynna walked on, enjoying an undisturbed stroll through town and spending ten minutes chatting to Essie, who was out shopping.

But the lull didn't last long. The next time Gwynna went out she saw her father talking to Jabez. Both men turned to watch her as she passed, Jabez with a gloating expression on his face and her father with that look he always wore when he had found a chance to earn some money.

She went back to Mill House filled with apprehension. They must be planning something and Jabez wanted her to know that, to worry. That would be why they'd stood where she could see them.

What was she going to do? She couldn't ask Mr Forrett's help, because she had no idea what they were planning.

Eli and Carrie left for Meldon to look at the music hall early one morning. The streets were full of operatives hurrying towards the mill, or going to work in the smaller businesses in the town. They hoped that in the crowds no one would notice them slipping into the railway station and waiting for the train.

'Eh, you've chosen a hard place to reach,' the station master said cheerfully as they booked their tickets. 'You'll be spending as much time waiting for connections as you will travelling. Know someone in Meldon, do you?'

'Going to see an act there,' Eli said.

The man beamed at him. 'That's good news. You keep them shows going, Mr Beckett. Me and the missus were there on Saturday and we right enjoyed ourselves. Not as good as the Pride, of course, and I could have done with a pot of beer, but still, it made a nice night out.'

'We're going to call the new place the Phoenix,' Eli said.

The man frowned. 'What sort of a name is that?'

'A good one. It's supposed to be a bird that burns itself once a year and rises out of its own ashes.'

The man wrinkled his nose. 'Sounds silly to me. Any road, folk will still think of it as the Pride, an' I doubt you'll change them.'

Carrie hid a smile, not wanting to rub it in. This was just what she'd told Eli.

They got to Meldon after a frustrating hour and a half of changing trains and moving from branch line to main line then back to a small branch line again. The town, which was just a bit larger than Hedderby, was situated between Rawtenstall and Blackburn, not a long thin town this time, but one which nestled in a circular valley. The station was on higher ground to the south of it and as they came out of its entrance, they could see down what looked like the main street into the town centre.

They had no need to ask their way to the theatre, because once they got to the end of the street, there it was, at the other side of the big square which seemed to be at the heart of Meldon.

'The Majesty.' Eli read the big gold letters, leaning his head back to stare up at the theatre's façade.

'It's very like ours will be,' Carrie linked her arm in his and they walked round the square, gazing across at the little theatre from different angles.

Eli sighed enviously as they got back to the front of it again. 'It's a nice-looking building and seems well built. I hope ours will look as good as this one day.' He turned to smile at his wife. 'I think we've been worrying over nothing.'

'Perhaps.'

He looked at her in surprise and waved one arm towards the theatre. 'Why "perhaps"? It's there, large as life, hasn't fallen down or anything.'

She wrinkled her nose and studied it, head on one side. 'I know, but let's find out a little more. We'll go and see if there's someone we can talk to about it.'

The front doors of the theatre were open as they'd so often opened the doors of the Pride in the mornings to air the place, so they went into the foyer. 'Is anyone there?' Eli called out.

A man stuck his head out of a door. 'We're not open till later to sell tickets and we don't need any more acts.'

Eli walked forward. 'We're not customers. I'm Eli Beckett and this is my wife, Carrie. We own a music hall too. In Hedderby.' He held out his hand.

'John Chidworth.' The man shook hands and nodded politely to Carrie. 'What can I do for you, Mr Beckett?'

Eli explained, ending up, 'We thought it best to come and check up on one of the theatres our architect's built, just to be on the safe side.'

'Very sensible. Would you like to look round?'

They followed him, stepping round the steaming buckets of dirty water belonging to two women who were cleaning the place ready for the next show, going down to look at the cellars, which were very different from what theirs would be like, much smaller and with several pillars breaking up the space. They ended up on the small balcony at the rear, staring down at the stage for a few minutes.

'Eh, I miss it,' Eli said softly.

Carrie squeezed his hand.

When they got back down to the foyer he turned to thank their host. 'I'm feeling a lot happier about Trevin now.'

'Trevin?'

'The architect, the one who designed this theatre.'

Chidworth frowned. 'It wasn't anyone called Trevin who built it, but Saul Barton. He's only young but he's making a name for himself with theatre architecture, and well deserved too. The builders said it all went according to plan.'

'But our man – he's called Maitland Trevin – had sketches of this place, good ones too, showing both the inside and the outside. Only the cellars are different. How could he have those if he wasn't the architect?'

'I don't know anyone called Trevin. Hold on, though.' Chidworth chewed on his forefinger for a minute then said, 'I think Barton's assistant, the one who did drawings and such, was called Maitland. Not Maitland Trevin, but Harry Maitland.'

'Short, balding, lost some teeth at the top right, talks *at* you as if he's better than you,' Carrie put in quickly.

The man grinned at her. 'You don't like this fellow you're describing and I have to say he sounds like our Harry Maitland. I didn't take to him, either.'

'You couldn't come over and see if it's the same man, could you?' Eli asked. 'We'd pay all your expenses.'

Chidworth shook his head. 'Couldn't spare the time. But I could send my eldest lad over. He'd recognise the fellow.'

They made the necessary arrangements, then Chidworth looked at the clock. 'Well, it's been nice meeting you, but I have to get on.'

Taking the hint they walked slowly back to the station.

'I'm hungry,' Carrie said. 'Look, there's a woman selling cups of tea.'

They went up to where the woman had her little cart with its spirit heater burning under a kettle urn. She washed out a couple of cups in muddy looking water, then filled them with tea and added a dash of milk and a teaspoon of sugar to each. Carrie was so thirsty she ignored the dirty streaks on the outside of the cup and gulped down the hot liquid with a sigh of pleasure.

A little further on they met a pieman crying his wares and bought a couple of pies from him, sitting on a bench at the station to eat them.

'I was sharp set,' Eli admitted. 'That filled the hole nicely, though I wouldn't have minded another.'

'There isn't time to go and find more food before the next train,' Carrie said. 'But that should hold you till we get back.'

They discussed their plans as they made the same tedious journey across country, changing trains and waiting around stations, not arriving in Hedderby until mid-afternoon.

'Who the hell *is* Trevin then?' Eli asked as they sat on the train looking out at more familiar scenery. 'Is he this assistant, do you think?'

'Whoever he is, he's a cheat. He must have stolen Barton's plans.'

'Well, we'll have to confront him, but it's what to do afterwards that worries me,' he admitted. 'We still have a theatre to build.'

'We'll find ourselves a real architect and get on with it.'

He sat with head bowed. 'Will we have enough money, though? I paid him partly in advance. I think that blow on the head addled my brains, Carrie.'

'We'll think of something,' she said stoutly. 'You'll see. The main thing is that you're all right now.'

'But I'm not. We both know I'm not.'

She could only hold his hand and sit as close to him as possible until the train pulled into the station. Athol Stott had done more than destroy a music saloon when he'd set the place on fire, he'd seriously damaged a good man.

★

Lucas went to see the lawyer the very next day. He explained the situation and Jack Burtell listened intently, clearly believing what Lucas was saying.

'I think we should tell the police sergeant,' he said. 'The new police force is doing its best to keep order in the town and it's been noticed that strangers have been coming and going, causing trouble.'

'I've no proof of anything.'

'You should still tell him. He's quite young to be a sergeant, and he got there because he's a clever fellow not because he's stupid.'

Lucas frowned. 'I just wonder whether it'll cause even more trouble if I'm seen going into the police station.'

Jack leaned back in his chair, thinking, then said, 'You may be right. Come and see me tomorrow afternoon. Use the back gate. I'll make sure the sergeant is here to talk to you.'

'I don't suppose he'll be able to do anything.'

'You never know. But you were right to come and see me. If you're ever in trouble with Hungerton, don't hesitate to send for me.'

Lucas got home to the heartening news that another lady in the town wanted a stick wagon, this time a bigger one for her two small children. Ted had taken the order, writing out the lady's name and address.

Lucas smiled as he sorted through his storeroom. He'd have to buy some more wood, but these wagons brought in a good profit, at least.

And he'd designed the special infant's chair for Mr Forrett's little daughter. He got the sketch out and studied it. Perhaps when he went round to the mill to show this to Mr Forrett, he'd manage to see Gwynna.

That thought was enough to lift his spirits.

★

The meeting with the sergeant was quite brief. In Jack Burtell's presence Lucas explained what had happened so far and how he was being harassed by men whom he assumed to have been sent by Mr Hungerton. The sergeant listened intently, nodding his head a few times and asking an occasional question.

'You say Declan Heegan has been helping you?'

'Yes. A great deal.'

'I don't know what to think of that man. I've been warned about him by more than one person yet I've found him very helpful.'

Jack grinned. 'There's nothing like having a famous brother for making you smarten yourself up – or sending you to the devil. I believe Declan has chosen the former alternative.'

'Is that what's causing this change of attitude?'

'I reckon so.'

The sergeant nodded then turned to Lucas. 'I'm grateful for the information. I happen to believe in law and order – and not just for the rich – so I'll keep my eyes open. If you have any further trouble, I'd be grateful if you'd come to me rather than taking matters into your own hands.'

He left by the front entrance, while Lucas slipped out of the back door. He hated this secrecy. And he wasn't at all confident that the sergeant could help him.

18

After the visit to Meldon it took Carrie and Eli a few days to make arrangements for John Chidworth's son to come to Hedderby and identify Trevin, because they had to make sure the architect would be there. Luckily Trevin gave them the excuse they needed by asking for a meeting, so they arranged to see him.

Young Johnny Chidworth arrived in Hedderby mid-morning, as arranged. He strongly resembled his father, though he still had the thinness of young manhood. He ate a huge piece of Essie's cake with relish, then went for a stroll into town with Raife, pulling his hat down low over his eyes as they approached the site.

'There he is,' Raife said. 'The fat fellow with the sour expression.'

Breath hissed into Johnny's mouth and he stopped walking in his excitement. 'It's him all right, only we knew him as Harry Maitland.'

Trevin looked across at them just then.

'Keep moving and don't stare,' Raife chided him.

'Sorry. Is he still watching us?'

'Yes.'

As they began to make their way back to Linney's, Raife said suddenly, 'I think he's sent someone to follow us.'

'What are we going to do?'

'Keep moving and don't look back. We'll pop in to see a friend of mine.' Raife kept a firm hold on Johnny's arm and led them past Linney's to a small terraced house in one of the lanes. When a woman opened the door, he said quickly, 'Throw your arms round the lad and pretend he's your nephew Peter, will you, Mary? I'll explain in a minute after we shut that door.'

Chuckling she did as he asked, exclaiming loudly at how lovely it was to see her nephew and asking if her sister was better now. Then she ushered them inside. Raife explained what was going on and she peered through the window.

'He's standing just down the road. Well I never!'

'Can we go out the back, love?'

'Yes, of course. But next time there's a show on, you owe me a ticket.'

'My pleasure.' He led Johnny outside and back to Linney's, well aware that the young man was nearly bursting with excitement.

As soon as they entered the kitchen, Johnny said, 'It's him, Mrs Beckett, definitely him. He isn't an architect, just a general assistant. Thought a lot of himself, he did, when he worked on our theatre, but the men didn't like him. I didn't like him, either. Dad heard Barton sack him towards the end, he said they'd had a right old dingdong about changes Maitland had made to his instructions. We didn't see the fellow again after that.'

'You're sure of that?' Eli asked.

'Cross my heart and hope to die!' Johnny solemnly matched his actions to his words.

'I wonder how he got hold of the plans,' Eli mused.

'There were some papers stolen a few days later. They never did find out who took them, or why. They were only drawings, most of them.'

Eli, who had moved to stand staring out of the rear window, walked out into the yard without a word.

Carrie distracted young Johnny with more food, saying

casually that her husband always went outside when he needed to think about something. When the lad had finished eating, she thanked him for his help and paid him the fare money.

Raife looked out of the window. 'I'll just check the street then walk with you to the station, lad.'

Carrie went out to join Eli in the back yard, finding him kicking at a chunk of coal that must have fallen out of a scuttle, hands thrust deep into his pockets, face twisted by an almighty scowl.

'I've mucked things up badly, haven't I?' he asked, without turning to look at her.

She went to link her arm in his. 'It is a bit of a mess, but we'll sort it out together, love.'

'How?'

She couldn't lie to him. 'I don't know. Maybe we should just let Trevin carry on for a bit till he's done what we paid him for, then find another architect to take over?'

'Who?'

'What about the man you were talking to, the one who's guardian to Stott's children?'

'Channon? I don't think he's a theatre architect. He said something about building houses.'

'Well, at the very least he'll know how we can find someone who does understand about building theatres.'

'Does nothing ever stop you?' he asked. 'You're a wonder, Carrie Beckett, a real wonder.'

'Come and play with Abigail while I help Essie with the housework. You know that always cheers you up and she loves being with her daddy.'

He grinned at her suddenly. 'You always think up some way to keep me occupied so that I don't brood.'

'I try to help.'

'I know. It makes me feel loved and I seem to need that

at present.' He rubbed his temple. 'My head's aching today. I think some fresh air would do it good. And there's a real feel of spring so I don't think Abigail will come to any harm if I take her out with me, do you?'

'She's getting very heavy to be carrying when you go walking.'

'Maybe we need one of those stick wagons like Gwynna's got? Only we'll need a bigger one, because your sister's baby will be coming back to live here soon and there'll be three children to take out then.' He hesitated. 'Does your sister ever ask about Leah?'

'No. Marjorie's letters are about how well she and Hal are doing and where they're playing next. She wasn't cut out to be a mother, was she? I could never hand my child over to someone else to raise. We're lucky we found such a good wet nurse for Leah.'

'Chalk and cheese, you two, sisters or not.' They turned and began walking towards the house.

'Why don't you go and see that carpenter while you're out and order a wagon? I'll go and wrap Abigail up warmly and you'll need your scarf, too. There's still a bite to that wind.'

He was smiling as he set out with his daughter in his arms. If anything could make the nightmares recede, it was Carrie.

Lucas looked up as a shadow fell across the open doorway of the workshop. 'Eli.' His expression softened into a smile. 'And Abigail. My, she's growing fast, isn't she, nearly as fast as Gwynna's Libby.'

'Aye.' Eli shifted his daughter to his other shoulder. 'There'll be three little 'uns at Linney's soon, so Carrie wants one of those stick wagons like the one the Forretts have, with seats in it, a bigger one though.' He saw Lucas's face brighten. 'Business slow?'

'Aye. You'd think I'd got the plague.'

'I heard someone's been trying to cause trouble for you. Surely they can't get to everyone who needs carpentering done?'

'They're making a fair fist of it. Hungerton's sent men here to intimidate people. If it wasn't for Declan Heegan and his friends, I'd have been in serious trouble before now.'

Ted came through into the workshop, whistling cheerfully, saw his brother-in-law and smiled a greeting.

'How's this young rascal doing?'

Lucas ruffled his apprentice's hair. 'He's doing well.'

Joe peeped round the edge of the door that led into the house. 'Want any jobs done, Mr Kemp?'

'Doesn't my aunt need you?'

'Not yet. I've to go to the shops with her later, that's all.'

'Then come and practise taking the nails out of those pieces of wood you hammered them into yesterday. You can straighten the nails up and use them again. You show him how, Ted.'

When the boys had gone out into the back yard, Lucas said thoughtfully, 'I'd better get Joe into a school, because you're nothing if you can't read and write nowadays. But I wanted him to settle down here first. He's still terrified underneath that we'll throw him out so he daren't act like a normal lad and get into mischief.'

'It was kind of you to take him in.'

'I can't bear to see children living on the streets, fending for themselves. What this town needs is an orphanage. The union workhouse for our group of parishes is too far away for relatives to visit, and anyway they're severe with the children in those places, cruel even. I hate to think of that.' He shrugged, embarrassed to have let his feelings show. 'Well, how exactly do you want your stick wagon made?'

'You've got me there. I haven't the first idea what to ask for. Do you think Forrett would let me see his and then you could tell me its finer points and how you'd adapt it for a bigger wagon?'

'Why not? He's not a bad chap to deal with unless you work for him in the mill. We can walk across to the mill now, if you like. I've got nothing else to do.' Lucas went to get his over-coat and hat. 'Here, let me spell you with Abigail. She's heavy.'

To Eli's surprise, his daughter went to a near-stranger with every sign of delight. 'You've a way with children.'

'I like them.'

As the two men strolled across town, Eli was greeted by nods and smiles from nearly everyone they met, and several stopped to admire Abigail and comment on how she was growing into a 'real little girl' now. At the mill yard they were lucky enough to catch Forrett coming out of the office and he came across to find out what they wanted.

'Easy enough, that.' He took them over to look at the stick wagon, which was kept in a shed at the rear of the house and they found Gwynna kneeling by it, strapping Libby in and singing softly to her. She didn't hear them approach and continued her song in a tuneful voice.

Lucas stopped walking so abruptly at the sight of her that Eli banged into him and let out an exclamation, which inter-rupted her song and made her blush.

'Mr Beckett wants to get a wagon made, so I said you'd show them how ours works, Gwynna.' Forrett waved one hand at the little vehicle then went back to work.

'Carrie wants one made for Abigail and the other two,' Eli explained. As he examined the wagon he became aware of the currents flowing between his two companions, and watched them covertly. Each avoided looking directly at the other and their only remarks were about the wagon, but you couldn't mistake the way they felt about one another. Gwynna and Lucas, eh? Carrie would be interested, he thought, hiding a smile.

'Why don't you sit Abigail next to Libby and see how she likes it?' Lucas suggested. 'There's plenty of room.'

They did so then Eli pushed the wagon out across the mill yard. 'It rolls easily enough,' he commented as the silence between the other two lasted too long.

'It's really easy to push,' she admitted. 'Libby's too big now to carry far, though she isn't as big as your Abigail, is she? I'm looking forward to her walking and I love it when they start talking.'

At first the infants were more interested in one another than where they were going, but gradually Abigail began to look around her as they progressed along the street.

By the time they got to the other end of town, Gwynna had taken over the wagon again and the two men had come to an agreement about making a bigger one to fit three children. Eli took his leave.

As Lucas turned to say goodbye, Gwynna said, 'I'd better go back now and— Oh!' She stopped moving and turned pale.

Lucas swung round quickly to see a man standing on the next corner, leaning against the wall and not troubling to hide the fact that he was watching them. When Lucas looked at the young woman beside him he saw real fear on her face. 'I'll walk you back to the mill, shall I?'

'I'd be grateful. I keep seeing Jabez when I come out for walks and he – well, he frightens me.'

'Just a minute. Isn't that the fellow who attacked you in the train?' He frowned. 'Jabez? Now I know why he seemed familiar! He's a groom at Hungerton House. His family must have lived in one of the villages on the other side of the big house, because I don't remember him as a lad. Mind you, with those sidewhiskers of his, it's a wonder even his mother recognises him now.'

She shuddered. 'I remember those sidewhiskers rubbing

against my face when Jabez tried to force himself on me.' She touched her cheeks as if they were still sore.

Lucas felt anger rise swiftly. 'I'll grab him and haul him before the police. You can lay a complaint and I'll bear witness that he was the one who attacked you.'

She hesitated then shook her head. 'I'd rather not. If it gets out, people will only say I egged him on. They always blame the woman. And if Mrs Forrett hears about it, she'll dismiss me for sure. She's only waiting for an excuse.'

'I hate to see fellows get away with things like that.' Lucas stopped as something occurred to him. 'What's he doing in Hedderby anyway? Doesn't he work for Hungerton any more or is he . . .' his voice trailed away, then he finished what he'd been saying, 'the one who's been causing all this trouble for me as well?'

'I wouldn't be surprised. He's a horrible man! His sister is Mrs Forrett's maid and I've seen him talking to her. I'm sure he's planning something, the way he always stands where I can see him, but I can't refuse to take Libby out for walks, can I?'

'What time do you take her out?'

'About this time of the morning.'

'I'll come with you from now on.'

It was her turn to stop. Flushing slightly, she said, 'I'd like that and I'm grateful for the offer, but we'd better not. Mr Forrett won't want me to keep seeing you while I'm working.'

'Then Mr Forrett should protect you himself.'

'I don't want to tell him about Jabez.'

Lucas got a stubborn look on his face.

She took his arm and shook him slightly. 'Lucas, please promise me you'll not tell him! I've got to keep this job or I'll have no future as a nursemaid – and I love what I do.'

'I'll see.' He stayed beside her all the way back to Mill House, glancing over his shoulder, annoyed to see Jabez openly following them.

Gwynna managed to ignore that because she enjoyed Lucas's company. She asked him about the business and was sad to hear of the problems Mr Hungerton was causing for him, then at his prompting, she talked about her own family, ashamed of her drunken parents but with fond memories of her brothers and sisters. Her sisters were working long hours in the mill now, so she never saw them on the streets, though she kept her eyes open for them in case.

'It seems we're both in trouble with that horrible man,' she said sadly as they stood by the mill gates and Jabez leaned against a wall opposite. 'Why can't he leave us alone?'

'Who knows? Hungerton seems to enjoy causing trouble. Gwynna, lass . . .' He looked at her earnestly, 'Promise you'll come to me if you need help.'

She smiled shyly up at him. 'I promise.'

The quietly spoken words hung between them for a moment or two, then she straightened up and said goodbye, pushing the little wagon across the yard again. When she got to the house, she couldn't resist turning round.

Lucas was still standing just inside the gate. He smiled and raised one hand in a final farewell then strode away.

'Got yourself a young fellow, have you?' a voice said from just behind her.

She jumped in shock and turned to see Mr Forrett. 'Just a friend. Lucas and I both used to work for Mr Hungerton and . . .' She bit back further words.

'And what?' he prompted.

'Nothing, sir.'

He grabbed her arm and swung her round. 'Finish what you were going to say. There are things going on in this town that I don't like and if you know something about them, I want to hear it.'

So she found herself explaining it all, telling him Lucas's story as well as her own.

Mr Forrett nodded his head several times. 'That explains a lot.' Then he grinned at her. 'I don't mind you seeing that young man, lass, as long as you do it openly. He'd be a good catch for you.'

She looked at him uncertainly. 'Lucas hasn't ever . . . it's not like that.'

He threw back his head and laughed. 'I'm not too old to recognise young love blooming, Gwynna. And I'll always be grateful to you for what you've done for my Libby. I'd never try to prevent you from finding happiness.'

Blushing hotly she hurried inside, surprised at how kind Mr Forrett could be sometimes.

On the Sunday of the trip to Manchester, Jeremiah studied Maria's appearance. He wanted to say how lovely she looked, but changed it to the safer, 'I like your new clothes. I love that shade of lilac shot with grey.'

She stroked the silk fabric of her sleeve and smiled down at the full bell of her skirt. 'I fell in love with the material and it has made up well, hasn't it? It was a bit extravagant, though.'

'No, it wasn't. Your husband kept you short of money.' He hesitated, then added, 'Just as my father does with my mother.'

There was a clattering on the stairs and the boys came down.

'You two look splendid!' Maria proudly put an arm round each of her sons and gave them a hug.

Jeremiah was pleased by the lads' new clothes, which were also grey, a shade neither dark nor light, because Maria was still very stubborn about no one wearing mourning for Athol. The boys' suits consisted of trousers, quite full with two tucks at the lower edge, which would be excellent for letting down as they grew, their mother had assured him – as if he cared about that! There were tunics to match their trousers, cut tight to the waist and then with a pleated part which reached to the knees. Their white shirts had frilled collars which showed over the tunic tops.

He'd seen other children from the more comfortable homes wearing such outfits and was glad the boys would not look different from their peers now. It had surprised him how shabby Maria and her children were, apart from their Sunday best.

'I like these trousers,' Benjamin announced. 'I can run about in them more easily. That skeleton suit was too tight, even when it was new.'

'Skeleton suit?' Jeremiah looked questioningly at Maria.

'A tight-fitting single garment, which is why they call it a skeleton suit.'

He consulted his watch. 'Well, let's set out.'

As they made their way through the streets he was aware of people staring at them and raised his hat to ladies he recognised from church. But he noted which of them ignored Maria. He saw her flush a couple of times in embarrassment at being cut dead, and was relieved for her sake when they reached the station.

While he bought the tickets, he could feel the excitement emanating from the boys. Turning, he smiled at them. 'Come on! We'll go and wait on the platform. The train shouldn't be long.'

But the boys had to go and peer over the edge at the iron rails, then walk up and down, studying every detail of the station's appearance. He watched them indulgently because it was only natural that lads should want to explore, then realised that Maria was watching him anxiously. 'I'm not going to get angry with them for behaving like lads,' he said quietly, pleased to see her relax a little.

The journey passed quickly, with the boys occupying the

window seats and pointing things out to one another, or turning to ask him questions. They took a cab from the station and as they drew up at his friends' house, Jeremiah became aware that the boys had fallen silent.

'Is something wrong?'

It was Isaac who answered. 'Are you sure they want us to visit them?'

'Of course I'm sure.'

'Other boys in Hedderby throw things at us if we go out on our own.'

Jeremiah closed his eyes for a moment, hating to think of what these two had suffered over the years, were still suffering. 'Well, my friends' children only know that you're my wards. They know nothing about your father. So just play with them, talk to them, act naturally.'

'We've never played with other children before,' Benjamin said.

'Then this is a good opportunity to learn. Be kind to one another and you'll do all right.' Jeremiah helped Maria out of the cab and the boys jumped down on their own, standing a little distance behind the adults, but close to one another.

Andrew had already opened the door and was beaming at them, while Sissy was waiting in the parlour to greet them, flanked by her son and daughter.

The four children eyed one another solemnly, then Sissy said, 'Why don't you take your guests out into the garden to play, children?'

After the boys had followed their young hosts out, Jeremiah said in a low voice, 'The boys' late father kept them very isolated, with only a governess and a dog as companions. They're not used to playing with other children.'

'Poor things,' Sissy said warmly. 'I'll ask Cook to keep an eye on them from the kitchen window. But I think the dog will make a bond.' She turned to Maria and smiled. 'I'm so happy to meet you, Mrs Stott. Perhaps we can let the gentlemen leave us to talk about their jobs while we gossip about clothes and children? I'll just see Cook first.'

Her hostess was so warmly friendly that Maria soon relaxed and found herself discussing the latest fashions, enjoying the novel experience of having her new clothes admired and even being urged to talk about embroidery, which was one of her hostess's interests.

In the study Andrew looked at Jeremiah and gave him a nudge. 'You didn't tell me you were in love with her.'

He was startled. 'Is it so obvious?'

'It is to those who know you. And about time too.' Andrew looked carefully at his friend then added, 'You won't let your father stop you?'

'No. But I'm afraid Maria is so badly scarred by her marriage that she'll be hard to win. Indeed, I've heard her say she'll never marry again.'

'That'll change as she gets to know you better.'

Jeremiah wasn't too sure about that, but he forgot his personal worries as the talk turned to Andrew's latest project and Jeremiah's plans for the future.

Riding home in the train Benjamin said wonderingly, 'They let us play with their toys.'

'Their dog knows all sorts of tricks,' Isaac added. 'We'll have to teach Migs a few.'

'When they come to visit us, you'll have to let them play with your toys,' Jeremiah said.

'We don't have as many as them,' Benjamin said.

'We'll have to buy you some, then.'

Isaac looked at his guardian. 'Will they really want to come and see us?'

'Yes, of course. You got on well with them, I think, and their parents are very good friends of mine.' He turned to look at the boys' mother. 'You won't mind my inviting them to visit us, will you, Cousin Maria?'

She smiled smugly. 'You won't have to. I've already invited them. They're coming to see us in a fortnight's time.'

It wasn't until she was in bed that she let herself shed a few tears of joy for the blessed normality of that day, for the way the boys had been able to act like children. All due to Jeremiah.

Who would have thought that Athol's choice of guardian would turn out so well?

Jeremiah was such a lovely man, a little shy perhaps, not used to showing his feelings, but . . . lovely.

19

Mr Forrett stopped Gwynna the next day as she was pushing Libby out for a walk. 'Wait a minute and I'll come with you.'

She blinked in astonishment and couldn't think what to say to that.

He walked more quickly than she could comfortably manage with the stick wagon and she found it a struggle to keep up with him. He didn't say anything or offer to help her push it, and as soon as they got to the main part of Market Street he stopped. 'I'll just nip into the bank. You go ahead till I catch you up. You should be all right on your own in this part of town.'

She hadn't gone more than a hundred yards when Jabez stepped out of a side street and blocked her way. As she tried to move round him, he grabbed the handle of the wagon, jerking it roughly from her and making Libby cry out in fear.

'Stop it! You're frightening her.' She tried to take it back.

Jabez laughed and shoved her away so hard she fell over, then he shook the wagon again, really hard this time.

Before she could get up there was a roar of fury and Mr Forrett erupted on to the scene. He punched Jabez on the nose, then yelled, 'Get Libby out of the way!'

Gwynna dragged the wagon hastily to one side as the two men began fighting in earnest. It was soon obvious that although Jabez was a strong man, James Forrett was a more experienced fighter who knew a few tricks to stop an opponent in his tracks.

'Hey! Stop that fighting!'

To Gwynna's embarrassment the police sergeant came running across the road, holding his tall hat on, the skirt of his unbuttoned uniform coat flapping around him. With a muffled moan at the show this was causing, embarrassed by the way people had stopped to gape at them, she watched as Forrett feinted skilfully then jabbed his right fist hard into Jabez's midriff, choosing his spot carefully.

As the younger man let out a surprised, 'Oof!' and bent over, clutching his middle, Forrett clasped his hands together and used them to knock his opponent to the ground. The younger man lay there writhing and making occasional muffled noises as he tried desperately to regain his breath.

'You're just in time to deal with this fellow, Sergeant.' Forrett picked up his hat and dusted it down, then brushed the front of his jacket.

'Seems to me you dealt with him quite adequately, sir,' the policeman said with an involuntary smile. 'I hope there's a good reason for this brawling.'

'A very good reason. He's been annoying my maid for several days now, pestering her every time she goes out. So I followed them and today he put my daughter in danger.'

'Is this true, miss?'

Gwynna nodded.

'Then you'd better come and make a complaint against him.'

Even as she looked pleadingly at Mr Forrett, Lucas came running up to join them. 'What happened? Are you all right, Gwynna?'

'Yes, thank you.'

'She's about to make a complaint against this fellow.'

'About time too. He's the one who attacked her on the train a few weeks ago. The station master reported the incident to you, didn't he, Sergeant?'

'Yes. I remember it clearly. Do you know him, Mr Kemp?'

'We both do.' As Lucas looked at Gwynna, his expression softened and his feelings for her shone in his eyes. 'Tell him what happened, love.'

She looked at him for a moment, smiling slightly, then turned back to the sergeant. 'Jabez works for Mr Hungerton. I used to work for him too and so did Lucas. But when Mr Hungerton found out I'd once had a baby, he dismissed me.' She faltered to a halt and blushed, expecting him to look at her disdainfully, but his expression was as respectful as before.

'Go on, miss.'

'Since then Jabez has been following me, attacking me, and I don't understand why.'

The sergeant's voice was harsh. 'I can't be doing with louts who attack decent young women.' He leaned down and hauled her attacker to his feet, keeping the man's arm twisted behind his back once he was upright.

'She's not – *decent*,' Jabez wheezed. 'She's a – whore.'

Forrett stepped forward quickly to stop Lucas from thumping him. 'She only went with one lad and that was out of love,' he said mildly. 'I knew Patrick. He'd have married her if he hadn't been killed.'

They all turned to stare at Jabez as Lucas demanded, 'Why are you following her? Is this on Hungerton's orders?'

Jabez was still struggling for breath. 'I don't like – such as her – associating with lasses as really are decent. It's not – right.'

'You're the one who broke the law, not her. I'd not call that decent behaviour.' The sergeant turned to the others. 'Let's get him back to the station and lock him up, then I'll take your statements.'

'I don't want him arrested,' Gwynna put in hastily. 'It'll put *me* in a worse light than him. *Please*, Mr Forrett, Sergeant, you know it'll not do my reputation any good.'

There was silence, then the policeman said quietly, 'We'll discuss this at the police station, if you please, miss. Are you free to come with us, Mr Forrett? And you, Mr Kemp?'

'I'll be delighted to,' Forrett said. 'This lout needs to understand that he'd better leave me and mine alone.'

Gwynna wondered whether to tell Mr Forrett that Betty was Jabez's sister, but decided not to. She didn't want to make the other girl lose her place. She knew how much it meant to her to be a lady's maid. Betty still wasn't friendly, but she had stopped being openly hostile, which made life a lot easier.

The sergeant put his prisoner in a cell and after some discussion it was decided that Jabez should be warned to leave Gwynna alone and to stay away from Hedderby from now on, or he'd be charged with assault. He was brought out and told, and not even the presence of two men standing protectively at either side of Gwynna stopped him from throwing a dirty look at her, a look which said he'd still do her harm if he could.

'If you lay one finger on my –' Lucas stopped abruptly as he realised what he had been going to say, then smiled and said it anyway, '– *my Gwynna*, you'll have me to answer to. I reckon men like you should be locked up and the key thrown away.'

'You're a fine one to talk. You're a thief, you are!' Jabez threw at him. 'Everyone knows you stole some tools from Mr Hungerton when you left and if you hadn't had a fancy lawyer, you'd have been locked away like you deserved.'

'Are you mad, making accusations like that when you've just been let off with a warning?' the sergeant demanded in tones of outrage.

'I'm loyal to my employer, who's been tricked and cheated by these two.'

Forrett went and stood very close to Jabez, saying slowly and emphatically, 'Shut up and listen, you. You're getting away lightly this time, for Gwynna's sake, but you won't if you come near my daughter and her nursemaid again. And I'm not nearly as fussy about sticking to the law as the police are, believe me.'

'You heard what he just threatened, Sergeant!' Jabez said. 'If anything happens to me, I'll call you as a witness.'

'I didn't hear a thing.'

There was another short silence, then Forrett said, 'Now, I've a mill to run. I can't waste any more time on rubbish like him.'

'I'll have him escorted to the station and put on a train,' the sergeant assured them. 'Constable, lock him away then go down to the station and find out the time of the next train to Sutherclough.'

'I've clothes at my lodgings.'

'Tell the constable what you've got and he'll pick them up for you. You're not getting out of here till we take you to the train.'

As they left the police station, Forrett grinned at Lucas. 'Why don't *you* walk Gwynna home? You can spare a few minutes, can't you? That wagon only goes slowly and I've work waiting for me.'

'Oh, I've plenty of time to spare,' Lucas said, unable to keep the bitterness out of his voice.

Forrett looked at him but said nothing, then turned to Gwynna. 'Cheer up, lass. You'll be safe from now on. That lout won't dare show his face in Hedderby again.'

As they walked along, Lucas said quietly, 'You don't look happy.'

She looked up at him. 'I'm sure we haven't heard the last from Mr Hungerton. Aren't you, Lucas?'

'Yes. It's well known he'll go to any lengths if he feels himself slighted. Stupid old fool he is! If I had money like him I'd not waste my time being spiteful.'

'What would you do?'

He paused for a moment, head on one side, then said, 'I'd do something about the children, the ones who live on the streets and the poor ones who don't get enough food.'

'What a lovely dream.'

'That's all it is, a dream! Where would a fellow like me get the money to do that sort of thing?'

'Lucas . . .' She stopped, afraid to ask the question.

'Yes?'

She wanted so desperately to know, she risked everything and asked, 'Why did you call me "my Gwynna"?'

He stopped her pushing the wagon by laying his hand on hers. Picking up that hand he slowly raised it to his lips and pressed a very gentle kiss on her palm. 'Because it felt right. Did you – mind?'

Her smile lit up her whole face. 'No. I loved it.'

They stood there for a moment or two, with him still holding her hand. Neither was aware of the passers-by or of the drizzle that had started to fall gently on the little town.

'Can I come and take you out walking on Sunday?' Lucas asked.

'I'd love that. In the afternoon? I'm free from two to four.'

'I'll be waiting outside the mill at two.'

They continued walking, not saying anything. But a smile lingered on both their faces for long after they'd parted.

Going walking on Sunday afternoon was an official declaration that they were courting.

When Lucas got back to his workshop, he had to pull himself together and think what work to do, because he'd been thinking of Gwynna all the way home. Slowly at first, then with his usual brisk purpose, he assembled the pieces of wood needed for Eli's stick wagon. Patiently he showed the boys what he was doing and winked at Ted as he let Joe help them with the simplest tasks.

His aunt came to the house door to watch them for a few minutes and when he went across to her, said quietly, 'You should have bairns of your own, Lucas love. You've got those two boys eating out of your hands.'

'They're nice lads.' He looked at her, hesitated, then said it. 'I've met a lass, started courting.' He saw anxiety beneath her smile and added, 'You'll like her and it won't make any difference to my looking after you.'

'I'd like to meet her. Why don't you bring her to tea?'

'I will.'

'I hope she's worthy of you, Lucas. You deserve the best.'

'She *is* the best.'

'Who is she?'

'Gwynna Jones.'

Her expression changed. 'She's not . . .'

'She had a baby by the lad she loved, if that's what you were going to say.'

'I wasn't. I was going to ask about her parents. There are some drunkards called Jones.'

He sighed. 'They're her parents but she has nothing to do with them now. She lives with the Linneys when she isn't living in with an employer. They think a lot of her, the Linneys do.'

'That's nice then. As long as she isn't like her mother. Now, your uncle wants to see you when you've a minute.'

'I'll come straight away.' He turned to give quiet instructions to the boys and went into the house.

Fred was sitting beside the kitchen fire looking thoughtful. His colour was good now and his eyes clear.

'You're looking better all the time, Uncle.'

'Aye. Seems the Lord doesn't want me up there yet.' He lifted one hand, spreading the fingers. They didn't open far, but previously they hadn't opened at all. 'Every day summat gets moving again in this owd body o' mine.' He stared at the hand as if he'd never seen it before, then let it drop on to his lap again and asked, 'How's the business coming on?'

Lucas shrugged. 'Slowly. It's only to be expected.'

'Could you put some wheels on a chair so that you can push me out? There are places I need to go, people I want to see.'

'Yes. Eh, I should have thought of it sooner.'

'I wasn't ready to go out before and even so, I'm not looking for'ard to showing this to everyone.' He gestured to his face which had a distinct droop at one side. 'Any road, that's summat I shall just have to thole, because it can't be changed. I want you to take me to the pub tonight. I've a few friends meet there regular and it's about time I found out who's really a friend.' He looked steadily at his nephew. 'I think I can drum up a few orders, whatever yon sod is doing.'

'Are you sure you're up to it?'

'Aye.'

'We'll give it a go then.'

'But I think them stick wagons and such would be a good way for you to go as well.'

'I'm not really a cabinet maker.'

'No, but you're more than a carpenter, what with the carving and all. Mebbe you should think about making stick wagons and stuff like that, selling them in other towns, putting announcements in the papers? And mebbe if you do, I'll be able to help you a bit from now on. It fair goes against the grain for me to be dependent on your charity.'

'You're family. And anyway, it was your money bought this place as well as mine.'

'That thought's been a comfort to me. But now it's time for us both to act, fight back.'

Lucas went back to the workshop feeling very happy that his uncle was well enough to try to help him.

Soon afterwards the third good thing of the day happened. The priest came in, carrying the piece of carved wood Declan had borrowed from him a few days ago.

A dazed Lucas found himself with a commission to carve some woodwork to beautify the Catholic church.

'How much will you charge for it?' the priest asked.

He spread his hands helplessly. 'I don't know. Perhaps you have some idea?'

The priest looked at him thoughtfully. 'I've already asked a friend of mine, who's had something similar done.' He named a sum that made Lucas gasp with pleasure. 'Will that be a fair price, do you think?'

'Yes. Very fair.'

'Then we'll both be happy.'

Was it possible Hungerton had failed? Lucas wondered as he went back to work. He gave a wry smile as he suddenly remembered the job in London and how upset he'd been to give it up. Well, one door had closed but another had opened.

Then he remembered how powerful Hungerton still was, how obsessed about getting his own back.

Would the new door be allowed to stay open?

Selwyn Hungerton intercepted the post. 'I'll just take out my own letters, Tythe, then I'll pass the rest on to my father.'

The butler hesitated, received an icy look and handed them over.

'I know he likes to get the post first, but I don't appreciate having my letters inspected each time.'

Selwyn took the letters into the room he used as a study and sorted quickly through them. One of his father's letters caught his eye and he sucked in his breath sharply. 'The little minx!' He removed the letter, tucking it quickly into an inside pocket, then picked up the rest of his father's letters and carried them through to the breakfast parlour.

'Here's the post, Father.'

'What are *you* doing bringing it in? That's Tythe's job.'

'I happened to pass him and took them from him.' He deposited the pile of missives in front of his father, picked up a plate and went to fill it.

'You've taken yours out!' The tone was angry.

Selwyn closed his eyes for a moment and prayed for patience. 'Of course I have.'

'I like to see what comes into my house and as long as I'm master here . . .'

'Please stop now, Father, and think what you're saying. When you were my age – which is forty-one, let me remind you, not fourteen – would you have tolerated having your correspondence inspected? I'm sure you wouldn't. And I won't tolerate it, either. If that's a condition of living under this roof . . .'

There was a long, pregnant silence as their eyes met. For once his father was the first to look away, shaking his head and muttering something under his breath.

'And don't blame poor Tythe. He was most reluctant to hand over the letters.'

After he'd eaten, Selwyn returned to his study and opened the letter which his daughter had sent from her new strict school to her grandfather, a letter that shouldn't have been possible after the arrangements he'd made. As he'd expected, she was pleading for her grandfather's help in taking her away from 'this terrible place where I cry myself to sleep every single night'. Selwyn breathed deeply in annoyance. He was paying very high fees to have Jane strictly supervised and was furious that she'd managed to get a letter out.

Pulling a piece of paper towards him, he wrote a terse note to the headmistress, putting his daughter's letter in the envelope as well. He went out to the stables and asked his groom to post it for him because he knew his father went through all the letters waiting for the post, as well as the ones that came into the house.

He had refused point-blank to tell his father in which boarding school he had placed Jane, but he'd have to intercept the mail every day from now on, just in case the little minx managed to smuggle another letter out.

As Selwyn was walking past the window of the library he heard his father exclaim in annoyance and start to berate someone. He hesitated then moved quietly forward to listen.

What he heard made him even angrier. It was more than time to stop this nonsense, only he hadn't yet worked out how to do that.

20

'You're looking more tired by the day,' Carrie said one morning.

Eli continued to get dressed. 'I'm all right.'

'You're not all right, love.'

'Well, I can't do anything else about the sleeping, so what can't be cured must be endured. I was having a ponder during the night. What do you think of my going to see that architect who's taken over at Stott's, doing what we said and hiring him officially to check on the building work?'

'Yes. I was going to remind you.'

When he'd gone out she went to find Raife, her usual confidant. 'I think it's a good sign, Eli not leaving it to me to do everything. Don't you?'

'I do, lass. It's wearing you down. You've been looking strained for weeks.'

Eli went to the site first, as he did every day, trying to keep an eye on things and make sure the work was done properly. The sun was shining with some real warmth in it, but that brightness only seemed to magnify the worries that were seething in his tired mind. The cellar walls had been completed quickly, with bricklayers from further down the railway line travelling to Hedderby every day. Old folk would marvel at travelling so far to work every day, but younger men were getting used to it now. Eli couldn't understand why local men hadn't been used and knew that had caused some bad feeling in the town.

After studying the work he caught the foreman's hostile gaze and moved on. He didn't like that fellow any more than he liked his master. And the men hired from Hedderby to do the unskilled work for the tradesmen were a rough lot. He could have found better ones himself but when he'd suggested it, the foreman had made it clear that he didn't welcome any interference.

At the house where Stott had once lived Eli paused, wondering if he was doing the right thing, then he took a deep breath and pushed open the gate. Mr Channon could only say no, after all.

But if he did, Eli didn't know what he'd do next.

After breakfast Jeremiah went to work in the bedroom turned office because he wanted to design a very special family house, one for Maria, the boys and himself – and big enough for more children if his hopes were fulfilled. Below him he could hear Renny pottering about in the back room, which no one else went into now, not even the maids. He could hear Renny's deep voice, but couldn't make out the words. A tangy smell of herbs burning seemed to be wafting up through the window, which was open on this fine day. He sniffed it, trying to work out which herbs exactly.

When a maid knocked on the door and said there was a man to see him, Jeremiah left his sketches reluctantly and went downstairs. 'Mr Beckett, isn't it?'

'Yes. I wonder if I could ask your professional help?'

'I'm not really ready to start work on anything yet.'

'It's advice I need not a building designing, and I'm happy to pay for it.'

Jeremiah guessed then that Beckett still had doubts about the work going on at the new theatre. He wanted to refuse to get involved, didn't need any more trouble in his life, but looking at the other man's anxious expression, he couldn't do that, because there were things that worried him about that building – things which raised questions about public safety. You couldn't ignore that. 'Come upstairs to my office.'

When the two men were seated, Eli explained the whole situation as he saw it. '. . . So I don't think the man is a proper architect. Only he's started work now and I've paid him a goodly sum in advance, so if things are all right, then maybe it's best to let him continue.'

Jeremiah nodded slowly. 'Very well.'

Eli beamed at him. 'You'll do it?'

'Yes. I'll meet you there this evening after they've left for the day. But I don't want you to talk about this to anyone.'

'Except my wife, who's a partner in every way.'

'Very well. I'll show you out.'

As they went downstairs there was a smell of burning from the back room, an acrid smell like the one that had filled Eli's nightmares for months.

'What . . .' Jeremiah ran towards the back of the house and threw open a door. Instinctively Eli followed. The room was full of smoke and Renny was lying unconscious on the floor in front of the fire. The hearthrug was smouldering.

'You see to him!' Eli dragged Renny off the rug, then rolled it up, ignoring the smouldering patches, and ran out into the hall with it. By that time people were moving towards the back room. 'Someone open the front door quickly!' he yelled and when Mrs Stott did that, he ran out and threw the rug on to the lawn.

When he turned round, he saw her waiting for him at the door and started back. But the visions of burning that bedevilled his sleep had suddenly filled his eyes, and he seemed to hear crackling flames, feel them around him. His steps faltered and he came to a stop.

Only when someone touched his arm did he manage to

shake off the nightmare visions and see the world around him once again. He realised it was Mrs Stott who was standing close to him. She was like Carrie, seemed to bring him the feeling of clean air and sanity once again. 'Sorry.'

'Are you ill, Mr Beckett?'

'No. I get – memories of the fire – they make everything blur around me sometimes.' He concentrated on breathing deeply and gradually everything steadied again. 'I'm sorry. How is your servant?'

'I don't know. I came to help you if you needed it. My housekeeper is with Jeremiah and Renny.'

'Shall we join them, find out what happened?'

Renny was fully conscious again, sitting on a sofa. He brushed away offers of drinks of water or a lie down and looked across at his mistress. 'I'm sorry, Mrs Stott. I felt dizzy. Must have been the herbs I was burning. I was trying to sweeten this room.'

She opened her mouth as if to speak, then closed it again, shaking her head helplessly.

'It's *him*, isn't it?' Jeremiah asked suddenly. 'It's as if he's haunting this place.'

She looked at him with despair on her face. 'I suppose so. I didn't think I believed in that sort of thing . . . before. But evil seems to linger in this room like a miasma. I can't sit here.'

Eli too could feel something evil in the room. And that made anger rise in him to think that anything of Athol Stott's wickedness could still be lingering.

'Will we never be rid of that man?' he demanded, unaware that his voice had risen to a near shout. 'I still dream of the flames he lit when he burned down our music saloon, can't get them out of my mind!'

Renny moved across to stand beside him and touch him, and the gentle pressure of his hand did more than anything to bring peace to Eli, peace such as he hadn't felt for weeks.

'He hurt a lot of people,' Renny said gently. 'But as time passes, it *will* fade, I promise you.'

As Eli walked home he was amazed to realise that he believed what Renny had said. He was normally a sceptical man, didn't believe in ghosts – but today he had felt *something*. He was grateful he didn't have to live in that room, or even the house that contained it.

When the visitor had gone, Renny slipped quietly out into the garden to seek nature's peace and Jeremiah joined Maria in her sitting room. They sat down and looked at one another.

'Ought we to leave this house?' Maria asked. 'Go and live somewhere else? I shall never use that room again.'

'It might be a solution.' He hesitated then looked at her. 'Would you like to leave?'

She shivered and looked round. 'Very much. But where would we go?'

'Would you want to stay in Hedderby?'

She gave this a moment or two's consideration, then nodded.

'I'd like to stay here too – with you.'

Her mouth fell open in shock and she moved instinctively backwards, fear on her face.

He spoke rapidly, trying to prevent her from saying something which would end the hopes that had been slowly growing in him. 'I shan't press that point in any way, I promise you, but I enjoy being with you and I think you feel comfortable with me. Surely you could give me a chance, see how things develop – between us?'

She shook her head and her voice came out more shrilly than usual. 'I meant what I said. I shall never remarry. Never.'

'That would be a great pity. Your boys need a father, a caring, loving father, and you need loving too.' He stood up and left, instinctively knowing it was no use to try to press his suit at this point. He could only hope that living together as they did, she would learn to trust him.

It had hurt him to see her recoil from him at the mere thought of marriage.

That night after the men had stopped work, Eli and Carrie went to meet Mr Channon at the site, taking with them the drawings, which they'd managed to 'borrow' from Trevin again on the excuse of using them to design posters for the grand opening.

'I wonder what it'll look like when it's finished,' she said.

'You've seen the drawings.' Eli tapped the roll under his arm.

'Yes, but this doesn't quite feel like the drawings we chose. He's changed some things, I can tell that, even though it's only partly built.'

'Good evening.'

They turned to greet Mr Channon.

He unrolled the drawings and studied them, then walked round the site, examining the work done so far. The cellar walls were in place and the labourers had started filling in the earth behind them. He began pacing up and down, counting, muttering, referring to the sketch, which Eli and Carrie were holding for him.

'I'd like to take the sketches home with me and study them tonight, if you don't mind. There are differences in the actual building.'

'Trevin wants the sketches back in the morning. He didn't like leaving them with us.'

'What time does he usually arrive?'

'On the nine o'clock train.'

'I'll bring them round to Linney's by eight o'clock, then.'

He walked away before they could question him further.

'What do you think of him?' Eli asked.

She stood with her head to one side, considering. 'He feels – honest. He doesn't smile much, though, does he? And he looks rather sad. But he thought the building seemed a bit different from the sketches too, so I wasn't mistaken.'

'You never are about things like that.' He rubbed his stomach and grinned at her. 'Let's go home and have our supper.'

'*Dinner*,' she mocked. 'Genteel people call it dinner in the evening.'

'I doubt I'll ever be genteel then. To me, dinner is what you eat in the middle of the day.'

They found Renny waiting for them at Linney's, with a package.

'This may help you to sleep, Mr Beckett. Steep a spoonful in boiling water and drink the liquid half an hour before you go to bed.' With a gentle smile, he walked away, leaving Eli to call out his thanks.

They opened the package and studied the contents dubiously.

'Shall I try it?' Eli asked.

Raife came across to sniff the dried herbs and smiled. 'Reminds me of summat my mother used to drink when she couldn't sleep. Eh, it's a long time since I've seen this stuff.'

'Is it safe?'

'Safer than that laudanum some folk use. Can't hurt to try this once, can it?'

And although Eli didn't sleep soundly, he slept a bit better and didn't have any of the lurid nightmares that drove him to walk the streets.

Renny brought the sketches round at eight o'clock. 'Mr Channon wondered if you could go and see him later this morning?'

'Yes, of course.'

★

Jabez fumed and fretted about his ignominious dismissal from Hedderby. Mr Hungerton wasn't pleased about that. Indeed, the old man seemed angry at the whole world lately, including Mr Selwyn, who was usually a favourite of his father's.

As Jabez worked in the stables, he wondered yet again how to finish the job that had now become a personal quest, not only to redeem himself in his master's eyes, but also to get revenge on that slut. Lucas Kemp was no doubt enjoying her favours. He should give other men a turn. Jabez's sister was no help – and just wait till she came home on a visit, wouldn't he give her what for! Putting on airs as if she was better than him now that she'd got a fancy new job!

He noticed Mr Selwyn walking along the path to the stable yard, a white envelope in his hand and wondered what he was doing there, since he wasn't dressed for riding. Putting down the curry comb, Jabez crept out along the back and heard Mr Selwyn say, 'Go and put it in the post straight away. If anyone tries to stop you, tell them you're on an errand for me.'

Jabez knew this was his chance to make Mr Hungerton trust him again. The only reason Mr Selwyn could be sending his groom to the post was to keep what he was sending private.

He waited until the other man had gone riding off into the village, then went to the head groom. 'Mr Hungerton wants me to do an errand for him.'

He grinned as he too rode towards the village. Magic words they were, 'Mr Hungerton wants . . .'

He took a roundabout way into the village, not wanting to make Mr Selwyn's groom suspicious. When he got there, he tied up the horse and strode confidently into the little post office run by an elderly spinster. 'Has the post gone? Thank goodness! Mr Hungerton wants me to get his letter back.'

It was as easy as that. He studied the address on the envelope. It was addressed to a school. It'd be about Miss Jane. All the servants were aware that Mr Hungerton didn't know where she'd been sent and had quarrelled with his son because of it.

Jabez grinned all the way home, couldn't wait to see his master and give him this. He'd be in high favour again now.

Gwynna felt shy as she got ready to meet Lucas on the Sunday afternoon. She'd kept an eye on the weather all morning, terrified it'd rain and spoil their walk, but although there was an occasional cloud to cover the sun, there was no feel of rain in the air.

When Betty came up to care for Libby, she looked down her nose. 'Cheap and nasty, that skirt of yours is. Can't you afford better than that?'

Even though she knew the other girl was only trying to make her feel uncomfortable, Gwynna couldn't help glancing down anxiously at the blue skirt she'd made herself. 'You're just jealous because you haven't got a young man.'

'Jealous? Of you going out walking with a thief? Never!'

But as Gwynna watched her, Betty lifted Libby up and gave her a cuddle, and the little girl smiled and cooed at her. 'When you're being nasty, I always try to remember how good you are with children.'

She had the satisfaction of leaving Betty gaping at her in shock, and that boosted her morale.

It was boosted still further when she saw the expression of admiration on Lucas's face as she walked towards him. He was waiting for her outside, wearing his Sunday best and clutching a cap in his hand.

'Hello, Gwynna. I thought we'd go up on the tops and come down the back end of town.'

'It'll be nice to stretch my legs a bit. You can't walk fast when you're pushing a wagon.'

He offered his arm and she took it self-consciously, hoping they wouldn't meet anyone she knew, not this first time. Today she just wanted to enjoy herself and get to know him better, small things like what was his favourite meal, what his life had been like as a lad. She wanted to know everything about him, really.

As soon as they got out of the town, he stopped and took her hand in his. 'You have nice capable hands.'

'Nice and red from the work I do.'

'There's nothing to be ashamed of in working hard, lass. How is that baby going on?'

'Not so much a baby now. Libby took her very first steps this week. Her father's that pleased.'

'You love children, don't you?'

'Yes. I've always had them around me, from when I was little myself and had to look after my sisters.'

'You've had a hard life. Lost the man you loved, lost his baby too.'

She had to ask it. 'You don't mind about that?'

'Of course I don't. I've known for a long time. What happened?'

'After Patrick died, I didn't have enough food because my parents took my wages for drink. And then the baby was born dead.' She looked into the distance for a minute. 'It was a little girl. She was so tiny and still. She never breathed, not once.' She blinked her eyes. 'What are we talking about this for? You won't want to hear about it.'

He stopped again and put his arm round her shoulders. 'I do. I want to know everything about you.' He gathered his courage in both hands and said the words that had been dancing round his brain for days. 'I love you, Gwynna Jones. I'm not best placed to do anything about it for a while, but one day . . .'

She let herself say the words too, because they made it feel real to her. 'I love you too, Lucas, with all my heart.'

'That's grand!' He picked her up suddenly and swung her round as if she weighed nothing, then he pulled her to him and kissed her.

Not shy now but eager for his kisses, she twined her arms round his neck and forgot the world for a few blissful minutes until the sound of voices made them both come down to earth with a jolt.

Holding hands they set off walking again, following the accepted route for courting couples. They met a few others up there on the same errand and exchanged self-conscious smiles with them.

The walk was over all too quickly and as they were making their way back down to the town she asked anxiously what the time was.

He pulled out a pocket watch, opened it and said, 'Half-past three.'

'Eh, where has the afternoon gone? I've to be back by four.'

'We'd better get a move on then.'

By the time they reached Mill House, she was rosy-cheeked and a little breathless, but with five minutes still to go, they lingered at the gate talking.

From an upstairs room Betty saw the edge of Gwynna's blue skirt through the little gate, with a trousered leg beyond it, and felt jealousy sear through her. No lad had ever come courting her because she wasn't pretty like Gwynna. She wasn't free with her favours, either.

Jabez was right. The girl was a slut and shouldn't be working in a respectable household. She was surprised Mrs Forrett put up with it.

A smile settled for a moment on her face as she suddenly

got an idea. Her mistress mostly did as her husband told her, but she could grow very stubborn at times and she didn't like Gwynna. Maybe Betty could find ways to set Mrs Forrett even more strongly against the other girl. It was worth a try. No one could blame her for that, could they?

21

'Don't you think you'd better see Mr Channon alone?' Carrie asked.

'No. You and I are partners. We both spoke to him at the site and we'll both speak to him now.' Eli gave her a quick hug and stepped away, repeating, 'Together in this, as in everything, love.'

She resisted the temptation to pull him back and ask why a quick, almost furtive hug was the nearest he got to touching her at the moment. Whatever had upset his peace of mind after the fire had also stopped him showing his love for her, which was hard when they'd been so loving before. She'd just have to be patient and hope he'd recover fully one day. Surely he would?

The two of them were shown into the front room at the Stott house, which seemed enormous to Carrie. There was such elegant furniture in it that she wished she had time to look at it properly.

Jeremiah came forward to greet them. 'Please sit down and I'll give you my professional opinion on the theatre building so far.' He waited until they were seated then said in his quiet way, 'I don't think your Mr Trevin is a trained architect, nor does he truly understand the principles of constructing build-ings. And you were quite correct, Mrs Beckett, when you said that what he's doing differs from the sketches he showed you in several important ways.' He proceeded to list these, then finished, 'But what worries me most of all is having only a single layer brick wall lining the cellar and such a narrow patch of ground supporting so much of the building just above it. If I'd been building that, I'd have put in a double wall, well reinforced, and I'd have had more supporting pillars beneath the stage as well. Indeed, I'd not have made the cellar so wide.'

They looked at him in dismay then turned to one another, clasping hands instinctively.

'It's my fault,' Eli said. 'I've ruined us. Can you ever forgive me, Carrie love?'

'*You* haven't ruined us. It was Athol Stott who did that.' Then she remembered that Mr Channon was a cousin of Stott's and glanced at him guiltily.

Jeremiah met her gaze steadily. 'It's all right. I know what my cousin was like. But it is possible to rescue the building even now if you stop work and redo the design and foundations. It'll add to the cost, though, I'm afraid.'

Eli was starting to feel as if he was stifling. 'The trouble is, I paid Trevin quite a lot of money in advance when I signed the contract with him, and I doubt he'll return it. I'm not sure I'll have enough left to finish off the building if we have to start again. And to make matters worse, it's not just our own money, but my cousin Joanna's as well.'

'Could you perhaps find another investor?' Jeremiah asked.

'We didn't want someone else telling us what to do.' Eli could no longer bear to sit still and jerked to his feet.

Feeling helpless, Carrie watched him pace up and down the room, despair in every line of his body.

'Was the music saloon profitable?' Jeremiah asked.

Eli stopped walking for a moment. 'Yes, very.' Without waiting for a reply he went to stand by the window, which was slightly open. There seemed to be more air there and he was having difficulty breathing, as well as trying to ignore the desperate urge to run outside.

Jeremiah hesitated. 'I may be able to help you find an investor. But I'll need to know more about music halls first. I've never even visited one. Until I came here, I thought they were dens of vice. But I'm hearing differently from so many people that I now know I was misinformed. Perhaps you can tell me where to go to visit one?'

'We can do better than that.' Distracted from his own problems for a moment or two, Eli turned to smile at Carrie. 'We'll take you into Manchester ourselves. Eh, love? It'll do us good to have a night out.'

She nodded. 'It will indeed.'

Jeremiah looked from one to the other. 'I'd like that. And perhaps you could also tell me something about the financial side of owning a music hall? Do you have figures, accounts, to show exactly how profitable yours was?'

Eli gestured to his wife. 'Carrie's the one who understands the details of that, though you'll just have to take her word for it at the moment, because our account books were burned in the fire.'

'Of course. I'd forgotten that.' Jeremiah studied her curiously. 'Most women wouldn't be involved in that side of things.'

'She's not "most women",' Eli said proudly.

Carrie did a quick mental calculation of what figures she'd need to produce. 'If you come round to Linney's tomorrow afternoon, I'll have some summaries ready that will give you a good idea of how things work.'

'I shall be happy to do that and—' An idea suddenly occurred to him. 'I think I'll invite my cousin Maria to join us on our visit to Manchester, if you don't mind. She'll enjoy an outing, I'm sure.'

When the visitors had left, Jeremiah went to find Maria, eager to invite her out. She was in the kitchen discussing menus with Cook, but turned to smile at him.

'Could I have a word with you, Maria?'

'Yes, of course.'

'Perhaps out in the garden? It's such a lovely spring day.'

He escorted her outside and they began to walk round the vegetable garden, admiring the recent spurt of growth, the promise in the young green plants.

At the far end she stopped. 'What did you want to talk about?'

He hadn't thought it'd be difficult to invite her, but now he was having trouble finding the words. 'Er – I'm advising the Becketts about the new building. There are problems and the man in charge isn't as capable as one would have expected. But I've never visited a music hall, so they're going to take me into Manchester one evening to visit one. I – er – wondered if you'd like to join us?'

She looked at him in astonishment. 'I've never been to one, either. Are you sure you want me to come with you?'

'Of course I am. I enjoy your company.'

That made her go very still. Her eyes searched his face and she seemed to see the feelings for her he was trying to hide. 'I've told you before. Don't enjoy my company. Go out and meet other ladies. Enjoy *their* company. I'm too – damaged.'

He grabbed her arm and was horrified when she cringed away from him as if expecting him to hit her. 'Maria, no! I'd never hurt you. *Never.* All I wanted was some company for the evening, someone to discuss things with afterwards. And I thought you'd enjoy an outing.'

She stopped trying to pull away and her breathing quietened down, though her breast was still heaving and small shudders were running through her. 'I'm sorry. You see how it is, how he's left me.' She glanced over her shoulder towards the windows of the library. 'I feel as if he's still in there, still watching every move I make.'

'I can understand that. And the room makes me uneasy too. But although I might wish to – to take matters further between us eventually, I'd never force you into anything you didn't want. Surely you know me well enough to understand that by now?'

She nodded, but her eyes still showed fear.

'Then will you come? Mr and Mrs Beckett will be with us, it'll all be perfectly respectable. And it'll do you good, I'm sure.'

'Very well.' She bit her lip then, as they began to walk back to the house, stopped again to ask, 'What do ladies wear to visit these places?'

'I have no idea. Perhaps you could ask Mrs Beckett?'

'Yes.'

'It's for the evening after tomorrow.'

'So soon?'

'The sooner the better. Their personal situation is very difficult and needs resolving. They've paid that charlatan who's supposed to be building the new theatre quite a lot of money in advance, you see, and they may not have enough left to finish building it.'

Her expression softened instantly. 'I feel guilty about that because it was Athol who ruined them. They lost everything in that fire, personal things as well as the business. Insurance money won't compensate for so many losses, I'm sure.'

Jeremiah hesitated, then said it. 'I'm thinking of investing in the theatre, both money and my professional skills. I could work with someone who understands theatrical architecture and – well, it's time I started work again.' He smiled into the distance, talking mainly to himself. 'Coming here, being needed by the boys and you, has been one of the best things that has ever happened to me. I was lost and sad before, just drifting, but I've never been so quietly happy in my whole life as I have here.'

Quietly happy. Maria carried those words in her heart for the rest of the day. To be quietly happy was her ambition too. Strange that a man had said those words.

She put on her mantle and bonnet and walked into town. She knew where Linney's was. She'd go and call on Mrs Beckett, ask her advice about what to wear.

In his local pub Declan was approached by a man he'd never seen there before. The stranger was well though not richly dressed, and was nicely spoken. There was something in his accent, however, which said he'd learned to speak that way in the past few years, because every now and then he stopped in the middle of a word and corrected his pronunciation of it.

'I gather you're quite a power in this town, Mr Heegan,' the stranger began.

'I have some influence among the Irish community,' Declan allowed, raising his drink and taking a careful sip.

'Yes, well, you've been well recommended and I'm employed by a gentleman who is prepared to pay quite highly for your services.'

'Oh? Who would this gentleman be and what does he want me to do?'

The man hesitated, then leaned closer and lowered his voice still further. 'My client doesn't wish to be named, but he knows you've been preventing certain attempts to attack and ruin Lucas Kemp and Gwynna Jones.'

Declan paused with the pot of beer partway to his mouth, wondering if they were trying to buy him off and prevent him helping Lucas, and if so, how much that was worth. He took a sip and put the pot down, waiting for the man to continue.

'You could earn a great deal of money if you were to undertake a small task or two for my client.'

'I'm prepared to consider the matter – if the money is tempting enough. But I'd need to know exactly what was involved first. I won't break the law, not for anyone.'

The man leaned back and smiled, though the smile didn't reach his eyes. 'I'll arrange a meeting for you with my client, then. He wishes to explain his needs in person. Would two nights hence suit you?'

Declan nodded.

'I'll come and pick you up here, then take you to meet him.'

'I'll bring a friend with me, if you don't mind.'

'We'd rather you didn't.'

Declan shrugged. 'In that case I'm not coming.'

His companion hesitated, then said, 'One friend only, who will wait outside the house, and no others are to follow us.'

'Agreed.'

When the man had left the pub, Declan let out a long, low whistle.

One of his regular drinking companions came across to join him. 'Who was that?'

'Someone wanting me to do a job.'

The other man spat into the sawdust on the floor. 'Moving in high circles now, aren't you, me boy?'

'Not too high to drink with my old friends.' But even as he said it Declan knew it wasn't true. If he did make something of himself, as he hoped, he would be looking at a different way of life. He never had liked fellows who spat like that, especially indoors. Dirty, it was. He scowled down at his beer. The trouble was, his wife wasn't the sort who could make the change to a better way of life. She was a shrew and stupid with it, wasn't even pretty now. Why the hell had he married her?

He let out a mirthless snort of laughter as he answered that. He'd married her for the usual reasons, because she was carrying his child and because his Mammy and the priest had cornered him about doing the right thing by her. There was also the small point that if he stayed in Hedderby without marrying her, her brothers and father would have beaten him senseless.

Now, both her brothers had moved away and her father was dead, but Declan was still lumbered with her until 'death us do part'. And Ruth was never ill, for all her complaining and whining. Well, he wouldn't be getting any more sons on her, that was sure, because he couldn't even bear to touch her now, had even bought himself a separate bed on the pretext that she was a restless sleeper and kept him awake. They had a decent house with a water tap in the scullery, so she had no excuse for not washing herself regularly. And if she thought he didn't know about the nips of gin she took in the evenings, never enough to make her drunk, but enough to make her stumble over her words and decisions, she was even more stupid than he'd thought. And his sons were like her, stupid, at least they seemed so to him, on the rare occasions he tried to talk to them. He didn't spend time at home if he could help it.

He realised the man next to him had spoken and was waiting for an answer. 'Sorry. I was thinking about something. What did you say?'

'I said I wished the music hall was still there. I could have done with something to cheer myself up tonight.'

'Aye. So could I.' And every other night, too.

James Forrett looked at his wife and didn't even try to hide his disgust. 'What's so important that you have to interrupt my dinner, woman? Make it quick. I have to be back in the mill in a few minutes.'

'I don't think it's right for a girl like that Gwynna to look after our child and live in our house. She has a bad reputation in the town. I want her dismissed.'

'What's brought this on so suddenly?'

'What do you mean, what's brought it on? I didn't want to employ her in the first place and well you know it.'

'Rubbish. You couldn't wait for someone to take the baby off your hands.'

'I didn't know what she was like then.'

'Well, I'm pleased with her work, so you'll just have to put up with her being here. It's not as if you see much of her, because you rarely go near your daughter. If Gwynna hadn't come, I'm not sure Libby would have survived your tender ministrations and those doses of Dr Godfrey's Damned Cordial you poured into her. I'll always be grateful to the lass for that.'

'Being grateful is one thing, continuing to employ a female like her is another.'

'Has Betty been stirring this trouble up?'

'I don't need a maid to tell me what's right and what's wrong, thank you very much.' Nenny sighed. 'I wish the sale of the mill hadn't fallen through. How much longer are we to live like this, so close to all that clanking machinery and dust? No wonder Libby didn't thrive. It's *your* fault she was so sickly. I'd have thought by now you could have found another buyer. I was *so* looking forward to living at the seaside.'

He looked at her with loathing. She was still coming to him every day for her dose of that damned stuff and yesterday had begged him for more. He'd been so angry he'd given her what was left in the bottle. At least when she took the stuff she didn't nag him as much. Her speech was always slightly slurred and though she was going out and about, meeting the other ladies she called 'friends', she wasn't any happier. Nenny had brought him money at a time when he needed it, but he'd paid for that every day of his life since. She was no wife for a lusty man and was growing vague and disoriented under the influence of the laudanum.

'What if I send you to the seaside to finish your recovery?' he asked. 'It's very fashionable to go there and with the weather getting warmer . . .'

She brightened up. 'You'd let me go away on my own?'

He'd pay a fortune for her to go away, he thought bitterly. But he knew she wasn't capable of managing a separate life, so his daily responsibility for her would never end unless he found someone else to take it over. 'Maybe I will let you go. I'll look into it. You're not fully recovered, that's for sure.'

'I'm a lot better since I've had Betty to look after me.'

'I'll send her with you, don't worry.' He didn't like the girl, not at all. There was something sly about her and it reflected in her face, making it uglier than it needed to be.

'When can I go?'

'When I've found out where to send you.'

The idea of getting rid of his wife was growing more and more attractive. There were homes for foolish women like her, he was sure of it, places where she'd be looked after, spoiled even, and where he would never have to see her again. He didn't care what his daughters said. The longer he and Nenny stayed together the unhappier they made one another, and you only had one life.

A good thing he was a wealthy man and could afford to do this decently. He felt sorry for poor men who had no choice but to put up with unsuitable wives until one of them died.

But in the meantime he wanted to keep an eye on both Gwynna and Betty, and find out what the hell was going on in this town lately.

Gwynna overheard her mistress talking to Betty about dismissing her and didn't know what to do. She wanted to keep the job, loved Libby, but the atmosphere was uncomfortable any time Betty was around. The other girl didn't trouble to hide her disdain these days and had a sly air of triumph about her, as if she knew something that Gwynna didn't.

This morning it was raining so she couldn't take Libby out for a walk, which was a pity, because the child was teething and had been crying intermittently for the past two days, waking up during the night as well. Mrs Forrett had sent Betty upstairs several times to complain.

Mr Forrett had come up, too, and when he'd seen how tired Gwynna was, had taken his little daughter off her hands for a while. You couldn't doubt that he loved her.

Having played all sorts of games and sung herself hoarse, Gwynna put Libby down for her nap. But a few minutes later the child started crying again, at first a low, miserable sound gradually building up into a roar of anger at being laid in the cot.

Betty appeared in the doorway again. 'Mrs Forrett says can you *please* stop that baby from crying.'

Gwynna joggled Libby around in her arms. 'I'm doing my best, but you know what they're like sometimes. She's teething, poor little thing.'

'You're stupid not to give her some cordial. It keeps them quiet at times like this.'

'I don't believe in it. Anyway, they need to cry to develop their lungs.'

'Well, other folk don't need to listen to them going on and on. Mrs Forrett is getting very angry with you.' She stamped off down to her mistress's room.

What did the two women do in there for so many hours? Gwynna wondered, walking up and down with Libby in her arms. When the child had quieted a little, she sat her in the special baby chair and went downstairs to get her a drink of warm milk and a crust to chew on, hoping that would keep her quiet.

Betty was in the kitchen getting her mistress a cup of tea, so Gwynna had to wait for what she needed. She went to the bottom of the stairs a couple of times and listened but couldn't hear anything.

When she got back to the nursery, she found Libby asleep, slumped in her chair. Putting down the cup of warm milk she went to pick the baby up, intending to put her to bed. She smelled something and sniffed. What was it? She sniffed again and frowned. It smelled like Godfrey's Cordial. She looked down and saw a stickiness around Libby's lips, put her fingertip in it and licked it off.

It *was* the horrible sickly stuff! As she studied the child more closely, she saw that Libby was sleeping more heavily than usual, her breathing laboured, her colour pale when it had been rosy this morning.

Betty had been in the kitchen. Only one person could have given the child the cordial.

How much had Mrs Forrett given her?

Gwynna hesitated, wondering what to do. She sat with Libby in her arms, but the child's breathing grew laboured and she had developed a waxy look to her face that worried Gwynna. She carried Libby down to the kitchen. But one look at Cook's angry face made her abandon the idea of sharing her worries. Cook made no secret of the fact that she didn't like babies and insisted she knew nothing about them, didn't want to, either.

Gwynna went to the back door, hoping the fresh air would revive the child, but saw to her horror that Libby's lips had taken on a bluish tinge and she was hardly breathing at all.

What was she to do?

22

Jeremiah went to Linney's as arranged and found Carrie waiting for him on her own.

She began, 'Eli sends his apologies and—' then broke off. 'I don't want to deceive you, Mr Channon. Eli hasn't been himself since the fire and keeps getting nightmares about being trapped. Even in the daytime he gets them and has to go outside or he can't breathe properly.'

'It must have been a horrifying experience.'

'Yes . . . But you have to keep going, don't you?' One sigh escaped her, then her tone became brisker. 'Now, here are some figures I've compiled for you. They're fairly typical of the last few weeks of running the Pride.'

He was impressed by her neat rows of figures. If they were true – and he had no reason to doubt her – then a music saloon or hall seemed to be rather a good investment financially.

'I'm sorry I can't give you the exact figures,' she said when he'd finished studying her careful lists, 'but you could go to the bank and confirm how much we paid in every week. That would go some way towards proving that I'm telling the truth, wouldn't it?'

'Would you mind if I did that? Not because I doubt you, but because I'm cautious by nature.'

'Not at all. In fact, I'll come with you to tell them it's all right to give you the figures.'

As they walked through the streets he couldn't help noticing how freely she strode out, so that he didn't have to slow his steps to match her pace. He'd never met anyone like her, but wondered what it would be like to be married to such a person. He'd rather have a gentler woman, one like Maria. He tried to push that thought aside, but it never left him completely because the more he lived in the same house, the more he came to value her qualities and character.

The owner of the bank frowned at Carrie. 'I'd have preferred to see *Mr* Beckett here today.'

'Well, you've got me and you know I do most of the paperwork.'

Throwing her a disapproving glance, he took them into his comfortable office and sent for the ledgers. A clerk struggled in with some heavy, leather-bound books and set them down on the desk.

'Here's the page summarising Mr Beckett's account,' the banker told Jeremiah, ignoring Carrie. 'As you can see, money came in very steadily.'

Mr Beckett's account, Jeremiah thought with a sudden urge to smile. It was *Mrs* Beckett who dealt with the money. Eli had been the one to run the music saloon and act as Chairman, whatever that meant. He would find out tonight. 'Yes, they seem very much as you indicated, Mrs Beckett. You're clearly good at figures.' He nearly laughed out loud at the sourness of the banker's expression.

Feeling optimistic and cheerful, he walked home. He hadn't felt like this for a long time – if ever – because he'd always been under his father's thumb. That was ridiculous for a man his age, but it was hard to go against one's upbringing.

Desperately worried for the child, Gwynna carried her across to the mill office, to the only person with the sense to make a decision. To her relief Mr Forrett was there. 'Sir, I'm worried about Libby. Look how pale she is, hardly breathing. I can't rouse her.'

She told him what she thought had happened and he too tried to rouse his daughter, but couldn't.

'We'll send for the doctor,' he said.

'I could run to his house with her. That'd be much quicker.'

'Aye. And I'll come with you. I want to hear what he says.'

They hurried through the streets and as Gwynna found her burden slowing her down, he lifted his daughter into his own arms without breaking his stride.

Mrs Pipperday opened the door, took one look at them and called for her husband.

The doctor too tried to rouse the child, but failed. Within the hour Libby had slipped from life and the doctor looked up from her tiny body, his expression sad. 'I think it was the Godfrey's Cordial,' he said. 'It's dangerous to give such a heavy dose to a child of this age.' He turned to frown at Gwynna. 'Surely *you* didn't give it to her?'

'No. I never would.'

'I know who gave it to her,' Forrett said grimly. 'Her mother.' He wiped away a tear with the back of his hand but another followed. 'She takes that filthy stuff herself, doesn't know what she's doing half the time. I've tried stopping her and she's always found ways to get hold of more.'

'It must have been a massive dose. Libby was a healthy infant, well cared for.'

Forrett stared at the doctor in sudden horror. 'Yesterday Nenny nagged so much about needing more that I gave her what was left in the bottle to shut her up.' He groaned and covered his face with one hand for a moment, then stood up. 'Give Libby to me. I want to take her home.'

'Should I not call the undertaker to do that?'

'You can ask him to come round to my house in an hour's time, if you will. I want to say goodbye to my daughter, and then . . . then I'll have to deal with my wife.'

Gwynna followed him to the door. He looked sideways at her. 'Was that maid of my wife's involved in this?'

'I don't think so, sir. Betty was in the kitchen with me when it happened and she'd gone down there before I even left the nursery.'

He nodded. 'So it's got to be Nenny who did it. Just her.'

He began walking and Gwynna stayed by his side, not saying anything. What could you say? Every now and then a tear rolled down her cheek and she brushed it away automatically. She saw people staring at them but didn't care. If you couldn't weep for the death of a child, when could you weep?

As they arrived at the mill, the men in the yard stopped work to stare at the sight of their master carrying a baby. But Forrett ignored them and something about his set, grim expression must have warned them not to approach him.

Gwynna opened the front door and as he went inside, he said quietly, 'You stay down in the kitchen with Cook till I call for you.'

'Yes, sir.'

Still carrying his child's body, James strode up the stairs and Gwynna watched him till he was out of sight then went into the kitchen. She sank down at the big, scrubbed table, suddenly overcome by grief and began to weep, sobbing so hard that Cook came across to pat her on the back.

'What's up lass? What's happened?'

'She's dead, Libby is. The mistress gave her some of that horrible cordial. Too much. And it killed her. We've just come back from the doctor's.'

'Eh, never!'

Betty came hurrying down the back stairs, her face white. 'I think he's going to kill the mistress. What on earth's happened?'

Gwynna looked up. 'She's killed Libby.'

Betty stared at her in shock. 'How could she have?'

'She gave her some cordial to quieten her while I was down in the kitchen, only she gave her too much and killed her instead.'

'No!' Betty sank down on the nearest chair. 'That lovely little baby, dead. I can't believe it.'

As she fell silent, the only sound in the room was Gwynna's stifled sobbing.

The housemaid came creeping in to join them, looking terrified, and the four women waited, not saying a word.

When Forrett went upstairs he paused outside his wife's bedroom door to take a deep breath. He mustn't murder Nenny, though he felt like doing so every time he glanced down at his dead child.

He pressed a kiss on Libby's pale cheek, then turned the handle and slammed the door open. The two women inside turned round, mouths dropping open in shock. 'You, get out!' he roared, pointing to Betty, who edged past him and rushed downstairs.

Nenny stared at him in blank bewilderment. 'What's wrong, James?' she faltered.

'This!' He thrust his daughter at her and she took the child from him.

'Shhh. She's asleep.'

'She's not asleep, you fool, she's dead.' If he hadn't caught the little body, Nenny would have dropped it.

'What has that girl done to her?'

'*That girl?* Gwynna hasn't done anything. It's *you* who killed her, you stupid bitch. How much cordial did you give her?'

'Just a drop or two, James, that's all. She wouldn't stop crying. My head was hurting.'

He closed his eyes and reined back his anger. *Wouldn't stop crying!* And for that his child had died.

But the anger and pain welled up again. He knew if he stayed a minute longer he'd throttle the stupid woman, so he left, slamming the bedroom door behind him and carrying his daughter's body up to the nursery. There he laid her in the cot, then fell to his knees by the side of it and began to weep, great heart-rending sobs that nearly tore him apart.

Downstairs the four women in the kitchen heard the bedroom door slam shut, heard footsteps go upstairs, then heard the dreadful sound of a man's agony.

Gwynna stopped crying. No one moved or said a word. After a minute of listening, her heart clenching in sympathy for him, she stood up.

'Where are you going?' Cook asked.

'Upstairs to the master.'

'You'll never!'

'He needs someone.'

Gwynna climbed slowly up the stairs, wondering what to say to him. At the top she hesitated. Perhaps he wouldn't want any comfort from her. But she couldn't leave him alone with his grief, just couldn't.

Outside the nursery door she stopped and looked inside, then went across to the man still kneeling there and knelt down beside him, compassion overcoming her doubts. Putting her arms round him, she began rocking him slightly, murmuring to him as she would have done to a child.

After a while he seemed to realise she was there and he clung to her, muttering incoherently, weeping on her shoulder, so that she felt the dampness of his tears. It was a long time before he stopped, then at last he pulled away from her, trying to wipe the moisture from his eyes and cheeks.

She fumbled in her pocket and pulled out her handkerchief, already dampened by her own tears.

He sat back on his heels, took it from her, wiped his face

and blew his nose. He gestured to the cot. 'She was so small, so helpless. You couldn't help loving her.'

'I know. I loved her too.'

He gulped back another sob, rubbed his eyes and got to his feet. 'Will *you* lay her out for me?'

She stood up. 'Yes, of course. It'll be an honour.'

He looked at her with a bitter twisted expression on his face. 'Why didn't I marry someone like you, someone who'd love their children? I might have a daughter to love me in my old age if I had.'

There were footsteps on the stairs and the housemaid came to the doorway, looking ready to run away. 'If you please, sir, the undertaker's here.'

'Show him into the parlour. I'll be down in a minute.'

As James went down the stairs, he opened the door to his wife's bedroom. She shrieked in fear at the sight of him and cowered away. He didn't say a word, just took the key from the inside of the door, closed it on her and locked it, slipping the key into his pocket.

'You'll kill no more children,' he muttered.

Downstairs he spoke to the undertaker, then he sat, just sat, because he couldn't seem to find the energy to do anything.

No one dared disturb him and when the overlooker came across to ask what was happening, Cook told him about Libby and suggested he manage without the master today.

Lucas was horrified when he heard about Forrett's little daughter dying, and utterly disgusted when he heard how it had happened. He sat in the workshop thinking of the waste of that young life, then began to worry about Gwynna. She'd loved Libby, no one could have doubted that. How must she be feeling?

He waited until after tea then made his way round to Mill

House. The workers had gone home and the square, five-storey building loomed above him in the dusk, all its dazzling gas lights out now, except for two in the yard. The front door of the house, he saw, had a big black bow on it and all the blinds were lowered.

'What are you doing here?' a voice said, a voice that sounded husky and raw.

He looked again and saw Forrett, sitting on a packing case in the far corner of the yard underneath the lamp that burned there all night. Without hesitation he walked across. 'I'm sorry for your loss, Mr Forrett. Libby was a lovely little lass.'

'You're the first to dare speak to me since the undertaker left,' Forrett said, his words slurred. 'Gwynna's sitting with Libby. I don't want the child left on her own. The others scuttle out of the way when I go into a room, or stand there as if they expect me to murder someone. You'll want to see Gwynna, I suppose.'

Lucas perched on the nearest packing case. 'Yes. She'll be upset and I didn't think anyone would have time to care about her.'

Forrett stared at him solemnly for a minute or two from swollen, red-rimmed eyes, then nodded slowly. 'You're right. But she's coping, your lass is. And she's the only one who's been able to offer me any comfort. I shan't forget that. Just as I shan't forgive my wife.'

'Did Mrs Forrett know what she was doing?'

'No, not really. She was doped by that damned cordial. A fine wife she is! And I dare say the stupid woman will live to be ninety just to spite me! But I'll make sure she doesn't harm anyone else, by hell I will. She's lost what few wits she had to that stuff, so I'm going to have her locked away in a home for rich lunatics. I went back to see Pipperday once I'd worked out what to do. He says he knows a place and he'll make the arrangements for me.

He agrees it's for the best, because Nenny isn't to be trusted again.'

His voice faltered and he sat in silence for a minute or two, then said sadly, 'But that won't bring Libby back, will it? I was too busy making my fortune to enjoy my other children, but I was enjoying her. Her little face used to light up when she saw me.' He gulped and fought to control himself.

Lucas laid a hand on his for a moment, offering silent sympathy.

'I was going to sell the mill and take Libby to grow up somewhere healthy by the sea. I've even found another buyer for it. Ironic, isn't it? Now I don't know what to do with myself. What do *you* think I should do?'

'I don't know. Do you want to live on your own at the seaside in a place where you know no one?'

Forrett stared blindly across the mill yard then shook his head. 'I'd go mad from boredom.'

'Then perhaps you should stay here and keep the mill going. But . . .' Lucas hesitated, wondering if he was being presumptuous.

'But what?'

'You could do some good in your daughter's name. There are children living on the streets in this town without families to care for them. They starve to death in winter, did you know that? Why don't you do something to help them?'

Forrett stared at him as if he'd suddenly grown horns and a tail.

'I'm sorry. It was just a suggestion.'

'It was a good one, a damned good one.' James rubbed his eyes tiredly. 'I've never cried like that before. Men don't cry, do they? But I did today. It tires you out, though. I think I'll go to bed.'

'Can I speak to Gwynna for a few minutes?'

'Yes. I'll send her down to you. Stay in the yard or people

will talk.' Forrett vanished into the house and a couple of minutes later Gwynna came outside, saw Lucas and ran into his arms. She didn't weep, but she held him as if she'd never let go. He didn't want her to let go.

'Come and sit down. There are some packing cases over there.' Once again he sat in the corner, but this time with his arm round the shoulders of the woman he loved. 'I came to see how you were.'

'Sad. So very sad.'

He hugged her close. 'You'll not have a job now. Have you thought what you'll do?'

'Not yet. I'm still too shocked by it all.'

He'd thought it would be hard to say, but it wasn't. 'Would you marry me instead of finding another job? I can't offer you anything but hard work, can't even offer you a house of our own, but—'

She turned her face up to him and said simply, 'Yes, please.'

So he held her close again. This wasn't a time to celebrate or even to share a kiss. But the simple warmth of her body against his, the knowledge that she loved him and was going to be his – all his other troubles paled before the joy that brought, the sense of the rightness of it all.

Life wasn't going to be easy for them, but he was going to fight back against Hungerton and his bullies. He had a lot more to fight for now.

As she walked into the station on Jeremiah's arm, Maria saw a gentleman of her acquaintance stop and stare at her in shock and disapproval. She inclined her head, but he turned away without acknowledging her and continued up the street. No doubt he'd tell his wife he'd seen her going out in the evening with Jeremiah. Well, let him!

She had nothing to be ashamed of in her relations with Jeremiah. Unless it was shameful to admire a man, to wish she had met him before she met Athol, to wish she were unmarked by her marriage. As always her hand went to her cheek on that thought, but she knew that the blackest marks left by Athol were on her mind and emotions. It wouldn't be fair to bring that darkness to a decent man like Jeremiah.

The other two were waiting for them. Maria looked down at her clothes then questioningly at Carrie, who gave her a quick nod of approval. She doubted either man had noticed this exchange but it made her feel better about her appearance.

On the train they talked about Mr Forrett's poor little baby, because gossip had wasted no time in spreading the news of how the child had died. An accident, some said. Criminal or insane behaviour on the mother's part, others whispered. Where was the nursemaid when this was happening? others whispered.

'Let's forget all that sadness now,' Eli said after a while. 'Let's just enjoy the evening.'

It was still light when they arrived in Manchester and took a cab to the People's Concert Hall in Lower Mosely Street. It was brightly lit, with crowds of cheerful people going inside, and it took Maria's breath away to see so many happy faces.

'It was only opened two years ago,' Eli explained, 'so it's a good example of a modern music hall. They say it can hold three thousand people. Just imagine that!'

'Just imagine serving food and drink to so many!' Carrie saw Maria looking at her in slight puzzlement at this remark and explained, 'It's my responsibility to arrange that side of things and to supervise the cleaning the morning after. People can make a right old mess when they're enjoying themselves.'

'You work in the music hall?'

'Yes. I love it.'

'I feel as if I've been imprisoned inside that house for most of my adult life,' Maria confessed suddenly. 'I wish I need never go back there again! I hate the place.'

'It must have been hard for you,' Carrie said. 'But you survived. And so did your sons. That's what counts.'

'But it's left its mark on us.'

Carrie shrugged. 'We're all marked by something in life. You just have to move on and keep doing your best.'

Maria stared at her thoughtfully. It was such a simple philosophy of life. Was she forgetting that other people had had a hard time too? She glanced quickly at Jeremiah. He'd had great unhappiness in his life as well, yet he was prepared to plan for a more normal future, even to express an interest in her. She felt her cheeks grow warm at that thought and the sudden longing it brought to feel safe and loved as she had during her childhood.

They were shown to the best seats and ordered their drinks and food.

When the show started Maria completely forgot her troubles, watching in delight and amazement as acrobats tumbled and contortionists twisted themselves into impossible shapes. A group of minstrels with darkened faces came on next and sang lilting songs, with the audience joining in the choruses.

Two beautiful young women followed them, singing gentler melodies, their voices blending in such sweet harmonies that tears came into Maria's eyes.

A man dressed like a tramp, with his toes sticking out of his boots and his top hat lacking a lid to it, sang a comic song about the Penny Post.

'That's old stuff now, happened years ago,' whispered Eli. 'He should find himself some new songs about what's happening today.'

The man went on with a song praising the queen, full of patriotic words. Sentimental as it was, it made Maria feel proud to be English.

And finally the Lancashire Nightingale came on stage.

'She's getting fat,' Eli said disparagingly, 'and showing her age.'

But the star of the show could still sing beautifully and as the glorious notes soared, Maria felt Jeremiah take hold of her hand and could not, for the life of her, bear to pull hers away.

'Well?' Eli asked as they sat in the train rattling home through the dark countryside. 'What did you think, Mr Channon? Was it a lewd and immoral performance? Were the crowds drunken and debauched?'

'No. Though there were a few who'd had more to drink than was good for them.' He smiled reminiscently. 'I think it was a decent evening's entertainment and I enjoyed myself tremendously – as did the rest of the audience.'

'That's the whole point of it, giving people pleasure. I love doing that, love everything about music halls.' Then Eli's face clouded over. 'I don't know what I'll do with my life if I don't get mine back again.'

23

Libby's funeral was a lavish event, with the operatives from the mill given time off to walk in two lines behind the hearse. Some of the women were weeping. There was something so touching about the tiny coffin.

But when people saw no sign of the child's mother in the carriages following the hearse, they began to whisper to one another. One lady, bolder than the rest, asked James where his wife was as they were walking into church.

'She's not well,' he said and refused point-blank to discuss the matter further.

It was noted how prominent a role the nursemaid played, even riding to church with her master in the carriage, ahead of his daughters and their husbands. Immediately people began to recall the scandals about Gwynna Jones and wonder if she was Forrett's mistress. But if so, why was she riding in the carriage? He had never flaunted his mistresses in people's faces before. Had grief turned his brain?

After the ceremony, however, a young fellow who had also attended the funeral came up and put his arms round the weeping girl and Forrett spoke to them both for a few moments, patting the young man on the arm as if he was a young relative. This confused everyone.

Although no expense was spared on the funeral itself, no invitation had been issued for the town's gentry to return to Mill House. After shaking hands with everyone at the church door, Forrett drove back alone, this time without the nurse-maid, who went off with the young fellow.

Once they arrived at the house, James led the way into the parlour and poured everyone a drink of port wine, over-riding his daughters' refusals with a curt, 'We all need something more strengthening than cat lap today. I've a few things to tell you.'

His elder daughter Alicia took the glass and sipped it distaste-fully. 'Where's Mother? I nearly died of embarrassment when I realised she wasn't in the carriage with you. And to have that maid there instead, well, it was an insult to the whole family.'

'That maid saved your little sister's life a while ago when your mother nearly killed her the first time, and I honour her for it. She tried to save Libby this time, too. She's a grand lass, Gwynna is.'

Alicia sniffed in disdain. 'I dare say she's very worthy, but still . . .' Then she suddenly realised what he had said. 'What do you mean by Mother "nearly killed her the first time"? Surely you're not implying . . .'

Her sister Diana interrupted as Alicia's voice faded, repeating the question on everyone's mind. 'Where *is* Mother?'

'She's locked in her bedroom. Her maid's with her.'

'*Locked in?*'

'Aye. For her own safety.'

'She isn't *mad*!'

'I think she is.' He stared down into his glass, then suddenly tossed its contents down his throat and went to pour himself another. 'Your mother was so unaware of what she was doing that she killed your little sister. I don't intend to give her the chance to kill anyone else.'

'It was an accident, surely?'

'An accident that'd not have happened if she'd been in her rightful senses. It's the laudanum, you see. You all knew she was taking it, but now, she can't live a day without it.'

They all fell silent.

'It's addled her brain,' he said.

Diana began to weep against her husband's shoulder.

Alicia's husband drank his glass of port and in answer to the unspoken question in James's eyes, held it out for a refill.

The silence continued until Alicia asked, 'You're sure of that, Father?'

James nodded, relapsing still further into the accent of his youth. 'Aye, that I am.'

'Do people know?'

'They guess.'

Horror filled her face. 'Mother won't be tried for murder, will she?'

'No. Rich people can get away with murder.'

'What are you going to do with her?'

'I'm going to send her to a place for ladies who've lost their senses and let her drink as much of that damned stuff as she likes. She'll die happy, at least.'

Four people stared at him in shock and dismay.

'Can't you – keep her here?' Alicia faltered.

'No, I damned well can't. If you must know, I can't abide the sight of her after what she's done. How I've kept myself from throttling her, I don't know.'

'But—'

'She's going to live in a big old house in the country, where ladies who are a danger to themselves are looked after very carefully. Dr Pipperday knows the place and assures me that they don't ill-treat their patients.'

Alicia clutched her husband's hand. 'I shall die of shame!'

'Not you!'

She stared at him resentfully.

'A home of rest, they call it. And they charge a damned fortune. You'll be able to visit her there whenever you want.' He poured himself another glassful, studied it and added,

'But I shan't go there again once I've delivered her to them.'

After exchanging glances with her husband, Alicia asked, 'What shall *you* do afterwards, Father?'

'What I've always done. Run the mill that you two so despise. And . . .' he paused deliberately, watching their eager gazes, their hope that he would give them some of his money all too obvious, 'I'm going to found an orphanage in Hedderby in memory of your little sister. It'll be called the Libby Forrett Orphanage. That'll make some good come out of her death, at least.'

An hour later, having failed completely to persuade him to change his mind, having visited their mother briefly, to find her as wild-eyed and incoherent as they'd been told, James's daughters left the house in some dudgeon.

'They're more upset that I'm spending their inheritance on an orphanage than about anything else,' he muttered to himself as he closed the front door behind them. 'I'd better set up a trust for the place, or they'll close it down once I'm dead.' He turned to find Gwynna waiting for him at the bottom of the stairs, dressed in her outdoor things, her eyes reddened and swollen from weeping. His daughters hadn't cried for their sister once that he'd seen.

'I'm packed and ready to leave, Mr Forrett. I came to say goodbye.'

'I've made up your wages, lass. Come into the parlour.' He went to the mantelpiece and took down an envelope, folding her hands round it. 'There's a bonus in there to help you set up with your young man. I want an invitation to the wedding, mind.'

She smiled at him, then her mouth wobbled for a minute and she surprised them both by giving him a big hug before going back to wait in the kitchen for Lucas to come and fetch her and her things.

As he sat alone in the front parlour, James reflected bitterly that neither of his daughters had attempted to hug or kiss him during their visit. Not once. Then he poured himself another glass of wine in a deliberate attempt to drink himself into oblivion.

Only he never could get too drunk to know what he was doing, because it made him sick first, so eventually, after he'd vomited over the front steps, he made his way unsteadily upstairs and flung himself on his bed fully clothed.

But his sleep was fitful, filled with images of his daughter's pale, dead face. And his living daughters' angry faces.

Declan went to meet the stranger as arranged, not at all sure whether he wanted to be involved in this. He liked Lucas Kemp, dammit, and didn't want to do anything to hurt the man. He liked Gwynna too, had known her first lad slightly and been sorry when Patrick had been killed. That lass deserved better of life this time round.

But money was important, too. Declan's brother Bram was making quite a name for himself, topping the bill with his wife at music halls round the country. Declan was jealous of that, because his brother's success had under-lined his own lack of it – though at least he was doing better these days than he had in the past. But Bram was set fair to be *rich*!

Declan ordered a pot of beer for himself and one for his friend Kelvin, but he hadn't any real desire to drink tonight, wanted to keep his mind clear, didn't want anyone tricking him into doing something risky. It was by the grace of God – he crossed himself quickly and furtively – that he'd not wound up in prison during the past few years and he didn't intend to do anything from now on that would put him there. He didn't mind bending the law a bit, but he wasn't going to break it.

The stranger had to speak twice before Declan realised he was there. 'Sorry. I was miles away then.'

'If you'd come with me now, Mr Heegan?'

'Drink up, Kelvin me boy.' Declan followed the stranger outside and the other trailed behind them.

On the afternoon following the funeral of that poor little baby, the Becketts went down to the site to confront Maitland Trevin. Eli had slept badly again and was looking worn to the bone. Without saying a word, because he was very touchy about his condition, Carrie linked her arm in his and matched steps. He laid his other hand on hers and as they walked they were conscious only of one another.

The site was busy, with the cellar completely walled in now, though the wooden floor hadn't been started above it. One of Trevin's bricklayers was working on the main floor, constructing the high side walls for the stage area, while the other was working on the outer walls of the music hall.

'The fellow certainly gets things done quickly,' Eli said regretfully.

'But not safely,' she reminded him. 'Where's Mr Channon?'

They looked round but there was no sign of him.

'We can start without him.' She nudged her husband to warn him and said loudly, 'Ah, good morning, Mr Trevin. We'd like to speak to you about something.'

'Good morning, dear lady . . . Mr Beckett. It's looking good, isn't it?' He waved one hand towards the two labourers filling in earth behind the cellar walls to the left, and then flourished it to the right, where another labourer was carting bricks to the bricklayer. 'I'm glad you've come today. I don't like to press you, but it's time for the next payment. Perhaps that's why you're here?'

She hated his smile, which never reached his narrow, watchful eyes. 'We received your invoice and we'll talk about payments later. First—' Out of the corner of her eye she saw something moving and glanced round, relieved to see a tall, familiar figure approaching.

Eli took over. 'Ah, here's Mr Channon. We asked him to join us today, Mr Trevin, to give us the benefit of his experience, since he's an architect too.'

Carrie saw Trevin stiffen as Eli greeted Jeremiah and then performed the introductions.

Trevin took the initiative. 'What's this about? Why do you need to bring another architect here?'

Eli waved one hand to indicate the building work going on. 'Because we're not happy with what you're doing.'

'*What?* How dare you say such a thing? And what do you know about such matters, anyway? I've fulfilled all my obligations to you, am building your theatre quickly and efficiently and—'

'But are you building it safely?' Jeremiah asked in his deep voice. 'I don't think so. I'd like to inspect those cellar walls and the foundations too. I can't agree that a single brick wall will be enough to support the downwards pressure from the side walls above it.' He tried to move forward but Trevin stepped in front of him, barring the way.

'I resent this and I have no intention of admitting you to the site. What's more I shall lay a complaint before the Architects' Institute about your unprofessional behaviour.'

'Are you a member?' Jeremiah asked.

Trevin spluttered and grew red in the face. 'Of course I'm a member! I have been since it was founded.'

'Then why have you got its name wrong? It's the Royal Institute of British Architects.'

Trevin glared at him. 'Members abbreviate the name all the time. And I *shall* lay a complaint if you don't withdraw your criticisms.'

'Complain if you will, but I doubt it'll get you anywhere,

not if what I suspect is true. Now, my clients wish me to examine the site, which *they* own, so please let me pass.' For a moment their eyes met, the smaller man continuing to glare at him, then Jeremiah stepped round him and started walking across the muddy earth. When he got to the edge of the cellar, he found a rickety wooden ladder and began to climb down it, pausing to ask, 'Presumably you are intending to build a wooden staircase?'

'It's much cheaper.' Trevin remained at the top of the ladder. '*And* it allows for storage space beneath the treads.'

'A solid staircase would have provided extra support for the walls, however.'

Eli followed them, looking at Carrie with a grin as he turned round to descend the ladder. 'This is where skirts are not suitable. Wait for me here, love.'

She watched as Trevin chewed one side of his mouth then, without a word, clambered down the ladder behind the other men. He stayed at its foot, arms folded, looking to her like a bad actor posing in a tableau vivant.

Jeremiah walked round the circumference of the cellar, prodding at the mortar with a penknife and frowning as pieces of it fell out from between the bricks.

'Leave that alone!' Trevin yelled. 'Can't you see that it hasn't had time to dry yet?'

'Then why are you building the walls above?' Jeremiah went across to the side of the cellar, stepped on to a pile of planks and clambered nimbly on to the top of the retaining wall. To his alarm, its bricks shifted beneath his feet and he jumped quickly up on to the ground above it. He went up to the bricklayer who was building the side wall. 'Can you lend me a hammer?'

The man looked across at Trevin, then shook his head, so Jeremiah went back to pick up a hammer he'd noticed lying there on his way in. As he walked back round the edge, he followed the labourer pushing another wheelbarrow load of bricks. The fellow had obviously been drinking and was weaving from side to side as he shoved the heavy barrow along. For a moment it seemed as if he was going to overturn it into the hole.

'Watch what you're doing!' Jeremiah yelled.

The man turned to grin at him, flourished a mock bow then turned back. But he wobbled suddenly and found it hard to keep the heavy barrow balanced.

Instinctively Jeremiah moved forward to try to help him keep it upright, but at that moment the man's foot slipped on the muddy ground. With a wild yell he let go of the barrow and struggled to keep his balance, knocking against Jeremiah as he did so.

Jeremiah found himself falling sideways into the cellar. The barrow tipped over the edge, bricks cascading everywhere. The empty barrow hung for a moment on top of the wall, then tumbled into the hole. The wall sagged slowly, then gave way, trapping Eli and Jeremiah beneath it before they could move away.

Then, just as Carrie thought the fall had stopped, the labourer yelled in alarm. He started running in one direction and the bricklayer in the other as the earth beneath the upper wall gave way and fell on top of the rest of the debris, bringing some of the upper wall with it.

Not until everything had stopped slipping and sliding for the second time did she dare run forward to peer down into the cellar. She could see part of Jeremiah's still body, but Eli was completely buried by the rubble. Trevin lay further away, moaning and clutching his head.

The men on the upper level were keeping well back from the edge, cursing and making no attempt to rescue those in the cellar. Carrie turned to scream for help at the top of her voice. As people came running from the street, she took charge. 'Someone fetch Dr Pipperday! And you others come and help me. My husband's buried under that rubble.'

Kilting her skirts up, heedless of who saw her legs, she climbed nimbly down the ladder and with her bare hands began to pull away the bricks from where she had last seen Eli.

That same afternoon James went up to his wife's bedroom and banged on the door. Betty opened it with the key he insisted she wear round her neck to prevent Nenny getting hold of it. He looked beyond her to see his wife sprawled on the bed, gazing vacantly into space. 'She's taken more of that stuff than usual, I see.'

'Yes, sir. You said to let her have what she wanted.'

'She's easier to manage this way.' He looked across the room and bitter anguish filled his mouth with bile at the thought of what Nenny had done, as it did every time he saw her. 'I need to speak to you for a minute or two, lass. I'm sure you can safely leave her.'

He locked the door behind the maid with his own key and she followed him downstairs into the parlour, looking apprehensive.

'I'm taking my wife to her new home tomorrow. They have their own servants there, so you'll not be needed. But I want to thank you for looking after her so well, and I've put a bonus into your wages. There's a reference here too.' He handed her an envelope.

She gazed at him in dismay. 'But you said I could be her maid.'

'That was before all this happened. She's not safe to be left to just one person and she's cunning when it comes to getting hold of that damned stuff. I've given you good references, so I'm sure you'll soon find yourself another job. Or you can find yourself a lad and get wed, like Gwynna. Now, I have work to do.' He nodded dismissal.

Betty went back upstairs feeling hard done to. It made things even worse to think of Gwynna getting married to a fine-looking man like Lucas Kemp, a man with excellent prospects, while she didn't even have a job any longer.

When her mistress wouldn't do as she was told, she took out her frustrations by slapping Mrs Forrett.

She'd have to go home now and then her parents would take her money off her. And there weren't any jobs going in Sutherclough. You could only do her sort of work at the Hungerton House and they had plenty of staff already. Anyway, they worked you too hard there, in Betty's opinion. Looking after Mrs Forrett had been much more to her taste. She'd never had a job which offered her more freedom.

Not caring that the rough surface of the bricks grazed her skin, Carrie continued to pull them off Eli, tossing them to one side. Jeremiah was only partly buried and she'd already seen that he was breathing, so he could wait.

A man's voice behind her said, 'You two carry Mr Channon out. I'll help Mrs Beckett.'

She didn't even glance round, had recognised Lucas's voice, knew he was strong enough to work quickly, which was all that mattered.

When they uncovered Eli's head she bent over him and let out a sob of relief when she found he was breathing. 'He's alive.' For a moment she couldn't move as relief shuddered through her.

Lucas laid his hand on hers for a moment. 'You stay beside him and let me and my friend here uncover the rest of his body.'

She did as she was told, because she was still shaking. As soon as it was freed, she took Eli's hand in hers, worried by how cold it felt, by the fact that he was still unconscious.

But as long as she could see the pulse fluttering in his throat, she could hold back her fears.

Jeremiah was groaning now and starting to regain consciousness.

'How did that bloody wall fall down?' a man's voice asked. 'And look at the wall up there. If we don't watch out, the rest of it'll come tumbling down on us.'

The men directly involved in the rescue looked up.

'Better hurry up,' one said. 'It doesn't look solid. Here, you keep an eye on it, lad. Shout out if it looks like falling.'

'Let's have a look at it.' An older man went across to the cellar wall and examined it, his behaviour suggesting he knew what he was about. 'They've skimped on t'mortar and the foundations aren't deep enough,' he said. 'Stupid beggars. Even I know you have to build t'foundations stronger than that. And that one calls hissen an architect!' He looked round. 'Where's he gone? You'd think he'd be helping here.'

Those not involved in pulling bricks off the two half-buried men looked round, but could see no sign of Trevin or the men he'd brought into Hedderby.

'I saw him climb back up the ladder out of the hole,' someone said.

'Looks like they've all runned off,' said another.

'Well, we'll run after 'em. They're not getting away with this. They'll be making for the station, I reckon.'

Several of the younger bystanders left, pounding along Market Street enthusiastically.

Maria, who had been shopping in town when she heard of the accident, stood back to let them pass then hurried on to the site, pushing her way through the onlookers. She stopped at the edge of the hole and stared down to see Jeremiah lying there, blood on his forehead. For a moment her feelings threatened to overwhelm her, then she set her basket down on the ground and moved round to where she could see a ladder. 'Excuse me. Could you move, please. I need to get down to him.'

An older man barred her way. 'Better not, missus. Which fellow's yours? Oh, they'll be bringing *him* up directly. They've gotten all the bricks off him and he's started to come to.'

Dr Pipperday came to stand beside Maria. 'Do I need to come down?' he called to those working below.

'Nay, you stay up there, Doctor. We s'll all be getting out of here as sharp as we can. The rest of that wall doesn't look too safe.' He gestured to one side. 'What that architect fellow were thinking of, to build a great big wall like that so shoddily, I don't know. That's what comes of bringing in outsiders instead of us as live in the town.'

Dr Pipperday watched the men carry Jeremiah to the ladder and heave him up it, then took charge. 'Lay him down over here.'

Jeremiah was starting to regain consciousness now, but didn't seem fully aware of what was happening around him.

With a sob, Maria knelt beside him and clasped his hand as she waited for the doctor to finish his examination.

'He's not come fully to his senses yet, but he doesn't seem seriously hurt apart from the blow to the forehead,' the doctor said. 'Stay with him and keep him lying quietly, Mrs Stott, while I examine Eli.'

But he had to wait a few minutes until they'd finished freeing Eli, and when they carried him up, he was still completely unconscious, his forehead and chin sporting gigantic bruises, while blood trickled from the back of his head.

'I think his arm is broken.' The doctor felt it again. 'Yes, the bone is grating. I'd better set it before he regains consciousness. We need to get him home as quickly as possible.'

'You can send for my carriage,' Maria called, having over-heard their conversation.

A man looked at her curiously. 'Mrs Stott, isn't it?'

'Yes.' She looked at him, waiting for him to make some nasty comment.

'I'll run round to your house and tell them, shall I?'

'Please.' She bent over Jeremiah again.

He opened his eyes and blinked at her. 'Maria? What—?'

'Shh. You've been hurt. The doctor says you should lie still until you're more yourself.'

He moved his head and winced, trying to put one hand up to feel where he'd been hurt.

She grabbed his hand and kept him from touching the wound, which was bleeding sluggishly. 'Don't. You'll get it even dirtier.'

He kept hold of her hand. 'Did they send for you?'

'No. I was walking back from the shops and heard people calling to one another about what had happened. I knew you were coming here this afternoon, so I ran to find out if you were all right.'

Their eyes met and she flushed a little but didn't turn away.

'You do care,' he said softly.

She opened her mouth to speak but the words didn't come easily. 'Yes. I – didn't realise quite how much, not until you were hurt.'

'Then it was worth getting hurt for.' As if he understood how she was feeling, he added quickly, 'We needn't rush into anything, you know. I'm a very patient man.'

She nodded, then looked down at their joined hands. She didn't pull hers away. It felt good to hold his hand, good not to be alone any more. Perhaps she wasn't too badly damaged to find happiness again.

★

Carrie watched anxiously as Dr Pipperday examined Eli. 'He's going to be all right, isn't he?'

'He's a strong man and has a good chance of recovery, but I'd expected him to start regaining consciousness before now, I must admit. I'll just go and check my other patient.'

So she was left kneeling by Eli's side, praying as she had never prayed before, for him to recover. What was happening around her was a blur. She didn't even attempt to find out if Mr Channon was all right.

Someone came up to her. 'We've cotched that architect chap and brang him back.'

She stared at him blankly.

'What shall us do with him, missus?'

'Do?'

'Well, he were responsible for this, weren't he, that architect of yours? Stands to reason he'll bear the blame.'

'I don't know what to do with him.' She bent over Eli again.

'Leave her alone. Eh, he looks a goner,' one man whispered to another.

She turned her head to say in a low, furious voice, 'Don't you dare say that again! He's been knocked unconscious, that's all.'

Dr Pipperday came to join her. 'They've brought Mrs Stott's carriage. If you'll let us carry him to it, Carrie?'

So she had to stand back as Dr Pipperday used a strip of material to bind Eli's broken arm to his chest. Then there were plenty of volunteers to pick up the popular Chairman of the Pride and lay him on a seat in the carriage. At a gesture from the doctor, she got inside and he joined her.

The carriage set off, moving slowly, carrying them up the hill to Linney's.

Someone must have run ahead, because Nev was waiting to guide the men round to the comfortable rear room where Carrie and Eli slept. Abigail's cot had already been moved out.

Gwynna said quickly, 'I'll look after Abigail. She'll be fine with me. You stay with Eli.'

Carrie nodded. That was one advantage about big families. There was always someone to lend a hand.

The men laid Eli on the bed, nodded to her and left.

'Help me get his clothes off then I'll set his arm,' Dr Pipperday ordered.

The very calmness of his tone helped Carrie and she followed his instructions carefully, wincing as she heard the bone grate into place. But even then, Eli didn't move. She watched the doctor strap the arm to a small piece of board that Raife found for them.

'It's a good thing he was unconscious,' the doctor said, still in the same calm, conversational tone. 'Setting a broken bone is a very painful thing, otherwise.'

They stood together beside the bed.

'Shouldn't he be showing some signs of regaining his senses by now?' she asked.

'Yes.' He hesitated, then said quietly, 'It's not good that he's still unconscious. He must have had a very hard blow to the head.'

Dr Pipperday stayed for half an hour, but Eli was still not showing any signs of recovery so in the end the doctor had to go off to deal with his other patients.

Carrie refused all offers of help and stayed beside the bed with sick dread lying heavy in her heart. Eli had had a bad thump on the head during the fire and look what that'd done to him. How would this second blow affect him?

But she didn't let herself cry. She had to stay strong for his sake, had to believe that he'd recover, for her own sake.

Back at the site men were milling round, arguing hotly about what should be done. Jeremiah had recovered enough to sit up, leaning against Maria, but he still didn't seem to be thinking clearly. She looked at the man who'd been helping them and impulsively asked, 'You seem to know something about buildings?'

'Yes, Mrs Stott. I used to work as assistant to an architect in London, just for a few months. My name's Lucas Kemp and I'm a carpenter by trade.'

'Could you take charge here, please, until Mr Channon is better? Make everything safe so that no one will fall into that hole? I'll pay you whatever the going rate is, but I don't want J— Mr Channon to worry about anything and from what I saw, Mr Beckett is in an even worse state, so he can't deal with this.'

Lucas nodded. 'I'll be happy to do it. Do you know what caused it?'

'No, I have no idea what happened this morning. But I do know that Mr and Mrs Beckett weren't satisfied with the standard of the workmanship and Mr Channon was advising them about that.'

Lucas looked across to where Trevin and his two companions were being held by a grim circle of men. He didn't want them to get away, despised people who did shoddy work. 'Would you mind if I brought the police sergeant into this, Mrs Stott? He can keep the architect and his men in gaol till Mr Beckett is conscious.'

Jeremiah groaned just then and her attention was distracted. 'Do whatever you think right, Mr Kemp.'

The carriage returned and with it instructions from Dr Pipperday to get Mr Channon home and to bed.

Lucas turned to see Declan stride up to the site and stand staring in amazement.

'Did you ever see the likes of this? How did this happen?'

'An accident plus faulty, skimped workmanship.' Lucas walked across to examine the remains of the wall the bricklayers had been working on. 'Just look at this. They've skimped on the lime and the mortar's not binding together properly. That fellow's got a lot to answer for.'

'Maitland Trevin, he's called,' Declan said idly. 'Or so he informed me one day when I stopped to see how things were going.'

Lucas frowned. 'Maitland? There was a fellow working on Mr Hungerton's stables called Maitland. It couldn't be the same person, could it? Only – how many people can there be going round pretending to be architects and builders?'

Declan let out a long, low whistle. 'Not many, I'd say. It'd be worth looking into.' He grinned. His new employer would be very interested to hear this, he was sure.

Lucas looked round, his mind back on the job at hand. 'Right then. I'd better get this place made safe. We don't want anyone else getting injured and you know what children are for playing on building sites.'

24

Since Eli still hadn't regained consciousness, Carrie stayed by his side. She dozed a little as she sat by the bed and Essie woke her gently in the middle of the night to tell her to go and sleep in the spare room next door.

'No! Essie, I can't bear to leave him. If anything happens . . .'

'If anything happens I'll call you.'

Carrie shook her head, tears in her eyes, her lips shaping another silent *No*.

'Then let me bring in a mattress for you to lie down on.'

Another shake of the head. 'I can't see his face if I'm lying on the floor. Just leave me be. *Please!* If you and the others will look after Abigail, that's all I ask.'

Essie went back to bed to worry to Nev about 'our Carrie'. That lass felt like a daughter to both of them, even though they were only her step-parents.

Early the next morning Dr Pipperday came and checked Eli's condition carefully. 'Apart from the broken arm, it's mainly bruises.'

'Then why is he still unconscious?'

'Sometimes, Carrie, after a head injury, the body simply goes to sleep and the person either recovers or,' he hesitated, then said it, 'slips quietly away.'

She stared at him numbly, swallowing hard. She hadn't allowed herself to consider the possibility that Eli might die until now. 'Is there *nothing* you can do?'

'No. I'm truly sorry. I wish there were. In these cases we can only leave the body to heal itself. He's young and strong, so he has more chance than most of recovering.'

'If he doesn't wake up, he'll starve to death, won't he?'

'Yes. But he'll die for lack of fluid intake first. Only if we try to force water down him, he may choke.'

When the doctor had gone, she sat down by the bed again and found herself talking to Eli, telling him how much she loved him, begging him to wake up, to come back to her and Abigail.

But he lay there without moving, except for shallow breaths that scarcely raised his chest, so that she had to watch very carefully to see the movement and know he was still alive.

Maria stayed with Jeremiah that first night, sitting in a chair by his bed, watching as he drifted in and out of consciousness. Every time he saw her sitting there he smiled and relaxed visibly.

She asked him questions mainly to check that he was in his right mind. 'Does it hurt?'

'Yes. But it'll get better.'

'Do you want anything?'

'A drink of water would be good, if you don't mind. I'm really thirsty.'

He struggled to sit up and wouldn't let her raise him. 'It's only a knock on the head, Maria. I'm all right, really I am. Or I will be in a day or two. You should go and get some sleep.' He drank the water and smiled his thanks as he was overtaken by a huge yawn.

'I'll keep watch on you tonight. Just in case.'

This time his smile was warmer if drowsy. 'I can't think of anyone I'd rather have looking after me.'

In the morning Maria went downstairs very early, before the servants were up, to get herself a cup of tea. As she passed the door of the library, it crashed open of its own accord, even though no one was near it. She fled to the kitchen and stood there, her heart beating with terror. Would she never be free of Athol? Would his ghost continue to haunt her?

It was some time before she had control of herself. She mustn't talk about such occurrences or people would think she was mad, like her husband had been.

But she felt jittery every time she went past that door. She didn't think she could bear to live like this for the rest of her life.

Betty returned to her family in Sutherclough, still furious that she'd lost her job and bitterly jealous that Gwynna had done so well for herself. Mr Forrett had been more generous than she'd expected so Betty kept her wages money where it would show and hid the rest in her spare shoes, rolled up in a pair of stockings. She wasn't telling her mother about the extra money and she definitely wasn't telling Jabez, or he'd be trying to take it from her. As soon as she could, she'd go into Manchester to a registry and see if she could find herself another job.

Jabez heard his sister was back and came round to see her, wanting to find out how things were in Hedderby. He was amazed to hear about the big accident, surprised too that Gwynna was going to marry Lucas Kemp.

'I reckon my master will want to hear about that. He won't like them two doing well for themselves, won't like it at all.'

'I don't like it either, but there's nothing we can do about them marrying.'

'Don't be so sure.' He laughed, a confident but nasty laugh.

She shivered. She wouldn't like to get on the wrong side of Jabez, felt sorry for Gwynna and Lucas. Jabez had always been like that, nasty.

The sooner she found herself another job, the better. It

came to her suddenly that she was happier when she was away from her brother. Perhaps she'd try to get a job in the south this time, right away from him.

Lucas got up early and went out to the site as soon as it was light, accompanied by Joe in case he needed to send a message to anyone. Ted and Uncle Fred were to keep an eye on the workshop. It had done Lucas's heart good to see how his uncle had brightened at the thought that he was needed and would be able to help.

Lucas found the night watchman walking up and down, beating his arms against his body for warmth, and paid him off. He turned to see two of the labourers who'd been working there hesitating near the entrance to the site. It was a good thing the drunken one hadn't turned up. There was no way Lucas would ever employ him.

'Is there any work today, sir?'

He looked round, estimating what needed doing. 'Yes. But I can only promise you today. We'll have to take it day by day. Three shillings a day?'

They both walked forward, nodding eagerly.

He set them to work, first to shore up what remained of the new upper wall so that it wouldn't collapse on anyone. He suspected it'd need pulling down, but didn't feel he could take responsibility for such a major decision. Afterwards, they were to clear the rubble from the cellar. He also warned them to keep onlookers off the site if they valued their jobs. 'That's just as important as clearing things up.'

Then he went round to the Stott house to find out whether Mr Channon was in a fit state to see him and give him further instructions.

Raife came round to the house early to say that Eli was still unconscious, which made Maria worry even more about

Jeremiah doing too much too soon. She went up to tell him and begged him to stay in bed.

'I'm all right this morning, Maria, just feeling a bit tired.'

'But there's no *need* for you to get up.'

'Maria, I'm all right, I promise you, apart from a headache. But if Eli hasn't recovered consciousness, I need to go to the site and ensure that everything is safe, that people can't fall into the cellar. I won't stay there long, I promise you.'

'I asked Lucas Kemp yesterday to do that.' Her voice was hesitant, as if she wasn't sure he'd approve of this.

He saw her sag in relief as he said, 'How clever of you! He's a sound craftsman and a man of sense, just the right person to ask. But I'm still going to check things myself, because from what you tell me, Eli can't. Now, I need to get dressed.'

She left him and went downstairs to find both boys waiting in the hall, eager to see Jeremiah and make sure for themselves he was all right. Lucas was also waiting patiently there too. 'He'll be down in a few minutes, Mr Kemp, then he wants to come to the site to check that it's safe. I'd appreciate it if you'd wait to walk there with him, in case he gets dizzy again. And please don't encourage him to stay for long. He really should be resting today.'

Jeremiah came downstairs ten minutes later, looking pale, with some of his bruises showing, but seeming steady enough on his feet. He shook hands with Lucas, turned to have a word with the boys, who were still hovering nearby. When he ruffled their hair they didn't wince, which he took to be a good sign.

As they walked into town, he asked Lucas about his past jobs, delighted to hear of the time spent working with Reginald Laing in London. 'I know Laing slightly. He's an excellent architect and has done some beautiful buildings. He must think you capable to have given you such responsibility.'

'I'd have stayed to work at a similar job he recommended me for if my uncle and his family hadn't needed me.'

'You have to look after your family.' After a few moments Jeremiah chuckled. 'You don't need to watch me as if you expect me to keel over at any moment. I've a hard head.'

'Even the hardest heads can be damaged.'

They both fell silent, thinking of Eli.

At the site Jeremiah walked slowly round, not missing anything. He commended Lucas on the steps already taken to make the site safer, and approved the employment of the two labourers for as long as necessary.

'Just one more thing you should know, sir,' Lucas said as Jeremiah prepared to return home. 'A group of local workmen stopped Trevin and his two so-called bricklayers getting on the train and the police sergeant has them locked up. He sent a man round to ask me what Mr Beckett wanted to charge them with, but I couldn't tell him. If nothing's done, they'll have to let them go. Only it wouldn't be right for them to get away with what they've done, would it?'

'Hmm. I'd better go and see the sergeant. Who knows when Beckett will be in a fit state to deal with this?'

'Should you, sir? I mean, you're still rather pale and Mrs Stott was worried about you. Why don't you go and see Mr Burtell, ask him to deal with this? He'll know what to do.'

'Good idea.' Jeremiah walked slowly down Market Street and Lucas watched him go, worried that the other man was doing too much. Then he saw a couple of lads sneaking on to the site from the back and turned to yell at them to stay away or he'd tan their backsides for them.

Joe behaved impeccably that day, not going into any area which Lucas forbade and staying as close to him as he could. Lucas knew the lad idolised him and felt humbled by that. If only he could help more children like Joe. He'd tried to suggest it to Mr Forrett, as a way of helping him out of his grief for his tiny daughter, but the mill owner probably wouldn't do anything about helping Hedderby's street urchins.

Well, one day Lucas would and he hoped Gwynna would understand that and want to join him in such valuable work. He couldn't help smiling at the thought of her.

Joe watched Lucas carefully, as he always did. 'You allus smile all soppy like that when you're thinking of *her*,' he said.

Lucas looked up and grinned at him. 'When we get wed, she'll be living with us. I hope you'll be on your best behaviour for her, young man.'

The boy nodded solemnly. But when Lucas had turned back to work, he began to worry that Gwynna wouldn't want him living with them. After some thought he decided to go and see her later, to make sure she knew how well-behaved he was. He didn't want anything happening to get him thrown out of his wonderful new home, where you got warm clothes and good food every single day.

At Linney's everyone walked around the house quietly, worried about Eli and about Carrie too.

'That girl hasn't left his side for more than a minute since they carried him into the house,' Essie said to her husband and Raife. 'She'll be the one collapsing next if she doesn't get some rest.'

'Would you leave Nev if it were him lying there unconscious and you didn't know whether he was going to live or die?' Raife asked.

She shivered and shook her head, casting a fond look at her husband.

'Then leave Carrie be.'

But Essie couldn't stop worrying. 'She's talking to him, though, acting as if he can hear her. Did you ever hear the like?'

'Perhaps he can,' Nev said. 'It'll do no harm and it'll make her feel better to let her feelings out, I'm sure.'

Gwynna came in carrying little Abigail. 'We had a lovely outing. That stick wagon is really easy to push, even with two of them in it. Raife, will you hold Abigail while I fetch Leah in?' She went back out for the other baby, a plump happy child recently returned from fostering by her wet nurse, and they could hear her laughing and playing with the infant, making a game of lifting her out of the wagon.

'I don't think I've ever met anyone who's as good with childer as that lass,' Raife said, dandling Abigail with her feet on the floor. 'Eh, I reckon this one will soon be walking. Look at her push with her feet.'

'They soon grow up, don't they?' Essie said. 'Sylvie should be waking up from her nap soon. Wouldn't it be nice if they all had a nap at the same time? It's a good thing we've got that lass back or we'd have had to hire someone with three little 'uns under foot. They're more trouble than I'd expected, not that I grudge the effort.'

Gwynna beamed at them as she came in and overheard this. 'Well, you don't need anyone yet. You've got me till I get wed.' She sighed happily at the thought.

Next morning Jabez waited till he knew his master would be alone then slipped into the big house through the French windows of the library, a room where old Mr Hungerton ruled supreme. 'They're getting wed, Kemp and that slut,' he announced even before he'd closed the window behind him, knowing it would infuriate the old man.

Hungerton scowled blackly as he took this in. 'We'll see about that. For all his faults Kemp is a decent fellow and he doesn't deserve to be tied to a female like her. Besides, when I get him back to work here, I don't want *her* around. I'll find him a decent lass, someone like your sister, perhaps.'

He sat drumming his fingers on the desk, then got up to pace the room.

Jabez waited patiently for instructions, knowing his employer didn't like to be interrupted when he was thinking what to do. As if he'd let Kemp marry Betty! He didn't want to be related to someone who didn't know where his own best interests lay.

When Mr Hungerton stopped walking and looked in his direction, he became instantly alert.

'This is what I want you to do . . .'

As dusk was starting to shadow the streets Gwynna left Linney's to walk across to Lucas's workshop. She was going to have tea with his family and then they were going to discuss a date for the wedding. Essie had suggested waiting for Ted to accompany her, but it was only five minutes' walk away and she was too excited to sit still once she was dressed.

'It's not even dark yet. Nothing's going to happen to me on a lovely evening like this, with other people out walking.' As she went out into the street a cool wind blew and she had to hold her newly trimmed bonnet on carefully because she didn't want to arrive looking untidy. She didn't notice the man following her until just at the last minute when something made her look round. But by that time it was too late and he'd grabbed her, putting one hand over her mouth to stop her calling out and dragging her into a narrow ginnel that ran between two houses.

She struggled desperately but he seemed enormously strong and she was unable to do more than gurgle in her throat and kick out futilely.

Out of sight of the street another man was waiting and even in the darkness of the ginnel she recognised Jabez.

'Now you'll get what you deserve, you slut,' he gloated.

Still smiling, he bent and tied her feet together, running

his hand up her leg and laughing as she tried in vain to jerk away. Then he stuffed a gag into her mouth and the other man twisted her round while they tied her hands behind her back. She felt helpless and terrified now. Why were they doing this?

The bigger man tossed her over his shoulder. 'Go and get the carriage, Jabez lad. I'll wait till you're at the end of the ginnel then bring her out once the street's clear.'

'Mr Hungerton will be pleased, Len. He'll pay you handsomely.'

'As long as I get my turn with her.'

'You will. We all will. He's promised.'

As she heard this, Gwynna tried again to struggle, but Len told her to stop that or he'd knock her senseless. You couldn't escape if you were senseless so she stopped wriggling.

If there were even half a chance of escaping, she'd be ready for it.

But what if there weren't?

Terror lodged like a lump of ice in her belly.

Joe had been waiting outside Linney's for Gwynna, desperate to talk to her and make sure she'd let him stay with Lucas. He was about to go across to her when he saw a man following her. Alerted to that sort of danger by his time on the streets, he quickly slid into the nearest shadows and watched anxiously.

Why hadn't she noticed the man? The boy wanted to call out to her to look round and get away, but was afraid of such a big fellow.

He moved up the street after them, slipping from one patch of darkness to the next, clapping a hand to his mouth to hold back a cry of dismay when he saw the bully grab her.

When they disappeared from sight, he ran across the street and risked a peep. The ginnel was too narrow for him to dare follow them down it. They were out of sight round the far corner, but he could hear something, so waited. Sounds seemed to echo between the high walls of the houses and as he listened carefully, he heard the men planning to take her away in a carriage. He knew he couldn't keep up with horses, so ran off, muttering the words of the last sentence he'd overheard to himself, 'Mr Hungerton will be pleased. He'll pay you handsomely.'

He burst into the workshop shouting for Lucas, his voice shrill with desperation.

Ted came out of the storeroom. 'He's having a wash for when Gwynna comes. What's the matter?'

'They've took her away.' Chest heaving, Joe darted into the house, pushing past Aunt Hilda and throwing open the scullery door to where Lucas was just getting dressed after his wash.

'They've took her away!' he shouted. 'Come quick! They've took your Gwynna.'

Lucas heard the fear in his voice and knew this wasn't a lad's exaggeration, so hurried out with him. 'What happened?'

As they ran Joe explained what he'd seen and repeated the words he'd memorised, Lucas felt sick with fear for Gwynna. He didn't doubt what had happened. Mr Hungerton had struck again. Who else was there who had it in for that poor lass?

But when they got to the ginnel all they could see was the rear lamp of a carriage disappearing into the distance far along the road.

'We'll never catch up with it,' Lucas muttered. He stood still, thinking hard, then set off running again, yelling, 'Go straight home and wait for me, Joe.'

He went first to Jack Burtell's, hammering on the front door and bursting in past the maid who opened it. Without waiting to catch his breath, he gasped out what had happened.

'Dear Lord, what are we to do?' Jack exclaimed. 'Can you get a train and go after them?'

'It's a few miles from the station to the house and there's not a cab to be had there because it's a tiny village. I think we'd be better finding a carriage for ourselves here and going after them in it.'

'You seem to have thought it out. Am I to come with you?'

'No. I want you to go and fetch the sergeant then both of you come after us separately. Can you get hold of a carriage for that?'

'Yes.'

'I'm going to ask Mrs Stott to lend me her carriage. I may not manage to overtake those sods before they reach Hungerton House, but I won't be far behind them.' He could only hope he'd get there in time. As he ran through the streets, he bumped into Declan.

'Wait! Lucas, I need to speak to you.'

'You'll have to run beside me. I can't stop.'

'What the hell's happened?' Declan fell into place beside him.

'I'm coming with you,' he said when Lucas had finished his tale.

'What did you want?'

'To tell you something about Trevin, but it can wait.'

By that time they'd reached the Stott house and Lucas had decided that Declan would be a good man to have at your side in a fight. He hammered on the front door, tried the handle and burst inside without waiting for anyone to answer.

The maid who'd been coming to open the door let out a shriek at the same time as Jeremiah appeared in the doorway of the dining room. 'Kemp! What's the matter?'

Lucas could have groaned at the need for another explanation, but got through it as quickly as he could.

Maria, who'd been listening from just inside the room, joined
Jeremiah in the hall. 'Of course you can take the carriage. Isaac,
run out and tell the coachman we need the carriage quickly.
Both horses. Fast as he can.'

The lad was off.

'I'll go with you,' Jeremiah declared.

'You're not fully recovered yet!' Maria protested. He'd just
been saying how tired he was and deciding to go to bed
early.

'We'll be quicker with just the two of us, sir,' Lucas said
tactfully. 'Less weight for the horses to pull.' In fact, he didn't
think Jeremiah was well enough yet to be of use.

Declan stepped forward. 'And if you don't mind, I'll drive
the carriage, ma'am. I know how to, don't worry. Same
reason. Less weight for the horses.'

'But there are only two of you,' Jeremiah worried.
'Hungerton will have several manservants to call on for help.'

'We stopped at Mr Burtell's on the way here. He's going
to get the sergeant. Even Mr Hungerton won't dare defy a
policeman. Only we can't afford to wait for them, for
Gwynna's sake.'

Fifteen minutes later they were off, driving through the
night, both sitting up on the coachman's seat.

If only we arrive in time! The words kept repeating themselves in Lucas's brain.

Declan was thinking it a rum thing that he'd be able to
report to his secret employer in person about the latest
developments.

Selwyn knew his father was up to something, but the old
man was wily, and although Selwyn watched for Jabez coming
and going, he didn't see him. His own groom, Fuller, said

there were times when Jabez was not to be found and the head groom had been told he was working directly for the master and was to be left alone. After some thought Selwyn asked Fuller to keep his eyes open and report anything unusual.

There was only him to deal with his father now, because Robert swore he'd never come back and their mother was holding on to life only feebly. They would all be glad when she died, harsh as that sounded. What sort of life was it, lying there like a helpless infant, being washed and kept warm, not even knowing what was going on around you? His concern about both her and his father had made him change his plans and stay at Hungerton House, but he'd sent his wife and little son off to her sister's. If there were going to be any upsets, better she wasn't involved in her condition.

That evening his father was even more fidgety than usual during dinner, saying he was exhausted and would go to bed early. Selwyn was relieved when the meal ended. It was hard to keep up a conversation with a man who didn't really listen to anything you said. He followed his father out, then realised he'd dropped his handkerchief and went back to retrieve it instead of going straight upstairs.

As he was about to leave the room, he saw through the narrow gap at the edge of the door his father look round furtively then disappear into the library instead of going upstairs. Selwyn stayed where he was until the door had shut behind the old man. Why had he pretended to be tired? Was something going to happen tonight? He wondered whether to send a message to Fuller, but decided that sending a maid out to the stables might also warn Jabez, so went out quietly through the front door. Nothing like seeing to things yourself if you wanted them done properly.

His groom was sitting with two others chatting quietly and

mending some harness. There was no sign of Jabez. Selwyn fidgeted for several minutes but in the end the men put their work away and went yawning to their beds.

'Fuller!' he called in a low voice.

The man turned, looking surprised. 'Mr Selwyn!'

'Shh! Where can we talk without being overheard or seen?'

'The new tack room, sir.' He picked up his lantern and led the way through the quiet stables to the part that had been rebuilt after the collapse.

'Have you seen Jabez tonight?'

'No, sir. But that's not unusual. The younger men don't sit with us older ones after work.'

'Can you find out if he's here?'

'Yes, sir. Just let me light another lantern for you and—'

'Never mind that. I'll be perfectly all right in the dark. Just go and find out quickly.'

Fuller disappeared and Selwyn sat down on one of the stools. He sniffed appreciatively, enjoying the smell of leather and wax, with faint undertones of clean straw. As he was sitting there, he saw through the window a carriage come up the drive and halt for a moment or two before turning off towards the woods.

What the hell was happening? Who could that be at this hour of the night? He couldn't see clearly enough to make out any details of who was inside the carriage, but it was one of theirs, the older one kept for servants.

Then he heard footsteps coming towards the stables. It must be the person who'd got out of the carriage. On a sudden impulse he moved from the window to crouch behind a rack of saddles, then heard a man's deep voice call out in shock. Damnation! Whoever it was must have bumped into Fuller.

Straining his ears, he heard a couple of dull thuds and some grunts, followed by what sounded like someone falling.

Had the person attacked Fuller? He hesitated, wondering whether to go out and help, then held back. Better to find out what was going on and then end this stupidity once and for all.

25

There was enough moonlight for Declan to see his way but he refused to push the horses harder. 'We could have an accident.'

'And while we're trotting along so tamely, far worse could be happening to my Gwynna.'

Declan looked sideways. 'Sorry, lad. I can guess how you're feeling, but what would we do if we lamed the horses? We'd be even later then.'

Lucas bent his head, fear roiling his stomach, and anger too. When he raised it he spoke more mildly. 'I didn't know you could drive.'

'There's a lot people don't know about me. Pays to keep a few secrets.' He stared ahead, watching the horses' rumps. 'I'm all right with these two because they're getting on, have lost their spirit – if they ever had any – but I wouldn't like to drive spirited ones. I'm not that good at this.'

'Turn left at the next crossroads.'

This was accomplished in silence then Declan asked, 'What plans have you made for when we get there?'

'To stop before we get to the gatehouse, leave the carriage and cut across the fields so that they're not aware of our arrival.'

'And then?'

'Find out what's going on and decide whether to kill Jabez or not.'

'You'll not kill anyone.' Declan's voice was calmly certain. 'You're not a killer.'

Lucas's voice was tight with frustration. 'I might be if they've hurt her.'

'Hungerton's rich and powerful. He'll have men there who'll swear black is white if he tells them to. You'd better not get into any fights.'

'Why do you think I asked Burtell and the sergeant to come after us? I hope and pray they'll not be far behind.'

'He might be too late to see what's going on, though. If they're not actually hurting her, we should wait till they arrive.'

Lucas sighed. 'I can't promise anything till I make sure she's all right.'

Gwynna jolted around in the carriage. Once she fell to the floor between the two men and Jabez laughed. 'That's where sluts like you belong.'

She couldn't even answer because they'd left the gag in her mouth. She felt as if she couldn't breathe properly, but wouldn't let herself panic. They hadn't touched her yet. Maybe they were just trying to frighten her.

But when Jabez at last leaned down to haul her back up on the seat, he made free of her body in a way that filled her with terror. His deep breathing and the gleam in his eyes told her how impatient he was.

'Why don't you go and ride outside?' he said to his companion. 'Give me a little privacy.'

'No. Mr Hungerton said not to touch her till we got her back.'

'How will he know?'

'Because she'll struggle and you'll mark her. Haven't you the sense you were born with? Our master makes a bad enemy.'

Jabez sighed. 'I've been wanting this bitch for months.'

Just then the carriage slowed down and they looked out of the windows.

'We're turning into the gates. You won't have much longer to wait.'

'I'll go and tell him we're back. You drive on.' Jabez rapped on the roof and the carriage slowed down. He got out and spoke quietly to the man driving it, then closed the door and let the carriage move on.

Gwynna could only hope that someone would hear the noise of the vehicle and come out to investigate. But even if they did, she'd not be able to call for help.

The carriage came to a halt and the man who'd captured her opened the door, picking her up as easily as if she were a sack of chaff. He tossed her over his shoulder so carelessly that the breath was driven from her and she had to struggle for air.

Jabez walked quietly across to the stables, lust making him careless so that he didn't see Fuller until he bumped into him.

'What are you—'

'Damnation!' He punched the other man in the jaw, then kicked him in the head for good measure. Stupid old fool! Always fussing and complaining. He looked around, listening intently. Was anyone else around? What bad luck to bump into that man of all the stable staff. Fuller had always had a down on him.

Only when he was satisfied that Fuller was unconscious and that no one was coming to investigate the noise, did Jabez move on.

He peered through the library window and saw Mr Hungerton dozing in front of the fire. Tapping on the pane of glass he waited until the old man had jerked awake, then slipped quietly inside the room. 'We got her, sir.'

'Good.' He stood up. 'We'll go out to the cottage straight away. I want to tell her to her face why she's here and warn her not to say anything afterwards if she values her freedom.'

Jabez didn't allow any of his feelings to show on his face, but he wondered if the old man was losing his wits as some old people did. Did Hungerton really think he could do what he wanted with Gwynna and then expect her to keep quiet about it afterwards? Jabez was damned sure she wouldn't. He'd made his own plans, would get a good price for her in a brothel he knew in Manchester – but only after he'd had enough of her. The old cottage was some distance from the house, never used now. She'd be all right there for a few days.

And so would he.

He helped his master up.

'Give me your arm. I'm not as steady on my feet as I used to be.'

Slowly they walked out of the house towards the cottage.

'Stop here,' Lucas said.

Declan reined in the horses.

'We go that way, across the field.'

'I'll just put the nose bags on them. That'll keep them quiet.' He patted the horses and saw them standing quietly munching, then turned to see Lucas in the distance, striding across the field. Pushing his way through the hedge, he ran to catch up with his friend.

Selwyn followed Jabez, keeping well back. He watched him go into the house, realising now how the groom had been able to communicate with the old man. Only after the library window had shut tightly did he go back to see if Fuller was all right.

The groom was beginning to regain consciousness and after telling him to go and get help once he was able to walk, Selwyn stood up. He wanted to see what his father was up to, and he didn't want the old man to see him till he was ready.

His caution in moving from one hiding place to another paid off. He saw the library door open and was able to hide behind some shrubs and watch his father go past on the arm of Jabez. He let them get quite a way ahead before he attempted to follow, and even then, he kept himself out of sight.

It was soon obvious that they were heading towards the old woodcutter's cottage, which was in a poor state and should have been knocked down years ago.

He had reached the side of the cottage before he noticed two other men making their way across the home field, two large fellows. He couldn't see them clearly because he was short-sighted and never had he regretted that as much. Were they coming to join the ones inside the cottage? What the hell was his father planning? He erred on the side of prudence and looked round for a hiding place, slipping round the side of the building and crouching behind the water butt.

As they drew nearer to the cluster of buildings behind the big house, Lucas put one hand on Declan's and pointed to a cottage on its own, which was showing lights. 'That place hasn't been used for years, but there are lights there now. Could be where they've taken her.'

'Let's go and have a look.'

Taking care to move as quietly as possible, they turned and made their way towards the cottage.

Gwynna lay on the floor while the man who'd carried her in busied himself lighting two lanterns. He ignored her completely and she looked round desperately for something to saw her bonds off with. But the minute she started wriggling away from him, he said sharply, 'Stay still unless you want a good thumping.'

She stopped and watched him, fear of what they were planning making her shiver. When she heard footsteps she hoped for a minute that someone had come to see what was going on, but the hope died the minute the door opened and old Mr Hungerton walked in, followed by Jabez. He wasn't surprised to see her, so he must have known she was here.

'Sit her on that chair and tie her hands to it,' Hungerton ordered.

Jabez picked her up by the front of her bodice and thrust her on to the chair more roughly than he needed to. As he undid her hands and tied them to the chair arms, she cried out from the pain. But of course, she could do nothing but make a muffled noise in her throat.

Hungerton took another chair, which rocked precariously on the uneven floor.

'Let me, sir.' Jabez stepped forward and found a more level space then helped his master to sit down.

'Take the gag out of her mouth.'

Hungerton was looking at her as if she was a dirty black beetle. It terrified Gwynna to see such hatred.

'If you make any noise, he'll hit you hard. Nod if you understand that, girl.'

She nodded.

Jabez removed the gag, grinning at her, then stepped back.

'You have to learn that women of your sort don't belong in decent households, let alone marry decent men. You have to be taught what your place in the world is. A whore like you looking after *my* grandson! The thought of that still makes me sick.'

'I'm no—'

A heavy hand knocked her sideways and made her bite her tongue. 'Quiet, you. Just listen to the master and don't speak until you're told to.'

'Therefore,' Hungerton went on, 'you will be used as a

whore should be, both as punishment for contaminating my household, and to make sure you learn to be obedient to the sort of men who'll be using you from now on.'

Horror filled her but she didn't speak.

'Do you understand?'

She pressed her lips together.

'*Do – you – understand?*'

She wouldn't give them the satisfaction of replying and though Jabez slapped her again, she kept her mouth closed.

'I'm sure she understands, sir, and I'll make sure she's trained to be obedient before I take her to Manchester and dump her on the streets.'

Mr Hungerton smiled, that thin, savage smile which made those who'd offended him want to run away and hide. 'Get to work, then.' He leaned back in his chair.

Jabez stared at him in shock. 'Sir?'

'I want to watch her being humiliated.'

'Do it in front of you, you mean, sir?'

'Have you lost your wits? I said so, didn't I?'

Jabez hesitated, looked at the other groom, who gave the slightest of shrugs, then turned to Gwynna. Somehow he couldn't stir up the same hot desire with his employer watching in that cold, nasty way of his. He just couldn't. For some things you had to be private.

He reached out to touch her breast, hoping this would rouse him.

Outside, able to see and hear what was happening through the worn shutters which were hanging at a drunken angle over broken window panes, Declan grabbed Lucas's arm and whispered, 'Wait! He's not hurt her yet.'

'And he's not going to.'

'Look at him. He can't do it with that old sod watching.

Damned if I could do a public performance in front of a man like that, either.'

'They're all watching him. It'd be a good time to break in.'

'Wait. See what they do next. Give Burtell time to get here.'

'I'll not let them hurt her.'

Inside the cottage Jabez was still hesitating. He fondled Gwynna's breast again, pinching the nipple hard until she squirmed, and still he felt nothing. Looking sideways, he swallowed and confessed, 'I don't think I can do it with people watching, sir.'

Hungerton looked at him in disgust and turned to the other man. 'Then *you* do it.'

'I'm sorry, but I'm the same, sir. I can't do it in public.'

'Then I shall have to show you how.' He got up, walked across to the chair to which Gwynna was tied and flapped one hand. 'Untie her and hold her down on the floor for me.'

After a moment's hesitation they did as he'd asked.

As the old man began to unbutton the flap of his trousers, the two men's attention was distracted. Gwynna chose that moment to start struggling and screaming, thrashing around to such effect that it was all they could do to hold her down.

Selwyn had found a door hanging at an angle at the side of the house and crept through it into the house to listen to what his father was planning. If they discovered him eavesdropping, they were hardly likely to hurt him, but he didn't want to make his presence felt until he knew exactly what was going on.

What he heard made him feel sick with disgust.

At the sound of Gwynna's screams, Lucas threw off Declan's hand and burst into the cottage. All three men swung round and he didn't hesitate, but punched the nearest, who happened to be Jabez, grabbing him to knee him in the groin a second later.

He turned to see Declan dealing with the other man, so shoved Hungerton out of the way and knelt beside Gwynna, who began sobbing and calling his name.

'You're all right now, my little love.'

'Look out!'

He turned just in time to see Mr Hungerton swiping at him with a chunk of wood. Rolling Gwynna to safety he took a glancing blow on his shoulder. With a growl of anger, he kicked out and knocked the old man off his feet. Then he stood in front of Gwynna to protect her.

Outside the door Selwyn stepped back, so disgusted by his father's behaviour that he felt physically sick. He stumbled to the side door and gulped in the fresh air, then stilled as he saw two more men running across to the cottage, followed by others coming from the house. He squinted, trying to see clearly, and as they got closer realised that one of them was wearing what looked like a police uniform.

Bile welled in his throat. Now everyone would discover what his father had been doing. He couldn't bear the thought of the scandal that would create.

Before he could decide what to do, the two leading men had burst into the cottage by the front door.

He went back inside through the rear door again.

Who were the newcomers? Were they here to help his father or were they friends of the carpenter fellow who had once worked here?

As soon as he was inside the cottage, the sergeant roared at the top of his voice. 'What the *hell* is going on here?' and so authoritative was his tone that everyone stopped moving to stare at him. 'I'm a policeman and I order you to stay where you are.'

Mr Hungerton pulled himself painfully to his feet. 'I'm glad to see you, Sergeant. These two men,' he indicated Lucas and Declan, 'kidnapped this young woman and when my men and I tried to rescue her, they attacked me. I want you to arrest them for assault. They need locking up where they can't injure honest citizens.'

'They didn't kidnap me!' Gwynna cried. 'It was Jabez who kidnapped me and Mr Hungerton told him to do it.'

'Are you going to take the word of a slut against that of a gentleman?' Hungerton demanded, drawing himself up. 'Because if so, I'll call in the magistrate and you'll be in trouble yourself.'

Jabez began to grin, for all that he was still half-bent and clutching his tender private parts. Money always talked.

Lucas itched to punch the groom's face again. '*You* know I wasn't anywhere near when she was kidnapped, Sergeant. As Mr Burtell will bear witness.' He looked across at his former employer, feeling no fear of him now, only hatred. 'A lawyer's word should also be worth something too, don't you think, Mr Hungerton?'

'I'll fetch the magistrate, shall I, sir?' the other groom asked. 'He'll soon sort this out for you.'

Jack moved to stand beside Lucas and said in a low voice, 'Don't say anything else. Leave it to me.'

'I shan't need to,' Lucas said angrily. 'The magistrate will be the same one you met last time and he's a friend of Hungerton's. We all know that money can buy anything. What do you bet that he'll find a dozen other witnesses to speak against me by the time this comes to trial?'

'Get off with you, fellow.' Mr Hungerton pointed towards the door. 'Take one of the horses and fetch the magistrate straight back.'

Selwyn could bear it no longer. Steeling himself to the most distasteful scene of his life, he walked into the room. 'Wait!' His voice wasn't nearly as loud as the sergeant's but it had an equal ring of authority.

'Ah, Selwyn, my boy,' his father began, 'can you just—'

'You, sir, are disgusting,' his son said. 'Kindly button yourself up and then keep quiet. I've been listening outside the door and if you think I'll let you blame these young people for a crime *you* planned, you've gone completely mad. I'm not sure you haven't gone mad anyway.'

As Hungerton hastily buttoned up the flap on his trousers, and subsided on to the nearest chair as if his legs would no longer hold his weight, people ran up to the cottage door and called, 'Do you need help, sir?'

Selwyn answered. 'Thank you, but no. Just a misunderstanding. Get back to bed now, but ask Smythe to attend us in the library in a few moments.' He waited till they'd all gone, then turned to the people crammed into the small room. 'I'd prefer to deal with this in the house. If you'd all kindly follow me? And Sergeant, please make sure these two villains don't try to escape.' He indicated Jabez and Len.

Lucas held Gwynna as she wept silently against him in sheer relief, shivering now. He looked across at the old man. 'Your own son said it: disgusting! You're lower than the worst scum on the streets, you are.'

Hungerton jerked as if he'd been hit, then twitched and slid sideways off the chair.

Selwyn wondered if this was a ploy to gain sympathy, but couldn't bear to touch his father, so snapped, 'Jabez, see what's wrong with your master, then help him to the house.'

'Yes, sir.'

Lucas swung Gwynna up into his arms and joined the strange procession that made its way across to the house and into the well-lit library. Selwyn Hungerton led the way at a brisk pace, entering through the French windows.

Jabez and Len struggled inside after him, carrying Mr Hungerton. 'I think he's had a seizure, sir.'

Selwyn went to check on his father, then rang the bell. 'Please bear with me a moment, everyone, then we'll sort this out.' When Smythe answered the bell, he told him to fetch someone to carry the old man up to his bedroom and then send for the doctor. He stood by the fireplace and waited until his father had been carried out, not even looking in the old man's direction.

Only when the door had closed behind Smythe did he speak. He turned first to Gwynna. 'I'm deeply sorry and ashamed that you've been treated like this, young woman. Thank God we got to you before they'd hurt you.' When she didn't answer, he asked in horror, 'They didn't . . .'

'They didn't rape me,' she said, 'but they ill-treated and terrified me. I want them brought before the law for that. I won't allow them to get away with this.'

There was a murmur of agreement from Lucas and Declan.

'If we do that, and believe me, I understand how you feel – but if we do that, mud will cling to you as well as to my family. I'm hoping we can reach an agreement about how we deal with these two.' He indicated Jabez and the groom.

Jack Burtell stepped forward. 'I'm the lawyer acting for Lucas and Gwynna. What are you proposing?'

'I'll pay out an agreed sum of money in damages if everyone will keep quiet. I'm not proud of making this offer, but so many lives will be ruined if it gets known what happened, that I'm hoping you'll persuade your clients to agree.'

'That means these two will go scot-free,' Lucas pointed out.

'No. I intend to make sure they enlist in the Army. Believe me, they'll have a hard life there. I'm sure you two will agree that's better than hanging them or transporting them to Australia? A living punishment, if you like.' He turned back to the sergeant. 'Will you allow us to do that?'

'Yes, sir. I think it's an excellent solution. But I'll need to see them do it.'

Jack turned to Gwynna. 'Will that suit you?'

She nodded.

'Well, it won't suit me. I don't want any money from a Hungerton,' Lucas said, soul-sick that he was forced to agree to these terms to protect his beloved.

Gwynna tugged at his arm. 'I want the money. It won't wipe out what happened, but we can do what we want with it. If we don't take it, the Hungertons will get away too easily.'

And suddenly it came to Lucas what they could do and he could feel a smile creep across his face. 'I've changed my mind. Mr Burtell, will you get us as much money out of them as you can.' He began moving towards the door. 'I'm taking Gwynna home now.'

Declan moved to join him and as Jabez looked round quickly, Selwyn said, 'One minute more,' went to the desk and pulled out a revolver which he levelled at the two miscreants. 'Now you may take your young woman home and leave the rest to me, with the help of your lawyer and the sergeant. I'd be glad of an excuse to use this, believe me.' He smiled at Declan. 'And thank you, young man, for the help you've given me. You'll receive the agreed sum.'

'Thank you, Mr Hungerton. It was a pleasure.'

Lucas looked at Declan in surprise. 'You were working for *him?*'

His friend nodded. 'I didn't do much, but he wanted someone to keep an eye on you.'

Both moved at the same time to shake hands, then they all left, Declan whistling softly as they walked.

By now Gwynna had recovered enough to walk beside Lucas as they crossed the field. 'What made you change your mind about the money?'

He stopped walking, looking down at her with his loving expression showing clearly in the moonlight. 'It's not for us, it's for the children.'

'I don't understand.'

'Children like Joe, orphans, fending for themselves on the streets, or ill-treated in the poorhouses. If we had some money we could buy another house and make a home for some of them.'

She looked up at him, mouth open, eyes glowing with admiration. 'What a *wonderful* idea!'

'There's no hope for you two,' Declan said, but he was smiling too. Then he suddenly remembered something. 'I forgot to tell Mr Selwyn something. I won't be long.' He ran back to the house and explained about Trevin.

Selwyn Hungerton's eyes lit up and he turned to Jack. 'Could you act for me on this? I want that fellow thrown deep into gaol, so that he can't build any more places that fall down.'

Jack grinned. 'I'll be delighted to do that. And if he has any money left, we'll get that back for my clients.'

When Declan rejoined his friends, he was smiling broadly.

As the carriage pulled away, with Declan driving it and the others inside, Gwynna nestled sleepily against Lucas. 'It's nearly dawn. Look at the sky.'

He looked out of the window and pulled her closer. 'It'll be a brighter day dawning for us. I think I must be the happiest man alive.'

They sat quietly together, watching the sun gradually climb above the horizon to their right as the horses clopped tiredly home. By the time they reached Hedderby, the sun was sitting proudly on top of the moors, in a sky streaked with red and gold.

'What did I tell you?' he said. 'Look at that dawn! It's the best of my life.'

26

Eli woke up suddenly, wondering where he was. He blinked as the daylight streaming through the windows hurt his eyes.

'Eli?'

He turned his head, an action which took a huge effort, and saw his wife sitting beside the bed looking haggard. 'Carrie love. You look dreadful. Have you been ill?' To his surprise his voice came out raspy and he felt more thirsty than ever before in his life.

'No, you have. Are you thirsty?'

'I could drink a gallon.'

'Dr Pipperday said you were to have a little water every ten minutes if you woke up.'

'If?'

'You've been unconscious for over a day, Eli.'

He found himself so weak he had to let her help him drink, then he lay back on the pillow. 'We've got to clear up the mess from that fire. If Athol Stott wasn't already dead, I'd be tempted to kill him myself.'

She looked at him in puzzlement. 'Fire?'

'At the Pride.'

'Eli, love, that happened months ago.'

It was his turn to stare at her. 'What do you mean? It happened yesterday – no, you said I'd been unconscious for over a day, so it must have been the day before.'

She took his hand and said gently, 'The fire happened months ago, love. We've started building a new music saloon. Surely you remember?'

He shook his head and winced as if it hurt. 'No, I don't remember. As far as I'm concerned the fire happened last night . . .'

Dr Pipperday was summoned and gave it as his opinion that the blow to the head in the accident had caused Eli to lose his recent memories. He waited till his patient had dropped off to sleep again, then said quietly to Carrie, 'Probably, given the problems he's been suffering during the past few months, it won't be a bad thing if he never remembers anything about that period.'

'As long as he's all right.'

'I'm sure he'll be fine.' He patted her gently on the back as she struggled not to weep for sheer relief and left Essie to persuade her to get some sleep.

It took days for the family to help Eli catch up on what had been happening since the Pride burned down. He looked better every day and within the week was walking round, a little paler than usual, getting tired more quickly, but apart from that nearly his old self.

They were delighted to hear that Selwyn Hungerton intended to prosecute Trevin for the collapse of the stables he'd built. Jack said they might get some of their money back at the same time, but Eli doubted it.

At no stage did he suffer from the memories of the fire which had made his life so miserable. Every night he curled up against Carrie and slept as soundly as a child. By the end of the week he was making love to her tenderly and beautifully, making her weep with joy at having her husband back in every way.

The thing which made him most bitter of all, however,

was that he couldn't remember several months of his little daughter's life.

Jeremiah took charge of the building site, going to confer with Eli as soon as Carrie allowed it, and suggesting they employ a real theatre architect to design a new building, then he would supervise the building, and make sure it was done properly this time.

Eli leaned back in his chair. 'Carrie tells me I paid that fellow good money.'

'Yes.'

'I must have been mad.'

'Let's say you were not yourself.'

'And she says you suggested us taking you on as a partner?'

'Yes. I've looked into it and I'd be very happy to be involved. I'm about to set up my practice again, too.'

'I don't want anyone telling me what to do in the music hall,' Eli growled.

'I don't want to tell you how to run it. I want to be involved in building it, then leave my money to grow in value under your capable control.'

'How do you know it'll grow in value?'

'People still talk about the Pride and how wonderful it was to go there. They tell me you're an excellent Chairman, with the loudest voice in Lancashire.'

Eli couldn't help feeling pleased at that compliment. He just wished he knew the man better. As far as he was concerned, he'd only just met Jeremiah Channon. Though Carrie said she liked him and he trusted her judgement. He stood up and went across to the window, itching to be doing something again. 'I'm bursting with ideas, not just for the Pride, but for building other music halls. If we had several of them, we could book acts for seasons and send them from one to the other.' He looked sideways, waiting for mockery and finding only agreement.

'I'd be happy to work with you on building them.'

On impulse Eli stuck his hand out and the two men shook. 'I'm sorry I don't remember you, but I don't intend to forget anything from now on.'

Jeremiah walked home feeling a sense of excitement, eager to share his news with Maria, but when he went inside he could tell that something had happened. 'What's wrong?'

'It's that back room. Benjamin went in to get a book and he got badly frightened, said he could hear his father's voice.'

'That does it.'

'Pardon?'

'I've been thinking for some time that you should leave this house. Renny tells me the evil, as he calls it, cannot be cleansed from it and certainly, there is a sense of anger and evil here that I too can sense.'

'But where can we go?'

He took his courage in both hands. 'You can marry me and we can rent a house until I can build a new one for us, a house where there will be no ghosts of past inhabitants.' He held his breath, waiting for her answer.

She stood very still, then slowly nodded. 'I will marry you, Jeremiah. I found out when you were hurt how much I cared for you.' She looked towards the back of the house and shivered, then looked back at him. 'How soon can we move?'

'As soon as I find another house to rent. Then we'll burn this place down – a fitting end for it, don't you think? Renny says it will cleanse it of spirits as nothing else would.'

'How soon can we move out?' she asked simply.

He moved forward then and took her in his arms, kissing her gently, feeling her first stiffen against his embrace then relax and kiss him back. He prayed that one day he'd banish all the shadows from her life.

As evening fell Eli prowled up and down the house, then turned to Carrie. 'That's it! I'm going out. I'll go mad from boredom if you keep me penned up here any longer. Go and get your coat.'

'Where are we going?'

'Down to the Pride, of course. I want to picture how it will be when we've built a proper theatre. It's a pity that theatre architect fellow can't come till next week, but as soon as he does, we'll start things moving. And if we did one Saturday concert at the church hall, there's no reason why we shouldn't do others, is there? You'll have to remind me of the details, though.'

She began to chuckle as they walked down the hill towards the site.

'What are you laughing at?'

'You, love. I'm so glad to have the old Eli back again.'

When they got there, she pulled him to a halt and whispered, 'Look.'

Lucas was standing there with his arms round Gwynna. As they watched, he bent his head to kiss her.

Carrie made a soft sound of approval in her throat and Eli grinned. 'Why do you never kiss me like that?' He pulled her into his arms and kissed her soundly, not caring who saw them.

When they broke apart the two young lovers had gone and they were alone with their dreams for the future.

'Do you still want to call it the Phoenix?' she asked.

'Call it the Phoenix?' he asked in amazement. 'Why should I want to call it that? It's got a name, and a damned good one too. It's the *Pride*.' He began to hum the tune Raife had written for their first music saloon and Carrie joined in the chorus.

She's the Pride of Lancashire, boys,
She's the Pride of Lancashire.

'Once it's built, we'll have a splendid opening,' he said.
'The biggest party this town has ever known.'

As Lucas and Gwynna walked home together they met James
Forrett, strolling down the street, hands thrust deep into his
pockets.

'Ah, there you are, Kemp, Gwynna. Have you time to come
back with me? I want to discuss something with both of you.'

At his house he installed them in the front parlour,
beaming. 'Well, young fellow, I've decided to do it.'

Lucas's head was still full of the wonder of kissing Gwynna.
'Do what?'

'Open an orphanage and call it after my daughter.' His
smile faded to be replaced by a look of deep sadness. 'You
suggested it to me after Libby died, but it took me a while
to think it out. I can't do it on my own. Let alone I have a
mill to run, what do I know about children? If I build an
orphanage, will you two run it for me?'

He had Lucas's full attention now.

'I have another job to go to, assistant to Mr Channon, the
architect.'

James's face fell.

'But I'd be happy to be involved, and I have an uncle who
needs a job that won't require physical work, plus a wife-to-
be, who is wonderful with children. I'm sure that between the
two families, we'll be able to run the place for you.' He paused,
then added severely, 'But it must be a happy place. I don't
want the children caned or made to behave unnaturally, or
fed poorly. I want them to be happy and healthy.'

James nodded, smiling again. 'You can run it how you
want, as long as it bears my daughter's name.'

As they walked back to Linney's, Lucas said in wonder, 'I can't believe how perfect life is suddenly – well, almost perfect.'

'Why do you say "almost"?' she asked innocently.

'Because of you. You're not my wife yet. My life won't be perfect till we're married.'

She gave him a glowing smile. 'Essie's full of plans, but I think we can make her bring them forward. It takes only three weeks to call the banns.'

'They'll be three of the longest weeks of my life.'

Exactly three weeks and two days later, Lucas Kemp married Gwynna Jones, then walked back through the streets with his new wife on his arm and his friends and family following behind them, ready to celebrate at Linney's. His parents and brother had come to the wedding, but he felt closer to the Prestons and his uncle now than he did to them.

When everyone raised their glasses to drink a toast to the newly married couple, he thought his heart would burst from joy and had to blink his eyes to dispel the tears.

As soon as they could, he and Gwynna slipped away to the cottage they were going to live in until the orphanage and its superintendent's quarters should be built.

'Whatever happens to us in the future, wherever we live, I'll always remember this night,' he said, as he carried her across the threshold.

'So will I,' she whispered, and when he put her down, she kissed him and pulled him towards the stairs.

Contact Anna

Anna Jacobs is always delighted to hear from readers and can be contacted:

BY MAIL

PO Box 628
Mandurah
Western Australia 6210

If you'd like a reply, please enclose a self-addressed, business size envelope, stamped (from inside Australia) or an international reply coupon (from outside Australia).

VIA THE INTERNET

Anna has her own web domain, with details of her books, latest news and excerpts to read. Come and visit her site at http://www.annajacobs.com

Anna can be contacted by email at anna@annajacobs.com

If you'd like to receive an email newsletter about Anna and her books every month or two, you are cordially invited to join her announcements list. Just email her and ask to be added to the list, or follow the link from her web page.